THE LAST DRUID

BOOK ONE

Cover Art Design by Geka @premadesbygeka

Dedication

No matter how lost you get, you'll always find your way back home.

Triggers

Childhood Trauma
Graphic Sex
Invasion of Privacy
Gore/Blood/Violence
Kidnapping
Claustrophobia
Anxiety

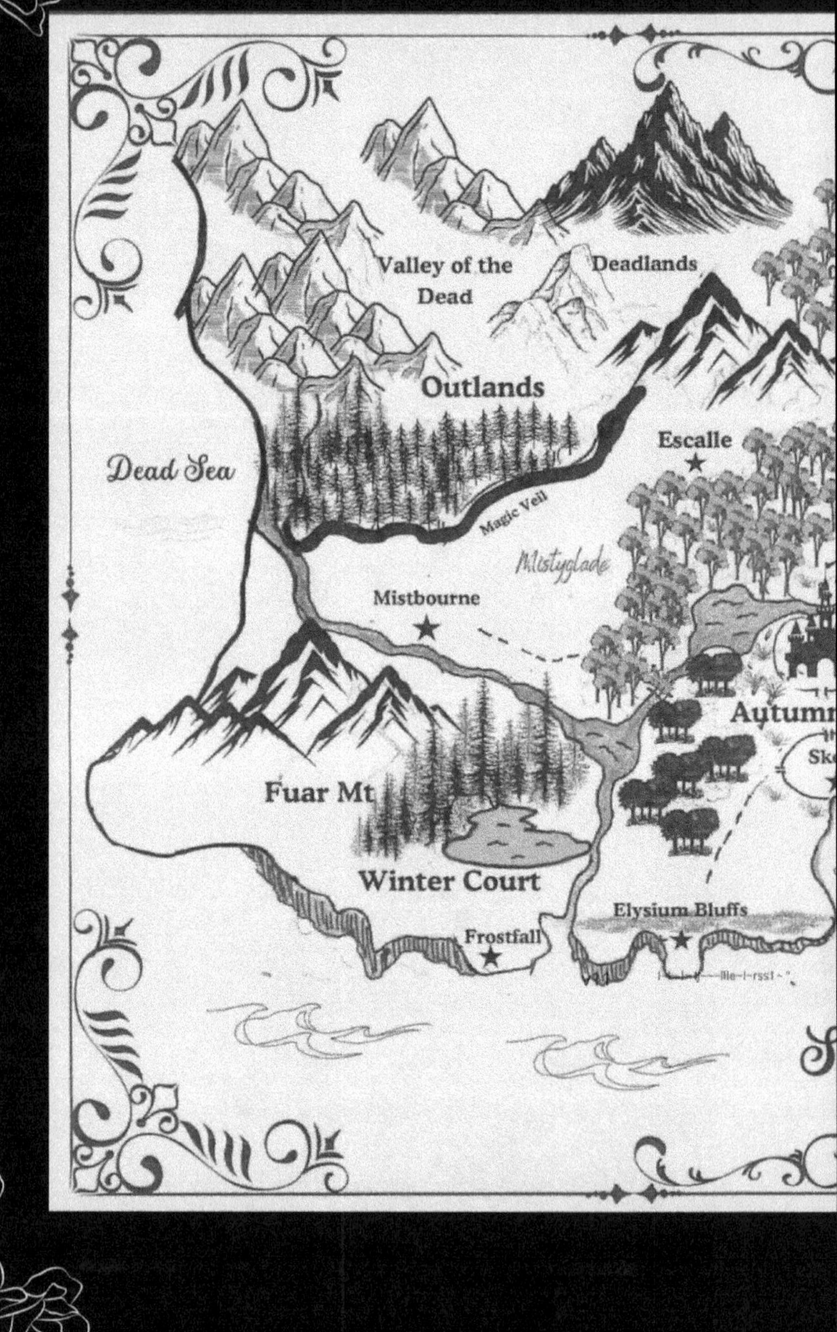

Valley of the Dead
Deadlands
Outlands
Escalle
Dead Sea
Magic Veil
Mistyglade
Mistbourne
Fuar Mt
Winter Court
Elysium Bluffs
Frostfall

Spring Court
StoneWillow
Pinehelm
Ethereal Peaks
N
W
E
S
Sea of Starlight
Summer Court
City of Starlight
Mermaid Bay

Prologue

Radio Broadcast

"The search for the missing hiker, Everly Baker, is being put on hold as weather conditions worsen. The search is anticipated to recommence at daybreak. However, following extensive efforts by ground search and rescue teams, aerial searches, infrared flights, and canine search teams, the search for the missing hiker will be scaled back. None were able to pick up any trace of the young hiker.

Details surrounding Everly's disappearance are still unclear. The young woman, age twenty-five, was out hiking with two of her friends when she seemingly disappeared from the popular track. The group had originally intended to hike to the summit of Talluna Mountain and complete the round trip in a single day. The terrain was not challenging, and this was not Everly's first time hiking the well-known trail.

Everly is of average height, with long blonde hair, and brown eyes.

Anyone with information should contact Mountain State Park rangers."

Chapter One

Everly

The sun's rays dance through the canopy of trees, creating a blanket of warmth on my face. Tilting my head back, I let my eyes fall shut and the fresh forest air flow over me, calming my soul. Whenever I am in nature, I feel a deep sense of connection and joy that I can't find anywhere else.

The sound of my friends catching up reaches my ears, and I can't help but smile. They sound like elephants stomping through the forest. Mia and Scarlett aren't usually fans of hiking, but the gorgeous weather made them eager to join me today. It's the first nice day we have had weather-wise in a few weeks, and we've decided to make the most of it. As we venture through the winding forest path, I confidently lead the way. Having completed this trek numerous times, I am well acquainted with the optimal route.

However, Mia and Scarlett seem to hold a different opinion. Their audible panting is unmistakable compared to my breathing.

In an attempt to hide my amusement, I tightly press my lips together, knowing that they would unleash their wrath upon me if they caught me smirking at them.

I am starting to get hot though. Slipping my arms from the straps of my backpack, I drop it to the ground and pull my long sleeved thermal over my head. I tie it securely around my waist before reaching for my backpack, leaving me now in just my tank, skinny jeans, and favorite hiking boots. The backpack I have is easy to carry because there's only a water bottle, some snacks, and a change of clothes inside. I learned in my early days of hiking to travel light.

As I round the next bend in the trail, a strange tingling sensation rushes over my skin. It's as if I walked through one of those thick spider's webs. The remnants of it cling to me, creating an unsettling sensation on my skin.

"Argh . . ." I wipe my hands over my arms, neck, and face. "I hate spiders."

Squirming with a mix of anticipation and anxiety, I turn to my friends for reassurance. If there is a spider crawling on me, I want it gone immediately. My vision blurs momentarily, little specks of white floating in front of me but I blink, and it's gone.

As I refocus, I'm met with empty space.

Where did they go? They were right there . . .

Nervously, my hands grip the straps of my backpack and I let out an anxious laugh, walking back the way I came. "Okay, guys. Very funny."

I stop and listen, but the only sound I hear is the gentle rustling of the leaves as the wind blows through the trees. Even the chirping of the birds has come to a stop. I feel my muscles tighten and my breathing speed up as my anxiety starts to increase. I take several deep, calming breaths, trying to slow my rapid heartbeat. The last thing I need is to have a panic attack halfway through a hike. Wiping my clammy hands on my jeans, I slowly turn in a circle.

Where did they go?

My friends are incredibly understanding and compassionate when it comes to my past and my struggles with panic attacks. They constantly go out of their way to create a safe and supportive environment for me. Their empathy and thoughtfulness truly make a difference in my life, reminding me that genuine friends prioritize your mental health and well-being above all else.

I'm not quite sure what triggers my episodes, just that, every now and again, a feeling of emptiness settles in my chest like a heavy weight. I feel incomplete, as if there was a piece of me that has gone missing. Even though I can't explain why, it's there, leaving a lingering sense of dread behind. I sometimes detect this urgency that I'm supposed to be somewhere, but I never can think of where.

Shaking my hands out in front of me, I roll my shoulders, getting myself under control. Then I take a good look around, my eyes catching on the vibrant colors of the flowers. My brows drop. This isn't the way I came. I look around again with clarity and notice subtle differences in the scenery. Though everything seems to be the same at first glance, it's not. It's too early in the season for wildflowers, and I know there won't be any on this trail for at least another month. Everything around me seems . . .

Brighter.

"Guys?" I call out again.

Nothing.

The silence is deafening.

Feeling a sudden sharp pinch on my leg, my eyes quickly scan the ground, desperately hoping it isn't a snake. Instead, I'm met with a pair of furious– Wait, what exactly am I looking at?

Tilting my head to the side and squinting slightly, I try to make sense of what I'm seeing. If I were a child, I might have believed it was a fairy, but as an adult, I know better. Fairies aren't real, right? Could I have possibly taken a fall and hit my head?

The fairy, small enough to fit in my hand, has light brown hair adorned with leaves and twigs, which are braided down her back. Her wide sapphire eyes seem almost too big for her face as she stares at me. Agitated, her shimmering translucent wings flutter, creating a cascade of sparkles in the air. Her delicate face twists into an angry scowl, making her look extremely furious. Suddenly, she emits a growl that resonates like sharp bells in the air. And then, to my surprise, she opens her mouth, revealing two rows of sharp teeth.

Instinctively, I take a step back, only to stumble over a small fallen branch. Panic courses through me, causing my muscles to tense up, but I somehow manage to swiftly regain my balance before toppling over. Suddenly, the fairy flies toward my face, and I let out a surprised squeak.

"How dare you tromp through here destroying homes?" she snarls.

My gaze automatically drops to the ground in confusion. I see the stick that I stumbled on, and to the side is a fairy circle of colorful mushrooms, much larger than any I have ever seen. One in particular catches my attention because of its caved-in side. I indeed did stand in what looks to be a small home, but not for the fairy, for something even smaller.

Crap.

Heart in my throat, I instantly drop to my knees on the moss-covered ground to get a closer look.

“There wasn’t anyone inside, right?” I ask.

I duck down trying to get a look inside, the coolness of the ground soaking through my jeans. I realize then that I am on the ground, and looking for what exactly?

When there is no reply, I peer over my shoulder at the fairy hovering in mid-air. The short yellow dress she wears seems to flow over her skin, it’s extremely distracting. She is frowning in what I can only assume is bewilderment before replying.

“No one was in there. Now, if you stomped on the other one with your stupid giant feet, then it would be a yes.”

Sitting back on my haunches, I rub my temples. “I’m so sorry.”

The fairy’s sapphire eyes open wide in incredulity, and she glances about. What did I do now?

“Did I say something wrong?” I ask, dropping my hands to my legs.

Her extremely large eyes blink twice before she snaps from her stupor.

“You're human!” she shrieks, flying a little closer.

Still kneeling on the ground, I glance around in confusion. “Uhhh . . . yeah . . .”

“You’re going to be eaten alive here,” she gasps.

“By bugs?” I question.

The fairy shakes her head at me. “How did you get here?”

I frown and think back. “Where is here?”

“You’re in Faerie.”

I slowly stand up, unable to stop my laughter. When the fairy doesn’t laugh, my smile falls. “You’re not serious, right?”

“Do I look like I’m joking?”

"But I can't be here. Here doesn't exist." Panic laces my words, and I come off sounding slightly hysterical.

"Well, clearly, you're wrong," she replies, rolling her eyes at me, and crossing her arms over her chest.

"But . . . how do I get back?" I ask, a slight tremble in my voice.

This can't be real, right? I must have touched a nightshade plant or fallen and I'm lying unconscious somewhere.

The fairy's sapphire eyes soften only marginally. "I'm not sure, but I can take you to someone who will."

My heart races as I try to decide what to do, my head full of conflicting thoughts. If this is really happening, how did I get here? How do I get home? Do I blindly trust an adorable but nightmarish fairy? What choice do I have?

Everything happened so suddenly. I am supposed to be enjoying a day out with Mia and Scarlett, laughing and joking around and soaking in the crisp mountain air. Not standing in the enchanted land of Faerie. I can feel it, a profound shift taking place within me, as the realization sinks in that my life will never be the same.

Chapter Two

Everly

I push a branch aside, feeling the dampness of the bark on my hand as I step over a fallen log. The rough texture scrapes against my palm, leaving a faint trace of moisture behind. The forest is dense, the canopy above swallowing most of the sunlight casting everything in a dim, green-tinged glow. There is no specific path that we're following as we make our way through the undergrowth. Which I find more than a little disconcerting Normally, I enjoy hiking. There's something about the rhythmic crunch of leaves underfoot, the crispness of the air, the satisfaction of reaching a destination. But this—this is different. We're wandering. Or at least, that's how it feels. Nothing but trees stretching endlessly in every direction.

Beads of sweat drip down my forehead, sliding down the bridge of my nose before I wipe them away with the back of my hand. The air is humid, wrapping around me like a second skin. Every step feels heavier, more deliberate, like the forest itself is pressing down on me, urging me to turn back. But there's no turning back. A sense of unease worms its way through me, threading through my veins like ice. My skin prickles as if unseen eyes are watching from between the trees. It's irrational. I know that. And yet, I can't shake the feeling. y breath comes a little faster, my senses sharpened to every sound—the rustling of leaves, the occasional snap of a twig, the distant caw of a crow overhead.

I don't understand what's happening, and I am doing my damn best to keep a level head. But my grip on calm is slipping, unraveling with each step forward into the unknown. My fingers curl into fists at my sides, nails pressing into my palms, grounding me in something tangible. But I know I will freak out soon. It's inevitable.

My mind wanders to my two best friends. A sense of worry engulfs me, and I hope Mia and Scarlett are safe and sound. Those two are always out of their element when it comes to the great outdoors; true city girls through and through. However, I know they must be in a state of panic searching for me. A heavy burden of guilt pulls at my heartstrings, leaving a lingering ache in my chest. I wish I could reassure them that I'm alright.

"How much further?" I grumble, shaking off another spider-web.

The fairy spins around, her hands on her hips, and I can feel the heat of her glare. I take a deep breath, feeling my throat tighten as my mouth suddenly goes dry.

How can something so tiny be so terrifying?

I feel the urge to burst out laughing, but I swallow it down and press my lips together firmly.

"Stop complaining or I'll leave you out here all alone to fend for yourself, and trust me, you wouldn't last the night."

My mouth drops open. "That's the first time I've complained."

The fairy raises an eyebrow in challenge and my shoulders slump. "Fine. Can you at least tell me your name?"

"You don't know a thing about the fae, do you?" She lets out a deep sigh, her expression exasperated.

I shrug. "Should I?"

I finally catch up to her and pause to catch my breath. She isn't exactly setting an easy pace.

"Well, the three main things to remember, especially for humans," she says, raising one finger. "One, do not say sorry or apologize. If you do, it implies that you owe them a favor. You don't want to owe a fae anything, especially a favor. It's the same as thank you. Don't say it. We find it disrespectful as it diminishes our act of kindness, which in turn makes us angry."

She must see me preparing to argue the point because she sighs heavily. "If you must . . . say, 'I appreciate what you've done.'" Another finger. "Two, never ask a lesser fae their name. It's sacred. Names hold power. We won't give it to you. The high fae are different. You cannot control them by knowing their name."

I open my mouth to ask her to elaborate, but she flies up to me, holding up another finger.

"Three. Us fae are selfish, spiteful, manipulative, and easily offended creatures, so stay quiet and don't step on any more homes."

My face heats in embarrassment, and I bite the inside of my cheek to stop from saying something I might regret. The fairy gives me a long, assessing look before turning away, her voice floating back to me. "Almost there, and you can call me Nix."

"Nix," I say, testing the name out on my tongue. It's different, definitely not a name I've heard of before.

"My name is Everly."

Nix keeps going without acknowledging me, and I groan in frustration. I am utterly spent, my eyes heavy with exhaustion, and my body slick with sweat.

"Is there a stream nearby, somewhere I can get a drink?" I ask.

My water bottle has long since emptied and my throat is parched. I can feel the sweat dripping down my neck and back, and would love to splash some cool water on my face.

Nix either doesn't hear me or chooses to ignore me as she continues on. After ten more minutes, Nix pauses beside a towering, hollowed out tree, the insides looking like a dark cave. The thick green glistening moss that blankets the bark gives off a faint musty smell.

"You can wait here. I will go the rest of the way alone."

My eyes widen in shock and disbelief. "You're leaving me here?"

Anxiously studying our surroundings, my fingers trembling as I grip the straps of my backpack tightly. The trees are thick here, and I can feel the coolness of the shade and the dampness of the soil. We are still deep in the forest, and although we haven't come across anything, I know they are there, watching me. I wrap my arms around myself and shoot a desperate and pleading look at Nix.

"You will be fine. Stay hidden and you won't be bothered." She gestures to the tree.

I peer into the dark, hollow space and shake my head. "I'm not getting in there."

"Why?"

"I don't know what's in there."

"Uh, nothing . . . "

"You don't know that!" I exclaim.

"Look, the quicker I leave, the quicker I can get help. Now stay here and stay quiet. You'll be safe. Do not leave the tree. Okay?!"

For such a tiny creature, she sure is formidable and bossy. I puff out my cheeks. How did I get myself into this?

"How long will you be gone?"

Nix smiles, revealing her sharp pointy teeth. "As long as it takes."

"Comforting," I mutter slowly, crouching into the cramped space.

It isn't as bad as I thought it would be, but I still hate small, dark places. I blame that on my horrible foster brother, David. That wanker locked me in the damn closet too many times to count. He left me there once for a whole day, while my foster family went out. My continuous pounding on the door left my tiny arms aching, and the sound of my desperate screams for help made my throat sore. My voice was strained and hoarse for two days afterward. After that day, I had kept track of the weeks, counting down until I was freed from that place.

"Don't die," Nix says, breaking me from my trip down memory lane.

I startle. What the hell?

"What kind of parting words are those?"

"Honest ones," she replies bluntly, shrugging her tiny shoulders in response. Watching as she turns to leave, I take my pack off and drop it to the ground next to me. Then I remember my water bottle.

"Wait!"

When she faces me, I shake my water bottle. "Is there a stream where I can fill this up?"

Nix lets out a weary sigh and slowly shakes her head.

"Damn." Defeated, I plop into the dirt and feel the cool dampness seep into my clothes. I scrub my hands on my jeans, leaving behind smudges of dirt. The ground under me feels like a soft cushion. Which is nice, but extremely unsettling. Nix looks back at me one last time before she disappears into the forest and a trail of sparkling, golden glitter follows after her.

Chapter Three

Everly

Alarmed, I jolt awake and take a sharp, audible breath. The sound of a branch snapping nearby has me jumping to my feet, my eyes wide open and alert. From my spot at the back of the tree, I peer outside, but it's so dark I can barely make out my hand in front of my face.

How long was I asleep?

I take several slow, measured breaths and focus my attention on the sounds of the forest around me. But the only sound that seems to fill my ears at the moment is the rapid beat of my heart. Another loud snap breaks the silence, and I instinctively crouch down. Whatever is out there wants me to know it's there, and that thought terrifies me.

Moving closer to the entrance, I cling to the opening of the tree for support.

Squinting into the darkness, I try to make out anything in the night. I blink a few times, struggling to get my eyes to adjust and focus as I desperately search for any source of light, but the darkness is overwhelming. I can hear my breathing increase, and know that if I don't calm myself down, I am going to have a full-blown panic attack. Just because I can't see anything doesn't mean I'm trapped. Trying to keep my breathing even, I peer into the night, my fingers digging into the rough bark of the tree as I lean further forward.

The night sky is a blanket of darkness without even a star or sliver of moon to be seen through the canopy of trees. My entire body tenses up with fear as the heavy, oppressive darkness seems to close in around me thicker than before.

"Calm down, Everly. You're fine, it's just the dark," I mutter to myself.

Holding my breath, I lean further out of my hiding spot, needing to know I'm not trapped within the tree. That I can escape if I want or need to. A tremor runs through me as an icy chill wraps around my body, sending goosebumps scattering across my skin. Surely Nix will be back soon. She must have been gone for more than a few hours now if it's this dark already.

Suddenly, the sound of a low menacing growl comes from my right, and I feel a hot, heavy breath on the side of my face. I freeze in terror, too afraid to move.

The creature lets out a loud huff, and the hair around my face moves, startling me into action. I scramble backward, landing hard on my backside, pushing myself deeper into the cavern of the tree. My breath catches as my back hits the rough bark and I can't go any further.

Holy crap, what is out there?

My eyes are fixed on the opening, straining to see through the darkness. I catch sight of two glowing crimson eyes, all the air leaving my lungs at once. I can feel its piercing glare locked on me, and my lungs start to ache as if engulfed in flames.

The outline of the creature is barely visible through the opening, but I can see it is huge, like a bear. As the creature stalks closer, a wave of dizziness overwhelms me and a surge of alarm courses through my veins. Frozen in fear, I watch as it takes another slow and deliberate step toward me.

One more step and I would be sharing the same space with that thing. My heart is beating wildly causing a cold sweat to break out across my skin.

Don't pass out. Don't pass out. Don't pass out.

The creature takes another step then stops abruptly; it seems to struggle as if something is holding it back. It lets out a really pissed off growl and slams against what looks to be an invisible barrier across the entrance of the tree. Now I know why Nix said I would be okay as long as I didn't leave the safety of the tree.

The creature stops striking the barrier and begins pacing in front of the entrance. I can see a bit better now and can make out the mist puffing from its mouth as it paces back and forth, a low grumble coming from its direction every now and again. It is really pissed off that it can't reach me, but a sense of relief sweeps through me, knowing it can't enter.

With my back firmly pressed against the wall of the hallow tree, I hug my backpack to my chest, never taking my eyes off the entrance of the tree, and the darkness beyond it.

I groan, feeling stiff and achy, my head begins to pound with an oncoming headache. I have been staring intently for hours while my head keeps bobbing and my eyelids droop from exhaustion. The creature gradually retreated to the trees a while ago. I can't sense it anymore. Closing my eyes, I take a deep breath and roll my neck slowly from side to side.

Just as I'm about to drift into sleep, I abruptly wake up, startled by the sensation of tipping over. The harsh impact of my head against the rough bark of the tree fills the air with a resounding thud. Frustration seeps through me as I grumble, my palms pressing against the ground as I return to a seated position.

"Crap," I mutter.

I stare out through the opening of the tree and gasp at the magnificent view. Sunlight has begun streaming through the canopy of trees, lighting the world beyond my hiding spot in a blanket of warmth.

Vibrant, colorful wildflowers cover the forest floor, creating a calming environment, different from the one of the night before.

Were they there yesterday? I don't think so.

The peaceful sound of the birds chirping fills the air, and I pause to take it in. My lips curl into a smile as I listen, my eyelids falling closed. That's when I hear another noise. A noise that has a rush of anticipation pulsing through me.

Was that . . . a stream?

But Nix said there wasn't one nearby.

I listen closely, and I'm one hundred percent sure it's a stream or creek. I can hear the tranquil sound of water trickling and gurgling with ease now. Excitement fills me and I jump to my feet, swiping up my pack, and making my way to the entrance. Glancing around, I see no signs of danger and the coast appears to be clear. Not to mention the forest is alive with birds and insects, which usually means there are no predators close by.

Shaking my hands out, I try to steady my nerves, but still, the buzzing in my stomach intensifies. I draw in a lung full of fresh air before stepping out into the open and releasing it slowly. I wait a heartbeat and when nothing comes charging out of the trees or bushes, my shoulders slump in relief. Swiping my sweaty palms on my jeans, a new sense of purpose fills me as my thirst returns with a vengeance.

"Okay, Everly, pull your shit together and get yourself some bloody water."

Chapter Four

Everly

It doesn't take me long to find the small stream, its shimmering surface visible even from a distance. I've walked maybe eight minutes from the tree, so I should be able to find my way back easily enough. Taking my pack off, I drop it to the ground, before sinking to my knees at the water's edge. The water looks so damn inviting, the surface glimmers where the sun hits it through the trees. I cup my hands, grabbing a handful of water and splash some on my face, rubbing all the sweat and dirt away. My next handful goes to my mouth, and I slowly sip at the cool water. As I drink, I can feel a cool, soothing sensation that helps to alleviate my headache. When I'm done, I turn and drag my pack closer, grabbing my water bottle so I can fill it up.

Submerging the bottle in the stream, I watch the bubbles rise to the surface, and wait for it to fill. Casting a quick glance around, I'm captivated by the vibrant sights that surround me. The small stream, about eight feet wide, flows lazily, its gentle current gliding over smooth rocks. The air is filled with the soothing sound of trickling water, complemented by the faint rustle of leaves in the breeze. A delightful aroma of damp earth and fresh foliage fills my nostrils. The entire area is alive with color, from the bark of the trees to the mossy ground below. Every detail of this place seems to glow with beauty. Vibrant flowers, delicate ferns, and intricate designs of trees and vines create an enchanting array of beauty.

Sensing a slight disturbance in the air, I look to my left and freeze. A slight jolt runs through me like an electric shock. My mouth parts. There, standing a few meters away, is a fox. Not a regular fox, this one is cobalt blue with strange white markings on its head. The tips of its pointed ears are pure white and so is the tip of its bushy tail. Its intelligent silver eyes glow with deep curiosity as it watches me. The cool water laps around my hand, as if trying to draw my attention away. The fox tilts its head down to look at the stream, as if it were considering something.

With my eyes focused on the fox, I make a conscious effort to stay perfectly motionless. I'm completely in awe of this creature. Excitement bubbles up; I've never seen a fox before, let alone one that looks like this. It is absolutely magnificent.

I remain perfectly still, unsure of what I should do, but also wanting this moment to last a bit longer. The fox flicks its bushy tail once before turning and bounding into the trees without making a sound.

I release a deep breath and carefully remove my hand from the cold water, sealing the lid of my water bottle with a click. I go to turn away when something in the water catches my attention. Frowning, I lean in closer to the surface of the stream. My heart skips a beat as a shock of awareness makes my stomach lurch suddenly. It's almost as if I'm looking at a face, but logically I know that isn't the case. The water isn't deep enough for someone to be hiding beneath the surface, but it isn't my reflection either.

I roll my eyes, and shake my head in frustration as I lean back on my haunches. "I'm going mad. Obviously dehydrated," I mutter.

Standing, I brush the dirt off my knees, and pick up my pack. I should probably get back just in case Nix shows up. Which hopefully will be before nightfall. I have no desire to spend another night out here alone.

I trudge back the way I came, stopping to admire some of the flowers along the way. I catch sight of some wildlife; normal looking deer, birds, and what look to be rabbits, but are a light shade of purple.

I am awestruck by the size of the trees, their branches stretching high above me to create a breathtaking canopy. As I tip my head back to admire them, I notice the leaves on the trees are a kaleidoscope of various shades of green, and the trunks twist and twirl as they reach up to the sky. We don't have trees like this back at home.

When I reach the tree that Nix left me in, I lower myself onto the cushiony soft grass, and lean back against the tree and wait. I had no desire to climb into the hollow just yet. My stomach rumbles loudly, reminding me that I haven't eaten in a while. I'm actually not sure how much time has passed since Nix left or how long I've been here. Rummaging through my pack, I find three granola bars and a red apple. I devour the apple immediately, but decide to wait a while before eating the granola bars, just to be safe. I might be here longer than I expected.

My headache has eased, and I'm feeling somewhat better. I tilt my head back, feeling the rough bark of the tree snagging on my hair as I rest it against the trunk. Suddenly, all the air escapes from my lungs as I release a blood-curdling scream.

The piercing sound echoes through the air, sending birds flying from nearby trees. My heart pounds in my chest as I leap up, adrenaline coursing through my veins, my flight response kicking into high gear. I spin around, eyes wide with fear. I can't recall ever moving with such urgency before.

What on earth was that creature?

About halfway up the tree trunk, there is a man gripping the tree with bulging, milky gray eyes and sunken cheeks. He's hanging upside down, his threadbare clothes barely concealing his skin, which has taken on a grayish hue. The sound of his long fingernails scraping against the bark fills the air, making goosebumps spread over my exposed skin. With slow blinks and a peculiar tilt of its head, the man slowly descends the tree, creating an eerie and unsettling sight.

I swallow roughly over the lump in my throat, as I slowly back away from the tree. Every step I take seems like an eternity, my heart racing and my palms sweating. My instinct is to escape, but I can't break my stare from the creature watching me, its head tilted at an unnatural angle.

When it reaches the ground, it remains on its hands and feet, its neck twisting to keep track of me. Adrenaline and dread shoots through me, sending my pulse racing, and I know I'm in danger. Without a second thought, I turn and run.

My feet pound the dirt as I run as fast as I can, back toward the stream. From behind me, I hear a loud screech echo off the trees, and the birds fall silent around me. The sound of the whatever-it-is crashing through the forest behind me—its bellows of outrage—makes the hairs on my neck stand on end.

Shit, shit, shit.

What should I do?

Suddenly, the image of the tree pops into my mind; its safe, dark cavern. I know that if I try to loop around, I risk getting lost and potentially being caught by that thing. I let out a shrill scream and cover my head as an object forcefully collides with the tree beside me, sending shards of bark flying in all directions.

I don't waste time looking behind, instead, I quicken my pace, veering to the left. My eyes are drawn to the stream up ahead, and I aim for it. I can't put it into words, but an unexplainable urge tugs at me, drawing me toward it. The stream comes into full view, and I can't ignore the captivating sight of the water, adorned with glistening ripples that seem to sparkle under the sun. However, I don't allow it to distract me. Without a moment's pause, I draw in a deep breath, and with a burst of adrenaline, I propel myself into the air. I gracefully land on the other side of the stream, feeling a rush of satisfaction. Another screech echoes through the air, sending a rush of pinpricks all over my body. I can hear the creature gaining on me. The wind rushes past me as I continue running. I don't peek back when a shrill wail pierces the air, followed by the unsettling sounds of someone choking and thrashing in the water.

Despite the heavy ache in my chest, I push myself to keep running. Only when I reach my limit do I finally slow down, collapsing onto my hands and knees in a clearing of tall grass. Overwhelmed by exhaustion, I crumple to the ground, my heart beating painfully in the confines of my chest. Rolling to my back, I gaze up at the sky, my skin slick with sweat. The sky is clear, and the clouds drift lazily overhead, as I lie here trying to catch my breath.

Everything hurts.

"Argh!" I yell, my cries ringing out in the open air.

Gasping for air, I can feel the heat of my tears streaming down my face. The rise and fall of my chest match the rhythm of my breath as I gulp in lungfuls of the crisp, cool air, my fingers finding solace in the soil beneath me. Despite my fatigue, I try my best to focus, but my mind struggles to bring my scattered thoughts together.

Hidden in the tall grass I wait for my heart rate to return to normal and for the feeling of sickness and light-headedness to subside. Gradually, I rise, feeling the stiffness in my body, and take in the sights and sounds of my surroundings. I don't know how long I have been here staring up at the sky, but now the sun is setting. I can see I don't have long left before the last of the sun is below the horizon, and I do not know where I am or what to do now. Without any resources, I am left defenseless; no food, no water, and no means of protection.

Nix will never find me, and there is no way I am going back to that tree now. What am I going to do?

I am totally screwed.

I watch the sun sink beneath the horizon, a chill running down my spine, and hear the distant call of an animal.

Chapter Five

Everly

I decide to stay where I am, but manage to stumble my way over to a fallen tree at the edge of the meadow. My skin crawls with unease as I stare up at the tall trees beyond it, the sound of the wind rustling their branches echoing my earlier experience. My imagination runs wild with the thought of what could be hiding in the branches, my mind conjuring up all sorts of images for me to spend the night stressing about.

My gaze sweeps around the meadow, taking in the way the long, tall grass sways and dances in the breeze. Looks like I'll be taking my chances sleeping out in the open tonight. But I'm not going to put myself in a situation where I can be cornered. I slump down against the fallen tree, hugging my pack to my chest. A headache teases at my temples, but I push it away by sheer will, and instead focus on the smell of the nearby wildflowers. I let my eyes drift shut as I inhale their sweet aroma, letting it soothe my senses enough for me to drift off to sleep. The gentle buzzing of the crickets is all that can be heard over the pleasant sway of the trees. It never would have crossed my mind that there would be crickets in Faerie. That was my last thought as I succumb to sleep, the weight of exhaustion pulling me under.

My eyes snap open as I jolt awake with no explanation. A sharp tingling sensation runs down my spine and the hairs on my neck stand on end, signaling a presence nearby. The tension in my body increases as I make an effort to pinpoint the source of my unease.

It better not be that red-eyed beast again.

I peer into the darkness, my eyes struggle to distinguish anything in the empty field before me. Slowly, I turn to my left where the forest begins, but the moonlight casts eerie shadows among the gnarled tree trunks, adding to the sense of foreboding.

I do my best to relax my breathing, and that's when I realize the air has become still. Even the crickets have stopped making noise. There isn't a single sound in the night. It's as if the forest itself is holding its breath.

I quickly stand up, bracing myself in case I need to run. I won't make it far in the dark, not without falling on my face, but I will not sit around and let myself be eaten either.

Nix's words float through my head; *You'll be eaten alive here.*

Without making a sound, I focus all my attention on the space around me. I become aware of a small disturbance in the air behind me, prompting me to spin around, my pulse thundering in my ears.

Standing on the fallen tree I have been leaning on is the shadowy figure of a man.

How did he get so close without me hearing?

"What do we have here?" he says in a language I don't know, but somehow understand perfectly.

"She's pretty." Another voice from my left, and immediately my eyes snap in that direction.

There are two of them.

The man standing on the weathered log leaps down, effortlessly landing before me without making a sound. Reflexively, I retreat a few paces, my eyes frantically darting back and forth between the two figures. The darkness obscures their features, yet their dangerous aura is unmistakable. Taking two more cautious steps backward, my body tenses as I unexpectedly collide with another person.

With a sharp intake of breath, I swiftly pivot my body to confront the unexpected intruder, feeling the rush of adrenaline through my veins.

Violet eyes stare down at me, sparkling mischievously. "Where are you going?" he asks, reaching for my face.

I back away, my heart pounding in my chest and a sick feeling twisting my stomach. The odds are definitely not in my favor. While I have some knowledge of self-defense, I doubt it would be enough to overcome three men. But that doesn't mean I won't fight back.

One of them lights a flame, illuminating the area, casting light all around. I turn to face all three men, my eyes darting between them. With the torch now lit, I can finally see their faces. Each is strikingly handsome, their features chiseled and defined, and their eyes varying shades of purple. The one nearest to me flashes a smile, but it's far from friendly. It is cruel and wicked.

My stomach knots, my fingers trembling with my fight or flight response pushing me to react.

The one closest to me turns his head to peer back at the other two, and I catch sight of his ears, their pointed tips standing out.

What are they?

I force down my fear, which is swirling inside of me like a tornado.

"What a treat to come across," snickers the one I bumped into.

Again, that odd language.

"How did you get here, and all alone?"

"Lonely women are so much fun."

The one closest to me lunges forward, his hand stretching out to reach for my arm. The moment his cool fingers make contact with my skin, a surge of heat engulfs me, and I can feel the heat of his desire like a knife slicing through my skull. Instinctively, I scramble backward, desperately trying to put some distance between us. In my rush, I lose track of the others, and accidentally bump into someone. Swiftly, a sets of arms wrap around me, their tight hold causing a surge of fear.

A primal scream escapes my lips as I forcefully throw my head back, connecting with his nose. The nauseating crunch echoes in my ears, followed by his pained grunt. I feel a sickening sense of satisfaction as he releases his grip, allowing my feet to touch solid ground. Without hesitation, I break into a sprint, my heart pounding in my chest.

Fingertips graze my back, sending shivers down my spine. I clamp my throat shut, fighting to suppress the scream threatening to escape.

I hear one of them angrily cursing, accompanied by the two others cackling with amusement, as if I have somehow made this a game for them. Their hollers echo through the air as they run after me. Adrenaline pushes me harder and faster than ever before. I'm in the middle of the clearing when one of the men cries out in pain. I glance back and feel a wave of relief as I realize they have stopped chasing me. My eyes have adjusted well enough that I can make out their forms in the distance. I stop running and drop into a crouch, hiding in the long grass. The gentle breeze dances around me, caressing my skin with its soft touch, almost reassuringly, as if wanting to soothe away any worries or troubles that may be weighing on my shoulders.

Taking slow, deliberate breaths, I carefully watch from my crouched position, feeling the dampness of the grass beneath my fingertips.

What are they doing? What happened to the third one?

Both men are alert, their attention on the treeline, their eyes scanning for any movement. A piercing, high-pitched whizzing sound shatters the silence, causing my hands to instinctively fly to my mouth. My heart slams against my chest, and I gasp, witnessing one of the men crumple to the ground. My eyes lock onto something protruding from his neck, a chilling sight that sends shivers down my spine. Meanwhile, the remaining man swiftly crouches down in the grass, disappearing from my view. My heart pounds relentlessly as my eyes frantically scan the dense treeline, desperately searching for the unseen assailant responsible.

Seemingly materializing out of thin air, a colossal and obscured shadow emerges from the dense foliage. The very ground trembles beneath me as I witness the figure hurtling toward the exact spot where the previous man was crouched. My jaw drops in utter disbelief as the figure deftly retrieves a gleaming sword from their back, while the thunderous hooves of their massive stallion pound against the earth with an unimaginable speed. The last man attempts to rise, raising his hands in surrender, but the figure shows no mercy, swiftly beheading him with a single fluid motion of the sword.

Falling backward, I gasp and scramble to my feet, my stomach left somewhere on the ground. In a state of shock and panic, I run. I don't know if he realizes I'm here, but I need to get to the trees NOW.

The sound of hooves pound in my ear as I sprint for the trees. I don't stop running or risk a chance to look behind me. I can feel the vibrations of the ground reverberating up through my feet. Out of the corner of my eye, I glimpse a shape next to me as a figure leans down, an arm reaching out. A loud shriek of surprise escapes me right before I feel myself being lifted off the ground. For a moment, I'm suspended in the air, then I find myself seated on a massive black horse. I'm held tight as two powerful arms encircle me, taking the reins. I take several breaths, my chest tight as fear sets in. My mind scrambles, but before I can pull a single coherent thought into my head, a voice whispers in my ear, in a deep gruff voice.

"Are you alright?"

A tremor runs through me at the words and the way my heart flutters when he speaks. When I don't answer, one of his arms wraps around my waist, pulling me tight against his warm, hard body. I swallow in surprise as my hands grab a handful of thick, black mane.

"Are you hurt, Stóirín?" he asks again.

I don't know what that means, what he called me, but my chest warms instantly. I feel my throat tighten as I nervously whisper, "No."

"Hold on," he says, covering my body with his as he rubs the horse's neck and whispers something I don't quite catch.

My heart races, and I clench my hands around the horse's mane as it gathers speed. The wind whips my hair across my face, stinging my eyes with its chill. The horse's huge powerful hooves hammer the ground beneath us, as the stranger veers the horse to the right, heading for the mountains I spotted in the distance yesterday.

My body becomes more and more relaxed as the horse slows to a trot, the gentle movements making my eyes drift closed. My head nods forward, and I jerk back, only to feel my eyelids growing heavy again. I've never been so physically exhausted before; my body has been completely drained of energy. The arm around my waist moves up higher, banding under my breasts to keep me anchored to the solid body behind me, preventing me from falling. Even though I should be scared, his energy doesn't elicit the same sense of danger as the others.

"We're here," his deep smooth voice says softly.

I slowly open my eyes and am almost blinded by the bright lights lining the stone wall of the castle gatehouse. My eyes grow wide as I take in the impenetrable structure before us. We pass through the large wooden gates into an open courtyard. I try to twist in the saddle, but the arm around me is like a steel band securing my body.

"Easy. Don't want you hurting yourself."

"I'm fine," I reply, my voice husky from sleep.

The man releases his grip on me, his hands now firmly on the reins, guiding the horse. The rhythmic clopping of the horse's hooves fills the air as we near the majestic stone castle. I rub my eyes, trying to dispel the lingering haze of sleep and confirm that it wasn't just a dream. Despite my doubts, the castle remains right in front of me. A wave of shock and awe washes over me, as glittering torches flicker to life, the flames lighting the area in a soft, warm glow.

"Whoa!" I take in a sharp breath.

The man behind me lets out a deep, resonant chuckle that makes butterflies flutter in my stomach. Geez, get a grip Everly. This man just killed three men in the forest. Granted, it was to save you from something extremely unpleasant.

An impressive staircase looms before us, guarded by several stoic figures. The man tugs gently on the reins, and the horse obediently stops at the foot of the stairs. Without pause, he swings down, his feet hitting the ground with a thud. Nervously, I fidget on the saddle, feeling the leather beneath my fingertips. I can sense the weight of his gaze, but fear keeps me from meeting his eyes. I take a moment to steady myself before I turn toward him, my stomach in knots. My breath hitches as our eyes meet. He is gorgeous, like, totally mouth-watering gorgeous.

His deep chocolate brown hair falls in cascading waves, reaching past his shoulders. Parts have been braided in sections and gold jewels clipped in. A soft gust of wind ruffles the free hair, making it move in the breeze, its tips brushing lightly against his skin. His beautiful eyes hold me captive, the deepest violet eyes set off by a ring of silver and framed by the thickest eyelashes.

My eyes travel over his face, taking in the tattoo of intertwining vines around his left eye, near his temple. His jawline is sharp, and his lips appear soft and full. I'm speechless, unable to form any words or coherent thoughts. Quietly, he stands before me, hands outstretched, patiently waiting to guide me down from the horse. I'm completely transfixed as a smirk tugs at the corners of his mouth.

"Stóirín, are you coming?"

I jump in surprise and instinctively blink multiple times, coming out of my stupor.

"What is your name?" I blurt, and then remember Nix's words.

Oops . . .

He grins at me, the dimples on his cheeks giving him an extra bit of charm. "Maxon. My name is Maxon. And I will not hurt you. You have my word." He raises his fist, resting it over his heart.

I'm overcome with a feeling of calm the longer I stare into his eyes, and I can smell his sweet scent of leather and cedarwood, which somehow reassures me everything will be okay. The scent is both earthy and masculine, and makes me think of intimate nights in, reclining on the love seat, lights off, candles on . . .

My cheeks flush with warmth, and I give a small nod, lowering my head. Placing my hands on his shoulders, I allow him to effortlessly lift me off the towering horse. Maxon's hands, warm and comforting, encircle my waist as he guides me down, carefully settling me onto my feet. My hands trail down his arms, feeling the strength of his muscles under his shirt, before finally resting on his forearms. We remain like this for a prolonged moment, completely captivated by each other's gaze, until a throat clears nearby. I swiftly withdraw my hands from his arms and take a step back, causing Maxon's hands to release their hold on my waist. Unintentionally, I bump into the horse, and it lets out a soft snort, almost as if it's amused. Embarrassment floods my cheeks, causing them to heat up once again.

"Sorry," I whisper, turning and gently rubbing its neck.

Maxon steps up behind me, the heat from his body seeping into my back, as his arm reaches around me to stroke the horse's head. "His name is Storm."

I turn my head and peer up at Maxon, my breath catching in my throat at his proximity.

"Sir, the queen would like to see you right away."

Maxon doesn't take his eyes from mine. "Tell her I'm on my way."

I hold my breath as he lifts his hand toward my face, gingerly running his fingers through my hair, pushing some of it behind my ear.

"What's your name?" he murmurs, eyes locked onto mine.

"Everly," I whisper.

"Everly," he repeats softly, the sound lingering in the air. His voice has a unique and curious undertone, with both elements blending together around me, giving his words a distinctively different quality, one of affection.

Taking a step back, he turns, giving the other man a nod before moving up the stairs, leaving me behind. Anxiety washes over me as I glance around, unsure of what I was suppose to do.

"Miss, if you'll follow me, I will take you to your chambers."

I jerk my head toward the voice of a young woman who is now standing beside me.

"Where'd you come from?" I choke out, rubbing a hand over my chest in surprise.

The woman gives me a warm, gentle smile. It's hard to tell in this lighting, but her eyes seem to be a soft brown. Her curly hair is a chestnut color, the masses pulled back into a ponytail, with parts framing her face. Tilting my head to the side, I squint, uncertain of whether my eyes are playing tricks on me.

Are those cat ears poking out from her hair?

"Follow me," Her voice is low and sweet as she turns for the stairs.

Quietly, I fall into step behind her, my gaze moving from her head down her body and I gasp in surprise.

"You– you have a tail!" The words are out before I can stop them. I cover my mouth, my eyes growing wide. "Shit, that was rude."

Oh, gosh, I feel sick. I am not making very good first impressions.

The young woman glances over her shoulder at me and simply smiles, her long, brown spotted tail whipping back and forth. "That I do."

My shoulders slump with shame and exhaustion. I need sleep, food and a shower. In any order, I'm not picky.

Chapter Six

Everly

The wooden beams running along the high ceilings create an arch, giving the darker rough stone walls of the corridors a tall and regal atmosphere, while the plush carpets run down the middle of the smooth lighter stone floors, making it seem comforting and cozy.

My fingers itch to run along the emerald heavy velvet curtains that frame the gigantic arched windows, spaced evenly along the corridors. The young woman leads me through the castle and up several flights of stairs before coming to a stop in front of a large set of wooden doors.

I press my teeth into my lip to prevent myself from expressing my appreciation or inquiring her name. Nix's words repeat over and over in my head. Is it all fae who have these set rules, or just the fairies?

When I stop beside her, she pushes open the doors and waves me inside. “There is hot water in the bathroom and a change of clothes for you on the bed. I will be back with some food.”

I step inside, and she shuts the door with a resounding click, leaving me standing in the entrance of a room that’s bigger than my entire apartment.

Everywhere I look, there are hints of the medieval era, but the glow of electricity is unmistakable. Slowly, I make my way through the large room toward what I assume is the bathroom. A gasp escapes my lips as I step through the doorway, slowly rotating in place to take it in. The bath is sunken into the ground and could easily fit two or three people in it, and in the corner stands a shower with a huge waterfall-type shower head, and no curtain or doors blocking it from view.

As dirty and smelly as I am, I really don’t want to shower. The idea of getting undressed and being naked here seems to make me feel unsafe and vulnerable. Glancing down at my dirt-stained clothes, I let out a deep sigh. Maybe I can wash up and quickly change into some clean clothes. The woman did say some are laid out on the bed. I walk back to the bedroom and make my way over to the bed.

I giggle as I feel the luxurious, soft fabric beneath my fingers. They have to be joking, right?

The dress is gorgeous, and judging by the size, won’t fit my curvy body at all. My breasts are more than a handful, and my hips are wide. I am a true hourglass figure, and this dress is made for someone who is tall and slim.

I glance around but don’t see any other clothes. I lost my pack in the forest, so I don’t have a change of clothes with me from home.

Shrugging, I make my way back to the bathroom, deciding to wash my face and armpits at least. The basin is lined with several sparkling glass bottles. I carefully unscrew the bottle of pink liquid and take a deep whiff of its contents. The sweet, fruity scent drifts through the air, and I hum in delight, the fragrance instantly melting the tension from my muscles and making me feel at ease.

I glance up in the mirror, my eyes widening in shock, and my body freezes. My long, thick, blonde hair is a mess. I wince at the thought of trying to untangle these knots with no conditioner to help me. Instead, I reach up and artfully twist and knot my mess of hair into a loose bun, creating what one might think to be an intentionally disheveled look. It still looks like a bird's nest up there, but it's as good as it's going to get for now. I turn the tap on, and the sound of running water fills the room. I cup some cool liquid in my hands and splash my face. Oh my god, that was nice.

Removing my shirt and tank, I grab a washcloth and lather up some soap, standing in just my bra and jeans. I make quick work of scrubbing my face, neck, arms, and chest, getting the majority of the dirt and sweat off me.

"There," I whisper to myself as I dry off.

I look down at my clothes, which are stained and exude an unpleasant smell. The last thing I want to do is put them back on, but I don't really have a choice. With a deep, forceful sigh, I pull my tank back on, then make my way back into the room and collapse on the bed. I am so exhausted that I can barely keep my eyes open, yet my mind is wide awake.

A soft knock at the door has me jolting off the bed, looking for a weapon. I hear the handle turning, and my eyes dart toward the door as it swings open, my heart in my throat.

The woman from earlier backs into the room, pulling a cart with her. The sweet smell of food hits me, and my mouth instantly waters.

"Miss?"

I must have zoned out, completely focused on the food, because I didn't hear her speaking.

"Sorry?"

She's frowning, her face full of displeasure. "Were the clothes not suitable?"

"Oh." I laugh and wave her off. "The dress is beautiful, but it will not fit me." I gesture to my body.

The woman's tail whips back and forth as she stares at me. "I will find you something more fitting, then."

"Oh, you don't have to. I should go soon anyway. My friends are probably frantic."

She tilts her head as if trying to figure me out. Maybe she hasn't seen a human before. As I take a closer look at her in proper lighting, I realize that the shape and curve of her eyes, even down to the slit vertical pupil, are the same as a cat, which complements her ears and tail. It takes a moment to register that we're staring at each other, and a flush creeps up my neck.

"Do you know who those men in the forest were?" I blurt.

"Why do you ask?"

"I want to know why I understood them? They weren't speaking English, but I could still understand them."

"From what I overheard the soldiers saying, they were part of a group that call themselves Outcasts. They lurk in the forest, using their native tongue to confuse and prey on unsuspecting travelers."

I sigh, my thoughts jumbled as I try to make sense of it. That still doesn't explain why I could understand them, or why I could sense their intentions.

If Maxon didn't come along when he did . . . I shiver, recalling their wickedness. It seeped from their pores. The images of Maxon killing them flash in my mind, making my stomach twist.

"He killed them," I whisper.

"They would have left you for dead."

I jerk my head up in surprise, taken aback by her stern voice. It makes me uneasy that someone could kill so quickly and simply, without hesitation. It seems heartless. Though, the Fae described in stories are said to be cold and calculating. I try to think back to any stories I heard growing up.

From what I can recall from reading books as a child, there are two main courts among the Fae. Seelie, the Court of Light, is said to be bathed in a brilliant, golden light. While Unseelie, the Court of Dark, is cloaked in a deep, mysterious shadow.

The sub-courts are sectioned off and named after the seasons that linger in their territory; Summer, Autumn, Winter, and Spring. I'm not sure how it all works, but I don't think I'm in the gloomy doomy Unseelie court. Instead, I feel a sense of lightness and warmth.

I watch as she turns away, a sense of urgency propelling me forward, and immediately I move toward her.

"Wait. What should I call you?"

The woman slowly looks over her shoulder and cocks her head to the side as she studies me again. I try not to fidget under her scrutiny, she's freaking me out a little. Especially her tail, it's swaying back and forth methodically.

"Zaria," she finally answers.

"Nice to meet you. I'm Everly," I say, stepping forward and holding out my hand. Zaria looks down at my hand and then back up at me in question. I drop my hand, feeling stupid. I am so out of my league here.

"I will return with some clothes." With that, she's gone again.

With a deep sigh, I shift my gaze toward the array of food laid out on the cart, taking in the vibrant colors and tempting aromas. Everything on the cart looks so delectable that my stomach lets out a loud growl, as if urging me to dig in.

"Okay. Okay," I mutter, reaching out and picking up a fluffy pastry.

I take a small bite and the flavors burst in my mouth. Oh my god, this is amazing. I take another bite and another. I devour two more pastries before grabbing a handful of berries and taking a seat on one of the couches. I just finish my berries when there's another knock at the door and Zaria walks in. Her brown eyes sweep around the room and land on me.

"Here are some clothes. It was all I could find on short notice. I'm sure you can make them work until I can acquire something more fitting."

She places the pile of clothes on the bed and stands there, watching me. Thank you stalls on my tongue, and I hesitate.

"I appreciate the clothes and food," I say, standing up.

Zaria slightly bows her head and turns for the door.

"Wait."

"Is there something else?" she asks.

"Where am I?"

Zaria's eyes widen in alarm. "You don't know where you are?"

"Well no . . . I don't know how I got here, and I'm sure my friends are worried. You see, I was hiking with them and then I met this fairy. And she was supposed to be helping me, but she disappeared, and then I was hunted and chased through the forest by–"

Zaria steps toward me, raising her hand to stop my rambling.

"You're from the human realm?" she inquires, confusion creasing her features.

I nod and squint my eyes when I notice her hair moving. Shaking my head, I refocus. I must be losing my mind. "Do you know how I can get back?"

Zaria chews her bottom lip. "The gates have been closed. You shouldn't have been able to come through."

My spirits drop, and my heart falls to my stomach. "What? What do you mean?"

"Look, I will let the prince explain everything to you in more detail. Just, for now, get cleaned up and rested. I'm sure you're tired."

Prince?

"Wait. One more question. Why are your eyes different from the men?"

Zaria's eyebrow arches, and I hear the sound of my knuckles cracking as I twist my fingers together in unease.

"You mean the fae men you've met?"

"I don't know, but the ones in the woods and Maxon all had different shades of purple eyes."

"High fae possess purple eyes. The depth of color reflects their power. The darker the purple, the more power."

"What about Maxon? He has a silver ring around his?"

Zaria's eyes flare wide in surprise. "The silver ring means royalty."

My heart skips a beat and I jerk forward a step. "Royalty?"

"Yes, and you should not call him Maxon," she replies sternly.

I'm getting on her nerves, I can tell, but I have to ask. "And you?"

She lets out a deep sigh and slowly raises her shoulders in a shrug. "My eyes are brown because I am a shifter."

"A what?" My mind goes to all the romance books Scarlett had me read, and I can't imagine that any of them are real. "A shifter?"

"Yes, now, was that all? You should really get some rest."

It's on the tip of my tongue to ask what type of shifter, but I bite down on my lip. My shoulders slump in defeat, and I slowly nod in resignation. I watch as she quickly and quietly slips from the room. I grab the pile of clothes from the bed and sigh in relief at the brown pants and white shirt.

I shimmy out of my dirty clothing, leaving only my bra and panties on. The pants are way too big, so I cinch them with the drawstring at my waist and roll up the hems. The shirt is an old fashioned tunic with long sleeves, the fabric soft and comforting against my skin. It falls to my mid-thigh, so I twist it in a knot, tying it at the front.

Slowly, I walk back to the couch, feeling the warmth of the cushions beneath me as I snuggle in and close my eyes. With a full stomach and the comforting pleasure of clean clothes, my mood is significantly improved. As I begin to slip into slumber, a tranquil sensation washes over me, causing my body to unwind and a gentle heat to flow through my limbs. I utter a soft, satisfied hum. Despite finding myself in an unfamiliar realm, devoid of any familiar faces, there is an inexplicable sense of recognition. As if the very atmosphere embraces me, enfolding me in the delicate fragrance of nature.

Chapter Seven

Everly

I wake to the gentle sound of tapping on my door. With a groan, I sit up and blink a few times, trying to get my bearings. I squint at the light pouring in through the windows and hear the birds chirping outside. I must have been more tired than I thought.

The sound of knocking echoes through the room again.

"Come in," I call out, my voice croaky from sleep.

The door swings open, and Zaria enters. Today she's in a plain silk sage dress with long sleeves, accentuating her graceful figure. The dress has a modest V-neckline, and the color beautifully complements her darker complexion, enhancing her natural radiance. With every step she takes, it gracefully flows around her, exuding an air of grace and poise. I watch as her lips press together, forming a tight line that conveys both concern and indignation.

I quickly stand up, my skin tingling with a sudden awareness. "What is it?"

She frowns at me but shakes her head, her attention quickly darting to the door behind her as she clasps her hands in front of her.

"You need to come with me," she answers.

Okay, I don't like the way she said that.

"Where are we going?" I ask as I reach for my boots.

Zaria's face drops to the ground. "Queen Lavina wishes to see you."

"Okay," I reply cautiously. "Is that a bad thing?"

Without so much as a glance in my direction, Zaria turns toward the door. I quickly slip my boots on before following her out the room. As I step out into the hall, I see two men wearing sage-colored uniforms standing on either side of my door. The sight of their swords against their hips is jarring, as are the stern expressions on their faces. Their presence immediately sends a wave of goosebumps down my arms, and I can't help but wonder who they are and why they're stationed outside my door. Zaria seems unfazed by them, her gaze fixed ahead as she strides purposefully down the hall. I hurry to catch up with her, my mind racing with a flurry of questions.

What happened while I was asleep? Are these men a threat, or some kind of protection? I desperately need answers, but Zaria remains silent, which only adds to the mystery surrounding the situation.

I turn my head, noticing the guards trailing behind me. The glint of their armor catches my eye, adorned with a striking red and gold emblem depicting a majestic dragon. The sight jolts my senses, a vivid reminder that I have crossed over into a realm beyond the mundane human world.

"This way," Zaria's words draw my attention.

Anxiety bubbles up inside me, and the air gets heavy with unease, as if it's suffocating my every breath. The sound of my heartbeat echoes in my ears, a constant reminder of my racing thoughts.

I observe Zaria's tense shoulders; her steps are hesitant, cautious, as if she's navigating a treacherous path. I can almost feel the tension radiating off her, a palpable energy that adds to the suffocating atmosphere.

Up ahead, two more guards are stationed in front of the gigantic set of ornate wooden doors. I know that's where we are heading, because the guards become alert at our approach. My heart is thundering in my chest, and a chill runs down my spine, causing the hairs on my arms to stand on end as we draw nearer to the doors. Zaria peers over her shoulder at me, her eyes flashing like lightning. I wonder if she can hear it—my heart, that is. I stare at her in desperation, silently pleading for her to tell me that everything is going to be alright. But she turns back around, her tail lashing in what I can only assume is frustration.

I have a feeling that even if she wanted to speak, she couldn't. I am hyper-aware of the energy floating around me and it makes my limbs tingle with the need to run. Glancing past her to one of the guards, I am met with a menacing scowl that has my stomach lurching.

What did I do?

If I knew I'd be meeting the queen, I might have tidied myself up better. My palms are slick with sweat, so I wipe them on my pants. I'm sure I look like a homeless person, my hair a wild mess and my clothes wrinkled. I didn't take the time to brush my unruly hair; instead, it's still tied up in a haphazard bun. But after sleeping, part of it's falling loose again. I slowly push some hair behind my ear and fidget on the spot.

Zaria turns to me and gives me a soft smile, but I can sense her worry and it doesn't make me feel any better.

"You'll be fine," she whispers, knocking on the doors.

"Enter," a stern but feminine voice calls from the other side.

The two guards behind me brush past to grab the handles, and Zaria steps closer, discreetly squeezing my hand. There is a warning in her eyes, as she leans in close to whisper in my ear quickly, "Don't give her a reason to throw you in the dungeons."

Startled, I jerk back, my eyes widening at the incredulous statement. Before I have a chance to question her, Zaria swiftly passes me, her presence fading down the hall.

"Come on," one guard snaps, causing me to jump.

Taking a deep breath, I reluctantly step inside, my feet dragging as if weighed down by lead. Immediately, my gaze is drawn to the massive glass doors across the room, revealing a stunning garden beyond. My hands tremble, craving the sensation of running them over delicate flower petals. The intensity of this desire catches me off guard, and I pause, inhaling deeply in an attempt to steady myself. As I do, the most heavenly scent wafts in through the open doors, saturating the air. It is so potent that it almost feels tangible, as if I could taste it on my tongue. I don't realize I have zoned out until I receive a hard shove in the back, sending me stumbling forward. I twist my neck, shooting the guard a dirty look.

"Don't worry about him," a sweet feminine voice startles me.

How did I forget I was here to see the queen?

My eyes are drawn to her, and my breath catches in my throat. The queen is beautiful, her long black hair in an elaborate updo, and she has the same eyes as Maxon, the deep violet with a silver ring around the iris. She stands in the middle of a large living area, with walls of smooth, gray stone. The only color in the room comes from the vibrant rugs and tapestries that are draped across the floor and walls. There are many decorative touches throughout the room, giving it a distinctly feminine feel. The queen is wearing a long purple gown that trails the floor, white lace trimmings on the sleeve. Unlike me, she looks well rested and fresh. She gestures to the chairs around where she's standing, and I slowly make my way over to her, tucking some wayward hair behind my ear.

"So you're the human girl. Everly was it?"

I nod cautiously, unsure if I'm allowed to speak.

"I'm Queen Lavina."

"It's nice to meet you," my word trail off uncomfortably.

The queen hums sweetly and sits down. I mimic her actions, sinking into the chair's soft cushions. I let my fingers drift over the material, feeling its plush, velvety texture. The chair creaks under my weight, my hands drifting to the wooden hand rest, the smoothness of the wood gliding under my fingertips. A small, gentle sensation stirs within me, bringing a sense of peace.

"Drink?" the queen asks, surprising me.

The queen rises gracefully and moves to the side table to pour herself a drink, some kind of nectar from what I can tell. I frown and meet her gaze, my cheeks turning red in embarrassment when I realize I still haven't answered her.

I clear my throat and shake my head no. I really have to snap out of my daydreaming. It's a problem I've had since I was a child. As soon as I touch an object of my focus, I can feel the weight of the world slip away. So immersed in whatever I'm doing, everything else becomes background noise. The door on the other side of the room opens and a tall, skinny looking Fae man appears. His dark hair on the side of his head fades to silver to match his neatly trimmed beard. He approaches us and bows to the queen before his attention focuses on me.

"Everly, this is Nolan, my royal advisor. Nolan, Everly."

I swallow over the lump in my throat and drop my gaze, unable to stand the glare focused on me.

"Let's skip the small talk and get straight to the point. There is only one way a human can enter this realm." The queen turns her sharp eyes my way.

I stare at her blankly, waiting. When she doesn't continue, I frown. "Okay, what would that be?"

The fire in her violet eyes is unmistakable. I really need to think before I speak, but it's not like I've spoken to a queen before. The silence in the room is deafening as I realize I am way out of my depth. I hear the Queen of Hearts' words—*Off with her head!*—from Alice in Wonderland echoing in my head.

The queen moves closer to me, taking a sip from her glass, her eyes assessing me like a predator would its prey. It is at this moment I feel the full impact of her power. An involuntary tremor racks my body, her watchful gaze catching the movement.

"A high fae must have brought you here."

I shake my head, fingers pressing into the wood. "I can assure you, no one brought me here."

"Then explain to me how it is that you made it through the gate? A gate which has been closed for centuries."

"I was hiking the mountain with some friends and suddenly I was here. That's all I know. Maybe someone reopened it."

"Don't be absurd," the queen scoffs.

"I'm not. It was just a thought."

I turn my focus back to the window, and take in a deep breath of the sweet smell of roses and other wildflowers. I can almost feel the sensation of running my fingers over the petals of the flowers and my toes curling into the grass. A slight smile adorns my lips.

"Who are you protecting?"

My gaze swings back to her in alarm. "No one."

I can see it in her eyes, in the way they've hardened. She doesn't believe me.

My heart flutters, and dread curls in my stomach, making me nauseous.

The queen's smile is anything but warm and comforting. It is cruel and harsh, and makes my skin crawl. I don't like this woman. There is something lurking in the depths of her eyes, something that only time will reveal.

"I will find out one way or another, so you should spare yourself the pain and tell me now." She speaks as if speaking to a child, and maybe to her I am, but it doesn't stop my anger from surfacing at that moment.

"I am telling the truth. I don't know how I got here. I didn't even know *here* existed until two days ago!" I exclaim.

"Humans lie. It's all they do," she brushes off my comment with a wave of her hand.

I suppress my rising anger, the muscles in my jaw tightening, and speak through clenched teeth. "I don't lie."

"Somehow, I find that hard to believe. If you won't tell me who you're protecting, then you leave me with no other option."

The queen looks behind me to the two guards. "Take her to the dungeons, a few days in there should change her mind."

"What?!" I shout, jumping to my feet. "You can't just lock me up."

My body trembles as my mind fills with thoughts of being confined in a small, dark area, unable to escape. A sense of dread and claustrophobia rises, making panic pulse in waves as sweat breaks out on my palms and neck.

"Of course she can," Nolan says, speaking for the first time.

The guards stalk over and grab an arm each and turn me toward the doors. I dig my feet in, protesting. I won't be locked up, I can't. My breathing picks up and I try desperately to pull my arms free, but I am no match for these fae guards.

"Oh, and Everly?" Queen Lavina calls out as we reach the door.

I glance at her over my shoulder and I'm met with a cold, hard stare, her eyes sharp and her lips curled in a sneer.

"You won't be going home until you tell me what I want to know."

When I don't answer, her lips press together in frustration, and she gestures to the guards, turning her back on me.

Chapter Eight

Everly

I'm basically yanked from the room and down the hall, but not toward my room. No, I stumble slightly as the guards abruptly drag me off in a different direction. I notice an alcove up ahead, hints of a hidden staircase awaiting me with its ominous, shadowy steps.

Panic surges through me as I fight against the tight, unyielding grip on my arms, my heart racing. The truth hits me hard—I was a fool to assume they'd allow me to return home. Not that I have much to return to. The only family I have consists of Scarlett and Mia.

"Let me go," I snap, trying to pull free.

One guard elbows me in the ribs, making my breath catch.

"Enough," he growls through gritted teeth, his voice laced with venom.

As they tightly grasp my arms, a yelp escapes me, a combination of both shock and pain. I try to slow my thoughts as they pull me further down the hall. I know I'll end up in the dungeons, but I'm not about to make it easy for them. Maybe I can use my body weight against them. I've seen that done in movies, right?

Anything was worth a shot.

As soon as I feel their grips loosen, I fall to the ground, my legs giving out beneath me. Their steps falter and I manage to break free, stumbling backward. They spin on me, and I raise my hands, signaling them to stay back.

"Where are you going to run, human?" one of them taunts.

Glancing quickly to each side, I realize there is no other path to take but to turn back. The guards advance on me, their faces twisted with anger. A surge of energy rushes through me, and my body trembles with the force of the adrenaline that floods my system. Now I'm free, I have no idea what my next step is. I didn't think that far ahead. The realization that I can't outrun them leaves me feeling hopeless, but the thought of being locked up is even worse. My heart races in my chest as I take slow, deliberate steps backward, keeping my eyes locked on their menacing figures.

Suddenly, their expressions change, and a wave of confusion washes over me as they halt their approach and seem to straighten up. I cock my head to the side and blink, they aren't focused on me anymore.

I'm about to turn and make a run for it when a heavy hand suddenly clasps my shoulder, startling me. I twist my head and tip it up into the breathtaking violet, silver-ringed eyes of Maxon. His long, thick brown hair frames his face, and the sunlight only accentuates his good looks. His gaze flicks up to the guards, and in an instant, he is standing in front of me, shielding me from their view.

"What's going on here?" His deep, rough voice sends shivers down my spine as it resounds around me with authority.

"We are taking the human to the dungeons, Your Highness," one guard speaks up, a hint of fear in his voice.

Maxon's body tenses, the movement so slight I don't think anyone else would notice, but my face is mere inches from his back.

"On whose orders?" he growls.

"The queen's, Your Highness."

I'm caught off guard by the sudden flutter near my face, making me jump as my hair moves with the gentle breeze. It's Nix; her gaze intense and unwavering, her big, round blue eyes focused on me.

"She isn't going to the dungeons," Maxon states firmly.

"But Your Highness, the queen . . . "

"Leave the queen to me," Maxon barks, a wave of energy accompanying his words.

I take another step back and Nix's blue gaze is like a laser as she shakes her head in warning.

I widen my eyes at her. What does she want me to do? I have to get out of here.

I don't want to stay here and run the risk of being thrown into the dungeons. With a quick spin on my heels, I take off running in the opposite direction. The sound of my pounding footsteps is matched only by the pounding of my heart in my chest. The sudden shouts from the guards make me whip my head around, my eyes meeting Maxon's in a silent exchange. His alluring violet eyes seem to sparkle, and a mischievous smirk appears on his handsome face. I don't have time to process that expression.

Without warning, I collide hard with a solid chest, causing me to fall on my backside.

Ouch!!

I peer up into the silvery eyes of a huge man . . . with wings!?

My gaze moves slowly over the texture of his leathery wings and I swallow roughly. When I look closer, I can see two horns jutting out from underneath his light brown hair. He frowns down at me; his intense silver eyes seem to swirl like liquid. I swallow nervously and scoot away quickly.

The hulk of a . . . I don't know what he is, crosses his bulky arms over his massive chest and raises an eyebrow at me, waiting.

"Are you crazy?" Nix shrieks, flying up to me as I lean back on my hands on the floor.

"No, I was tested. Several times, actually," I snap.

Nix looks taken aback for a moment before she huffs and flitters up to stand on the hulking bat guy's shoulder.

Grumbling under my breath, I get to my feet, rubbing a hand over my sore butt.

"Where have you been?" I ask her.

"Looking for you."

I sense a subtle presence behind me, and I instinctively turn, shifting to the side, ensuring I never have my back exposed to anyone. That is a lesson that was ingrained in me since a young age, thanks to the various foster homes I was in. They were far from the safe havens people thought they were. Maxon, with his disheveled, tousled dark hair and his tunic clinging to his sweaty chest, stands before me. I look behind him and see the guards are gone, obviously having been dismissed. At that moment, it dawns on me that it is just the four of us, alone in this precarious situation.

"Did they hurt you?" he asks, his jaw going tight.

I give my head a shake, and his features relax, that twinkle returning to his eyes.

"The queen will be pissed if we go against her orders," the guy with the wings grumbles.

"I will go and see her," Maxon replies, putting his hands on his hips.

His attention focuses on me, his violet eyes locking with mine. Everything else seems to fade away as we stand there caught in each other's gaze. Something deep in my chest tugs, and I want to step into his arms. I trace the lines of his face with my eyes, taking in every detail: the entwining vines tattooed around his left temple, the delicate curves and swirls wrapping around his cheekbone; the way his thick, dark eyelashes frame his captivating eyes, which seem to have depths that could never fully be explored. My fingers itch to reach up and touch his full lips, just to see if they are as soft as they look.

I blink, caught off guard by the sudden clearing of a throat. Here I am drifting off again, only this time I've been hypnotized by a Fae. Not just any Fae—a prince. My face heats and I cross my arms over my chest in embarrassment. Maxon smirks, shifting closer, his hand reaching up to glide his fingers over my cheek in a featherlight touch.

My body immediately becomes rigid at the unexpected contact.

"Beautiful," he whispers, the silver around his eyes brightening.

A completely foreign emotion washes over me causing a soft flutter in my chest. I swallow roughly and step away from him, making his hand drop. There is a moment of awkward silence while I wait for someone to tell me what the hell is going on.

Movement down the corridor catches my attention, and I watch as Zaria hurries toward us, her long silk dress getting tangled in her legs. She curses, gathering her skirts in her hands as she runs.

"There you are," she pants, looking at me as she comes to a stop.

"Here I am," I reply, shifting on my feet.

"I thought for sure you'd be in the dungeons." Her tail whips around swatting the hulking bat guy in the chest. "I was looking everywhere for you, and you." She nod to Maxon.

Uncertainty fills me, I don't know what's going on or why I'm here. Who any of these Fae are, or who I can trust?

"Can someone tell me what's going on?"

"Why don't you tell us?" the hulking Fae questions.

"If I knew, I wouldn't be asking now would I, Batman!"

"Batman?"

I gesture to his wings, and he laughs, a rumbling sound coming from deep in his throat. Zaria lifts her hand to hide her smile and Maxon chuckles from next to me. Nix's eyes twinkle with amusement as I lock my gaze with hers. In a swift motion, she flies over and hovers before me, her wings fluttering softly in the air.

"I'm sorry I took so long, but my friend, Raiden here"—she gestures to the winged Fae—"was hunting, and it took a bit to find him."

Zaria steps forward. "We shouldn't talk here, not out in the open."

"She's right," Maxon replies. "We will go to my chambers."

I stand firm, putting my hand on my hips. "Why should I trust any of you?"

"I've saved you, twice now," Maxon counters, a smirk tugging at his full lips.

He has a point, but still . . .

I steal a quick look at Zaria, and she offers a slight nod in my direction. I feel my resolve waver, like a fragile thread about to snap.

Ultimately, I am entrusting my life to a group of complete strangers. And not just any strangers, but fae. It is a thought that I never could have fathomed before. And even though they appear to be genuine, I can't help but feel a sense of unease.

Chapter Nine

Everly

I'm guided through the corridors and up several flights of stairs to a separate wing of the castle. My eyes take in all the details around me from the high ceilings to the intricate details of the wooden banisters, and the cracks and imperfections in some of the smooth stonework. Every detail tells a story, a whispered secret I wish I knew.

Maxon pushes open a set of large wooden doors carved with golden vines similar to the markings on his face, and at his touch the carvings glimmer. My footsteps slow, my mouth dropping open in awe. We enter the room behind him, and the heavy doors close with a resounding thud. I notice a faint shimmer emanating from them, and as I do, a tingling sensation travels over my skin, causing me to instinctively rub my arms.

"What was that?" I ask, looking around the room.

"Magic," Zaria answers.

"My rooms are warded," Maxon adds.

It's like what I experienced before in the forest as I stepped through the gate. It's a familiar sensation. The others gather in the sitting area, their footsteps echoing softly in the room. Two additional doors on the opposite side beckon me to explore. A sudden urge to satisfy my curiosity consumes me. It's a weakness of mine, always drawn to places I shouldn't be. However, never did I expect it would lead me to another realm. A soft chuckle escapes my lips, and I see Zaria's ears twitching as she shifts her attention toward me.

I clear my throat, looking around at the group before me. "Why does the queen think a high fae brought me here?"

Maxon strides over to the double glass window, unlatching it and allowing the wind to blow in, causing the sheer curtains to sway gently in the breeze. I immediately feel a sense of calmness as the breeze wraps around me.

"In order to enter Faerie, a human must either be invited or possess their own magical capabilities to open the gates. Those on the other side aren't strong enough to open the gates alone. Only a handful possess the required magic to do so."

I blink and throw my hands in the air with exasperation. "Well, I didn't have anyone bring me here, and I'm not magic, so what else you got?"

Raiden, with his muscular physique, folds his massive arms over his chest and huffs out a disbelieving chuckle, the sound dripping with mockery, causing irritation to seep into my bones.

"It's the truth!" I snap.

"Well, if what you say is true, and no one invited you here, then we can only assume you hold some type of magic," Zaria argues.

"Doubt it," I mutter, plonking down on one of the velvet sofas.

"Could be you've just never noticed." Zaria shrugs.

Nix flutters closer. "When I found you, was that when you first arrived here?"

I nod my head, remembering her anger at me.

"I had been walking with some friends, then suddenly they were gone, or I was."

Nix studies me for a long moment before she speaks. "She smells and looks human. Maybe one of her friends sent her through the gate," she offers, turning to the others.

My mouth drops open. "No. No, no, my friends had nothing to do with this."

No way Mia or Scarlett would send me to Faerie on my own. I've been friends with both of them since college. We have been by each other's sides for close to five years. We were housemates for three years, and the bond we formed still stands strong.

"Some people are good at hiding who they really are," Raiden counters.

The insinuation is clear, making anger flare in my chest. I bite the inside of my cheek and shoot him a glare, but the swirling depths of those silver eyes give me pause. He is assessing me.

"Well, until we figure it out, you are under my protection. I will have you moved here, to my chambers," Maxon declares.

Stay here with him? No way!

My head whips around to him, my hair getting in my face as I send a scowl in his direction. "No, I'm not staying here."

Maxon clenches his jaw as he stalks toward me. "This is non-negotiable."

"Well, I say it is," I snap, standing up so I can face him on somewhat level ground. I spent my whole life being bullied and pushed around in foster care. I am not going to give in so easily.

"Everly." My name comes out in a low growl, sending a shiver down my spine, but not in fear.

I straighten my shoulders, lifting my chin in defiance. "No."

The tension between us grows as we stare at each other, neither relenting.

"She can't stay here. The court would have a fit." Raiden's voice is low and filled with disapproval as he looks at Maxon with a heavy frown.

Maxon grumbles under his breath, pressing his thumb and forefinger against his forehead, as if trying to stave off a throbbing headache.

Me, too, buddy.

"The timing of her arrival is suspicious. I don't trust her," Raiden adds.

Shock rolls through me, making my stomach dip. I can't believe him. "Well, I don't trust you either!"

"Humans are nothing but trouble," Raiden counters.

"Enough," Maxon breathes, stepping between us.

Raiden grumbles under his breath, and I can't help but poke my tongue out. Immature, I know, but he is pissing me off.

"Speaking of courts. Where am I?" I ask, looking up at Maxon.

He unfastens his sword, dropping it down on the table, and I watch as he rolls up the sleeves of his black tunic. When his eyes meet mine, I feel a sudden flutter in my chest as his intense stare holds me captive.

"You are in Skora. At the Castle Vesner," he answers roughly.

"Okay, that means nothing to me."

"You are in the Autumn Court," Nix explains, her tiny feet landing on the arm of the chair.

"The Unseelie Court," Raiden adds, crossing his arms. "This here is the crown prince, and I'm his personal guard. Zaria here works for me, keeping tabs on the staff."

"Personal guard? And here I thought we had been best friends since we were boys," Maxon says, smirking at his friend.

Raiden's wings flare outward slightly as he chuckles. "Yes, but my duty comes first. Your protection comes first."

"Good to know," Maxon replies, clearly amused.

"Only one guard?" I question.

Raiden's eyes quickly meet mine, but Maxon answers before he can. "I don't need a guard. I just keep him around for my amusement."

Raiden scoffs.

Nix grins wickedly, her eyes glinting with excitement. "You should witness the prince in action. No one would dare lay a finger on him."

Raiden stares at me, a serious expression crossing his face once more. I feel like his silver eyes are searching, trying to uncover my secrets. It makes me antsy and on edge. He is making me feel guilty for something I haven't even done.

"I don't know why I'm here, or how I got here, okay? So, stop looking at me like that."

Raiden grunts and turns his back on me to say something to Zaria. My eyes trace over the edges of his wings. They look so much like bat wings. I wonder if he can actually fly, if they'd hold his massive weight . . .

"Don't worry about him. He's just being cautious." Maxon approaches me.

My pulse jumps as he draws nearer, and I rest my hand on my chest.

"Can you really stop the queen from throwing me in the dungeons?" I ask.

Maxon's eyes harden, his jaw tensing. "You won't be going to the dungeons."

My mind flickers back to the unseelie part of the conversation, and I can't shake the dizzying sensation. Am I with the bad Fae? Unseelie is bad, right?

I stare at Maxon, the crown prince. He doesn't seem all that bad. I look at the others. None of them do. But looks can be deceiving. I don't know any of them, so who am I to say if they are good or bad? My internal monologue berates me for my lack of knowledge, causing me to feel even more incompetent.

"What do you mean by Seelie and Unseelie?" I ask, my voice barely a whisper.

"The Fae realm is divided into two main courts. Seelie, who reign over the vibrant Summer and Spring courts. Then there is us. The Unseelie who hold their power within the Autumn and Winter courts. You know, amidst the crackling of frozen twigs and the howling of winter winds," Nix sharp teeth show as she grins.

Clearly, she's waiting for my reaction. I roll my eyes and gesture out the open doors to the garden.

"It doesn't look that bad. The forest was filled with wildflowers."

"Yes, I noticed that," Raiden hums. "We rarely get flowers, our foliage more wavering between green, browns, and oranges."

"Skora is in the heart of the Autumn court," Maxon explains.

Tucking some hair behind my ear, I bite my bottom lip in contemplation.

"Just ask," Zaria chuckles.

I peek over at her and ask. "Aren't Unseelie bad?"

Nix guffaws, and Zaria presses her lips together to hold in her smile. I peer at Raiden, and he appears confused, while Maxon rubs his chin with a mischievous glint in his eye.

"Oh, we can be bad," he replies, his voice teasing.

Oh my god, that look has my stomach dipping violently. He is pure temptation, all wrapped up in sexy. Put a bow on him, and I'd unwrap him in a second.

I shake my head, trying to rid myself of these thoughts before I turn bright red. Zaria clears her throat and Maxon blinks, running a hand through his hair, a smirk tugging at his lips.

"Everly, there is no black and white when it comes to the morality of the Fae. Self-interest always guides our decisions. Unseelie is no more good or bad than Seelie. But in saying that, the Seelie high fae will trick you into your own destruction if given the chance," Maxon says.

"The high fae have the beauty of angels, but the hearts of demons. The Seelie more so, as they think they are set way above the rest of us." Zaria's response is nonchalant, her gaze moving to Maxon. "No offense, Your Highness."

Maxon smirks, his eyes sparkling with amusement as he tilts his head and shrugs. "None taken."

"Good to know," I reply, looking at each of them in turn.

I hear the flutter of wings and turn to see Nix landing on the chair next to me. Her large sapphire eyes that are shaped like innocent orbs, transform into slits of anger as she focuses her full attention on me.

"What I want to know is why did you leave the tree?"

The sudden change in topic catches me off guard and leaves me speechless.

"Well?" she demands.

I blink, taking a small step back from the full force of her fury. Honestly, she is terrifying for something so small and cute.

"I heard the sound of water. You may recall me telling you I needed water. You told me there wasn't any close," I reply, giving her a pointed look.

"There isn't," she says, her face scrunching in confusion.

I blink. "Wait, what?"

"There isn't a stream near the tree. The closest stream is a half day's walk."

"But I saw a stream. I washed up and filled my water bottle."

The room was suddenly filled with an eerie silence, leaving an unsettling stillness in the air.

"Are you sure?" Nix whispers.

"Yes."

Nix bobs her head, looking over at the others before returning her gaze to me. "Why didn't you return to the tree?"

The question has a shiver running up my spine, making me wrap my arms around my waist in an attempt to feel secure. I sense Maxon move closer to me, as if sensing my unease, and his touch on my shoulder immediately calms my anxiety. As I look up at him, I notice the warmth in his eyes and the gentle curve of his smile.

"What did you see?" he asks softly, almost coaxing me to speak.

A weak laugh escapes my lips. "I don't know. It was a horrible creature; one I hope to never see again. It wanted to hurt me. Its intentions were as clear to me as if they were my own." I pause, thinking. I sensed the intention of the Fae in the fields, too. Have I always been able to do that? Is it only bad intentions I can pick up on?

Maxon's gentle touch on my arm brings me back to reality, and I continue.

"I just ran and didn't stop. But I think something stopped it when I crossed the stream. I heard its screams, but I didn't dare look back. After a while, I finally reached the grassy field where you found me."

"What did this creature look like?" Raiden inquires.

I flick my gaze to his, and I'm momentarily mesmerized by the swirling silver depths. "A giant ass human spider, only with two arms and two legs. Its skin was gray and it had a deformed head. Milky eyes that were sunken in, gaunt looking, and fast—so fast. It was creepy. I could go a lifetime without seeing that again." I shudder.

"A deadling . . .", Zaria gasps. "They haven't been seen in–"

"Centuries," Raiden finishes, his gaze narrowing on me.

Zaria steps forward, basically pushing Maxon out of her way as she grabs my hands. "How did you outrun it?"

I shrug, giving her a weak smile. "I listened to my gut and ran for the stream. Once I crossed it, I was safe."

Zaria frowns, then shakes her head. "Well, I'm glad you're okay and you got away. Deadlings don't usually come to the surface."

At my look of confusion, she gives me a wary smile. "They don't come topside. They dwell underground in caves and tunnels. The fact you encountered one is more than a little unnerving."

"You showing up a week before Maxon is due to take the throne is even more unnerving." Raiden eyes me again. "The flowers and the deadlings coming out of hibernation, that's disturbing."

Zaria steps back, giving me some space, and I shoot her a grateful look. I have had a lot of information thrown at me today, and I'm not sure I fully understand any of it. I stretch my neck to the side, feeling the tightness in my shoulders and neck. My body is still recovering from the day before. I have never had to run for my life twice in one day, or ride a horse. Now I'm suffering the lingering effects.

"Well, I have no answers for you." I roll my shoulders and peer at Zaria. "I could really use that shower now," I say, smiling at her.

I need to get away from Maxon's and Raiden's penetrating stares. Their gazes are suffocating, making me feel trapped and exposed. Maxon's eyes are filled with a relentless curiosity, his mind seemingly racing with questions he wants to ask. It's as if he wishes to unravel every secret I hold, leaving me feeling vulnerable and uncomfortable in his presence. On the other hand, Raiden's is piercing and hostile, as if he sees right through me, finding me guilty of some unknown offense. His accusatory stare makes me feel on edge, constantly questioning my every move and motive.

"Of course," Zaria replies.

Maxon steps in front of me as I go to follow Zaria. "I promise you will be safe here. You won't end up in the dungeons."

From the corner of my eye, I see Raiden's head turn sharply toward us and Zaria's hands flying to cover her mouth. The subtle change in the air is confusing. Then I remember that Fae do not make promises. They are bound by their word.

"Maxon!" Raiden hisses.

Maxon ignores them, his eyes burning into mine. "What is it about you that has me so unguarded?" His head tilts as he studies me, but I don't know what to say. I've never had so much attention focused on me before. I like to stay hidden in the background.

My head tips back as Maxon takes another step closer, our bodies less than a foot apart. His violet eyes seem to penetrate my soul, leaving me feeling exposed.

"Why am I drawn to you?"

My heart skids to a stop at his softly spoken words. He feels it, too. The strange impulse, the instant chemistry.

Maxon's hand lifts slowly, his fingers ever so lightly brushing against my cheek and trailing down my neck, sending a tremor through me. I hold my breath, my heart beating wildly in my chest at his intense proximity. Maxon's fingertips lightly graze the back of my neck, sending a wave of warmth through me with each press of his fingers. I can see he is just as transfixed by me as I am with him. His eyes travel to my lips, and my stomach feels like it's doing somersaults. Desire burns hot in his gaze as it rises back to mine, and my body sways closer to him.

"Okay, that's enough," Raiden growls, stalking toward us.

I blink as Maxon drops his hand, my body swaying on my feet. Raiden slaps a heavy hand on Maxon's shoulder and turns him away. Shaking my head, I let out a long breath.

What is happening?

I feel Zaria's hand on my arm, a intense heat radiating from her palm as she pulls me toward the windows.

"Girl, you need to be careful."

"Huh? What do you mean?"

Zaria's stare lingers, making me shift uncomfortably.

"Is it hot in here?" I ask, pushing my sleeves up and fanning my face with my hand.

Zaria's eyes widen, and she moves to block me from the rest of the room.

"What's that?" she whispers harshly, looking at my arm.

I frown, glancing down. "What?"

Grabbing my wrist, she holds my arm out in front of me, her fingers running over my birthmark on the inside of my forearm. She glances over her shoulder to where Maxon and Raiden were conversing in low voices on the far side of the room.

Then she quickly tugs down my sleeve, her lips brushing against my ear as she whispers softly. "Show nobody this."

I jerk back, my eyes meeting hers. "What? Why?"

My birthmark is odd, I agree, but it's just a skin discoloration. I always thought it looks like a unique combination of a sun and moon, together in a winding pattern of vines. But that was just my imagination. Like when you make out shapes in the clouds. It's also a pale white color, unlike the deeper pigments of most. Unless you are looking closely, it's hard to make out against my pale skin.

"Not now. Please tell me you won't say a word. It's important, if the wrong person sees this, it could be very dangerous for you."

I stare at Zaria for a long moment, my mind filtering through the implications. Can the others not be trusted? Nix is watching us closely from the sofa still. Unease slithers down my spine and I nod, trepidation making my pulse pick up. The prince's gaze snaps to mine as if hearing my heart speed up. He frowns at me in question, but I look away.

"What are you two whispering about over there?" Raiden asks, sauntering toward us.

"I could ask you the same thing," I reply, crossing my arms, the birthmark now feeling like a burn under my shirt.

“I need to go and talk to my aunt,” Maxon says, making his way over. “Zaria will take you back to your room.”

“Okay,” I whisper.

Zaria links her arm with mine and smiles. “Don’t worry, she is in good hands.”

Chapter Ten

Everly

Back in my room, Zaria goes straight to the bathroom, and the sound of running water fills the air along with a soft, sweet, flowery scent. Nix flitters over to the cart of food and starts picking through the mass amounts of fruit.

"These are so good." She hums, biting into a blueberry. "Want some?"

I give her a small smile. "I'm okay."

Nix narrows her eyes and then shrugs, taking a bite from a grape.

Zaria returns, her eyes scanning the room. "Bath won't take long."

"I can't wait." Just thinking about a bath, I can almost feel the warm water caressing my skin and the gentle tickle of bubbles.

Zaria reaches up and pulls her chestnut curls back, twisting them into a knot on top of her head.

"Oh, wow!" I exclaim, walking closer and examining her hair.

"What?" Zaria asks, frowning in confusion as she retreats a few paces.

"You don't have ears!" I blurt.

Zaria rears her head back, her nostrils flaring as her eyes dart over to Nix. Following her gaze, and my eyes land on Nix, who simply sits cross legged on the food cart.

"I have ears," Zaria corrects, twitching the massive cat ears on her head.

"Yes, but not like everyone else."

"Well, no. When I got stuck in this form, my fae ears disappeared."

"I like your ears. They're cute," I reply.

Zaria's cat-like eyes blink at me, and I can't help but notice the pink flush that spreads across her tanned skin.

"Uhh . . . thanks."

I giggle at her skepticism, feeling a lot more relaxed now that we're back in my room and away from Maxon and Raiden's probing stares.

"What type of shifter are you?"

Zaria smiles softly. "You have a lot of questions, don't you?"

"Considering I'm in a completely different world, yeah."

"I'm a leopard."

"Can I ask how you got stuck in a half shift?"

When Zaria's face falls, sending a pang of guilt through my chest. "I'm sorry. I'm being nosey. You don't have to tell me."

Zaria's warm hand clasps mine, leading me to the sitting area where we settle on a comfortable sofa. Her gaze drifts toward the open window, her eyes fixed on the world beyond as she loses herself in contemplation. In the silence, it's easier to note that the air holds a faint scent of rain, hinting at an impending storm. I remain still, patiently waiting for her thoughts to find their voice.

"Most shifters don't shift until their sixteenth birthday. It's a huge celebration. We all gather, and the whole family is there to help guide and protect the process." She pauses, her eyes dropping to her lap where she twists her fingers. "It was supposed to be fun."

I stretch out my arm and gently cover her hand with mine. With a blink, she gazes up at me.

"When I was thirteen, I wandered too far from my parents when we were out collecting berries."

A feeling of unease snakes its way up my spine.

"I found myself in a tight spot when two Outcasts blocked my path and attempted to kidnap me. I was so terrified when they grabbed me that I couldn't control the shift that overtook me. By the time my parents arrived, it was too late. The damage had been done. I was left to cope with an early shift and no guidance. Leaving me stuck like this," she says, gesturing to her ears.

I scoot closer and grab both her hands in mine. Now I know why she spoke with such disdain when she mentioned the Outcasts earlier.

"I'm sorry you went through this. Is there not a way to reverse it?"

Zaria shakes her head. "My parents tried everything, but nothing worked. It's not all that bad, but it can be painful when the urge to shift comes and my body can't do anything."

The need to comfort her is overwhelming. Although she isn't yet a friend, I am tempted to hug her like I normally would, but instead squeeze her hands and offer a kind smile.

"I don't know what to say except I think you look beautiful," I answer honestly.

"Really?" Zaria blinks rapidly for a couple of seconds.

"Yes."

"Are you two done with the sob stories yet?" Nix yawns, stretching her arms above her head. "Because I'm tired. I have spent the last two days awake trying to find you."

"Now who is telling the sob story?" I interject, raising my eyebrow.

"Touché." Nix grins, putting her pointy teeth on display.

Zaria stands, clearing her throat. "Your bath should be ready. Do you need assistance?"

Shock renders me speechless, my face slack with disbelief. "To bathe?"

"Yes."

"Uhh, no, I can most surely do that on my own," I reply, standing.

"Don't drown," Nix quips.

Peering over my shoulder, I meet her gaze. "I'll do my best not to."

I shut the bathroom door behind me and close my eyes, breathing in the scent of jasmine and lilies. I slowly strip off the clothes I have on and step into the bath. The warmth of the water wraps around me, soaking into my skin, warming every part of me. I immerse myself in the water, laying my head back against the side. As I close my eyes, I can feel the bubbles completely surrounding me, and the gentle pressure as they pop against my skin. I let my hands float out in front of me, skimming the water. The gentle back-and-forth motion soothes my muscles. I take my time soaking in the bath. And despite my hair being difficult to manage, I am eventually able to smooth it out.

I walk back into the bedroom, and see Zaria's contemplative expression as she stares out the window.

"Where is Nix?" I ask, using the towel to dry my hair.

"I sent her to rest," Zaria says. "She has been up for days."

My gaze lingers on her, studying her every movement and expression. She seems worried. There's an air of uncertainty around her.

"What's wrong?"

"That mark on your arm. How did you get it?"

Confused, I furrow my brow and give her a questioning look. "It's a birthmark."

Zaria lets out a sigh and massages her temples. A long tense moment passes, and her hair shifts again as she tilts her head, catching the light just so. I step closer, squinting. I see her hair move again and two tiny bright orbs stare at me.

I gasp, and Zaria's eyes snap up to meet mine.

"You have someone in your hair!" I exclaim, pointing.

Zaria's tail whips back and forth behind her and she reaches up, holding out her hand. I watch in complete fascination as a tiny shape appears. The fairy is only the size of my little finger. Eyes that are mesmerizing, one a piercing blue and the other a vibrant green. Her tiny frame is draped in a brown dress that matches the color of Zaria's hair, and her light brown skin glows in the light. The tiny fairy gracefully steps on to Zaria's hand and she brings it to her chest, holding it in front of her.

"This is Asrai. She is a Willowroot fairy."

Asrai gathers her long brown hair over her shoulder as she blinks those unique eyes at me.

I step closer and lower my voice. "Hi, I'm Everly."

Asrai peeks up at Zaria, who smiles warmly at her, reassuring her. When she faces me again, Zaria holds her out to me. Slowly, I hold my hand out until our fingertips touch. Asrai steps to my hand and curtsies, then signs her name to me.

With my free hand, I sign back. *Nice to meet you.*

"You know Willowroot?" Zaria asks.

"Huh? What do you mean?"

"Willowroots don't speak. They use hand signals as a way of communicating. No one knows their language, not even I."

I shrug as Asrai beams at me and unfolds a beautiful set of butterfly-like wings from her back. The colors are a mixture of blues and greens, just as vibrant as her eyes.

"You're absolutely beautiful," I whisper in awe.

Asrai blushes and signs, *Thank you,* before she lifts from my palm and flies back up to Zaria's head, and sits down. Now that I know she's there, I don't know how I missed her in the first place.

"Look, back to your birthmark."

I freeze, trepidation making me shuffle nervously on my feet. "What about it?"

"It's the mark of the druid royal bloodline."

I raise an eyebrow at her. "You're joking, right?"

"Not at all."

I laugh, feeling a weight lift from my shoulders. "No, that's silly. It's just a birthmark. An odd discoloration, anyone can have one, it doesn't mean anything."

"It's not. The Druids were all hunted and killed twenty years ago. The King and Queen fell, but their daughter was never found. Everyone assumes she died, but what if . . . "

I chuckle at the seriousness in her voice. "Zaria, I'm not some lost princess. Believe me."

"But it would explain how you were able to cross through the gate."

"No, it doesn't."

"Even if you're not the druid princess, you must conceal your mark. The consequences of the queen or the wrong person discovering it would be fatal. All druid sympathizers were captured and exiled to the desolate outlands. Those who remain are now in hiding or have joined the Outcasts in the forest."

I swallow roughly, the sensation of unease settling in my stomach. "You can't be serious."

"Completely."

"Well, what do I do?" I ask, starting to panic. I didn't want to get hurt because someone might mistake my birthmark for something more.

"I have a magic concealer which will cover it, but you'll need to make sure you reapply it every morning."

"Okay. I appreciate it."

"Anything for the . . . "

I shoot her a dark look. "Don't say it."

Zaria presses her lips together and nods. "Fine, but I think maybe you should be trying to think of how you were able to cross through into this realm, because I bet it has something to do with that mark."

Shaking my head, I turn away in amusement, then head straight for the food cart. Now fully stocked, the cakes become my immediate fixation, their sweet smell wafting toward me. Cake is a weakness of mine. I grab a small plate and fill it with three slices of different cakes and a few strawberries. As I turn to take a seat, Zaria lifts an eyebrow at my plate.

"I have a sweet tooth."

"I can see that."

"Thanks for the clean clothes." I rub the soft tulle fabric between my fingers. This dress is a much better fit. The bodice fits me like a glove, with over the shoulder delicate cupped sleeves, and the flared bottom gives me a twirl-worthy silhouette.

"It looks good on you. I have sent some maids into the village with your measurements ready to stock you up with garments as we speak."

"Oh, there was no need for that. I'll be heading home soon." I'm thankful for the topic change because Zaria thinking I am some lost druid princess is absurd. That is, until I notice her expression.

"Now what is it?" I groan.

"The queen has forbidden you from leaving the castle grounds."

Chapter Eleven

Everly

Agitated, I pace back and forth in my chamber. Who does the queen think she is? I am not one of her subjects to be ordered around. I don't belong here.

Nix still hasn't returned, and Zaria left about ten minutes ago to find Raiden. Observing the group, it's clear how close-knit they are. Their interactions are fluid and natural, filled with an unspoken understanding and camaraderie. The trust they share is unmistakable, reminiscent of the bond I have with Mia and Scarlett. Those two are more than just friends to me; they're like sisters, woven into the fabric of my life with threads of shared experiences and unwavering loyalty.

A sudden, loud knock at my door makes my heart skip a beat as it echoes through the chambers. I quickly make my way over to the door, my fists clenched. With a deep breath, I swing the door open, ready to confront whoever waits on the other side.

My breath catches in my throat as I take in the incredible sight before me. Holy shit.

Dressed in all black, Maxon's violet eyes blaze with an intense heat. Clipped to his shoulders is a long black cape that drapes almost to the ground. Secured to his waist by a leather belt, a long sword hangs at his side, its hilt gleaming in the sunlight. My eyes run over the leather cuffs covering his forearms, each bearing the same markings as the tattoo on his face.

"Stóirín," he says with a grin, his eyes sparkling.

I quickly shut my mouth, realizing I had been gaping for a few seconds.

"Your Highness."

"Call me Maxon."

"But Zaria said–"

Maxon shook his head, some of his dark hair falling over his face. "I want you to call me Maxon."

Taken aback, I struggle to push the words out. "Oh, okay."

He stares at me with a strange expression, one that seems caught between amusement and curiosity. "I have training for a few hours, but after I can come and give you a tour of the castle if you'd like."

A thrill of excitement shoots through me at the thought of exploring the castle, and my anger is momentarily forgotten. "And the gardens?"

"Yes, and the gardens." Maxon grins.

The memory of Zaria's words before she left causes my smile to falter. "Why can't I leave?"

Maxon sighs and steps closer, our bodies less than a foot apart. Why do I want to take that final step and close the distance?

"The queen wants answers. If you're not in the dungeons, then you're to remain on the castle grounds until she has them."

"So, I'm a prisoner then?" I murmur, wariness creeping into my voice. Heat creeps up my neck and I take a step back.

Maxon doesn't like that. Moving quickly, he closes the distance once more, his hand raising to gently cradle my face. I freeze in place, my senses on high alert.

"No," he states firmly. "You are not a prisoner here."

My eyes search his and I can't seem to look away. "Then what am I?"

Maxon moves closer, our bodies only inches apart. My palms itch to reach for him, but I curl my fingers into my palms to resist the urge.

"I'm not sure yet."

My heart skips a beat at his softly spoken words.

What does that mean?

Dropping his hand, Maxon steps back, his hand landing on the hilt of his sword. "I will collect you after training."

Without waiting for a reply, he turns and swiftly makes his way down the hall, his black cape flowing behind him. Feeling defeated, I grip the door and swing it shut. Almost instantly I feel my mood darkening, I don't like being cooped up. Looking around the chambers, I ponder what to do until he returns. I walk over and run my fingers over the books lining a small bookshelf in the corner, but don't recognize any of the titles.

The balcony doors are open, and the gentle scent of jasmine drifts in on the breeze. Closing my eyes, I inhale deeply, taking in the fresh air. The sweet scent of blooming flowers fills my senses, and my sour mood begins to lift. I need to be outside. Wandering over to the balcony doors, I step out into the sunshine, the warmth of the sun soaking into my skin. This morning has been a rollercoaster ride of craziness, with almost being thrown in a dungeon and all. The thought of being locked up in the dark makes my skin crawl.

I step toward the edge of the balcony and feel the cool breeze on my face as I look out over the courtyard. I'm several storeys up, with no hope of finding a way to climb down. Not that I would, though I let the thought linger a moment longer before I push it away.

The courtyard is huge and also empty. Where is everyone? I expected the castle to be bustling with people, yet I've barely seen anyone apart from the guards and a few maids.

I make my way back into the room, finding the silence to be almost overwhelming. There has to be something I can do in here to pass the time. The large beautifully carved wooden wardrobe catches my attention. Making my way over to it, I pull open the door, disappointed to find it empty.

Zaria said she sent some maids to fetch me some clothes from the village. I wonder what the village looks like. I only really recall the forest, and then the castle.

I close the wardrobe and move on to the dresser, opening each drawer, but finding them bare.

Leaning down, I smell the candle sitting atop the dresser. The scent is strange and unfamiliar, unlike anything I have ever smelled before. I gingerly lift the candle, hoping to find the fragrance written on the bottom, but as I do, a soft click echoes through the room.

There's a faint rumble, and suddenly a part of the wall gives way, revealing a hidden tunnel. I stand frozen for a moment, my senses alert to the newfound mystery lurking just beyond the threshold. With hesitant steps, I approach the revealed entrance, the silence of the chamber pressing in around me like a heavy fog. I cast a wary glance over my shoulder before steeling myself to peer inside. Looking into the dark void that calls out to me, a sense of unease crawls down my spine. The stone corridor stretches out before me, a winding descent into the unknown depths below. Shadows dance eerily along the uneven walls, swallowing the feeble light that dares to intrude. The darkness is thick, and my eyes strain to see beyond a few feet.

Lost in contemplation, I weigh my options, torn between the safety of the room or the allure of the unexplored. I should remain here until Maxon or Zaria return, even Nix. But curiosity pulls me forward.

Taking a deep breath, I step into the tunnel and am immediately hit with the musty smell of damp stone and mildew. I realize I'm still holding the candle and turn back for a match or lighter, but don't see anything.

Shit.

Maybe I should stay where I am.

The thought of being trapped in this room fills me with anger, yet the prospect of venturing into an unknown, dimly lit passage is equally unsettling.

It could lead to the dungeons for all I know.

Still, I take another step, resting my hand against the rough stone wall which is cool against my skin. Cautiously, I move all the way into the passage, a thrill of excitement rushing through my veins. But with no light source, the foreboding darkness of the tunnel and its narrow appearance send my anxiety spiking.

Leaning against the wall to gather myself, I tip my head back and hear another click. My heart stops dead in my chest, then takes off in a gallop as I scramble upright. Before I get a chance to move, the wall slides back into place, enclosing me in pitch-black darkness.

"Oh, no, no, no, no," I mutter, my hands touching the wall in front of me.

A familiar knot forms in my stomach, causing a wave of nausea. I frantically feel along the wall, my palms become clammy and a cold sweat breaks out across my forehead. The fear that once haunted my childhood memories resurface, gripping me tightly in its icy grasp.

"Shit!" I gasp.

Even though I can't see a thing, white dots dance across my vision as my breathing rapidly increases. I need to get myself together. I lean over, resting my hands on my knees, and take deep breaths.

"You've got this, Everly," I chide myself.

This is a passage, a tunnel, and that means it leads somewhere. I'm not trapped.

Gathering myself, I stand upright, and using the wall as a guide, the fingers of one hand trace the rough surface as I grip my long skirt in the other. Navigating the steps in this dress is awkward, and the absence of sight makes it even more challenging. The only sound to be heard is my breathing as I descend further into the darkness. I take the stairs slowly, and though relief consumes me when my feet hit the bottom and I see light, it takes a conscious effort to control my emotions and not run ahead.

I step out into the sunshine and gulp down the fresh air. The soft breeze envelops me in its comforting embrace, and I savor the way it caresses through my hair and across my skin, cooling me in an instant. Unable to stand on my shaky legs a moment longer, I fall to my knees on the soft grass, my tulle skirt puffing around me like a pillow.

Oh my god, never again.

The passage behind me is partially concealed by plants, and as I study it, my gaze shifts upward to the intricate ironwork on the balconies above me, but I'm unsure which one is mine.

I'm fine. Everything's fine.

The garden is filled with the sounds of chirping birds, which somehow calms my mind. Pushing myself up from the ground, I notice the dirt that has collected on my skirt and give it a shake, dislodging the bulk of it.

Satisfied I'm alone, I step out from my hidden spot and look around the garden. My breath catches in my throat as I stand here mesmerized. Though my balcony has a view, the true beauty of the surroundings is lost from that height. The colors are so bright and vivid. Making my way across the grass to the stone path, I take in the various flowers. Some I recognize, some I don't.

As I walk through the garden, I trail my fingers over the velvety petals and leaves, taking in their different textures and scents. A sense of lightness washes over me, from the tips of my toes to the top of my head. Nature has always brought me peace and comfort, especially under the warm sun and in the crisp, fresh air. Being inside and confined always feels like a heavy blanket being draped over my shoulders, suffocating me.

Suddenly, the silence is shattered by the sound of voices, followed by boisterous shouts and cheers.

What on earth?

I pick up my pace, my heart racing with anticipation as I head toward the source of the voices. A large Victorian-style wrought iron gate at the edge of the garden reveals a crowd of people. As I draw closer, the sound of metal-on-metal rings through the air, piquing my curiosity.

Slipping through the gate unnoticed, I walk around the outskirts of the crowd, trying to get a view of what they're looking at. I stomp my foot in frustration, not able to see over the mass of people. Glancing around, I see some wooden crates next to a cart and make my way over. I'm spurred on by the round of cheers as I hastily make my way over to them and climb up.

Looking over the crowd I see a large arena with two men inside, both in fierce combat. I'm completely transfixed as their swords clash. One man loses his sword and I gasp as the other man sweeps him off his feet before pointing the sword at his neck. The crowd's roar is deafening, but my eyes are trained on the two men. My chest tightens as I watch and wait, unsure of what I'm about to witness. The swift relief I feel causes my shoulders to slump as the victor sheaths his sword and assists the other man to his feet.

Finally able to breathe again, my eyes wander over the crowd. They all vary in shapes and forms, most resembling regular men, but all have the pointed ears that mark them as Fae.

My breath catches in my throat when I see a dark figure step into the arena, drawing everyone's attention. A rhythmic stomping starts, the crowd's feet echoing through the air as Maxon strides confidently toward the center of the arena, his cape billowing behind him. My heartbeat keeps time with the stomping as the vibrations send a thrill through me. The feeling is electrifying. I've never experienced anything like it before.

Maxon's face remains impassive as he removes his cape and hands it to a young boy who swiftly dashes toward the arena's edge. Sometime since he left my room, he secured his long hair into a bun, highlighting the defined structure of his jawline. I stare transfixed as he draws his sword, swinging it around, his movements strong, powerful, direct.

He reminds me of the god of war.

Dark and formidable.

Another fae makes his way to the center of the arena, and he is huge. My pulse kicks up in fear when a grin spreads across the fae's face while he strips off his shirt. The crowd roars with excitement as the man's muscles bulge, and the stomping comes to a stop. Maxon stands there, his features carefully neutral, giving away nothing.

Both fae ready their swords, and I hold my breath. My body is pulsating with nerves, making me feel dizzy, but the thrill of excitement keeps me transfixed on the scene ahead. A horn blares, and in an instant, the two men are off, their bodies a blur of motion.

The hulk fae swings his sword in a wide arc, and a gasp falls from my lips. My hands fly to cover my mouth. Maxon swiftly sidesteps to avoid the swing, pivoting quickly on his feet, and unleashes a series of blows that cause the bigger fae to stumble backward.

Maxon's movements are fluid and practiced. Every strike is swift, precise, and calculated to perfection as he swings the sword, his gaze fixed on his challenger. I watch with bated breath for several moments. Their swords clash and dance in a lethal battle of skill and strength, his opponent fighting back with equal ferocity.

The crowd erupts again, their thunderous applause reverberating through the arena. Maxon's face remains stoic, focus unwavering. His challenger is struggling to keep up as Maxon surges ahead, with an unrelenting pace.

My understanding of sword fighting is minimal, but Maxon is clearly winning.

"Hey, what do you think you're doing?" an unfamiliar voice bellows.

I jump as a hand lands firmly on my forearm, and I'm yanked with surprising strength. My eyes shift from the fight to find an irritated man with bluish skin glaring up at me. Despite my efforts to pull free, his grip on my arm remains unyielding. His snarl reverberates through the air around us as he forcefully pulls me down onto the ground from the crates. I stumble when my feet hit the ground, but his firm grip on my arm keeps me from falling face-first into the dirt.

"Hey!" I exclaim angrily. "Let me go."

But the fae doesn't listen, beginning instead to drag me back toward the gate I came through. I try to halt my movement by digging my heels into the ground, but the slipper shoes Zaria gave me provide no traction. Argh! Crappy delicate fae shoes. I need my boots.

"I said let me go!" I snap, forcefully tugging on his grip.

As preoccupied as I am with fighting the fae, I don't immediately notice the stifling silence that has descended upon us. Abruptly, a dark shape looms over us, causing us to freeze in place.

In one swift motion, Maxon's arm encircles my waist, pulling me into his side. I feel my face heat as everyone's gazes lock on me.

Maxon's sword is now pointed at the fae's throat. "Care to explain what exactly you are doing with her?"

The fae swallows roughly. "She isn't supposed to be here, Your Highness."

The tension in the air grows thicker with every passing moment. I cautiously peer up at Maxon. His eyes are blazing in anger.

"Maxon?" I whisper, confused.

The sound of gasps and grumbles from those around me makes me press myself closer to Maxon's side, my fingers gripping the fabric of his black shirt. The arm around my waist gives a small squeeze.

"Do not touch her," Maxon growls. The sound is low and menacing, making my pulse skitter.

"It's fine," I try, but Maxon isn't listening.

"No one lays a finger on her. Understood?" he commands, addressing the soldiers in the arena.

The weight of everyone's stare bores down on me, and I can feel my face flush. I try creating distance between us, but Maxon isn't having any of it. Lowering his sword, he glares at the fae before nodding. Without hesitation, the fae turns and strolls away, disappearing into the crowd.

"That's enough for today. Tomorrow at dawn, everyone is to report here," Maxon declares firmly to the crowd.

Chapter Twelve

Everly

Everyone disperses quietly, and Maxon grabs my hand, leading me back toward the castle. I replay in my mind every detail of what just occurred. It all seems so surreal. How did he know I was there? He reached me in a matter of seconds, when he was completely focused on his duel.

Maxon's steps slow as he enters through one of the open double doors.

"Who let you out of your room?" he asks, the skin around his mouth tight, as we make our way down the main hall.

Snapping out of my stupor, I rip my arm free of his grip. "I thought you said I wasn't a prisoner?"

Maxon turns to face me. "You're not. But you're not safe without an escort."

I snort and cross my arms over my chest. "Sounds like a prisoner."

Maxon stands in front of me, booted feet braced shoulder width apart and arms crossed, almost mirroring my stance.

"If you want to leave your room, that's fine, but I have two hand-picked soldiers stationed outside your room for your safety and protection."

My frown deepens. I don't remember seeing anyone outside my room when Maxon stopped by earlier.

"How am I supposed to know that?" I snap.

Maxon appears no less dangerous than he did in the arena. It's clear by the fierce burn of his violet eyes that he is not happy. I should be scared. But I'm not. Out of everyone, he's the only person who makes me feel completely safe. Which is absurd.

"Where is Nix?"

With a shrug, I drop my arms, brushing past him to continue walking. I don't know the way back to my room, but I can't endure his stare any longer.

"I'm here!" Nix calls as she flies around the corner in front of me, leaving a shimmering trail of fairy dust behind her.

"Where have you been?" Maxon demands, pinning her with a fierce look.

"Zaria told me to go rest."

Maxon throws his hands in the air as he stops beside me. "You were supposed to be watching her."

"Well, I didn't think she'd be stupid enough to leave the safety of her room after almost ending up in the dungeons only a few hours ago."

"Well, you thought wrong!" Maxon snaps at her.

"Hey! I'm right here, you know!"

They both look at me in confusion.

"Yes, we know," Maxon replies.

My eyes narrow, and I let out a huff of annoyance, making my way toward the stairs.

"You're going the wrong way!" Maxon calls out when I go to turn left.

A low growl slips past my lips, and I spin going the other way. Wisely Maxon remains quiet as we climb the stairs in silence, but as we reach the top, two soldiers materialize in front of us, blocking our way. Shock and surprise are evident on their faces as they both look at me and then at Maxon.

"How–" one guard says in disbelief. His lavender eyes are wide as he stares at me. They have a pinkish tint to them, making them look like a blooming flower in spring. He runs a hand through his blonde hair, looking adorably confused.

The other guard's initial look of surprise quickly turns to one of displeasure, his eyes a shade darker and flashing with anger.

"How did you get out?" he glowered.

Maxon steps in front of me. "I will discuss this with you after I've spoken to Everly." Maxon moves past them, and I quietly follow, mouthing sorry to both of them. The blonde guard gives me a small smile, but the other remains aloof as he watches me.

Maxon opens my door then waits for me and Nix to pass before stepping inside and shutting the door. As the silence stretches on, I finally turn to face Maxon, searching for any sign of what he's thinking.

"So, care to explain how you were able to slip past the guards? Because I can assure you they are two of my best." Maxon folds his arms over his chest and leans back against the door. Despite the room's enormity, his commanding presence makes it feel small. Dressed in his black breeches, boots, and black shirt, even with his cape and leather cuffs gone, he still looks fierce and deadly.

I pause for a moment, considering my options. Even though I wanted to lie, I knew they would eventually discover the truth. Without a word, I turn and walk over to the dresser, pressing the small button ingrained into the wood. The sound of the wall parting fills the chamber, and my hidden passage appears.

"What the fuck?!" Despite her small size, Nix's voice echoes through the room.

I bite my lip as I turn around, my fingers twisting in the tulle of my skirt. "I went through here."

Maxon pushes off the door with a scowl, his footsteps heavy as he stalks over and brushes past me into the dimly lit passage.

Nix flies across the room and lands on the dresser. "I thought only the royal chambers had tunnels and escape passages."

"They do," Maxon rumbles, walking back into the room and pressing the button, sealing the door shut once again.

His eyes meet mine, and I feel a hitch in my chest. Why does he have to look at me like that? It makes it impossible for me to look away.

"Get whatever you need, you're moving rooms."

The rasp of his voice causes a wave of goosebumps to break out over my skin. "What? Why?"

Maxon stares at me with a strange expression, like he isn't sure if I'm being serious or not. "If you can get out, it means others can get in."

"You think someone would come through the passage for me?"

His chin dips, his lashes lowering, shielding his vibrant eyes. "I would rather not find out."

I look away and stare out the doors to the balcony. Everything is so different here. I have no clue what I'm doing. What if someone knew about those passages and came in here? But why would they bother with me? I'm nobody. Ghostly fingers dance along my spine as I stand here, my mind racing with fear and uncertainty.

Maxon's hand lands on my shoulder, making me jump. "Are you alright?"

Yes . . .

No . . .

I'm not sure.

My anxiety rises, and pressure bears down on my chest. What have I gone and gotten myself into?

"Hey? What's wrong?" Maxon's voice sounds concerned.

He steps closer. I instinctively take a step back, feeling a sudden rush of adrenaline. With him standing so close, my mind is completely scattered. Why do I feel like I'm not safe anywhere I go?

A nagging memory tugs at the back recesses of my mind. It's so close, yet so far, hovering just beyond my grasp. I know it's important, but I can't focus on it. Frustration rises quickly at feeling so helpless. I am powerless to do anything about the situation I've found myself in.

Maxon walks over to the door and gestures to someone outside. The faint sound of footsteps grows louder as the guards make their way inside. They both glance around the room before coming to a stop in the center. The blonde guard gives me a small grin, and I feel the tension in my body ease. Though the other doesn't acknowledge my presence, not even with a glance. His short and scruffy dark hair gives him a rugged appearance, as does the hint of regrowth on his face.

"Everly. This is Kian and Tristan. They are your bodyguards while you're here," Maxon introduces the two fae.

My cheeks flush at Kian's playful wink, but Tristan remains stoic with the same glare from before. His purple eyes narrow on me.

Seriously, what's he got to be pissy about? I'm the one trying to make sense of a world that is completely foreign to me. Until the queen has gotten what she wants, I am trapped here.

"We are moving Everly to my wing of the castle. I want you to scout ahead and pick a room, make sure it is clear."

"Yes, Your Highness," Kian says, bowing.

Tristan's frown deepens. "Your wing? Are you sure about that?"

Maxon growls, stepping up to Tristan. "It is not your place to argue. Everly is under my protection."

"Of course, Your Highness," Tristan mutters.

"Be discreet," he orders, then he turns to Nix, who is still perched on the dresser next to me. "I want you to find Zaria and Raiden. Bring them here. Once we are all together, we will move Everly. Kian, once a room has been secured, come back and inform me. Tristan, stay put and guard the room until we arrive. Understood?"

In unison, everyone murmurs their agreements. Kian and Tristan turn on their heels and briskly walk out of the room. Nix swiftly launches into the air, gliding toward the window, but suddenly comes to a stop.

"Should I tell them what's going on?"

Maxon shakes his head. "Wait until they get here. I don't want anyone overhearing."

With a sharp nod, she is gone.

"Do you really think I'm in danger?" I ask, walking over and resting my hands on the back of the chair.

Maxon wanders over to the balcony doors, with his hands casually tucked in his pockets. His back is to me as he gazes out over the gardens below. The gentle breeze makes the sheer curtains dance around him, softening his dark figure.

"I don't know, but I won't take the risk." His voice is barely above a whisper, but I hear it as if he were right next to me.

My heart pounds against my ribcage, its rhythmic thumping echoing in my ears as I move around the chair. Maxon must feel my presence closing in, because he pivots to meet me, his face a mask of indifference. The glint of the silver ring encircling his captivating violet eyes catches the light, ensnaring me.

I stop a few feet from him, my hands twisting together. "You don't know me. Why do you care what happens to me?"

Maxon tilts his head to the side like a confused puppy. "You feel it, don't you? The calm that takes over when we are near?"

I drop my eyes to the floor to hide the truth in my face. I do feel that, but I also feel my pulse race and butterflies swarm my stomach. And the way the world falls away when our eyes lock, like a moment frozen in time.

Maxon steps closer, his finger going under my chin, tipping my head back. "You do feel it, don't you?"

My eyes search his, and I open my mouth to answer, his gaze dropping to my lips. The way his eyes flare sends a scorching swell of hot fire through my veins, and I suddenly wish he would kiss me.

Unable to form the word, I take a small step back, needing some space. My eyes slowly roam over his face and I tilt my head, studying the vine-like tattoos on his face.

"Why the tattoos?" I ask, curiosity getting the better of me. I need to change the subject.

Maxon contemplates the question, his attention unwavering.

"They aren't tattoos. When I was young, I had recurring dreams of this mysterious pattern, as if it held some deep significance. I later drew it, and over time, it appeared on my face. I adorn my chambers with the same markings. I later learned that the patterns etched into the surface were actually a powerful protection rune. Beyond its surface meaning, the symbol also serves as a symbol of my mating."

That piece of information is so unexpected that it makes my eyebrows lift. Maxon smirks, sending a rush of butterflies swirling in my stomach.

"After the markings had formed completely, an oracle informed me that it was one half of my mate mark, and that when I find my mate and we link souls, she too will have the other half of the tattoo appear on her face to match mine."

"What do you mean, mate? Like I think I know with what I've read in romance books, but–"

My words are abruptly cut off, silenced by the intensity of Maxon's presence as he takes a step closer, his eyes piercing mine, burning with a fiery energy. The air crackles with tension, the silence amplifying the weight of his stare.

"Mate is our other half, the missing piece of the puzzle we must find. It's not predetermined or fate, simply souls being reunited."

"How do you reunite the souls?" I whisper hoarsely, trying to ignore the way my pulse is racing.

Maxon's lips turn up and he smirks down at me. "It happens over time. Mating is a dance of souls, where the gentle movement of bodies intertwining, echoes with the sweet symphony of two hearts beating in unison. In this sacred union, the sensation of becoming one, transcends the physical as their souls merge and intertwine, creating an ethereal bond that is beyond words."

"Oh," I whisper, trying my best to ignore the rush of warmth that spreads through me and settles in my lower stomach. So much for changing the subject.

My throat tightens as I swallow, and Maxon's attention is drawn to the balcony where the curtains sway. His pointed ears immediately catch my attention, adorned with multiple piercings that glimmer in the light, I'm tempted to reach out and touch them. Then, as if in a daze, I reach up and run the tip of my finger over the top of Maxon's ear. His head snaps to me, making me jump in surprise, and I go to lower my hand, but he clasps my wrist tightly.

"We have very sensitive ears," he growls, sending a shiver down my spine, but not in fear. I feel a fluttering sensation in the pit of my stomach, causing my thighs to involuntarily tense up. I quickly swallow, my tongue gliding over my lips. Maxon's intense gaze fixates on my mouth, and a deep, rumbling growl escapes from the depths of his throat.

The sudden sound of a sharp rap on the wooden door causes my heart to race and my body to jolt with surprise. Maxon loosens his grip on my wrist, allowing me to swiftly pivot and hasten toward a nearby chair. The presence of Maxon in my life is a perilous mix, a constant threat to both my emotional well-being and physical health.

"Enter," Maxon calls, his voice sounding gruff.

Zaria and Raiden step into the room, followed by Nix. Zaria takes me in and then fixes her gaze on Maxon with a sharp intensity.

"What did you do?" she accuses.

"Me?"

"Yes, look at her," Zaria replies, her arm flying in my direction.

I frown at her, but my expression softens as Nix lands on my skirt, her weight barely noticeable as she looks up at me with her large, sapphire eyes. "She does look a little flush."

"That's enough." I stand, making Nix take flight. "I'm perfectly fine, thank you."

Raiden's massive arms are crossed, and his eyes shift from Maxon to me. I don't like the way he looks at me, his silver eyes taking in every detail.

"So, we have a breach?" he asks slowly.

"Yes," Maxon says as he walks over to us, and I make a conscious effort to avoid meeting his gaze. "There is a passage that leads to the garden."

"Zaria, who told you to use this room?"

Zaria's eyes widen on Maxon. "The duke, he told me to put the guest in here on Nolan's orders."

"How did the duke know I had someone with me?"

Silence falls around the group, my gaze bouncing between them.

"Who's the duke?" I ask.

"Only a pompous ass who thinks his farts don't stink," Nix says.

At the sound of Raiden's snort of agreement, Zaria spins around sharply to address them. "Hush, you two."

Maxon runs a hand over his hair, the strands falling back haphazardly over his face. "The duke is . . . "

"A pompous ass, like I said."

"Nix," Maxon growls, shooting her a look.

"What? I'm just saying what we are all thinking," she complains, pouting like a child.

"The duke is not someone you want to mess with," Maxon says cryptically. "The fact he knew I was bringing you here is concerning."

"We are moving her, then?" Raiden asks.

"Yes, I've sent Tristan and Kian to clear a room in my wing."

Raiden steps forward, but Maxon's raised hand stops him from arguing. "No one will know she is there, but I cannot leave her here. This is a matter of safety. I don't know if anyone else is aware of this passage, but I'm not taking that chance."

A shiver creeps across my shoulders, and I feel Raiden's glare zero in on me. I keep my mouth shut. Nothing I say will do me any favors.

"Why her?" Raiden asks, jutting his chin my way. It's clear by his dismissive tone he thinks I am nothing more than an annoying bug that has landed on their windshield.

"Raiden!" Zaria hisses.

But Raiden continues, "She shows up acting like she knows nothing, which is impossible, given she is *here*. She is trying to stay close to you, moving her closer is a bad idea." He shakes his head.

The air around me becomes charged with tension, causing me to stand up. Maxon's energy shifts, becoming more foreboding. I automatically place myself between Raiden and Maxon. My attention is fully focused on Maxon as he stops short. His dark brows lower as he stares down at me. I notice the tightness in his shoulders and the sharpness of his gaze. Raiden thinks I am a threat to Maxon's safety, and I don't know how to convince him otherwise. Without thought, I reach my hand out and grab his, letting my thumb stroke over his knuckles. With a brief pause, Maxon blinks twice before letting out a deep sigh.

"Why? Because she is innocent and a human, and the fae world is ruthless." His eyes drop to mine briefly, and the look in them seems distant. I don't like it. "And even if she wanted to, she couldn't hurt me." Maxon says, looking over my head at Raiden and dropping my hand.

I do my best not to wince. I don't know why, but those words sting a little. Or maybe not the words, but the tone. Mia always playfully teased me about my tendency to openly express my emotions. But it couldn't be helped. When it comes to my feelings, I'm an open book.

Zaria must sense my discomfort because she links her arm in mine, drawing me away from Maxon toward the door. "I will take Everly for a walk, and you guys can figure out the rest. Send Nix when you've sorted out a room."

Before anyone can protest, Zaria has already led me out into the hallway. As soon as the door closes, I feel my muscles relax.

"You okay?" she asks softly as we make our way down the hall.

A strange lump forms in my throat, making it impossible to speak, so I just nod.

Chapter Thirteen

Everly

Zaria strolls into my chambers the next morning with Kian, his arms full of garment bags. Tristan steps in and frowns at me before stepping back into the hall and closing the door.

"What's his problem?"

"You're human, and you somehow managed to slip away unnoticed," Kian says, drawing to a stop in front of the large wardrobe where Zaria is waiting.

"In my defense, I wasn't even aware you were out there."

Kian smirks. "He knows that, but his ego is bruised."

"I apologized."

Zaria chuckles. "Fae hold grudges."

"We do. It's a thing," Kian adds, standing there patiently while Zaria meticulously takes each garment from him and places it in the wardrobe.

Zaria continues organizing the garments, her fingers delicately smoothing out any creases as Kian watches her with amusement.

"So, what's Raiden doing today?" he asks, breaking the silence.

Zaria pauses for a moment but doesn't look at either of us. "How should I know?"

Kian raises an eyebrow, a mischievous glint in his eyes. "I assume you two were close. It was his rooms you were–"

My eyes widen as Zaria spins on Kian, her face red. "Be quiet."

"So, it's true?" Kian chuckles. "You and the captain."

Zaria squares her shoulders and swiftly grabs a gown from him. "I don't know what you're talking about."

My eyes dart back and forth between them in amusement.

"I need some popcorn," I giggle.

Zaria's attention snaps to me, a smile playing on her lips before she turns back to Kian and points her finger at him. "We aren't talking about this, now or ever."

"You're no fun." Kian winks.

I walk up to the wardrobe and peer at the rows of dresses.

"Why so many?"

"Need one for every occasion," Zaria shrugs.

"She is playing dress up with you."

"I am not."

Kian stares at her, and I laugh. "Well, I don't mind either way. They are gorgeous. I've never worn anything this beautiful, so I appreciate it very much. I didn't even get a dress for my prom."

Zaria frowns, her ears twitching. "Prom?"

My face heats, realizing they have no idea what prom is. "Prom is a formal dance held at the end of the school year for juniors and seniors. It's seen as a rite of passage. A memorable night for most."

"So like a ball?" Zaria asks.

"Exactly."

"Why did you not get a gown?" Kian questions, handing Zaria the last dress.

I shrug my shoulders, attempting to downplay the situation. "My foster parents used the money to go to a concert instead."

Truth is, I was devastated.

The prom was supposed to be a magical night, a chance to feel like a princess for once in my life. Yet, my foster parents had chosen their own desires over mine, leaving me feeling discarded and unimportant. Mixed in with my teenage emotions and hormones, it was a truly challenging time. I had to watch as my friends excitedly prepared for the dance, picking out their perfect dresses and discussing their plans for the night. It was a constant reminder of what I was missing out on, a stark contrast to the neglect I experienced at home.

Asrai peeks out from Zaria's hair and flies over to me. I hold both my hands out in front of me and she gracefully lands there.

'That wasn't very kind of them,' she signs.

"No, it wasn't."

"Wait, you can understand her?" Kian asks.

I nod and smile down at Asrai.

Her hands are moving again. *'You have lots of pretty gowns now.'*

"Yes, I do."

Asrai's wings flutter and she lifts from my hands and tugs some of my hair and giggles. *'You can wear them for the prince.'*

My cheeks heat and I sign back. '*There is nothing happening there. Now or ever.'*

Asrai's eyes seem to grow larger as she stares at me. '*You're lying.'*

"What are they saying?" I hear Kian ask Zaria.

"I know about as much as you," she replies.

Asrai returns to Zaria's head and settles in, her eyes like pools of blue and green, sparkling with mirth as she watches me.

Zaria places her hands on her hips as she stares at the rows of dresses. "Well, that's all the gowns, twelve in total. Plus, I have another trunk of undergarments and nightwear downstairs. Tristan is currently fetching them."

"Really, you shouldn't have. I don't need all this."

"The prince insisted you have everything. Plus, I enjoyed shopping for you. It was all extremely satisfying."

As I stand before Kian and Zaria, grateful for their kindness, I can't help but feel a mix of emotions.

Tristan suddenly reappears at the doorway, carrying a large wooden trunk. "What in Aine have you got in here?" he grumbles, making his way over and dropping the trunk at the foot of the bed.

"Nothing that concerns either of you. Now shoo." Zaria's tail flicks up, swatting Kian in the chest.

With one eyebrow raised, Tristan crosses his arms over his chest, his tone laced with annoyance. "Are you done bossing us around?"

Zaria rolls her eyes, completely unfazed by Tristan's perpetual grumpiness. "Almost," she replies nonchalantly, dragging out the word just to annoy him. "But you know, Tristan, you could learn a thing or two from Kian about letting go of grudges."

Tristan scowls, the furrow in his brow deepening as he crosses his arms. "I don't need lessons from him," he mutters, his voice dripping with irritation.

I bite my lip, trying to smother the laugh threatening to escape. Across the room, Kian grins, clearly enjoying the moment. He claps a firm hand on Tristan's shoulder and steers him toward the door with an exaggerated sigh.

"Let the ladies be, old man."

Tristan tenses under his grip. "I'm not old."

Kian smirks, casting a pointed glance at Tristan's perpetually furrowed brow. "Your frown lines say otherwise."

The door clicks shut behind them, leaving behind a brief silence before I turn to Zaria, still grinning. "They are the perfect grumpy-sunshine combo."

She blinks at me, her expression blank. "The what?"

"Never mind," I say with a laugh, shaking my head.

Some things just weren't worth explaining.

Chapter Fourteen

Everly

I've been left alone in the room for hours, the silence growing heavier with each passing minute. In the hall, Kian and Tristan stand watch, their presence a silent barrier between me and the outside world.

Zaria has her own tasks to attend to, so I don't assume she'll be with me constantly. She mentioned earlier that she had errands to run, so it makes sense that she's preoccupied. As for Nix, I haven't seen her all day either. Usually, she hangs out with me, but today seems different. It's unusual not having both Zaria or Nix around, but I know they'll be by later.

Since I left Maxon's room two days ago, I hadn't laid eyes on him, and a strong desire to be close to him makes my skin crawl. It's a bizarre sensation, one I can't say I've ever experienced before. But Zaria informed me that he's preparing for his coronation.

I walk out onto the balcony and feel the warm breeze against my face as I peer down at the vibrant colors of the garden. Maybe I can climb down . . .

My gaze sweeps across the balcony, and I notice the tendrils of vines clinging to the side of the castle walls. The lush green vines cascade down the side, they look strong enough to hold me. Hiking up my long tulle skirt, I sit on the stone ledge, the cool breeze playing with the hair around my face, carrying the scent of damp earth from the garden below. The vibrant green vines sway gently in the wind, their leaves rustling softly, as if beckoning me forward.

Am I seriously considering this?

A sense of restlessness writhes within, as if the walls of the room are closing in on me, urging me to go. But as I tug on the vine, feeling its sturdy grip in my hand, doubt begins to creep in.

Am I being foolish?

Is this reckless longing worth the potential risks?

The little voice in my head, a nagging reminder of caution, questions my motives.

No, I won't be confined to a room all day, not when there's a beautiful garden waiting below. Gripping the vine tightly in my hand, I can feel the adrenaline rush through my veins as I slip off the ledge.

"You got this, Everly," I mutter to myself, taking a deep breath to steady my nerves.

Inch by inch, I descend the vine, my arms quivering with the strain until I finally reach the next balcony and carefully land on it. Flexing my aching hands, I can feel the sweat trickling down my forehead as I peer over the edge, contemplating the two remaining levels below. The distance seems daunting, but the adrenaline pumping through my veins fuels my determination. Or perhaps I can quietly slip away through this room. I steal a quick glance at the door that opens into the room, and bite down on my bottom lip as I ponder my next move.

Curiosity gets the best of me, so I peek in the window and survey the room. Seeing it's empty, I quietly push open the doors and step inside. It's furnished similar to mine and seems to be where a woman stayed, based on what I can gather from all the jewelry and fabrics scattered about.

Not wanting to be caught in someone else's room, I quickly hurry toward the door, opening it up and slipping into the hall. I let out a deep breath as I softly click the door shut behind me. The tension in my body ebbs, and I look both ways down the wide hall, not seeing a single soul. A smile stretches across my face, and I start toward the stairs feeling a sense of triumph stirring in my chest.

Escaping my room and guards has given me a little bounce in my step. I look down, admiring the way my dress is flowing around my ankles, unable to help myself. I do a twirl, watching the skirt flare out around me, a small laugh escaping me.

Out of thin air, three fae women materialize before me. I jerk to a stop, my eyes flaring in surprise, but before I can speak, two of them forcefully grab my arms.

"Wait!" I rasp, desperately trying to break free.

A sharp tang of fear hits the back of my throat, and as if on cue, the third woman positions herself directly in my line of sight, causing me to lose focus on everything else. With laughter dancing in her eyes, she raises her hand between us, twirling it in circles, her lighter purple eyes deepening in color just ever so slightly. A cruel smirk twists her lips, causing my stomach to plummet. I feel as if something is taking the air from my body.

Opening my mouth, I attempt to scream, but my voice fails me. I can't breathe. Panic widens my eyes as the three women cruelly laugh and begin dragging me down the corridor.

Dammit.

I didn't intend to draw attention to myself by coming out here; I simply wanted some solitude in the garden.

They drag me to a door at the end of the corridor and forcefully toss me into the darkened room. My knees hit the ground with a force that sends a jarring shock through my body.

My throat finally opens, and I gasp, drawing in lungfuls of air. I glance nervously behind me, my heart pounding in my chest, and come face-to-face with the piercing stare of the leader. The dim light reflects off her icy eyes, sending a shiver down my spine.

"What does he see in you?" she sneers, her voice filled with disdain. "You're a weak, pathetic human. I am destined to marry the prince. Don't you dare stand in my way, you wretched filth."

I'm so confused, what is she on about? Before I can ask, they slam the door shut. Utter darkness engulfs me, and I scramble to my feet, lunging for the door. My heart races, and my palms grow sweaty as I push and pound on the door, but it remains immovable. I try to cry out for help, but no sound escapes my lips. Tears cascade down my face, and my claustrophobia amplifies, causing my chest to constrict in pain.

I sink to the ground on my knees, pounding my fist against the unforgiving wooden door.

"Help . . . " I breathe, unable to scream like I want to.

Even though I only caught a quick glimpse of the room, I know I'm in a small storage closet, and I can feel the walls pressing in on me. The air feels hot and suffocating as I struggle to calm my breathing. If I don't get myself under control, I am going to pass out.

"Please . . . " I sob.

My heart pounds in my chest, the sound echoing in the small space. The silence is interrupted only by the muffled sounds of my fists hitting the door, creating a desperate rhythm. The wooden door reverberates with each strike, but there is no response from the other side.

With every breath, the air feels thinner, suffocating me. I struggle to steady my breathing, fighting against the rising wave of nausea that threatens to overpower me. I can taste the metallic tang of fear in my mouth, my throat tightening with each passing moment.

Time feels distorted, as if the minutes stretch into hours within the confines of this suffocating closet. Desperation fuels my determination, pushing me to keep banging on the door, hoping for a miracle, praying for someone to rescue me from this claustrophobic nightmare. My muscles ache from the repeated exertion, and my trembling limbs betray my growing fatigue.

A whine escapes me, my forehead thudding on the door as I slump down in defeat. At the very moment the door opens and I spill out onto the marble floor, cool, fresh air licking my sweaty skin.

"Everly?"

Panting heavily, I blink up at Raiden, his formidable presence towering above me.

"Hey, batman," I rasp, my voice barely audible and my throat feeling dry and scratchy.

Raiden's big silver eyes roam over me. I'm sure I look like a hot mess. Squatting down, he reaches out, swiping the hair from my sweaty face, concern written all over his features.

"What happened?" he asks softly.

I let out a raspy laugh, as I roll onto my back and gaze up at the ceiling. It's a nice ceiling. High, too.

"Everly?"

"I was locked in the closet by some fae."

Raiden emits a low growl, and I glance at him, noticing his tense muscles. "Who?"

"Like I'd know," I retort, taking in a shaky breath.

"What did they look like?"

"It doesn't matter."

"When Maxon finds–"

"He won't be finding out. Don't worry."

"Don't worry?! Look at you, you're shakier than a newborn unicorn."

"You have unicorns here?" I ask, completely breathless. "I want to see a unicorn."

Raiden rises with a huff, his burly arms folding over his chest as I struggle to stand. As he predicted, my legs tremble uncontrollably, and I clench my teeth in an attempt to steady them.

"Why did you react like that?"

Placing my hand on the wall, I take a deep breath and let it out slowly. "What do you mean?"

Raiden waves his hand over my body. "Like that. Panicked, sweaty, trembling, hyperventilating . . . "

"Oh, that." I bite my lip and look away. "It's nothing."

"Tell me. Please?"

I look at him and arch an eyebrow. "Did you just say please?"

"Don't get used to it," he huffs, crossing his arms over his chest.

I chuckle and lean against the wall. I have no energy left to feel embarrassed or fight him on this. "When I was growing up, I used to get locked in small spaces a lot, sometimes for days at a time."

Raiden jerks forward a step. "What?!"

I shrug in an attempt to pretend it's not a big deal, but my pulse races at the thought of being confined. It was years ago, and I thought I'd put it behind me, but it seems the fear is as real now as it was when I was little. Though the fear may linger, I refuse to let it define me. I will continue to shrug it off, playing it off as no big deal, until one day, it truly becomes just that—a distant memory of a time long gone.

"Who did this to you?"

"Doesn't matter."

"Don't lie."

"I'm not."

"Not all scars are visible, Everly."

At his penetrating gaze, I sigh, "Fine. If you must know, my foster brother was an asshole. He would lock me in boxes or cupboards a lot. You'd think I'd get used to it after a while, but I never did. Things got especially worse after I was locked in the dark for two days before anyone realized I was gone. Now you know why I don't like small spaces."

The more I speak, the deeper the furrow between Raiden's eyebrows becomes. He looks furious. When he doesn't speak, just stares at me with those damn silver eyes, I become even more uncomfortable.

"Any chance we can get some food? Otherwise, I'm going to pass out. Preferably something sweet. I need sugar to revive me."

Raiden looks ready to argue, but my expression turns pleading, silently begging him to drop it. I didn't want to get into this right now or ever. "Please."

"Fine. This way." His arm comes out, and I grin up at him as I loop my arm in his.

"Why, thank you, good sir."

"Don't push it."

"You might be a big scary . . . bat man with horns, but you're just a big old teddy bear, aren't you?" I tease.

Raiden's grunt is music to my ears.

"Thanks for finding me," I whisper, my fingers tightening around his arm.

"You can thank Tristan. He was the one to inform me you'd disappeared AGAIN."

My eyes drop to the ground. "I just wanted to go down to the gardens. It makes me happy. You guys left me for hours," I murmur, feeling guilty.

"We have told you that it's not safe, but you refuse to listen."

"I know."

Kian and Tristan round the corner, their eyes widening on my disheveled state. I give them both a weak smile.

"Sorry to worry you both."

"Seems we had a reason to be worried." Tristan eyes my creased and sweaty dress.

I wave him off. "Everything turned out fine."

Raiden snorts, and I elbow him in the side.

But Tristan doesn't stop. "You aren't supposed to leave your chambers."

"I know."

"So why did you, then?"

"The garden looked too nice to pass up and I was getting agitated waiting."

"Are all humans as stupid as you?"

I can feel my eyes flare. "Wow, you deserve a high five for that one."

Tristan frowns, clearly confused. "A what?"

"A high five . . . in the face . . . with a chair," I reply, giving him a flat stare.

Raiden snorts again, shaking his head in amusement. Tristan still looks thoroughly confused as he looks off to the side, a muscle popping in his jaw.

"Look, the crown prince told us to protect you with our lives, and I take that seriously. If you want to see the gardens, ASK."

Kian steps forward. "We are glad you're okay. But he is right. Next time, please ask, and we will take you."

I look between the two fae soldiers that I only met a day ago and nod.

"Would you two please fetch Everly some food—something sweet—and meet us in the west gardens," Raiden says.

Tristan's eyebrows shoot up and Kian looks speechless.

"Sir, you don't want us–"

"Nope. I will take her to the gardens myself."

A tingling sense of awareness washes over me upon finishing the food Tristan and Kian brought me, making me sit up straighter.

"What is it?" Raiden asks from his position, leaning against the base of a tree. He has been silently sitting there, his hands carefully shaping a small piece of wood into something beautiful with a small carving knife. Not that he'll show me what it is.

I don't answer as I watch Maxon stalk around the corner of the garden, heading straight for us.

Raiden follows my line of vision and stands. "Finished the meetings already?"

"Yes. Thank fuck," Maxon exhales.

My eyes wander over him. He looks good, really good.

My dark prince.

Wait, what?

My dark prince, what made that thought pop into my head? He is definitely not mine. But still my eyes roam over the uniform. The black ensemble hinting at danger.

Maxon's gaze meets mine, and I feel a blush spread across my face. My fingers twist in my skirt and I look down at the grass.

"Mind if I join you?" he asks.

My head snaps back up to him. "You want to sit with me in the garden? Don't you have a sword to swing around?"

With a mischievous glint in his eyes, Maxon's lips curl into a playful smirk. "Swing my sword around?" he questions.

I pick up a grape and throw it at him. "Oh, shut up."

Raiden shakes his head. "I need to see a nymph about a dragon."

"I will take care of Everly," Maxon replies without looking at his friend.

"I'm sure you will," Raiden quips, sending me a slight smile.

"Bye, and I appreciate your help earlier," I respond, shifting on the blanket so my legs are stretched out in front of me, and rest back on my hands.

Raiden gives me a nod and starts walking toward the castle. “FYI, she wants to see a unicorn,” he tosses out over his shoulder.

Maxon chuckles, a wide grin spreading across his face as he lowers himself down to the ground. Taking a handful of grapes, he casually reclines on his side, his head propped on his hand as he gazes at me.

“A unicorn?”

“Are you teasing me?”

“Never.”

I narrow my eyes. “Well, if they are indeed real, then yes.”

I suppress the bubbling excitement that threatens to overwhelm me. I am going to encounter an actual unicorn. My heart pounds in anticipation. They better not be lying to me!

“They are, and I can take you to them, but not today.”

I sit forward, my shoulders slumping in disappointment. “Oh, okay.”

I lower my gaze and without me seeing him move, Maxon is suddenly next to me, gripping my chin and tilting my head back.

“Don’t give me that look,” he growls, his eyes darting between mine.

“What look?” My voice trembles.

“I’d give you the whole fucking world on a silver platter to never have you look sad again.”

I blink startled by his words. “I didn’t mean–”

Maxon leans in closer, cutting off my words, his eyes flashing in warning. “Don’t you dare say you're sorry.”

“I wasn’t.”

"Good," Maxon releases my face, and I take a quivering breath, feeling a wave of relief wash over me. The man was intense.

Maxon leans back on one arm and rests the other on his bent knee. "I will take you to see the unicorns, just not today. It's a half day's ride, and we have a ball tonight."

That makes sense. It's already the afternoon, definitely too late to make the trip. "Wait, did you say a ball?"

"I did. It's not every day that a human gets to attend such a prestigious event in the fae realm. I want to make sure you look the part, so I had Zaria run to Skora and fetch you a dress. Not that you need to worry. You'll outshine everyone there, I'm sure."

Heat invades every cell in my body at the compliment.

"Thank you. But are you sure it's okay for me to come? I don't want to impose. Plus, I'm not that comfortable in crowds. It would probably be better if I stayed in my room."

Maxon tips his head back and laughs. "Now you want to stay in your room?"

I glare at him. "Yes. Plus, I can't dance."

Maxon smirks, clearly enjoying himself. "Well, it's a good thing I'm here to teach you, then."

"What's with the dragon? Is that the royal crest?"

Maxon looks taken aback. "You do realize you shift conversations rather abruptly, right?"

He was right. It's something I've done since I was a child. It's like if I don't ask the moment it enters my mind, it will disappear.

"Sometimes."

Maxon looks out over the garden. "In fae lore, the dragon symbolizes ancient power, wisdom, and guardianship. The dragon depicted on my family's royal crest symbolizes the lineage's connection to these virtues. The dragon embodies strength, often associated with the ruling authority, and signifies protection of the realm and its inhabitants. It's not just a symbol of raw power, but also intelligence and the ability to navigate both the physical and mystical realms with grace and precision. Legend has it that the dragon was revered among the fae for its ability to command the elements and maintain harmony within their world. My family, a long time ago, ruled with the dragons by our side. It's said that they bestowed gifts upon the heirs to the throne, but they have long since disappeared."

"Do you have any of these gifts?"

Maxon raises his hand between us, and I watch in awe as it erupts into flames. The flames dance and flicker around his fingers. The intense heat radiating from the fireball causes the air to shimmer, distorting the space around it. I can hardly believe what I'm witnessing.

"You just summoned fire into your palm." Mesmerized, I lean forward, my eyes locked on the hypnotic display of elemental power. Maxon's face remains calm and focused, his expression betraying nothing of the immense energy he wields. It's as if he has tapped into a hidden wellspring of magic, unleashing a force that defies the laws of nature.

I move onto my knees and reach forward to feel the heat of the flames. "It doesn't hurt?"

"Not at all. How can something that's part of me hurt me?"

Maxon slowly lowers his arm, the flames receding until only faint embers remain. My mind races with questions, curiosity mingling with a hint of fear.

"Do all fae have this type of magic?"

"No. Only a few high fae possess the ability to manipulate one or even two elements. On the other hand, certain fae possess alternative forms of magic. Let's consider Nix, for instance; she has the power to utilize her fairy dust in order to fashion exquisite gems."

"Wow. Okay. How is your magic chosen? Do you know what it is?"

"Our magic, especially those with elemental magic, reflects who we are in our soul."

"I can see that," I reply.

Maxon's fire magic, a mesmerizing spectacle, mirrors his essence flawlessly. The fiery glow in his eyes emits an intense heat, granting a fleeting glimpse into the abyss of his very being. It's as if danger and untamed nature are personified in him. As my thoughts wander, I recall the encounter with the fae who ensnared me earlier. With a mere wave of her hand, the air vanished, leaving me breathless. Could it have been her magic that had done that?

Chapter Fifteen

Everly

Zaria curls the last strand of my hair, just as a loud knock echoes through the room.

"Just a minute!" Zaria calls out.

Standing up, I give her a grateful smile.

"Go on, take a look." She pushes me toward the huge mirror.

As my eyes catch my reflection, my steps falter, and my eyes widen.

"Holy shit." My jaw drops in surprise, and I step closer to the mirror.

Zaria chuckles behind me, but I can't tear my eyes from my reflection.

"Oh, wow," I murmur, touching my cheek.

I rarely wear makeup unless the occasion calls for it, but I hardly recognize myself. My gaze moves over my reflection, the light playing off my features. Half of my thick blonde hair is pinned back, and the long, loose strands cascade down my back in perfect waves. The rose gold gown is stunning, its sweetheart neckline showing off my collarbone and shoulders. The gems on the bodice sparkle like stars in the night sky, catching the light with my every move. Gems have also been sewn along the bottom of the gown. They seem to climb up the dress in an intricate pattern almost the same as the tattoos on Maxon's face.

"I love the delicate capped sleeves," I whisper, reaching up and touching the delicate fabric that hangs from my shoulders.

"You look like a princess," Zaria says, coming up behind me.

"Thank you, Zaria. You've done an amazing job. This dress, just wow." I pause, looking at Zaria in the mirror as she packs away the supplies. "Aren't you going to get ready?"

As soon as I speak, her wide brown eyes shoot to mine, and her furry ears twitch in response. "Umm."

"Aren't you coming?" I ask, suddenly nervous.

Zaria shakes her head. "I'm just a servant. I don't attend balls."

I furrow my brow, trying to make sense of it. "But Maxon is your friend."

"He is, but he is my king first."

"I'm coming in!" Raiden calls out, before stepping into the room. His silver eyes go wide when he spots me. "Well, you polish up nicely for a human."

A light laugh falls from my lips, and I do a spin. "That's the nicest thing I think you've said to me."

Raiden shakes his head, his lips curling up into a small grin, softening the features of his face. His wings are folded neatly against his back, adding a regal touch to the black fabric of his formal soldier's uniform. A gold and red dragon symbol is etched onto the chest over the heart.

"You look quite dashing in that uniform."

It's my first time seeing Raiden in a soldier's uniform. While the other soldiers and guards dress more formally, Raiden usually wears simple black breeches and a tunic which he's ripped the sleeves off. His sword is missing from his back tonight, but I'm sure there's a weapon somewhere on him. Who am I kidding? He is a weapon.

"Would you train me to use a sword?" I blurt.

Raiden looks startled for a moment before laughing. "What?"

"I want to learn to use a sword. If I am to be stuck here, I wish to learn how to fight. You don't expect me to just stay in my room all day and walk the gardens?"

"Well . . . "

"Please." I am not above begging if I have to.

"Fine. It would probably be a good idea, anyway."

Unable to stop my burst of excitement, I fling my arms around Raiden's neck and hug him. The big brute stiffens at the contact, and I pull back, thankful for the heels, as his height is really imposing. I give him a reassuring pat on the chest.

"Sorry," I chuckle. "I'm a bit nervous."

Raiden clears his throat and nods to Zaria. "We should be going."

Zaria walks over, grabbing my hands in hers, and I catch her quick glance at my arm. My birthmark burns under the makeup she used to cover it.

"Be careful tonight. The court is full of vipers."

I give her a soft smile and squeeze her hands. "I'm sure everything will be just fine."

"We've got her," Raiden says.

Zaria lets go of my hand with a nod. "Okay."

Raiden opens the door, and we step out into the hall, my nerves abuzz with excitement as I hook my arm in his, leading me down the hall toward the stairs.

"How many are coming?"

"At least a couple hundred. This is for the noble fae, the lords and ladies mostly. A pre-coronation party."

My heart speeds up. A couple hundred?

"So why am I attending?" I croak.

"The queen insisted you attend."

"Why?"

"That's the question, isn't it?" Raiden replies cryptically.

We walk in silence down the stairs, Raiden helping keep me steady in the heels. At the far end of the hall, I can see the massive double wooden door leading to the grand hall. The guards bow as we approach and pull open the doors, allowing us to pass.

A rush of excitement courses through me as we come to a stop at the edge of the balcony. The opulent grandeur of the ballroom is accentuated by the sweet, melodic strains of music that fills the air. Crystal chandeliers cast a warm, ethereal glow over the swirling couples, their elegant gowns and tailored suits adding to the timeless allure of the evening. It's the most magical thing I've ever seen.

"Come on," Raiden says, hooking my arm in his and leading me toward the grand staircase.

I can't seem to stop the way my heart picks up as I gaze around the large ballroom, searching for him. My eyes catch on a set of silver ringed, violet eyes and it feels like the world stops spinning. A million butterflies burst to life in my chest, leaving me breathless.

Maxon looks up at me from below, his eyes tracing over every inch of me. The heat of his stare feels like a physical caress, making my cheeks flush.

Damn it, I need to get myself under control.

Maxon starts through the crowd toward us, never taking his gaze away. I can't help but admire how the black suit hugs his body in all the right places, emphasizing his masculine physique. The black shirt is undone midway down, showing off his tanned and muscled chest. The black clothing seems to bring out the intensity of his features. Plaits woven with gold rings are scattered through the length of his dark brown hair. My eyes roam his face, taking in every detail. The three sword earrings in his left ear, glinting in the light. The way some of the free hairs frame his features.

"He really should be more careful. You both should," Raiden mutters.

I have no idea what he's talking about, trapped as I am in Maxon's gaze—unable to look away or speak.

Maxon's eyes sparkle like gems as he stops at the base of the stairs to wait for us. When we finally reach the bottom, Raiden releases my arm, and Maxon's hand finds mine, his grip firm and comforting as he smirks down at me.

"You look absolutely stunning tonight, Stóirín."

Unable to hold those intense eyes a moment longer, I drop my gaze. "Thank you," I whisper.

Gosh, is it hot in here?

Without a word, Maxon turns, pulling me toward the dance floor. Panic begins to set in. I didn't know any of these fae dances.

He can't expect me to dance, right?

"Stop worrying. I've got you."

He faces me, his palm sliding around my waist to pull me closer, our bodies fitting together seamlessly. My first steps are hesitant, but soon fall into a smooth dance, Maxon spinning me around, leading me into each step with perfect grace.

The world around us melts away, leaving only the two of us twirling, spinning, and gliding across the floor. I am so content in this moment; a feeling I'm not familiar with. His eyes brighten and we remain locked in each other's stare.

Maxon pulls me closer, and the warmth of his body sets my heart to a racing pace. Moving his face closer, his cheek brushes mine, his warm breath on my neck, his hand firm against the small of my back. My heart races faster as I marvel at the sensation of being so completely enveloped in his presence.

As the music swells, reaching its crescendo, our bodies press together in a fiery embrace. He leans me back over his arm, my head falling back slightly and eyes closing, my body surrendering to the magic of the dance and the irresistible pull of the man in my arms.

My smile is so big that my cheeks hurt, but I can't seem to wipe it off my face. "That was amazing," I laugh, my fingers digging into his arms.

Maxon's eyes are warm and tender as he grins down at me, slowly lifting me upright before stepping back and releasing his hold on me. "I'm glad you enjoyed the dance."

Out of nowhere, a fae man appears and whispers something into Maxon's ear. Maxon's eyes narrow, and his jaw clenches as he gives the man a curt nod.

His attention returns to me, and he sighs in frustration. "The queen wishes to see me."

"Oh, okay. I'll find Raiden."

Maxon appears torn as he looks around, and I feel a pang of guilt.

"I will be fine," I assure gently, resting my hand on his arm.

Maxon peers down at me, something flickering in the depths of his eyes before he nods. Turning, he makes his way through the crowd toward the dais where the queen is conversing with a few other fae.

With a deep inhale, I square my shoulders and survey the room. Raiden is leaning against one of the massive marble pillars around the edge of the large ballroom, his hawklike gaze watching everything. I start making my way over when someone steps in my path. I look up into the cool, calculating eyes of a tall fae with dark hair.

"You must be the human. Everly, isn't it?"

"Yes, that's me. The lowly human," I reply with a tight smile.

The fae's eerie smile makes me shiver with unease. I can't quite put my finger on it, but my gut is telling me that there's something off about him. His unsettling eyes continue to rake over my body, making my teeth clench and anger burn in the pit of my stomach.

"I can see why the prince has taken a liking to you. I, too, like curvy women."

"Excuse me?" I growl, feeling my face heat.

"Have I offended you?"

Before I can answer, another voice cuts in. "You always aim to offend, Duke Wallcliffe."

I turn my head and see a dark skinned fae with long black hair and tattoos covering every inch of exposed skin. He is not dressed formally like the rest of the guests, but in breeches and a plain white tunic. I can't help but lean in closer and stare at the tattoos.

"Are they moving?" I ask in awe.

The newcomer chuckles. "Yes, my markings move. You must be Everly."

Our eyes meet, and I respond with a nervous smile. "Yes, and you are?"

The fae bows at the waist. "Forgive me. My name is Nero. I've actually just been given a name other than the usual phantom, changeling, puca, or shapeshifter. It's nice."

"It's a pleasure to meet you, Nero," I reply, purposely ignoring this so-called Lord Wallcliffe.

"Would you care for a dance?" Nero asks.

"I was conversing with this young lady first," Duke Wallcliffe argues, trying to step between us.

"I would love to." Grabbing Nero's hand, I basically drag him away from that horrid man.

Nero chuckles as we move into the next dance. "I thought you could use a rescue."

"Is he always so rude?"

"Yes." Nero's eyes take on a hard edge as he looks in the direction of Duke Wallcliffe.

"Even though that was a simple answer, it seems ominous."

"Just stay away from him." Though his voice is gentle, the warning is unmistakable. Nervously, I swallow and give a nod.

Nero lifts my hand and I twirl, the skirt of my dress flaring out and sparkling like gems in the sun. Pulling me in close to his chest, a grin spreads across his face.

"You're an excellent dancer for a human. I wouldn't think you'd know this dance. It is a traditional fae dance."

I jerk in his grasp. He's right. I've been dancing, my body moving freely and without thought.

"It's okay, Everly," Nero whispers. "You will remember when the time is right."

The music comes to a stop, and with a final bow, Nero retreats and disappears into the crowd. I am at a loss for words, and my body feels frozen in place.

What did that mean?

My eyes dart to the birthmark hidden under the makeup on my arm, and a sudden sense of urgency courses through me. My eyes dart around, searching for any sign of where Nero went. I have a gut feeling that he possesses the answers I am seeking. I push through the crowd of fae, but I can't see him.

Damn it.

I catch sight of Maxon next to the queen, conversing with two Lords. With a sigh, I spin on my heel, intent to find Raiden, but bump straight into another lady.

"Shit. I'm . . . " I hold my tongue as Nix's words of warning about fae debts come to mind.

The fae woman snarls, her eyes piercing straight through me as she pokes me in the chest with her sharp nails. We stare at each other for several long moments, neither breaking eye contact. I recognize her immediately, it's the fae woman who threw me in that small storage room.

She is dressed to the nines, in a slinky red dress, her dark hair curled around her shoulders as it falls to her waist. I notice the other women around her have fallen silent, keenly watching our exchange, with smirks on their faces.

"Don't you have something to say, human?" she spits the last word as if being human makes me less than the dirt beneath her shoes.

Biting my lip, I shake my head. No matter what I say, the outcome of my situation remains the same.

Where is Raiden?

The fae's eyes flare and she raises her hand. Is she planning on slapping me?

Without giving me a chance to react, Maxon appears in front of me. He moved so fast that I didn't even see him leave the dais. And now he firmly holds the wrist of the female fae in his hand.

"Lay a finger on her again. I dare you." His dark, menacing tone cuts through the air.

The female's eyes grow wide as she stares at Maxon.

"You can't mean to protect this– this human . . . "

His jaw flexes as he stares down at her. "Touch her again, and she will be the least of your worries, Madeline."

I might have stopped breathing as I stand here motionless. I'm not sure why, but the air in the ballroom feels charged with hostility, making me hesitant to divert my gaze. Maxon releases Madeline's wrist, and he purposefully positions himself a little closer to me.

Taking a swift glance around, I observe a sudden hush that has befallen the room. All eyes are fixed on us, their penetrating stares resembling those of vigilant hawks. My attention is drawn to the queen, whose expression displays obvious disapproval and indignation. The radiant light from the chandelier illuminates her violet eyes, sending a shiver down my spine. The weight of the consequences for disrupting the ball suddenly feels daunting, and I am painfully aware that I may have to bear a substantial price for my actions.

I sense someone approach and meet Raiden's gaze through the crowd. A wave of relief washes over me, and my shoulders instantly relax. The large fae moves gracefully through the crowd, his wings tucked tightly against his back. Raiden gives me a small wink, as if sharing a secret, before extending his elbow to me. Grateful for the rescue, I slip my arm in his and give him a weak smile. Maxon looks over his shoulder at us and Raiden bows slightly, and I dip my head.

"I will escort Miss Baker to her rooms, Your Highness."

Maxon gives a sharp nod before his piercing gaze meets mine, and I feel a lump form in my throat. His eyes wander across my face and down before settling on the spot where Madeline poked me. I look down and see a thin trickle of blood. Damn, she has some sharp claws.

Maxon's jaw is clenched so hard that a muscle in his cheek pops, and his eyes turn so dark they look like pools of inky blackness, with only the silver color flaring with magic. As much as I want to take his hand, to comfort him, I know it would only escalate the situation. It seems that he is barely managing to keep his anger under control.

Drawing in a shallow breath, I allow Raiden to lead me through the crowd toward the doors. The whispers and furtive glances in my direction do not go unnoticed.

Raiden gently pats my hand. "Pay them no mind."

Chapter Sixteen

Everly

There is a soft knock on my door the next morning and I walk over, expecting to see Maxon or Raiden.

"Kian? Come in."

Kian bows, giving me his usual easy-going smile. "The prince has been called away. I'm not to let you out of my sight until he returns."

I roll my eyes and cross my arms in defiance. "Well, Raiden was going to start training me today. Will you help me?"

Kian's eyebrows shoot up in surprise. "You?"

I let loose a laugh at his look of shock. "Yes, me. I'm not all that helpless. I learned to defend myself at a young age, but I lack technique. Or the ability to use a sword."

Kian gives me a once over, taking in the black guard breeches and the white tunic Zaria had given me. I also have the dagger Raiden handed me last night when he dropped me at my room, it was tucked into the waistband of my pants. I asked Zaria if she could get a couple of outfits made for me. I spent hours last night drawing up some designs that, while still pretty, will be acceptable to fight in and will hide my daggers.

"Okay, I can run through some things with you."

I let out a tiny squeal of excitement and then clamp my lips together in embarrassment. "Sorry."

Kian laughs, his lavender eyes taking on a more pinkish hue. "I like your enthusiasm. You'll need it." He winks and turns for the door, holding it open for me.

I don't like the sound of that.

"After you, my lady."

The clang of steel against steel echoes through the arena as we make our way over to the far corner out of the way of the others that are training.

"Maybe we should train in the garden?" I say nervously, looking around at all the men staring our way.

Kian shrugs off his coat and starts rolling up the sleeves of his tunic. "Scared?"

My gaze whips back to him. "What? No!"

"Sounds like it," he says, smirking.

A low growl escapes my lips as I place my hands on my hips. "I just wasn't expecting a crowd."

Kian's gaze softens. "It will be fine. No one will bother us."

He turns and walks over to a small wooden table and picks up two sticks. Facing me, he tosses one at me. I panic for a moment then instinctively reach out to grab the stick, raising an eyebrow in confusion.

Wooden swords?

"It's necessary for you to master the basic movements first. To use a sword correctly, the movements must be as natural and fluid as the flow of water in a river."

I look down at the wooden sword, studying the grain of the wood and the rough edges. It's still surprisingly heavy.

"Okay. But I don't think I'm ever going to be as fluid as a river."

"You will if you are determined. We will also have to work on your endurance and stamina."

I lift my gaze, and I notice the mischievous twinkle in his eyes. The innuendo sinking in, I bite my bottom lip and shake my head, trying to hide my amusement.

"You're a turd," I chuckle.

"What?" Kian asks innocently.

"I'll have you know my stamina is just fine."

"Could always be better though."

My face flushes, and I narrow my eyes at him. Deciding to give me a break from his flirtiness, Kian takes up a stance next to me. "I want you to follow my movements."

I watch and copy as Kain gracefully moves through a series of fluid moves. After going through them with me several times, Kain drops his sword.

"Continue," he orders.

I nod and focus ahead, going through each move he's shown me. Kian watches and corrects me when needed. I can feel the sweat rolling down my forehead and back, as I go through each movement. The weight of the wooden sword makes my muscles shake with exertion.

"Okay. Enough."

I let out a weary sigh, my arms falling heavily to my sides. The muscles in my body ached in protest as I fight to catch my breath.

"You did well, but we will take a break from the sword. Want to do some hand to hand?"

I nod, unable to speak just yet.

"Okay, but first, one lap of the arena."

"What?" I shriek.

Is he serious?

"Endurance, remember." He smirks and takes off jogging.

I tip my head back and groan before running to catch up. I may hike a lot, but cardio really isn't my thing. Once we complete a lap, Kian turns to face me and bursts out laughing.

"What?" I pant.

Shaking his head, he hands me a glass water bottle. "You are as red as a beet."

"Shut up."

Kian tips his head back and laughs. "Okay. Hand to hand combat is all about fundamentals. Balance, control, and instinct."

With lightning speed, he demonstrates a quick jab, his fist snapping out like a viper. "This is your golden snitch. Jab, cross, hook. Practice these until they're second nature. It's all about precision, not power."

I raise an eyebrow at him in question. "Golden snitch?"

"Someone got a hold of the Harry Potter books and brought them back for me. Found them to be quite addictive." He winks as he pushes his blonde hair from his face, and I'm slightly annoyed to see he hasn't even worked up a sweat.

"I didn't picture you as a reader."

"It's always the quiet ones, right?" he says with a wink.

"Sure, whatever you say."

Kian grins and motions for me to start. With a nod, I adopt the stance he shows me, my feet shoulder width apart, weight evenly distributed, my fists clenched, knuckles up.

"Good. Now, imagine your challenger is right in front of you. Jab." I follow his lead, my fist shooting out with newfound purpose. It feels clumsy at first, but with each repetition, my movements grow smoother and more focused.

Kian stands off to the side with his arms crossed over his chest and watches me closely. Offering pointers and corrections as I practice the basics. "Don't announce your punches. Keep your shoulders relaxed until the last second. And don't forget to breathe. That is the most important thing."

Throughout our movements, Kian emphasizes the significance of proper footwork, circling and angling to gain an advantage.

As we continue on, time seems to slip away, and I have no idea how long we have been training. Every muscle in my body aches, but I push through the pain, refusing to be some helpless human.

"Right, good. We can take a break for lunch. It looks like you could use it."

I don't need to be told twice. Panting heavily, I collapse onto the dirt, the warmth of the sun heats my face as I gaze up at the sky. Wiping the sweat from my brow, I realize that my body is aching in places I didn't even know existed.

"If you're up to it, we can work on defensive maneuvers tomorrow. I can show you how to block and parry, using your arms to shield yourself from an incoming strike. Your arms are your first line of defense. Protect your head, your body. Keep your guard up."

Kian comes to stand over me, his shadow blocking the sun. "Sound good?"

I grunt in response and a grin lights up his face. “I think it’s great you're willing to learn how to fight.”

“You do?”

Kian holds out his hand to help me up. “Yes. You should always know how to protect yourself.”

I grip his hand, and he heaves me to my feet. As I’m brushing the dirt from my pants, someone runs toward us. Another guard.

“Kian, the queen wishes to see the human.”

“Everly,” Kian states.

“What?”

“Her name is Everly.”

The guard looks affronted, but refuses to acknowledge me. “Right. Well, the queen wants to see her. Now.”

“We will be there shortly,” Kian replies, waving his hand at the guard.

I wait until the guard is out of earshot before speaking. “Why does she want to see me? Other than when I first arrived, she has been avoiding me. Frankly, I don’t even understand her insistence that I attend the ball last night.”

“The queen’s motives are never clear.” Kian shrugs on his jacket and attaches his sword to his waist. “But we must not keep her waiting.”

My stomach chooses this moment to grumble and groan. “I hope this doesn’t take long. I’m starving.”

Kian winks and begins walking back toward the castle, and I hurry to catch up. Falling into step with him, I look around, noticing the guards and soldiers we pass each wear different uniforms. The guards wear the sage green like the maids, but the soldiers wear black and red. Despite the difference in color, both display the emblem of a majestic dragon. I can’t help but wonder if this emblem holds a deeper meaning or if it simply represents the royal crest.

"Why are the guards in different uniforms to you and Tristan?"

"Well, the guards are mainly stationed around the castle and take orders from the queen and Nolan. Soldiers are in the black and red because we are the army. We follow the crown prince and keep the Unseelie kingdom safe."

"Is it beneath you to play bodyguard and babysitter?"

"Not at all."

There is a hint of hesitation in his voice, but I decide not to press it.

We arrive at the doors to the queen's sitting room, and I struggle to suppress the unease clawing my insides. After what happened last night at the ball, am I in trouble?

Kian's knuckles rap twice against the door before he steps back, clasping his hands behind his back. I bite down hard on my bottom lip as we wait, nerves getting the better of me. The door swings open, and a young servant girl greets us with a polite bow before stepping aside to allow us entry. As we pass through, her gaze lifts to meet mine, and a flicker of recognition passes between us. Before I can say anything, she quickly averts her eyes and leaves the room.

"You may leave us," the queen says, dismissing Kian.

My heart jumps into my throat and fear skates down my spine, as I focus on the queen standing in front of us. The thought of being alone with her brings a feeling of immediate dread. Her animosity toward me is noticeable, and though she tries to play it off, it's clear she sees me as nothing more than a bothersome insect to be dealt with.

"I'm sorry, your majesty, but I am not to leave Miss Baker's side."

The queen's black hair falls down her back as she tips her head back and laughs. "Nonsense, boy. You may leave."

"With all due respect, your majesty, no." Kian refuses to back down.

My breath seizes in my throat, and my eyes widen. Is he crazy?

Worried for his safety, I am on the verge of intervening when he gives me a look that makes me think twice.

The queen's expression turns predatory as she strolls toward us. "You would disobey your queen?"

Kian bows with respect, before rising back up to his full height. "It's not that I'm disobeying you. But I will not disobey my king."

My eyes just about pop out of my head, when the queen's face turns red.

Vibrating with rage, her violet eyes take on a crazed edge. "He is not king yet," she snarls.

Oh, shit.

Despite the her fury, Kian stands resolute, his demeanor unchanging. My respect and gratitude for him soar to new heights.

The queen takes a step forward and my breath catches as she stops in front of me. I can feel the heat of her rage as it fills the air around us, and I watch in alarm as her canines grow longer. I'm tempted to squint my eyes and double-check, but I don't want to appear rude. I'm caught off guard when she grabs my chin, and I wince as her fingers dig into my skin. I can feel her warm breath on my face as she leans in, and I fight the urge to pull away.

"What is it about you"—she ponders—"that has the prince so fiercely protective?"

Kian moves, his muscles tense and ready for action. "Remove your hand, Your Majesty."

Would he really fight the queen for me?

I can't help but feel a sense of apprehension as her lips curl into a twisted, cruel smile. Leaning in, her lips brush against my ear as she whispers so softly that her words are almost indistinguishable.

"They cannot protect you all the time, child."

I feel the blood drain from my face and rapidly flow back in, nausea swirling in the pit of my stomach. Her fingers release their grip on my chin, and she steps back, crossing to her armchair to take a seat.

"Sit," she demands, not sparing me a glance.

I stand there a moment and consider what she'd do if I turn around and walk out. Kian gently nudges me, I begrudgingly make my way over to the chairs, and take a seat. I can feel Kian's protective gaze on my back as he takes up his stance behind me, making me feel so much more at ease.

"Now I want you to recall everything that happened leading up to you arriving here."

"I already told you."

The queen shoots me a look. "I want details. We are missing something. You arriving when you did can't be a coincidence."

I bit my lip as I think back. "Well, like I told you, I was out hiking with two friends. One second, they were behind me and the next second, they were gone."

"Who are these friends of yours?"

The corners of my lips turn down. "They are none of your concern." I will not draw Mia and Scarlett into my mess. I'm not sure if the queen has the means to send anyone after them, but I am not taking the chance.

"Well, they were the only other beings with you when you stumbled into my realm. I'm just curious."

"They had nothing to do with this. Maybe you should check your gates?"

Queen Lavina crosses one leg over the other, toying with her pendant as she rests back in her armchair. A slight smirk plays at the corners of her lips, making that sense of dread resurface.

"I have." She pauses. "They are sealed tightly shut. It also shows the gate was opened by someone from the other side."

"I did not open the gate," I grit, feeling my patience wane.

A wicked gleam enters Queen Lavina's eyes as she runs the pendant back and forth along the chain. "You care for these friends of yours?"

"You know I do," I reply, straightening my shoulders.

"Well, since I can't touch a hair on your precious head . . . "

I can't help the feral growl that rumbles from my throat, causing the queen's eyes to flash with a dangerous light. The silver ring lining her violet eyes seems to pulse with power, and I can feel her waiting for me to slip up and give her a reason to lock me away. As it stands, Maxon is the only thing that remains between me and the dungeons.

"You wouldn't dare," I whisper, my hands curling into fists on my knees.

The queen uncrosses her legs and leans forward. "I think you misjudge me."

I snort. "Unlikely."

Suddenly, the doors bang open and a very pissed off Maxon storms in. The black cloak of his uniform flows behind him as his heavy boots eat up the distance between us. His piercing gaze remains fixed solely on the Queen as he halts a foot away. I can feel the power rolling off him, and not for the first time, I wonder just what he is capable of. The air around him crackles with an unmistakable energy, causing my heart to race.

"This meeting is over," Maxon growls, glaring at the queen.

The tone of his voice is so icy that I can't stop the shiver that runs down my spine. He is totally pissed.

Queen Lavina stands, her expression soft and innocent. It's all an act, and it makes my skin crawl. It's like she strives to please him and keep him content. Why?

So he doesn't question her?

"You know I'm only doing this to protect our people. I must know what she is hiding."

"Kian, take Everly to the gardens. I will meet you there shortly."

Kian bows and tilts his head at me, beckoning me to follow. I hesitate, glancing over at Maxon, but his entire focus is on his aunt. I swiftly rise and walk past Kian, who firmly closes the door behind us. Quietly, we make our way down the hall toward the gardens.

"Is she always that intense?" I murmur, not wanting to speak too loud in case someone is listening.

"Yes."

I have so many questions about the queen, about how she ended up in power. What happened to Maxon's parents? Why he is only now assuming the throne. But I keep my mouth shut. Thoughts of the young maid from earlier filter through my mind.

"Who was the servant girl who let us into the room earlier?" I ask Kian.

Turning to look down at me, he frowns. "Eve?"

"Green, brown eyes, darkish skin and black hair?"

"Yes. That is Eve. She is a shifter."

The name doesn't seem familiar, but her eyes—I know those eyes. But that doesn't make sense. I've never been here before.

It's official. I am finally losing my mind.

"Most of the maids here are shifters," Kian continues, nodding to a guard stationed at the door as we pass through.

"Why?"

"Their social standing has been deemed inferior, and they are categorized as part of the lower class."

Anger ignites in my stomach, and I draw to a halt. "That's ridiculous!!" I exclaim, my hands flying to my hips as I glare at him.

Kian holds his palms up. "I didn't say I agreed. And before you ask, neither does the prince. He plans on changing that as soon as he takes the throne. It wasn't always this way."

"What do you mean?"

"A long time ago, it wasn't just us high fae ruling Faerie. The druids ruled over the forest, the fae over the cities. During this time, there was equality. It didn't matter who or what you were. The druids were fair and kind. They, how would you put it . . . " He pauses for a moment. "They kept the high fae tempered. Kept order among the groups. Those Outcasts who attacked you didn't exist until the druids were hunted to near extinction. They banded together in protest of the death of their king and queen. Over the years, some have become thieves and felons. Now, any who follow the druids remain hidden among us, too scared to reveal themselves."

My mind whirls as I go over this new information. "Why would you hunt them?"

Kian looks down at me, the pink hue of his lavender eyes seems to deepen with an emotion I can't name. "A prophecy. It's always about prophecy," he mutters.

"What is the prophecy?"

Kian stops next to a rosebush, the white flowers in perfect bloom. I can't help but reach out, letting my fingers trace the soft velvet petals as I wait. I know it's silly, but it feels as if the flowers are reaching for my touch.

"It was said that a druid would be born who possessed power greater than any before her." Kian's voice drops to a whisper drawing my attention.

"It was from the whispers of ancient trees and the murmurs of the sacred groves.
A druid born under a crescent moon's gentle glow, shall wield power unmeasured in realms both high and low.
With magic deep within, she'll rise, her destiny unknown,
To shake the faerie realm, where mystic secrets are sown.
Her heart a beacon of the woods, her spirit strong and free,
She'll dance with stars and call the winds.
Beneath the moon's enchanting light, she'll rise to claim her throne,
Uniting realms of faerie, her power fully grown.
With wisdom, love, and courage, she'll mend what once was torn,
For in her hands, the faerie world shall be reborn."

The hair on the back of my neck stands on end and goosebumps spread across my skin, the feeling making me uncomfortable. Kian steps closer, the intensity in his gaze causing my breath to quicken. He has this knowing look in his eyes, as if he holds a secret I am not privy to.

Kian reaches his hand out, his fingers grazing my arm exactly where my birthmark is hidden under the tunic. I draw in a sharp breath, my brows lowering, and I take a step back.

"When you're ready, princess." His words catch me off guard, and my body locks up, just like it did during my encounter with Nero last night.

"There you are!" Maxon's voice rings through the garden.

Kian steps back, and my attention drops to the ground as I try to compose myself.

"Everything okay?" Kian asks.

Maxon's voice is barely audible as he mumbles something to Kian and steps up to me. His finger lifts my chin, and I'm struck by the seriousness of his gaze. It's as though he can see right through me.

"Are you okay, Stóirín?"

I feel a pull toward him, and I want nothing more than to take that last step and wrap my arms around him. But I don't.

"I'm fine," I whisper.

I lean into Maxon's touch as his finger trails across my jawline. I feel a surge of warmth in my chest and my stomach flutters as he pulls me closer with his other hand on my waist.

"I'm worried if I let you out of my sight, you'll disappear on me," Maxon murmurs. His warm breath skates across my cheek as his head drops closer. My eyes drift shut, and I take a shallow breath, my body tingling with anticipation. Maxon's lips barely brush mine when a throat clears loudly, making me jump, my eyes flying open.

How did I forget we weren't alone?

Chapter Seventeen

Everly

Heart pounding in my chest, I take a step back, looking out over the courtyard. It's getting harder and harder to deny my feelings for him. The fact that I can't control my blush doesn't help matters at all. It's probably clear as day to everyone that I have feelings for the unseelie prince.

"I'm taking Everly into Skora. We will be back by nightfall."

That catches my attention, I look up as Kian bows before turning and heading toward the training grounds. My heart races as Maxon takes my hand and pulls me after him, the scent of the garden and the rush of adventure fill my senses.

"Where are we going?" I ask, struggling to keep up with his brisk pace.

Maxon's gaze catches mine over his shoulder and he slows. "I was going to take you to Skora. I heard you've been training all morning and haven't eaten. There is a place that does the best fried honey cakes with an assortment of berries and creams."

On cue, my stomach rumbles, and a blush spreads over my cheeks as Maxon smirks. I could swear the tattoos on his face darken for just a second, but it must be a trick of the light.

"That does sound good."

"Fae have a voracious appetite, and a particular fondness for sugary delights. Many of the dishes we serve have a distinctly sweet taste, so be prepared for that."

"No arguments here." I smile.

It's one thing I've always had, my sweet tooth is well known. Mia and Scarlett always teased me about how much sugar I eat. While diets have failed me in the past, my dedication to a meat-free lifestyle has never wavered.

"As long as I don't have to eat meat, we will be fine."

Maxon's eyes flicker to mine, seemingly caught off guard. "You don't eat meat?"

"Nope. Never." I see a building up ahead and people walking horses in and out.

A young fae boys meets us at the doors to the stable. "Storm is in a mood, Your Highness. He won't let anyone near him since you got back."

Maxon chuckles. "When isn't he in a mood?"

The young fae boy is clearly unsure of himself, his feet shuffling nervously in the dirt. "That is true, Your Highness," he says quietly and bows before disappearing.

I follow Maxon into the large stables, the smell of hay filling the air as we make our way to the back row of stalls. The sound of hooves pounding the ground grows louder, emanating from the largest stall. I peer into the stall and see Storm anxiously pacing back and forth, his nostrils flaring with each breath. Fear twists in my stomach when Maxon opens the door and walks in.

With a steady hand and unwavering focus, Maxon approaches the massive beast and holds out his palm. Storm's mane whips around as he shakes his head in agitation and nudges Maxon's hand with his nose.

"What's up with you?"

With each powerful stomp of Storm's massive hooves, the ground quivers beneath him as he nods his head up and down. Stepping inside the stall, I am immediately greeted by the sound of Storm's loud and steady breathing. He has an untamed, majestic beauty that takes my breath away. The black-maned beast has a powerful physique that commands attention. I can't tear my eyes away from his massive hooves, their size easily surpassing that of my head.

A true war horse.

Storm's nostrils flare, and he lets out an angry snort, clearly upset about something. I watch as he barges past Maxon, making me freeze in fear as he steps up to me, snorting aggressively. I feel the wetness of spittle on my cheek and raise my hand to wipe it off before meeting the horse's gaze.

"Geeze, thanks for that, Storm."

Storm's hoof strikes the ground, and I can feel the thud reverberate through my body. I cross my arms, raising an eyebrow at him. Staring into those dark, bottomless eyes, I can't help but close the distance and run my hand down his neck, feeling the warmth and softness of his coat. As the tension eases from his body, I sense a feeling of disappointment lingering.

"So, you're annoyed he left you and came to see me without you?"

Storm's head bobs dramatically, nearly pushing me off balance. Stepping carefully around him, Maxon approaches Storm's side and rubs his hand over his side.

"I'm sorry, Storm, but time was of the essence."

Storm turns his head away, as if giving Maxon the cold shoulder. My lips curl up involuntarily, but I quickly bite down on my bottom lip to suppress the smile. The horse is clearly upset at being left here. Maxon's hand strokes Storm's cheek.

"Forgive me? I was hoping you would take us for a ride?"

When Storm looks at Maxon, he nudges him playfully and knocks him back a step. I cover my mouth to stifle my laugh.

"Good. Everly hasn't eaten today. I was thinking about taking her to the markets. I knew my big strong horse would be up for showing a pretty lady around."

Storm's hooves stamp the ground as he dances, his thick mane whipping around him.

"You like the sound of that? Good."

Making a soft chuffing sound, he moves past us and trots out of the stall, his head held high. Maxon gives me a conspiratorial grin and follows Storm. I notice everyone giving the massive horse a wide berth when we pass, afraid to get too close.

As soon as we step outside, Maxon takes control of the reins and brings Storm to a halt. The war horse really is a thing of beauty, he is just like his rider. They both exude an aura of strength and power that demands respect from all those around them. My heart melts as I watch Maxon stroke the horse's neck and whisper something to him. The bond between the two is clear to see.

A young fae man with bluish skin and curly red hair, a startling color combination, rushes over. "Would you like some help, miss?"

Before I can answer, Maxon steps up behind me, his hand landing on my hip, causing a rush of warmth to flood my cheeks. The young fae's eyes widen before he bows and scurries away without another word.

Huh . . .

"You scared him off!" I accuse.

"I did no such thing."

Turning to face him, I brush my hair out of my eyes and smile. "Sure. Whatever you say, Your Highness."

I need to question Maxon about the queen's threats, I have to know if she would actually send anyone after my friends. But the memory of my encounter with the queen fades away as I gaze into those sparkling, jeweled eyes. A soft breeze picks up our hair and tosses it around our faces. I can smell the sweet scent of flowers and hay drifting in the air. I swear, it feels as if the wind itself is wrapping around me and pushing me toward Maxon.

Storm breaks me from my musings, nudging my shoulder, gently drawing my attention. I reach up and run my hand down his face.

"You are a stunning creature."

"Ready?" Maxon murmurs in my ear, the warmth of his breath sending goosebumps over my skin.

My heart trips over itself as I look from Storm to Maxon over my shoulder.

One side of his lips curves up in a devilish smirk, and my stomach clenches in response. An image flashes behind my eyes of us in bed together, his body moving over mine.

"Pray tell what it is you're thinking to make you blush so?" Maxon whispers in my ear, making me jump.

Clearing my throat, I tuck my hair behind my ear, nervously. "Nothing at all."

"Right." Maxon's hands grip my waist, and he lifts me with ease. I quickly grab hold of the staddle and swing my leg over, adjusting my position. As I feel the softness of Storm's mane under my hand, the excitement bubbles up inside me. In a matter of seconds, Maxon has taken his place behind me and is grabbing the reins, his chest pushed firmly against my back, his strong thighs bracing my legs.

Storm begins trotting down the hill toward the gates, and I try desperately to ignore the sensation of Maxon's arms around me. How nice it feels with his warmth surrounding me, like there is absolutely no space between us.

We pass through the gates and out onto the open road, a few soldiers and guards nodding in our direction. The distance between the castle gates and the village below isn't too far, but the green fields that lie between are beautifully alive with wildflowers in an array of colors.

"Wow, so many flowers."

"It's weird. We don't usually get wildflowers here."

"Why?"

Maxon leans in closer, making me tense. "We are in the Autumn Court, Stóirín."

"Oh, that's right," I breathe.

My fingers sink into Storm's mane, and I try desperately to control my breathing. It takes all my willpower not to turn my head and find his mouth. All too quickly, we have closed the distance to the village gates and are passing through. Cobblestone roads make up the street, which is adorned with charming little houses. A handful of fae idle and chat, a couple of them stealing a glance at us as we go by, inquiring stares tracking us. The few who are in close proximity to the road bow their heads in respect as we pass, but Maxon merely acknowledges them with a nod. I cannot resist allowing my eyes to linger on the grey skinned fae with horns and wings, which is an extraordinary sight that is far from my usual experiences.

Just as a wolf emerges onto the road, the echo of a woman's shout fills the air. My heart thumps frantically in my chest as Storm halts abruptly, narrowly avoiding trampling the creature. A frantic woman comes rushing out, looking completely frazzled.

"Oh, Your Highness. I'm so–" But before she can finish, Maxon raises his palm, silencing her words.

"It is fine. No one was hurt."

The wolf runs toward the woman, making my throat tighten with emotion. I watch in complete awe as a swirl of shimmering light surrounds the wolf, and it transforms into a young girl no older than twelve.

Maxon's gaze shifts to the young girl, who averts her eyes and lowers her head.

Maxon's voice is gentle when he speaks, making my heart beat a little faster. "Maybe just slow down when you approach the street, leanbh."

The girl's light brown eyes widen as she nods, the mother mouthing *thank you* to Maxon as she wraps her arm around her daughter, guides her back toward the house.

"What is leanbh?" I ask as we start moving again.

"It means my child."

My lips twitch. "That's so sweet."

Maxon's hand moves, and I feel the warmth of his palm as it flattens on my stomach. The heat of his hand seeps through the fabric of my tunic, igniting my blood. Desire washes over me, and the only thing I can think of is what our bodies would be like skin on skin.

Is it normal to have these kinds of reactions to a man? I don't think it is, but he isn't a man, is he? He's fae.

Turning the corner, my breath catches in my throat as I take in the magnificent sight before me. Nestled within the heart of the village are the markets. Sprawled like a labyrinth of wonders, its stalls and tents forming a colorful mosaic is a sensory overload.

Maxon gently tugs on the reins, and Storm comes to a halt beside a quaint garden in between two shops. Jumping swiftly from the horse, Maxon turns to me as I swing one leg over. Without any hesitation, his hands firmly grasp my hips, and gently lower me to the ground.

My hands automatically grasp his shoulders and trail down to grip his forearms. "Thanks," I say, smiling up at him.

"Anytime."

I step back, my pulse thrumming loudly as I clasp my hands together in front of me.

"Come on. I will take you to Láthair Milis. It's the best spot for sugary delicacies."

I nod eagerly, my mouth watering with the promise of delicious sweets. "Lead the way."

A mischievous twinkle appears in his eyes, and the side of his mouth turns up in a grin. Holding out his hand, he reaches for mine. Slowly, almost hesitantly, I place my hand in his. Without hesitation, he flips our hands, he laces our fingers together, the feeling of intimacy making my stomach flutter with excitement and apprehension.

"Nothing to be nervous about, Stóirín. You are safe with me."

"My safety isn't what I'm nervous about," I blurt.

Maxon stares back at me, almost curiously. "Dare I ask?"

My cheeks flush and I shake my head. "Let's go." I smile, trying to hide my emotions, but we both know how he is making me feel.

The aroma of exotic spices wafts through the air, enticing me to sample the culinary delights of foreign lands.

As we walk through the crowd, I am surprised to see a lot of different fae creatures. I see a few tiny pixies and I wonder if Nix knows them.

The merchants trade their wares, their voices weaving a cacophonous tapestry of languages and dialects. Some I understand, others I don't. It's on the tip of my tongue to ask Maxon why I can understand languages I've never spoken, but something holds me back.

We come to the end of one street and on the corner, a mysterious apothecary named Elören displays jars of glowing potions that sparkle like the afternoon sky. My curiosity gets the best of me, and I pause to investigate the peculiar jars and vials on the shelf.

Spells, maybe? Curses?

I hesitate to ask, not wanting to reveal my human nature. Nearby, an enigmatic fortune teller with a cloak as dark as midnight reads the future in the shimmering depths of a crystal ball, her words drawing a hushed crowd. I really want to see the fortune teller. Something about being in Faerie makes it all seem so real. Mia and Scarlett would always scoff at the idea of getting our fortunes read, calling it a scam and a waste of money. I'm the opposite. Always drawn in by the mystical.

Amidst the clamor, fae children dart around shoppers with wide-eyes, some tug at their parents' sleeves, begging for colorful trinkets and magical baubles. So many stalls are laden with vibrant fabrics and embroidered silks catching my eye. This must be where Zaria got the fabrics for the dresses she had made for me.

Maxon doesn't hurry me, instead letting me take in everything at my own pace. His hand is still firmly clasping mine, gentle and comforting. The sharp clanging of metal on metal resonates through the air as we pass the blacksmith. I watch in awe as he swings the hammer with precision, never breaking his momentum. The weapons and armor that line his walls are so intricate, they look fit for fae heroes and warriors.

"George is the best at what he does," Maxon whispers next to my ear, making me jump.

"His pieces are beautiful."

"They are."

Maxon tugs my hand, and we round the corner into a quieter street. "Here we are," he says as we stop in front of a sweet little shop that seems to be carved from a gigantic tree trunk.

Above us, the canopy spreads out, creating a natural roof, with pink and orange flowers delicately decorating each branch.

"Oh my gosh, it's gorgeous," I breathe, dropping his hand and peering in the small window. The shop is filled with baked treats and the smell . . . the smell is heavenly. The aroma of cinnamon, sugar, and chocolate waft from the open window, making me feel warm and cozy.

The door to the shop is much too small for Maxon or I to fit through, but I don't have to worry, because a short fairy walks out, holding several bags.

"Maxon, my boy!" she exclaims, her round face breaking into a joyful grin.

Maxon raises his hand, covering his chest, and bows his head. "Coraline," he replies almost affectionately.

The fairy's wings flutter with excitement as she holds up the bags for all to see. Her light pink eyes are like nothing I have ever seen before and are perfectly complemented by her purple pixie cut. What really fascinates me are her wings. The shimmering colors are so vibrant that they remind me of a rainbow after a storm.

Her wings are so captivating that I am oblivious to the fact that they are speaking to me. Maxon's hand lands on my shoulder, snapping me out of it.

"Everly, I'd like you to meet Coraline. She has been baking me sweets since I was old enough to walk."

Coraline steps forward, taking both my hands in hers. "Maxon has never brought any girls to meet me before." She gives me a coy wink before continuing, "You're a pretty little thing, aren't you? And not skin and bones like all those other court fae." Dropping my hands she flies around me. "You have a body."

Oh my god, bury me now!

Maxon chuckles. "Don't mind Coraline, she doesn't seem to have a filter today."

I smile kindly at the fairy. "I hear you have the best honey cakes."

Coraline's pink eyes sparkle in delight. "You're here to try my cakes?"

"Yes, please."

Turning, she picks up the bags she's placed on the ground and hands them to Maxon. "Here. I saw you coming and packed all your favorites."

Maxon's face breaks out in a broad grin, and I'm once again mesmerized by how handsome he is. He is a black knight, a warrior, a prince of the Unseelie fae, but he is soft and gentle and sweet.

"Many thanks, Coraline. I will take Everly to the old oak to try them."

Looking down at me, butterflies flutter madly in my stomach as he winks at me and takes my hand.

"Bye, Coraline," he says, pulling me away.

I swallow roughly and wave goodbye to Coraline. Her smile falters, and she tilts her head to the side, as if trying to understand something. She narrows her eyes briefly, before they flare wide in disbelief.

My stomach drops, and I quickly turn my head around and continue walking. What was that look?

The smell coming from the bags is so delicious that I can almost taste it and my stomach rumbles in response.

Maxon looks down at me with concern. "You really are hungry."

I shrug. "I'm fine," I lie.

"Well, we are here."

My mouth drops open at the sight in front of me. In the center of a large courtyard is an ancient oak tree with gnarled branches that provide a natural canopy. Musicians are playing haunting melodies on wooden flutes and stringed instruments off to the side. The dancers move in perfect harmony with the music, creating an enchanting atmosphere. Being in Faerie is like stepping into a dream, where everything is vivid and tangible, and reality is blurred with magic.

Chapter Eighteen

Everly

Maxon and I have absolutely demolished all the sweets in the bags. The powdery sugary delights were amazing. I've never tasted anything like them in my life. It's near impossible to stop at one, and I understand why Coraline gave us a full bag.

Watching the fae dance around the tree from where we sit, a soft smile plays on my lips. My stomach is full, I've had my sugar hit, and the music is beautiful.

Maxon nudges my shoulder gently. "Ready to head back?"

I raise my gaze to him and offer a nonchalant shrug. "If you want."

Maxon's eyes darken, he leans in, running his thumb over the corner of my mouth. Bringing his hand back, he puts his thumb in his mouth, sucking it.

"You had some sugar on your lip," he replies, his eyes completely focused on my mouth.

Desire burns deep in my chest, heating my entire body. I can't help but lick my lips, drawing my bottom lip between my teeth. Our bodies sway toward each other, my eyes fluttering. A loud shriek from a young boy running past jolts us, and Maxon stands, holding out his hand to help me up. My entire body is flush, making me want to hide from his gaze, but I let him pull me to my feet.

As we make our way back through the markets, we can't help but notice the newfound tranquility that has replaced the earlier commotion. Storm is still where we had left him earlier. When he spots us, he shuffles back and forth, letting out a soft whine. Maxon reaches into the bag and pulls out one remaining treat and holds it out for him. Storm leans in and sniffs it before gently taking it from Maxon's hand. Storm devours the treat and nuzzles into Maxon's chest, as he whispers something to him. The sweetness of the moment brings a rush of emotions, causing my chest to tighten.

Maxon helps me onto Storm's back and mounts behind me, his arms coming around me to grasp the reins. His scent wraps around me, and I let my eyes drift shut as I inhale the woodsy scent.

We slowly trot down the cobblestone street toward the gates that exit Skora and take us to the castle. The sun is beginning to set as we pass through the gates, and I'm in complete awe of the colors streaking across the sky like a painting, casting a surreal glow over the fields of wildflowers. The breeze is cool and refreshing, but it's also making it difficult to see as my hair whips around my face. With a grin, I reach up, pushing it back and twisting it over my shoulder. Suddenly, Maxon's cheek presses against mine, causing me to jump.

"You smell amazing, Stóirín."

"Uhh . . . thanks."

A deep rumbling noise emanates from him, sending a flash of heat through me. His hot mouth moves against the side of my throat, his lips and teeth dragging over the sensitive skin. There's a wicked sharpness there that steals my breath. My nails dig into his arms as I tilt my head, giving him more room.

Maxon gently sucks on my neck, a moan slipping from my lips. I want nothing more than to turn in his arms and have those lips on mine.

"Maxon . . . " I breathe, my breath forming a mist in the chilly air.

Sparks of energy move between us, and his grip on me tightens. His palm sliding up my body, I tremble at his touch. Gently, he takes hold of my chin to turn my face toward his, and I am struck by the desire in his violet eyes, which seem to glow in the dim light. I gasp as the silver ring around his eyes flares with heat and he slowly moves closer. I don't breathe as his mouth closes in on mine, nor can I stop my eyes from falling shut.

Suddenly, Storm lets out a loud neigh, causing us to tense and my eyes snap open. Maxon lets go of my chin and clears his throat, a twinge of disappointment filling me before he pulls away, creating distance between us.

"What is it about you that has me so twisted up inside?"

"If you find out, let me know," I whisper honestly.

Maxon drops his hands from my waist, grabbing the reins with a sigh, and I immediately miss the warmth and weight of his touch. The absolute ridiculousness of it brings a flush to my cheeks, even as I find myself yearning for more, craving the taste of his lips against mine once again.

However, Nix and Zaria were right—I can't let myself become entangled in whatever inexplicable bond exists between us.

"I better get you back." His voice is tinged with regret.

I nod, feeling a wave of emotions overwhelm me, and tears begin to sting my eyes, a lump forming in my throat. Damn emotions.

Adjusting my position in the saddle, I sit so I'm facing forward again and take a deep shaky breath.

The rhythmic thumping of Storm's hooves against the ground is the only sound as we ride in silence the rest of the way. The stables are empty now, only one young fae manning the doors. Upon seeing us approaching, he rushes to open them, and Maxon deftly grabs the reins as he dismounts Storm, leading him into the stables with me still perched on his back.

The stables are dark and quiet apart from the shifting of hay and the soft nicker of other horses every now and again. Reaching Storm's stall, I decide to try to dismount myself. It can't be that hard. Though Storm is significantly larger than the other horses. I can do it. I'm not sure, however, whether I can handle having Maxon's hands on me anymore.

With Maxon's back turned, I quickly swing my leg over and flip onto my stomach, prepared to make my escape. Holding my breath, I start to slide down but slip. A gasp escapes my lips as I instinctively tense, bracing myself for the impact with the ground. Powerful hands swiftly catch me, securely wrapping around my waist and guiding me safely to the ground.

Maxon presses himself against me, trapping me and causing my breath to quicken as a wave of heat rushes over me. It's becoming increasingly likely that I will faint if things continue at this rate.

He has this way of taking my breath away and making my heart race all with one touch.

"What do you think you are doing, Stóirín?" he whispers, against my hair.

That word again. I want to ask what it means, but I'm also worried. Worried it will make my heart beat even harder for a man I can't have. I also don't want to embarrass myself.

Maxon drops his head lower, lips skimming down my neck as his fingers tug at the neck of my tunic, baring my shoulder to his touch. Gently he bites down on the sensitive part of my neck, where it connects with my shoulder, eliciting a moan from me.

"Maxon . . . " I whisper hoarsely, my body flooding with desire.

"Yes?"

My eyes flutter shut as he continues to lay bites and kisses across my shoulder and neck.

"We– we need to talk," I stutter.

Maxon reluctantly takes a step back, and I slowly turn to meet his gaze. I cannot allow myself to keep getting distracted. Taking a deep breath, a sense of determination wells up inside me and I lift my chin a fraction higher.

"What did you need to talk about?"

"The queen."

Maxon frowns. "What about her?"

"She threatened my friends in the human world. Said if she wasn't allowed to torture me, then she would torture my friends to get me to talk."

Maxon goes still; the type of still that is predatory. Dangerous.

"She said that?"

"She hinted at that. I need to know if she was bluffing. Would she hurt my friends?"

The silver around Maxon's eyes burns brightly as he stares at me. He stares and stares and stares before finally speaking. "What else did she say to you?"

It doesn't slip my notice that he hasn't answered my question. "Nothing of importance. I only care if my friends are in danger."

"The queen can open the gates, but she won't."

"How can you be so sure?"

Maxon moves past me and unclips Storm's bridle, lifting it from his head. "I just know. Lavina is all bark, no bite."

"I don't think we see the same thing when looking at her. Or you do, and you just won't admit it to yourself. Otherwise, why would you barge into her chambers to rescue me yet again?"

Maxon flashes me a hard look over his shoulder, his jaw clenching. "I'm not blind to her ways. I will make sure the gates are guarded. No one will leave this realm and hurt your friends."

"Why can't I leave if the gates can be opened?"

Maxon's body stiffens.

"I know, because you need to know how I managed to stumble into this realm." I roll my eyes. "Kian said something to me today about the old druids and the prophecy."

Maxon's hands pause on Storm's buckles. "You have questions?"

I have plenty of questions, but no one seems to want to answer them. "Why were they killed?"

Maxon releases a deep sigh as he lifts the saddle off Storm's back and puts it aside. He grabs two brushes, tossing one at me. I catch it and step forward to help him brush down Storm's coat.

"The Seelie Queen, Anwyn, heard the prophecy first from a Seer. And in the beginning, she wanted this child for herself, wanted the druid princess to marry her son. The Druids refused this offer. After all, no one knew when this would come to pass. When the druid king and queen at the time had a daughter, the Seelie queen once again tried her luck, but the king and queen stood firm in their decision. Their daughter would marry whomever she wanted. This provoked Anwyn, causing her to veer off in another direction. If she couldn't have the powerful druid on her side, she would turn all others against them, scaring the fae folk with outlandish tales about how this druid would be powerful beyond what has ever been. The seelie king and queen deemed the druid's powers too dangerous to leave unchecked and opted to eliminate them, thereby extinguishing the royal bloodline. It then became a race to see who could capture and kill the druids."

Maxon pauses, his gaze dropping to the ground before his haunted eyes peer over at me.

"My father was against it at first, but somehow, he was persuaded to help them in the hunt. My mother tried to stop him, but someone was whispering in his ear, and he wouldn't listen to reason. Following my father's death in battle, my mother's health declined rapidly, and she passed away soon after. At the age of only five, I was deemed too young to take the throne, and thus, my father's sister was appointed to rule in my stead until I came of age. It basically comes down to power and who holds it."

The despondency in his tone is like a physical blow to my heart. I stop brushing Storm and turn my attention to Maxon, laying a comforting hand on his arm. "I'm sorry you lost your parents. I lost mine, too."

Chapter Nineteen

Maxon

We walk silently back to the palace, the weight of unspoken words hanging in the air, suffocating and thick. Everly, lost in her own world of thoughts, appears distant. My mind spins, reeling from her remarks about my aunt and the lingering questions about the druids. Memories of the past flood my consciousness, long forgotten until now. The absence of the druids has caused the prophecy to fade into the background like a distant echo. Why does it seem like her questions had a deeper meaning, and why would Kian have disclosed a prophecy that had long been forgotten?

By the time we reach the stairs, her legs are trembling, and I instinctively extend my hand for support. She hesitates for only a moment before taking it, her fingers curling around mine.

"Thanks." She looks up at me with a tired but radiant smile, her eyes shimmering like stars in the dim light. The sight steals my breath. "Kian sure got me working muscles today I didn't even know existed."

A quiet chuckle escapes me. "I'm surprised you wanted to learn."

"I won't be defenseless anymore." Her voice is soft, but there's an unshakable resolve beneath it.

Her determination sparks something deep in my chest. I feel it swell, a mix of admiration and something far more dangerous. My muscles tense, not because I doubt her, but because the thought of her needing to fight at all twists something inside me.

"I will help you train when I can," I offer, knowing I'd rather be by her side than let anyone else take that role.

She tilts her head, a teasing glint in her tired eyes. "Thank you, but I think you'd be more of a distraction."

The soft laugh that escapes her lips is a melody I could listen to forever.

As we approach her door, Kian is already waiting outside, standing with his usual silent vigilance. I nod in acknowledgment, but my attention stays on Everly. As we near the threshold, her gaze lingers on mine—warm, uncertain, something unspoken hanging in the air between us.

"Thank you for taking me out today. It was beautiful," she says, her voice quieter now, more intimate.

Stopping just outside her door, I reach up and gently tuck a strand of blonde hair behind her ear. Her breath catches at the touch, and I smirk, pleased by her reaction.

"Anytime, Stóirín."

Her brow furrows slightly. "What does that mean? Stóirín?"

"Little treasure."

"Oh..." A delicate blush blooms across her cheeks, her gaze lowering as she absorbs the meaning.

"Now go have a bath. It will relax those muscles," I murmur, reluctant to let this moment end.

Her eyes flick briefly to Kian, but he remains impassive, giving us what little privacy he can. Still, I can sense her hesitation, the way she lingers as if there's something else she wants to say.

I reach past her, pushing open her door with ease. As I pull back, I catch a whiff of her scent—soft, sweet, intoxicating. It takes every ounce of restraint I have to step away.

"Good night, Everly."

Then, forcing myself to turn, I stride down the hall toward my chambers, each step widening the distance between us. And I hate it.

I know it's impossible, but is she. . . I shake my head in frustration. She couldn't be . . . She's human. But the way my body and soul light up when she's near, the way I would break every rule to protect her. The night I found her . . . I grit my teeth, the fear I felt coming from her was my undoing. I slaughtered those fae without a second thought.

My mood sours the further away I get from her, and I push into my chambers, feeling the magic sweep over me. I walk straight to the balcony, needing fresh air to cool my blood. I should head to the tavern and work off this edge. I may not be able to have Everly, but I can have any other woman down there. As soon as the thought enters my mind, I dismiss it. There is no way I can be with anyone else. Everly consumes me.

I spend the next hour meticulously working on cleaning my sword. It's a welcome distraction, allowing my mind to focus solely on the task at hand. With a sigh escaping my lips, I slowly rise to my feet and stretch my arms above my head, feeling my muscles pop. Ripping my shirt over my head, I wipe the sweat from my face and head toward the bathroom.

The grinding sound of a shifting wall reverberates through the room. Adrenaline floods my veins, and I spin on my heel, raising my sword.

Hesitantly, Everly emerges from the darkness, her eyes taking me in, as mine do her. She looks like a goddamn angel. Thin delicate straps hold up her soft light pink night dress. My gaze travels down, following the material as it cascades down to her ankles, the silky fabric hugging every contour of her body and tying together at the front with a delicate ribbon. A low rumble vibrates in my chest as she adjusts the silk shawl that hangs from her arms, barely providing any coverage or warmth.

My arm drops, the sword resting in my hand as we stare at each other for a long moment.

"What are you doing here? How did you even know where the tunnel was or where it would go?" I am furious she's left her room again. "You're lucky the tunnel led you here."

Everly moves all the way into the room, and I swallow hard when I see her nipples through the fabric of her thin nightdress. Fuck . . . I tip my head back and count to ten, before bringing my eyes back to hers. Her soft gasp at the obvious magic and heat edging my eyes has lust burning through my body. But that doesn't stop her from taking another step toward me.

"I knew where I was going," she whispers.

"Really?" I sheath my sword and lay it on the table.

"Yes." Her eyes move over my torso, as if committing it to memory. I clench my jaw, my eyes briefly closing under her gaze that feels like fingers caressing my skin. "I could feel you. Something in my chest was tugging me here."

"You should leave," I grit out, my jaw tightening with restraint.

"Why?" Her voice is raspy, the word getting stuck in her throat.

"Because I'm trying really hard to hold back right now, when all I want to do is tear that dress off you and taste every inch of your body."

Everly's eyes widen in surprise, and then they darken, hinting at her hidden desires. I watch as she grips the silk night dress at her hips, her fingers tracing the delicate fabric. The electric buzz of desire and magic hums in the air as we stare at each other.

Fuck. This isn't good.

Since I first breathed in her floral scent, I've been making a conscious effort to control myself. It's been a fucking nightmare.

"I'll give you one chance to leave," I growl.

Everly's gaze is unwavering as she takes another step closer, her shoulders pulled back in defiance.

"So be it."

My eyes stay fixed on her as I unfasten my breeches and kick off my boots. With a smirk, I let my breeches fall and step out of them, turning to lounge back in the large armchair completely naked. I rest my elbow on the arm, feeling the soft fabric against my skin, and prop my head up with my hand. Everly hasn't moved a muscle. She just watches me, the flickering light from the fire dancing across her smooth, pale skin.

"Undress for me," I demand, my voice more gruff than normal. It's taking everything in me to stay seated, to let her make the first move.

Everly blinks twice, her eyes roaming my naked body, before she slowly reaches up and pulls the ribbon holding the front of her dress closed. As she loosens the ties, the dress slips off her shoulders and her gorgeous breasts spill out. Dusty pink nipples catch my attention as the fire casts parts of her body in shadows. Slipping her arms free from the dress, it falls to the floor like water flowing down her body and pools at her feet.

I swallow roughly, my eyes drawn to the spot between her legs. A low growl rumbles from my chest. She isn't wearing underwear.

Deliberately, her hands skim up her sides past her breasts and push her hair back over her shoulders. It is taking all my willpower to remain seated right now. I beckon her closer, needing my hands on her. Everly's eyes sparkle with desire as they slide down to my cock. I am so fucking hard I could hammer in nails.

"Come here."

I watch as her tongue darts out, swiping across her bottom lip before drawing it into her mouth. This woman is driving me mad. If that's what she is trying to do, she is succeeding. I fist my cock, giving it a hard squeeze. Everly's eye's track the movement, and her pupils dilate as she rubs her thighs together.

"Come here, Stóirín. Don't make me ask again."

Her eyes, still fixed on my cock, flash to mine as she swallows. The beauty in front of me walks over, stopping just out of reach. Before I can give her another command, she drops to her knees, surprise shocking me immobile.

Leaning over, her hands land on my thighs and her tongue darts out, dragging it across the head of my cock. My hips jerk in response as I draw in a sharp breath, my fist squeezing my cock again. Every muscle in my body tenses as she does it again. The sound I make is guttural, almost animal. Everly smiles coyly up at me and wraps her soft, delicate fingers around my cock. Without hesitation, I release my grip, letting her take control.

Keeping her eyes on mine, she slides her tongue from my balls up my shaft, my stomach tightening as pleasure skyrockets through me, and she takes my cock into her warm, wet mouth and sucks.

Fuckkkk . . .

Everly's mouth is fucking heaven. I grind my teeth together as her mouth moves over me. My hands grip the arms of the chair so forcefully that I hear the wood crack and splinter. Blood whooshes in my ears as heat rolls through me. I refuse to close my eyes as she tries to take every inch of me into her mouth, her tongue swirling around the head of my cock before drawing me back in. As her other hand glides up my stomach and over my chest, a gentle twitch courses through my body. The delicate touch feels as light as a feather, causing my head to spin. With a soft and teasing motion, her fingers effortlessly glide over my nipple, causing my hips to instinctively jerk in response. She repeats the motion, this time lightly pinching, eliciting a deep groan from deep within me. My grip on the chair releases, replaced by the firm grasp of her hair. The silky strands slip through my fingers, creating a tantalizing sensation as I gather them away from her face. The sound of her moan reverberates, vibrating through my very core, while her lust-filled eyes meet mine, intensifying the desire that surges within me. With her gaze locked on me, my self-control shatters, succumbing to the overwhelming passion of the moment.

I thrust upward, holding her head, my cock hitting the back of her throat. My eyes drill into hers as I thrust over and over.

Everly's hands brace on my legs as she moans and squirms, tears leaking from her eyes.

Fuck!

Pleasure crashes over me, and time stands still, caught in a whirlwind of desire and forbidden ecstasy.

But as much as I want to come in her mouth, there is something I want more. I pull her mouth off me and grab her, lifting her onto my lap. My hands sink into her blonde hair and my mouth slams down on hers, tasting myself on her tongue.

Nothing has ever felt quite like kissing her. I surrender myself completely, allowing the sensations to consume me, losing myself in the blissful chaos that unfolds when our lips meet.

It is sparks and heat and pure satisfaction, and I drink it in, absorbing the feeling as I devour her mouth.

She squirms on my lap, her knees on the chair on either side of my legs. My fingers move down her body and dig into the flesh of her hips, dragging her over my cock. She whimpers into my mouth, a soft plea. Unable to hold back any longer, I lean back and stare into her eyes as I thrust upward, driving into her wet heat.

Fuck, this woman will be the death of me.

"Maxon . . . oh . . . oh my God . . . "

A growl rumbles up my throat and my tongue plunges into her mouth, swallowing her cries.

Everly pulls back, her hands landing on my chest as I lift her and slam her down on me. My hips thrust up to meet her, and I grind her on my pelvis, hitting that bundle of nerves with each plunge of my cock. The sound of our bodies joining, and our moans bouncing off the walls is pure ecstasy. I never want this to end.

Her muscles begin to spasm and tighten around me, drawing a loud growl from my throat.

Fuck, she was made for me. Made to take my cock.

Tipping her head back, her eyes falling shut, and her long, silky hair tickling my legs. My mind is swimming and my body is heated with all that is her. With her breasts in my face, I lean forward, drawing one nipple into my mouth and sucking before biting down, then run my tongue over it.

"Maxon . . . " Everly's hands delve into my hair as she bucks on my cock. I move to the other breast, paying it the same attention.

Everly tips her face down to mine, her hands clasping my face as she kisses me in desperation. Beads of sweat form on our bodies, creating a slick sheen.

"Maxon, please," she begs, breaking the kiss.

I give her a wicked look and cover her mouth with my hand, the other arm wrapping around her waist tightly. Then I go feral, my hand muffling her screams as I really fuck her. My hips rise and fall as I move her over me. Her body shakes and quivers, then tenses as her inner walls lock down hard around my cock, her orgasm like nothing I've ever felt before.

I let out a grunt as a tingling sensation spreads through my body and I come hard, a growl tearing from my throat, and my canines extending. I want to bite her so badly, but I hold back. *Barely.*

My hips slow as she milks me for all I'm worth. My hand falls from her mouth and I kiss her like I need her to breathe. I kiss her until I feel dizzy and sated. Pulling away, I kiss down her neck, brushing her hair away from her face, my lips skimming over every inch of her skin I can reach, as if I could never get enough.

We sit here, both panting heavily and covered in a sheen of sweat.

My eyes meet hers. "Are you alright?"

With a dazed expression, Everly lets out a soft hum, swaying slightly. I wrap my arms around her, feeling the warmth of her body against mine as I pull her into my chest. I stay planted inside her, not wanting to move.

"Is it always like this?" she murmurs, her fingers pressing into my chest.

"Like what?"

"Explosive."

"With us, yes."

Everly bites her bottom lip, her expression turning wary. "What are we going to do?"

I know what she's asking, but I play it off, arching my eyebrow. "I can think of a few things."

Everly blushes, and once again, I am spellbound by the variation in color. My fingers lightly trace over her cheeks and then slide into her soft golden hair that shines like the sun. Cupping her head behind her ears, I bring her face to mine and brush my lips lightly over hers before pressing harder. This kiss is gentle, deliberate, soul consuming. I know now with the way my heart is pounding fiercely against my chest, and the surge of devotion originating from a sacred place that has always been reserved for her, that she is my mate, my destiny, the other half of my soul.

The realization sends a surge of protectiveness and possessiveness through me, making my chest swell with love so strong I struggle to draw in a breath. In this moment, there is no room for doubts or uncertainties. Only the raw intensity of our connection, the unspoken language of desire that weaves between us.

We pull apart, her forehead resting on mine, her soft breath caressing my face.

"You know what I mean," she whispers.

Running my nose up the column of her neck, I inhale the sweet smell of roses and springtime blossoms. "That's tomorrow's problem."

She nods, but I see the worry in her eyes.

Chapter Twenty

Everly

Maxon stands, his arms cradling me as he carries me over to his bed. I find myself looking at him intently; the way his muscles rise to the surface of his skin, at the full curve of his lips. He is extremely handsome, unbelievably powerful, and he is holding me in his arms like I am precious to him.

With a heavy sigh, I rest my head against his chest. "I should really go back to my room. If someone sees us . . . "

"No one will see us. You are safe here."

Maxon places me on the bed and climbs in behind me, pulling the soft silk sheets up over us. I roll over and snuggle into his side, feeling the warmth of his body against mine. Wrapping his arm around my shoulder, he anchors me to his side, creating a sense of intimacy and protection. I relax, drawing his strength and warmth as I listen to his strong, steady heartbeat under my ear. A wave of familiarity washes over me, and I can't help but feel like I have finally found where I truly belong.

"Maxon?"

"Yes."

The words I love you are on the tip of my tongue. But that's crazy. I have only known him for a week. How can I possibly be in love with him? Will he think I'm crazy? I don't want to scare him off, but the way he looks at me makes me think he feels the same way, too. Although, I'm too afraid to ask.

For the first time since I can remember, I feel like I'd found home. Could that be because I am so desperate to find that place to call home? Really, I have no clue what home is. I never had one growing up.

"Nothing," I reply, drawing lazy circles on his chest, following the patterns of his tattoos. The tattoos on his face seamlessly continue down his neck, with the vines gracefully curving around his chest and waist.

As Maxon's hand glides up and down my arm, my eyelids grow heavy, and I fight to keep them open. Eventually, I surrender to sleep, embraced by a comforting feeling of contentment and security.

The next morning, I awaken to the gentle streaming of light through the curtains and the soft caress of a breeze causing the sheer fabric to dance. I sink my back into Maxon's warm chest, a smile tugging at the corners of my mouth. I am sore. Deliciously sore. A good sore. I've never experienced sex like that before, and I think that was the first time I've actually orgasmed during sex. Which sounds absolutely crazy.

Maxon's muscular arm is wrapped under my breasts, keeping me close as if worried I'd disappear during the night. I can feel his gentle breath tickling the strands of hair beside my ear. His erection is pressed against my ass, and I can't help but wriggle a little. Maxon's hips instinctively thrust, his cock wedging between my ass cheeks, and he lets out a low groan as his arm tightens around me, pulling me flush against him. There is a pulsating ache in my core as my heart races. The anticipation fills every inch of my being. My fingers tremble slightly, betraying the rush of emotions coursing through me. With bated breath, I close my eyes, surrendering myself to the intoxicating desire that consumes me.

"Stóirín," his deliciously deep voice rumbles against the shell of my ear, sending goosebumps rippling over me and making my nipples hard.

A soft noise escapes my lips as I draw in a sharp breath, my hips rocking back. His touch sends shivers dancing down my spine, awakening a hunger I never knew existed. Every nerve in my body pulses with an extreme need, a magnetic pull toward him.

We dance on the edge of danger, a reckless tango in the darkness.

With each breath, I surrender to the invigorating thrill of his touch. The world fades into a blur of shadows as we become lost in our own universe.

Maxon's hand skims down my stomach as he places kisses along my neck and shoulder. My eyes fall shut, soaking in the sensations of his fingers and lips on my skin. He groans when his fingers get to my pussy, finding me wet and ready for him.

"Stóirín, you are perfect."

I draw in a sharp breath as his fingers move in slow torturous circles around my clit.

"Maxon . . . " I moan, my hand going behind my head to sink into his hair.

I rock my hips against his hand, my breathing labored. Maxon's hand dips lower and he sinks a finger inside of me, pushing in deep and then pulling out before adding another finger, heat coiling deep in my stomach.

Removing his hand, he lifts my leg slightly and pushes inside of me, his cock filling me in one deep thrust.

"Oh my god!" I cry out.

The heat from his cock and the silky smoothness instantly have me teetering on the edge. Maxon's mouth moves to my ear, his teeth biting down on my earlobe, causing me to clench around his cock.

"Will I ever get enough of you?" he growls, pressing his cheek against mine.

The words send my pulse into overdrive, and I moan, tightening my grip on his hair. Maxon lets go of my leg, our hips still moving in tandem as his hand wraps around my throat. In this moment of vulnerability, I turn my head blindly, guided solely by the magnetic pull drawing me closer to him. My senses heighten, and I can almost taste the electricity in the air. The world around us fades into a blur as my focus narrows down to the warmth of his breath on my face. Our lips meet in a passionate, possessive fire.

Everything ceases to exist, replaced only by the symphony of our intertwined breaths and the sweet touch of our lips. It is a dance of passion and vulnerability, a dance that speaks volumes without uttering a single word.

Maxon's rough hand cups my breast, his thumb stroking over my nipple, making my core tighten around him. His forehead drops to my shoulder, and I feel his body tense.

"Fuck," he snarls, the sound sending a ripple of desire through me.

He cups my breast and pinches my nipple, rolling it between his thumb and finger. The invisible string pulls taut and I break apart, my orgasm sending me free falling into the abyss. Maxon follows me over the edge as his hand moves to my hip to hold me still as he rocks against me, drawing out the pleasure moving through me. Everything goes black for a split second, and then the world comes back to life in a whirlwind of colors, leaving me panting for breath and completely boneless.

"I want to stay here with you in this bed all day," Maxon murmurs against my skin.

A giddy feeling consumes me, sending a swarm of butterflies fluttering in my stomach. Maxon's arms tighten around me, as we lie here entwined in each other. I soak in the moment, a lazy haze floating around us. The taste of his lips lingers on mine, etching itself into my memory, to be a constant reminder of the profound intimacy we shared in that single, electrifying moment.

Suddenly, a pounding starts on the door, and I startle. Maxon kisses my shoulder and stands just as the wall slides open and Zaria comes running in with Nix flying in behind her. In a moment of panic, I scream and hastily cover myself with a sheet. Maxon slowly lowers his sword as he takes in Zaria and Nix.

When did he get that?

Zaria and Nix pause, their wide eyes taking in our state of undress. Zaria snaps out of it quicker that Nix and rushes forward. "There you are! You need to come now."

Another round of banging starts at the door, and Maxon frowns. “What’s happening?”

“The guards found Everly’s room empty. They are searching for her.”

Panic drenches my body in ice.

“They can’t find me here,” I whisper, jumping from the bed.

Nix flies toward Maxon. “What were you thinking? She is human, you can’t . . . ”

Maxon's menacing growl stops Nix’s tirade, and she gasps, looking between us. Zaria grabs my arm and tugs me toward the hidden passage, my feet catching in the bedsheet, making me stumble. Maxon is there, his firm grip keeping me upright.

"Careful," he murmurs, his voice barely audible.

I tilt my head back, and his piercing violet eyes meet mine, and in that moment, I feel myself melting under his gaze.

Panicked, Zaria scrambles to grab my nightdress, her voice filled with urgency. “We have to go now. I will sneak her into my quarters and say I had her helping me with chores.”

Maxon releases his grip on me and softly nudges me toward the passage, while Nix swiftly flies past me into the abyss.

“Go. I’ll find you later.”

With one final look back, I slip into the tunnel, the darkness enveloping me as the wall seamlessly closes behind me.

Chapter Twenty-One

Everly

Following Zaria and Nix down the dimly lit passage, I can hear the echo of our footsteps bouncing off the walls. I attempt to gather the bedsheet tightly around me, careful not to let it touch the grimy floor. This experience takes the walk of shame to a whole new level. I feel a deep sense of embarrassment as anxiety gnaws at my insides, wondering what thoughts are running through Nix and Zaria's minds. I shouldn't care what they think but I do.

Instead of turning left toward my room, we take a right at the end of the passage. I'm amazed at how I successfully found my way through the narrow and dark passages and into Maxon's room. I didn't even know my new room had a secret passage until last night, and only then by accidentally bumping my desk chair into the wall, knocking a picture down. There, carved into the stone wall, was a button. Of course, I pressed it. And when the wall slid open, it felt as if an invisible force was gently guiding me forward, my every step accompanied by a faint whispering sound. Somehow, I knew I was going to Maxon, but I wasn't sure how I knew that.

When the wall slowly slid open, my breath caught in my throat at the sight of Maxon standing there, his bare chest glistening in the soft light. In that moment, my mind went blank, overwhelmed by the sight of him. All I yearned for was to trace my fingertips along his skin, savoring every contour and relishing the sensations that awaited. My mind is so preoccupied with thoughts of Maxon that I don't realize Zaria has stopped walking, and I accidentally bump into her, almost sending her tumbling.

"Sor–" But before I can finish, Zaria's hand covers my mouth, her feline eyes glowing otherworldly as she stares at me, then cocks her head like she is listening for something.

"I'll go first. Make sure the coast is clear," Nix whispers.

Zaria nods and then looks at me, her eyes wide, as she places her finger to her lips. I nod in understanding, and she releases her grip.

The moment Nix disappears around the corner, I notice a beam of sunlight streaming through the path she just took. Five minutes later, there is a soft whistle, and Zaria sighs in relief.

"Come on."

Hurriedly, we move forward, and Zaria pushes open a wall, peeking her head out before slipping through and waving at me to follow. I look around, but don't recognize where we are.

"We are in the servant's corridors," Zaria explains, reading my confused expression.

The narrow servant corridor is plain, and its unadorned walls have low lighting in sconces that shine with a dim glow, no windows in sight. Zaria's hand tightens around mine as she sprints down the corridor, the sheet slipping from my grasp, as she pulls me along.

As we turn the corner, she swiftly opens a small wooden door, tugging me inside before shutting it firmly behind us. Looking around the small room, I notice the cramped space occupied by a small bed, wardrobe, and a night table with a desk tucked away in the corner. Zaria moves toward the wardrobe, its wooden doors creaking as she pulls them open.

She rummages through it in a hurry, muttering to herself in frustration before turning and tossing a sage dress and apron at me. "Put these on."

I hold up the dress and arch an eyebrow in question. "Really? It has a hole for your tail."

"That's what the apron is for."

"Zaria, I'm at least two sizes bigger than you. Why not just take me back to my room?"

With her lip between her teeth, she anxiously sways her tail back and forth.

"Because the queen was on her way to your room. One look at you and she would know exactly where you'd been," Nix explains, making her presence known.

I look up and see her perched on a ceiling fan, her eyes gleaming in the dim light. Honestly, the contrasting old architecture and modern appliances really make my head spin.

"Okay . . . " I say, drawing out the word.

"I will tell the guards I had you helping me today. It's the only thing I can think of to explain why you were gone from your room so early. Kian is already aware. He's covering for us."

My heart skips a beat. "Does he know?"

"About you and the crown prince? I think he guessed. We knew you two were . . . " she trails off.

Nix flies down, her wings beating in agitation. "The prince's fondness for you and the timing of your arrival may raise suspicions, leading the people to believe that you are here to deceive him. If they desire your demise, the prince's efforts to protect you might prove futile. Zaria has already warned you to stay away, that nothing can come of this thing you two have, but no! You still wandered into his room last night!"

Disbelief wells up inside me, and my fingers instinctively tighten around the sheet. "Do you two think that? That I'm here to cause trouble? That I could hurt Maxon?"

Zaria steps closer, her eyes softening. "No, it's clear to me you care for him, but others won't see that."

I drop my head. "I don't know why I'm drawn to him. Whenever he's near, all I can feel is him. I don't even know how I was able to find my way to his room last night."

Nix tugs on my hair, and I raise my eyes to meet her fiery blue ones. "You're in love with him, aren't you?"

My eyes flare, and a swarm of butterflies fills my entire body, leaving me dizzy. I glance at Zaria, noticing Asrai peeking out from her hair. I offer a weak smile before turning my attention back to Nix. It's astonishing how such a tiny fairy can be so intimidating—I feel like a child being scolded.

"Yes," I whisper.

Nix shakes her head sadly. "You both know this can't work. You're human. No one will accept the two of you. All you're going to do is get your heart broken."

My chest cracks with an overwhelming whirlwind of emotions. God, I just want to see Mia and Scarlett. I feel a tear roll down my cheek, the weight of sadness heavy in my chest as I hurriedly swipe it away.

"Can I get dressed in private, please?" The words are barely audible.

I don't watch as they leave the room, remaining motionless until I hear the door click shut. I plunk down on the bed, tipping my head back, desperately hoping gravity will keep the tears at bay.

"Why am I here?" I whisper into the empty room.

I have never felt like I fit in anywhere, but last night with Maxon, I finally felt a sense of belonging. Am I being stupid?

With a sniffle, I stand up and slide the dress on, noticing its soft texture. The dress is a tight squeeze, barely managing to fit over my hips and my chest. I snatch up the apron and tie it around my waist, the bow at the small of my back covering the gap made for Zaria's tail. I walk over to the desk, picking up a small mirror to take in my reflection. My eyes are glassy, reflecting the emotions hiding beneath the facade. I reach up, lightly brushing my fingers over my lips as I recall how Maxon claimed my mouth. I truly love him, and now I don't know what to do. If only I could escape and go back to my world, leaving all of this behind. If one night with Maxon was all I could have, so be it. But I can't be around him and watch him move on. The thought makes me sick to my stomach. I wonder if someone in the village will be willing to help me cross through the gate. There has to be a way.

A soft knock on the door has me turning to face Zaria and Nix as they enter the room again.

"Oh, good, it fits," Zaria sighs, her shoulders slumping in relief.

I give her a small smile, running my hands over the soft material. "Just."

Nix flies closer. “We need to get you to the kitchen. Rayna is in there.”

"Oh, thank goodness," Zaria mutters.

“Who’s Rayna?” I ask.

“Rayna is my sister.” Zaria ushers me into the hall.

Nix follows me and gracefully lands on my shoulder, her wings delicately brushing against my hair. “Rayna is loyal and trustworthy. But we need to hurry.”

“If anyone asks, you wanted to learn how to bake the bread and asked to help us this morning. Okay?”

“Okay,” I agree, struggling to keep up with Zaria's brisk pace. The tight dress restricts my movement so much it makes it difficult to breathe. Stepping into a large room with stone walls, a wave of heat immediately hits me. Looking around the kitchen, I’m left speechless as my mouth hangs open.

The sheer size of this place is staggering, and the scent of warm bread fills the air, making my stomach growl in hunger.

“This place is massive.”

“This is just the bakery. You should see the food prep kitchen,” Nix says.

Zaria walks over to a young girl who looks like her twin, only minus the tail and ears. “Rayna, this is Everly. She has been helping us this morning in the kitchen.”

Rayna and Zaria exchange a knowing look, their eyes sparkling with mutual understanding. “Of course. So good to meet you, Everly.”

Then her hand reaches for the workbench, snatching up some flour and tossing it at me. I jump in surprise, my eyes immediately darting down to find the dress covered in a light dusting of flour.

“Umm . . . nice to meet you too?”

Rayna giggles, her brown feline eyes sparkling in delight. "Well, if you've been in here helping Zaria and me all morning, you have to look the part."

"That's very true." I smile.

Nix lifts from my shoulder, making her way over to a tray of pastries and sighing in delight.

"Come sit. I'll get you some breakfast." Zaria motions me over to a table.

"Shouldn't I be working?"

A soft chuckle escapes Rayna's lips. "It is all taken care of. Sit. I want you to try my newest creation. I call it the hummingbird."

Before I take a step toward the table, we all turn to the sound of a gentle knock on the door. Kian stands there, his hand resting on the pommel of his sword. His focus is on me, but he addresses the room.

"You ladies having fun?"

"Yes, we are. Would you like to join us?" Zaria offers.

The intensity in his eyes makes my heart skip a beat. He knows . . .

Kian steps into the kitchen and walks past me. I hold my breath, my fingers twisting in the apron. I don't know what I was expecting, but a knot forms in my stomach, making me feel uneasy. Kian waves me over and pulls out a chair, signaling for me to take a seat.

"Uhh . . . I don't think I can."

"Why not?"

"The dress . . . "

Suddenly, Nix starts laughing hysterically. I look over at her, powdered sugar covering her face and hands.

"Oh, no . . . " Zaria whispers and Rayna chuckles, tugging her sister's tail.

"You brought her here. This is your fault."

Kian and I exchange confused looks.

"What's happening?" I ask.

Zaria lets out a deep, exasperated sigh. "Nix has a sensitivity to sugar, which means she has to be mindful of how much she consumes. Give it a few minutes and she will be in a sugar-induced coma."

"Oh . . . That's understandable. Nix is tiny," I reply, captivated by the sight of the fairy rolling around on the table. Her eyes sparkle with delight, reflecting her genuine enjoyment. A smile spreads across my face, and I cover my mouth in amusement.

It seems to take Nix a moment to register my words, because she stands and staggers in my direction, finger pointed at me. "Hey, I'm not tiny."

"You are," Zaria argues, giving her a flat look. Clearly, she's unimpressed by the events of this morning.

"You look drunk," I add, biting my lip.

Kian clears his throat, and I look over at him. He holds a baked sweet roll out to me, carefully balancing it on a napkin. The sugar icing on top sparkles under the lights, resembling glistening crystals.

"Here, you must be hungry."

I quietly reach for it, taking it from his outstretched hand. "Thank you."

"You're welcome," he replies with a warm smile, thought it seems forced. "You can eat it on the way back to your room. We have training."

Chapter Twenty-Two

Everly

Like a movie on repeat, the memory of last night plays in my mind, each scene carved into my consciousness with vivid clarity. The way Maxon's eyes locked with mine, filled with an intensity that spoke volumes without a single word being uttered. The way our breaths mingled, our bodies moved and entwined.

But as much as I long to relive that moment, I can't escape the bittersweet reality that it was just a momentary encounter. One that left an indelible mark on my soul, yet remains forever out of reach.

"Again!" Kian bellows.

For the past twenty minutes, we have been fully immersed in our training session. Kian wasted no time in easing me into today's session. The warm-up was anything but easy. Within minutes, sweat dripped down my forehead, soaking into my shirt, while my muscles burned under the strain.

I swiftly dodge to the side, my body moving even faster than before, and raise my wooden sword to block his incoming blow. Kian swiftly spins behind me and swings his wooden sword, the sound of it slicing through the air serving as my only warning. My arms tremble under the weight as I deflect and execute one of the complex maneuvers he's been teaching me. Kian doesn't let up though, his strikes coming one after another. My wooden sword arcs through the air in a counterstrike, but Kian deflects it effortlessly, his movements precise, practiced—untouchable.

His attacks come faster now, an unrelenting storm of strikes that forces me to retreat step by step. Sweat trickles down my back, dampening my shirt. My fingers ache from gripping the hilt too tightly, but letting go isn't an option. If this were real combat, I'd already be dead.

"You're not concentrating. Again!"

I'm seething with anger, feeling my heart race like crazy, its thunderous beats echoing in my chest. The arena seems to spin around me, my vision blurred with fury. In frustration, I take a step away, and Kian releases an exasperated sigh, his breath heavy with irritation. With a frustrated gesture, he throws his arms up in the air, the sound of his exasperation provoking my burning anger.

"What?" I yell, spinning on him.

"You are not focused," he growls, his lavender eyes flared in annoyance.

"What has gotten into you?"

With each step Kian takes, eyes fixed on mine, his presence becomes more intimidating. "Last night was stupid and reckless. If you'd been caught . . . "

I swallow roughly, my throat feeling dry and constricted as my arms fall limply at my sides. "I don't know wha–"

"Now more than ever, you need to be able to protect yourself, princess."

"Don't call me that."

Kian's eyes drop to my arm, and I narrow my eyes at him, crossing my arms over my chest. Even though Zaria covered the birthmark, he still seems to know something is there.

I lean in closer. "Whatever you think you know, you are wrong."

"I highly doubt that," Kian huffs, stepping back. "Tristan will watch and make sure you get back to your room. I have something I need to take care of."

"Tristan?"

"The other personal guard."

"I know who he is, but I haven't seen him."

"You're not supposed to, princess."

With that, Kian snatches my wooden sword from my grasp and saunters off.

Does he call me princess to mock me, or is it more? Does he have the same assumptions as Zaria?

I rub my fingers over my forehead, the tension in my temples slowly dissipating. With a deep sigh escaping my lips, I reluctantly turn and make my way out of the arena. A few soldiers that linger nearby, pause their idle chatter as their curious gazes follow me. I do my best to ignore them, but it isn't easy. I've never been one to draw much attention, yet being the only human among them now makes me a spectacle.

The weight on my shoulders vanishes the moment I slip through the gates into the castle's garden. Now away from prying eyes I unzip my boots, and slid them off, letting my bare feet sink into the velvety green grass, reconnecting with the earth beneath me.

The vibrant hues of the flowers dance before my eyes, their petals swaying in the gentle breeze. A sweet floral fragrance wafts through the atmosphere, tickling my nose and invigorating my senses. With each step, the cool blades of grass caress my feet, providing a refreshing and rejuvenating sensation. As I reach the castle, quietly slipping through a pair of ornate French doors, a wave of sadness washes over me. Making my way down the hall, I can't help but get lost in my own thoughts.

How many days have passed? Does time move differently here?

The atmosphere in the castle is filled with anticipation as the main hall, where Maxon's coronation is to take place, is being transformed into a magnificent setting. Servants are bustling about, hanging luxurious drapes and adorning the walls with intricate tapestries. The air is fragrant with the scent of freshly cut flowers as arrangements are being meticulously crafted to adorn every corner of the hall. The chandeliers are being polished to perfection, their crystal prisms gleaming in the soft glow of the candles that will soon illuminate the room. It's clear that no expense is being spared to ensure that Maxon's coronation will be a truly majestic affair.

I turn down a quiet hall heading toward the stairs of Maxon's wing, not really paying attention to anything in particular. I frown at the sound of footsteps getting nearer, and twist around. However, the hall stands still and empty. I continue walking, gripping my boots tightly in my hand. If I swing them hard enough, they'll make a good weapon. I pass by a small alcove, and a sudden grip on my wrist causes my boots to slip from my grasp.

Adrenaline surges through my veins as I spin around, meeting Maxon's mischievous gaze. He places his finger to my lips and pulls me closer, his grip unyielding. The world blurs around us, the air crackling with electricity.

"We can't be seen!" I whisper harshly.

"We won't." Maxon swings me around so we are hidden in a small alcove, his entire body blocking my view of the hall.

I tilt my head back against the wall as he braces his hands on either side. Desire flickers like flames in his eyes as he lowers his head. In an instant, my pulse races, and I become acutely aware of the sound of my breathing.

His lips brush against mine, gentle and tentative at first, but quickly succumbing to the undeniable chemistry between us. A shiver runs down my spine, and my body responds instinctively, pressing closer to him as if searching for solace in his arms.

With each stolen kiss, time seems to stand still.

Maxon gently pulls back, both his hands cradling my face in his palms. "No matter how complicated it gets, I'm always going to choose you. I can't explain it, Everly, but I know you're mine."

"Seriously!" Nix shrieks from behind Maxon.

Reality crashes back as I grip his shirt tightly, my fingers sinking into the fabric of his tunic. The taste of danger lingers on my lips, a bittersweet reminder of our predicament.

Maxon groans, turning to Nix. "Why do you keep popping up?"

"Do you want to be caught? Is that it?"

I step out from behind Maxon and face Nix. In her wide sapphire eyes, a mix of surprise and disbelief shines through as she nervously tugs at her long, brown hair.

A rush of guilt surfaces. "I'm sorry."

"Do not apologize to her," Maxon growls, the warning clear in his tone.

Nix shakes her head, a look of uncertainty on her face. "I thought you'd both be smarter about this, but I'm really worried."

My heart drops, and I glimpse movement out of the corner of my eye. It isn't until this moment that I realize I have completely forgotten about Tristan.

Chapter Twenty-Three

Maxon

I notice the figure standing down the hall the moment Everly does and my body tenses, but it's only Tristan. I'm not usually caught off guard like that, but this woman has a way of distracting me like no other. I nod in his direction and Nix spins to see who I'm looking at, going pale.

"It's fine, Nix," I assure her.

Her face is so priceless, I would laugh if I didn't feel bad for her. I know she cares and feels somewhat responsible for Everly since she was the one to find her, but she has nothing to worry about when it comes to me or my men.

"It is not fine, Your Majesty," she snaps back, her tiny hands clenching into fists as she hovers in front of us. I watch from my periphery as Tristan makes his way over.

"Your Highness," he says, dipping his head.

"To appease Nix here, would you tell her what you told me?"

Tristan looks over at Nix. "I serve only my king. Everly is safe with us, and I do not believe she is here as a spy."

Nix flies closer to him, a vibrant trail of glitter following her, catching the sunlight. "Are you sure about that?"

Tristan's eyes flicker toward Everly for a second before refocusing back on Nix. "No offense, but she is a weak human. What harm can she do, really?"

Everly gives Tristan a flat look and snatches up her boots from the floor. "You, sir, are the fae version of menstrual cramps."

I can't help but chuckle as Tristan's face contorts in a comical manner, his brow furrowed in exasperation while his mouth opens and closes like a fish out of water. Everly tugs her boots back on, casting a glance at the small group gathered around us. There's a flicker of something unreadable in her eyes—curiosity, perhaps, or maybe amusement.

"Right, well, on that note, I'm taking Everly for a ride," I announce, slapping Tristan on the shoulder with a grin that I know will annoy him.

Though it's clear that Nix wants to argue—her lips pressing into a firm line, her arms crossing so tightly it looks uncomfortable—she remains silent. Her stormy gaze follows me as I step toward Everly, but I ignore it.

Eager to have Everly to myself, I swiftly take hold of her hand, the warmth of her fingers curling against mine sending a thrill up my arm. Without hesitation, I guide her outside, eager to leave the tension of the others behind.

"Wait," she says, tugging against my grip.

I pause in my tracks, spinning to meet her gaze. "What's wrong?"

Everly's cheeks turn a delicate shade of pink. It takes all my willpower not to reach for her face, to brush my fingers against her flushed skin and see if it's as warm as it looks. Her blush intrigues me—it always does. It draws me in like a moth to a flame, and resisting the temptation to touch her feels impossible.

She gestures to her training clothes, tugging at the hem of her sweat-dampened shirt. "I need to change."

I drag my bottom lip between my teeth, my thoughts taking a dangerous turn. Now all I can think about is peeling those clothes off her myself, the idea sparking a heat deep in my chest.

"You'll be more comfortable riding in those," I murmur, my voice dropping slightly.

"But I'm all sweaty," she protests, her nose scrunching slightly in an expression I find entirely too adorable.

Stepping closer, I slide a hand to her waist, my fingers brushing the fabric of her shirt. The heat of her body seeps into my palm, and I relish in it. "I don't mind."

Everly raises an eyebrow, her skeptical expression clear as she tilts her head. "That's because you're not the one covered in sweat."

I smirk, leaning in just enough that our breaths mingle. "No, but I wouldn't mind getting a little sweaty with you."

She gasps, and I revel in the way her pupils dilate, just a little, at my words. But she quickly recovers, rolling her eyes even as the corners of her mouth twitch upward. "You're impossible."

I flash her a roguish grin, squeezing her waist playfully. "And yet, you still put up with me."

She sighs dramatically but doesn't pull away. "Fine. But if I smell, it's your own fault."

If spending time with Everly means enduring a little sweat, I'll gladly suffer through it.

I smirk down into her enchanting brown eyes, which seem to flicker with sparks of green, like emerald gems shimmering amidst a mesmerizing fusion of earthy tones. It's as if a hidden universe lies within, where the warmth of brown intertwines with the vibrancy of green, creating a unique and alluring kaleidoscope of colors.

"Your eyes are truly stunning," I murmur.

"They are boring compared to yours."

I shake my head, my other hand naturally gravitating toward her waist, urging her to come closer until our chests meet ever so slightly.

"You are the most intriguing, beautiful creature I've ever had the pleasure of rescuing."

A playful spark lights up her eyes as she bites down on her lower lip, struggling to suppress a smile. The apprehension visible in her eyes only moments ago has vanished.

"Rescue many damsels then?" she asks teasingly.

I enjoy seeing this side of her, the one filled with playfulness and a relaxed demeanor.

"A few."

"Good to know."

I step back and take her hand. "Let's go."

"Where are we going?" Everly asks as I guide her over to where Storm is waiting patiently in the garden.

"It's a surprise."

"Hmm, I don't know if I like surprises anymore." She snorts in amusement.

"You'll like this one," I assure her.

Storm snickers softly when we approach, nudging Everly gently, demanding a pat. He really has taken to her. Stepping up behind her, I grip her waist and smoothly lift her up, ensuring that she is stable and secure on Storm's saddle. I make sure to adjust the stirrups to her desired length so that her feet are comfortably positioned. My hands graze her legs, tracing the smooth contours, and savoring every moment.

I swing on behind her, gripping the reins in both hands, my arms encircling her. Her sweet floral scent wraps around me, and I automatically lean forward to smell her golden hair.

"Really? I'm all sweaty." Everly laughs, leaning away from me.

"You smell amazing to me."

"Whatever."

Giving Storm a gentle pat on the neck, I click my tongue to signal him to start moving. Storm's ears perk up and he begins to move, his hooves hitting the ground with a rhythmic beat. I lightly pull on the reins, guiding us toward the forest and his soft trot causes us to sway gently together in the saddle.

My aunt may be insistent that Everly not leave the castle grounds, but she's with me, and I know she isn't a threat to me or my people. You just have to look into those alluring eyes to know there isn't a deceiving bone in her body.

We ride in silence, Everly's eyes catching on the array of sprites moving about, their tiny wings fluttering rapidly as they dart from branch to branch. Her amazement, knowing that this encounter is a rare and magical moment for her, brings a smile to my face.

The sprites' curious eyes are focused solely on Everly. They seem both fascinated and cautious, their bodies shimmering with a soft glow as they keep out of reach. They're whispering amongst themselves, their voices barely audible to us, almost like a whisper in the wind.

"It's not much further," I say.

Gently, I tug on Storm's reins, and he obediently stops, his hooves dancing restlessly beneath him. With a swiftness that comes naturally from years of riding, I gracefully dismount and land, immediately extending a hand to assist Everly in her descent.

"We have to go the rest of the way on foot."

Everly nods as she takes in her surroundings. I quickly unstrap my sword and tie it to Storm's saddle.

"You won't need that?"

"No, I have a weapon."

"Where?" she asks, running her eyes over my body.

"Right here." I gesture to myself.

Everly tips her head back, laughing. "Coming from any other man, that would seem absurd, but from you, I totally believe it."

Grinning, I give her a wink. "Come on, we still have a way to go."

As we make our way through the dense forest, Everly's hands brush along the vibrant ferns that densely populate the surroundings.

"They have really grown wild here," she breathes in wonder.

I tilt my head and study her, wondering what it is she finds so beautiful. The ferns especially have completely engulfed the area, rendering it nearly impossible to navigate without difficulty. I think they are more of a nuisance than anything else.

I can't stop my eyes from drifting back to Everly's face as we maneuver through the lush foliage.

"The tree's here are so different from the ones in the human realm."

"How so?"

Everly pauses, tilting her head back as her gaze drifts skyward. A soft breath escapes her lips, almost like a sigh of wonder, and I follow her eyes to the towering trees above us. When her gaze returns to mine, there is a spark in her eyes that has my chest tightening.

"Here, they just seem magical. The way the branches twist around, reaching for the sky, as if seeking the heavens. Vines and flowers delicately coil and embellish the earthy tones with vibrant bursts of color, and beams of sunlight that filter through the dense canopy, creating a dappled tapestry of light and shadow. It's just beautiful."

I cast my eyes up again, this time truly looking—not just seeing, but absorbing. I have walked through this forest my entire life, its towering giants and tangled undergrowth as familiar to me as my own breath. Yet, in this moment, it feels as if I am seeing it for the first time. How had I never noticed the way the sunlight dances between the leaves, or how the vines seem to weave themselves into delicate patterns, like nature's own form of art?

Her words settle over me, awakening something deep inside—a quiet realization of the beauty I've taken for granted.

Everly begins walking, her fingers brushing the back of my hand as she passes. The touch, though fleeting, has my pulse thundering. How is it that she is able to provoke such extreme emotions from me?

As we walk, I try to see the things around me as Everly does. The soft symphony of rustling leaves and chirping birds that accompanies our every step. And how the air carries the distinct scent of earth, mingling with the refreshing fragrance of wildflowers.

"Tell me what you see and feel," I ask, wanting to hear more of how she describes my world.

Everly smiles. "Well I see so many vibrant hues of green. I wasn't aware there could be so many shades. You've got the moss-covered rocks and fallen logs, the leaves from the different trees and ferns." Everly's eyes close, and she takes a deep breath before opening them again. "I feel the gentle breeze as it whispers through the trees, causing the leaves to dance and shimmer like emerald gems."

"What else?"

"Birds of various species flittering from branch to branch, their melodic songs filling the air. The occasional scurrying of small woodland creatures add a touch of whimsy to the already enchanted atmosphere."

"I love the way you see the world."

Everly drops her face so her hair covers the blush I know is spreading across her cheeks.

Up ahead, there is a massive fallen tree that stretches across the path. With one effortless leap, I land on the soft, cushioned surface. The moss and rot contribute to the crumbling texture. I look down and see Everly's gaze roam over the area, trying to find a way over. I squat down and hold my hand out to her.

Her bright eyes smile up at me. "Why thank you, good sir," she teases, placing her soft palm in mine.

With a gentle tug, I pull her up, her feet landing on the log next to me. Everly moves to step away, but I tighten my grip on her hand, not ready to let go. As I do, her foot slips and she shrieks, her panic slamming into me as if it were my own. Swiftly my arm bands around her waist, hoisting her against me.

"Don't know if I should hit you for making me slip or thank you for stopping my fall," she grumbles.

My grin grows wider as I tilt my face down to hers, unable to hide my amusement. "A thanks might be nice."

Everly laughs and pushes away from me. "I'm sure it would."

Stepping back, she glances down and readies herself to jump. Without hesitation, I jump down and spin around, prepared to catch her.

"Really?" She quirks her eyebrow at me in disbelief.

"You're right. You got this." I grin, turning and walking away.

Everly's clumsy movements create a cacophony of sounds as she jumps and stumbles before finally catching up to me. I can't fight the chuckle every time I hear her trip and mutter a curse under her breath. She is different from any other woman I have encountered before, her presence refreshing like a breath of pure fresh air. Unlike others, Everly isn't driven by a thirst for power or a desire to use me for personal gain. She also has a body that demands worship, with curves that drive me wild. Though it hasn't escaped my notice, she appears to have lost some weight since her arrival. That thought causes me to frown.

The scent of damp earth fills the air as I navigate through the maze of ferns, bringing a sense of tranquility to my surroundings. I smell the mist a second before it cools the air.

"Is that a waterfall?" Everly asks, her hand landing on my back as she catches up.

"Yes."

I clear a path through the large ferns, Everly steps into the small clearing where the sound of the waterfall fills the air. She draws in a sharp breath as she takes in the cascading waters, shimmering like liquid silver as they descend from great heights, forming a delicate veil of mist around the area.

A lush landscape, vibrant with hues of emerald and sapphire, surrounds the waterfall which spills into a serene, crystalline lake. The waters are a mirror to the sky above, reflecting the ever-changing dance of sunlight and the ethereal glow of the faerie moon.

"Look at this place . . . " Everly gapes in awe as she slowly makes her way across moss-covered rocks, softened by time and draped in verdant velvet, to approach the water's edge.

"You can wash off here. These waters are the purest in the land."

Her gaze swings my way, and she laughs. "You brought me here to wash?"

With a shrug, I reach for the neck of my tunic and pull it over my head, tossing it aside.

The resulting spark in her eyes captivates me, her smile so warm and genuine it draws me in. She also has this uncanny ability to put me at ease.

With a wink, I kick off my boots and unbutton my pants. Everly's eyes wander over my chest, desire flickering in her gaze. The sight of her biting her lip sends a jolt of lust through my body. Fuck, this woman completely owns me. I move toward her, letting my pants slip dangerously low on my hips.

I push some of her sun-kissed hair behind her ear, letting my eyes take her in.

"I love the way you look at me." I say, my voice low and rough.

"Well, you are the most gorgeous man I've ever laid eyes on," she murmurs, her fingers dancing up my abs to rest on my chest.

I bend my head down, skimming my mouth over hers. "I don't know what spell you've cast over me, but I never want to break it."

My mouth covers hers, a rumble sounding in my chest, as need and passion engulf me. Everly's hands grip my arms tightly as I devour her mouth. The blood rushing through my veins feels like it's on fire. Her hands slide up my arms to wrap around my neck, her touch like a sweet elixir, leaving a lingering warmth on my skin.

Breaking the kiss, I grab her tunic and pull it over her head, her long golden hair falling around her shoulders.

"So sweet, so beautiful," I whisper against the skin of her bare shoulder as I unclasp her bra, letting it fall to the ground. A grin spreads across my face as a tremor courses through her body, accompanied by goosebumps that follow my touch.

Stepping back, I swiftly remove my pants and take three large strides toward the water before diving in. The cool water wraps around me, invigorating every cell in my body. I can see clearly under the water and pull myself toward the middle of the lake.

Breaking the surface, I swipe my hair back and face the shore where Everly stands in only a pair of pink panties, her bare breasts on display. I let out a low groan, my dick growing hard at the sight of her. She is more alluring than any nymph or goddess I can recall. I just stare at her, taking in her beauty, the magic of this raw unfiltered moment. I want to remember everything I'm seeing and feeling, to be able to relive it whenever the dark tries to take over.

"It's nice!" I call out, flashing her a smirk.

She smiles, and I swear my heart stalls in my chest. I watch as she carefully navigates the rocks and slowly sinks into the water, her gorgeous body disappearing under the surface bit by bit. Swimming toward me, her golden hair floats around her in the water as she takes in the view. Those spellbinding eyes light up when she looks up at the waterfall behind me.

"It's so beautiful."

I grin, and when she is close enough, I seize her wrist, dragging her into my chest. Her arms loop around my shoulders as I keep us afloat. Her fingers glide through my hair, my eyes falling shut, and all the tension draining away at her gentle touch.

I run my hands over her arms, feeling the softness of her skin, and then down her back, tracing the curve of her spine. Gradually, I guide us closer to the cascading waterfall. Everly's head tilts backward as we draw closer, and she closes her eyes as the mist from the waterfall rains softly over us. I find myself reaching up and gently running my fingers along her cheek.

"I'm taking us through," I murmur in her ear.

Everly's head jerks back and her eyes widen in surprise, but before she can argue, I give a powerful kick, gliding us through the water. Her arms tighten around me, and she buries her face into my neck. The heavy stream barely lasts a couple of seconds, and once we are concealed behind the sheet of water, my mouth is on hers. My blood surges with desire and need as her soft, full lips move over mine, matching the need coursing through me. My hands encircle her waist, drawing her against me, moving her body over mine, creating delicious friction. The heat from her body compared to the cool water is a dynamic combination.

Everly moans into my mouth, her fingers sinking into my hair as she crushes her chest against mine, craving to get closer. Her hard nipples against my chest cause a growl to work its way up my throat. I bite down on her bottom lip, drawing it into my mouth, and wrap her legs around my waist. In one swift motion, I have her back pinned to the smooth rocky wall of the small cave. My cock slides over her pussy. The warmth coming from her is driving me fucking insane.

"I need you now," I growl, pulling back just enough to kiss down the column of her neck, sucking on the soft, subtle skin.

I love the way her head tips back and she moans "yes" in a breathy whisper.

My hands slide up her sides to cup each of her fucking gorgeous breasts, my mouth watering, and I bend, sucking one nipple into my mouth before moving to the next. Everly's legs constrict around my hips, desperately seeking that closeness.

"I need you, too." She reaches between us and wraps her hand around my cock, running her thumb over the tip, making my hips jerk.

"Fuck . . . " Gripping her jaw, I tip her head back and slam my mouth over hers as she lines me up and I drive in. Everly cries out, the sound echoing around us, and she tilts her hips to meet my thrusts. I take my time, gradually working my way deeper inside her. My entire body burns like it's on fire.

I let go of her jaw, drawing back so I can look into those gorgeous eyes of hers. The moment our eyes connect, my body jolts with recognition. My heart thumps hard in my chest as I move inside her, my mind trying to work through what I am feeling. Everly grabs my face in her hands, her lips eagerly pressing against mine. I increase the power of my thrusts, the water around us splashing against the rocks. A tingle starts in my gums, and I know my canines are lengthening, begging me to own her, bite her, make her mine. Could it be possible? My body and soul seem to think so.

Breaking the kiss, I drop my forehead to her shoulder, her nails digging into my back as she tries to match my tempo.

"Fuck . . . " I growl, my jaw tense and teeth gritted. "You feel so fucking good wrapped around my cock."

My teeth drag along her neck and I bite down, careful not to break the skin. Everly trembles in my arms, her pussy gripping my cock like a vice as she comes.

"Maxon!" she cries out, the sound going straight to my cock and ricocheting through my body lighting every nerve.

My body tenses and I explode, my pace slowing as I try to draw it out for as long as possible. This woman, with her captivating curves and fierce attitude, is becoming an obsession.

"Stóirín," I breathe, my hand stroking over her hair.

Everly's body relaxes as she leans into my touch, her eyes closing and a gentle sigh escaping her lips. I draw her into my chest, and we float together, wrapped around each other for a few long moments.

"Maxon?"

I hum in response, not wanting this moment to end, but judging by her tone, I don't have a choice.

"What are we doing?"

"Hugging. It's quite nice, don't you think?"

"You know what I mean."

I sigh and pull back enough to cup her face. "Honestly, Stóirín, I haven't the slightest clue. I can't explain it, but all I know is that I need you by my side."

"It's not possible, though. I'm human. I can't stay here."

"You can if that's what you want." I can sense her heart rate increasing with my words, the indecision weighing heavily in her eyes. I place a gentle kiss on her forehead, welcoming the warmth of her skin against my lips. "We don't have to decide anything yet. But I don't want to deny what I'm feeling either."

"You're going to be king in two days," she whispers.

A surge of protectiveness washes over me at her vulnerability.

"It won't change how I feel." I brush a kiss across her temple.

"The longer I'm here, the stranger I feel."

I frown looking down at her. "What do you mean?"

Everly's eyes dart off to the side, avoiding me. "It will sound stupid."

I curl my finger under her chin, drawing her attention back to me. "Tell me."

"I'm finding my energy is different." She sighs heavily, biting her bottom lip. "It's hard to explain."

"Try," I urge.

"I can sense the energy around me, especially when I'm outside. It's as if nature itself is reaching for me, brushing along my body, welcoming me. I feel alive, like . . . " She blinks and her cheeks turn rosy. "See? Stupid."

"No, it's not. Maybe you have some magic after all."

She blinks, then blinks again, shaking her head. I notice a flicker of uncertainty in her eyes, the color morphing from brown to a striking green for a split second before returning to normal. But I know what I just saw. Everly is more than she seems.

"Come on." I gesture for us to swim back through the waterfall.

Everly nods, and we glide through the water, feeling the weightlessness and the gentle resistance of the currents. Emerging on the other side, Everly's smile spreads across her face, exuding pure happiness.

"I love it here."

"I will bring you as often as I can," I promise.

Everly pauses suddenly, and I notice a shift in the air around her, making my body tense. My eyes scan the shore, searching for any sign of movement, but it remains empty.

"What is it?"

"That's the fox I saw that day by the stream."

I turn to where she is pointing, and sure enough, there is a frostflare.

"You see it, right?" she asks.

"Yes, it's a frostflare. They are extremely rare and never seen around here. They prefer the solitude of the deeper forest, where their blue and white coat allows them to disappear into the scenery. Rumor has it that the mythical creatures are guarding the ancient secrets hidden in the forest."

According to legends, the frostflares are said to possess otherworldly intelligence. Eyes, radiant like pools of sapphire, contain the knowledge of centuries past. They move with a grace that mirrors the dance of snowflakes on a winter breeze, leaving no trace of their movement. It's been a long time since one has been seen.

"To have one show you favor is a great honor and privilege. If this one is following you, then it must trust you. And gaining the trust of one is no easy feat."

Slowly, I swim toward the rocky shore. The air is thick with a sense of mystery, as if the very fabric of reality has been altered by the fleeting presence of the frostflare. I turn my gaze back to Everly, studying her intently. There is an undeniable connection between her and the creature, an invisible thread that binds them together. I know now for certain that she possesses a dormant magic, waiting to be awakened. But for now, she remains oblivious to her true potential. I won't rush her, though. She must unravel her memories and unleash her magic in her own time.

"It's gone," Everly pouts as she attempts to navigate the slippery rocks.

I reach out my hand and help her step out of the water. The sight of the water cascading down her body like shimmering stars has me hard again. I watch as droplets caresses every curve before pooling at her feet.

"We lost my underwear," she admits shyly.

"You don't need them." I pull her into me.

Immediately, she pushes up on her toes, her lips on mine. A groan sounds from my chest as my arms wrap around her waist, anchoring her to me. We stand there completely naked, and I want nothing more than to lay her down and take her again. But it's getting late, and I don't want her to get sick.

Drawing back, I look down at her. "You drive me fucking wild, Stóirín."

Everly bites her lip, trying to suppress her grin. A subtle pulling sensation courses through my chest, and I sense my magic intertwining with an unknown force, both reaching out to her. I close my eyes and concentrate on the feeling, and in my mind's eye, I watch as Everly's magic, her spirit reaches for mine, and the two energies entwine. My body jolts, and I feel her tense, a small gasp falling from her lips. My eyes flash open, and I stare down at her, a sense of wonder filling my chest, and it takes me a moment to realize it's her. I'm feeling her wonder.

There is no doubt in my mind she is my soulmate.

Chapter Twenty-Four

Everly

"What was that?" I whisper, trying to make sense of what I am feeling.

It's as if a powerful magnetic force has firmly clasped onto my heart, pulling me toward Maxon. A surge of sensations accompany the inexplicable yet undeniable tug. As if awakening from a slumber, something within Maxon has come alive, his mere presence becoming electrifying, his aura pulsating with a vibrant energy that seems to emanate a radiant glow.

Maxon's violet eyes are burning so brightly it's almost too much to look at. He seems to be trying to figure something out. His hands squeeze my waist and pull me closer and I'm fully aware we are still both completely naked, standing at the edge of the water. The air crackles with a charged intensity, filling my senses with a tingling sensation. I can't tear my gaze away from him, captivated by this peculiar and enchanting experience that has left me both intrigued and slightly unsettled.

"Maxon . . . "

"I don't wish to scare you," he replies, letting me go and turning to tug his pants on, before scooping up his tunic.

I frown at him, my confusion increasing, tightening my chest. Why won't he just tell me? I'm already in a world I don't understand, and I refuse to be kept in the dark about things I need to know. The air feels heavy with unanswered questions, and a sense of unease settles over me. Maxon tugs the tunic over his head and I'm almost sad to see that muscled chest disappear, but he looks just as attractive clothed.

"You won't. I feel the safest when I'm with you. For some reason, I trust you."

There is a noticeable fire in his eyes as they abruptly shift to meet mine. A deep, guttural growl rumbles from his throat, causing me to shift uncomfortably on my feet. Is he mad at me?

"I'm not mad at you," he growls.

My eyes widen. I did not say that out loud.

Maxon runs his hand through his long hair before picking up my tunic and stalking toward me. He slips it over my head and holds it so I can slip my arms in easily. Beneath his intimidating exterior, the unseelie prince of darkness has a surprisingly soft demeanor.

Maxon lets out a grunt as he bends down to retrieve my pants. Can he . . .

"Can you read my thoughts?" I question, though I'm afraid of the answer. God, it would be mortifying if he could.

"I cannot read your mind, but I can read your emotions as if they were my own, so I can decipher them."

"Have you always been able to read me?"

Maxon shakes his head, sitting down to lace up his boots. "No."

"No?"

"Not until a moment ago." Maxon replies, standing. "Let's go."

"But, what was that? That feeling that moved between us."

"I think our souls touched."

"What?" I balk.

Maxon stalks forward and I'm in too much shock to move. His warm hands cup my face, tipping it back. He presses his lips to mine, his mouth hungry and urgent. My heart is beating so hard in my chest I feel like I'm going to pass out. And yet the touch of Maxon's hands on my face, at once gentle and possessive, grounds me in the present moment. The warmth of his touch radiates through my skin, seeping into my very being. Every nerve ending comes alive, pulsing with desire.

As our lips part, there is an undeniable sense of vulnerability that hangs in the air. The intensity of our connection is evident, and a new bond has been forged. Uncertainty still lingers within me, but I cannot deny the wonder that pulses through my veins.

At this moment, I am terrified by the prospect of Maxon being able to read my emotions.

"Don't be frightened," he whispers, placing a soft kiss on each cheek.

My eyes flutter closed at the tenderness of his touch, and contentment fills my chest as I reach up, gripping his wrist and looking into his eyes.

"I'm not frightened for the reasons you're probably thinking. It's just having someone else know what I'm feeling. It's going to take some getting used to."

"You can feel me, too."

My eyes widen at his words. "I can?"

Maxon chuckles, dropping his hands, and I release his wrists. "Close your eyes."

I do as he says. I sense his movements, but keep my eyes closed. Maxon moves around me, and his breath skates over my ear as he whispers, "What are you feeling right now?"

So many things.

Rolling my shoulders, I try to concentrate. I feel content in this moment, a little nervous, but something else; I follow that feeling and a purple thread opens up in my mind. It lights a path, and I follow it to another heartbeat. Maxon . . .

I feel an overwhelming rush of protectiveness.

Chapter Twenty-Five

Maxon

I help Everly finish dressing before lifting her into my arms. The warmth of her body against mine is intoxicating, as is her scent—a delicate blend of roses and jasmine. Her legs wrap around my waist, her soft hands cradle my jaw, as she leans in for a kiss. I will never get enough of her. Every moment with her is a sensory overload, an addictive fusion of desire and connection.

As we pull apart, our foreheads rest together, breaths mingling in the quiet intimacy of the moment. The setting sun bathes the sky in hues of orange and pink, its beauty only amplifying the magic between us. My fingers trace the curve of her jaw, savoring the softness of her skin. Entranced, I slide my fingers through the silky strands of her sun-kissed hair, captivated by its golden glow. I can't help but reach for her, drawn by an irresistible force, as if my body and soul crave nothing more than to be near her.

Lowering her to the ground, I take her hand, our fingers intertwining. A warm, electric current hums between us, heightening the awareness of our connection. Smiling down at her, I brush my thumb over her cheek, mesmerized by the velvety softness of her skin.

"We should make our way back to Storm," I murmur.

"Okay," she replies softly.

The air feels crisp as we walk hand in hand, surrounded by a forest that teems with the melodic chirping of birds and the gentle rustling of leaves in the breeze. Rays of sunlight filter through the dense canopy, casting a warm glow upon our path. As we navigate through the labyrinth of towering trees, the soft rustling of leaves underfoot harmonizes with the whispers of the wind, as if nature itself is speaking in a language beyond our comprehension. My gaze sweeps across the forest, and I notice that it seems to part, creating a clear path, as if nature itself is guiding us back to Storm.

Storm is exactly where we left him, his excitement clear when he sees us emerge from the thick foliage.

"Storm," Everly says affectionately as she approaches.

Dropping my hand, she reaches out and runs her hands over his cheeks before stepping closer and resting her forehead on his nose. My heart thumps hard at the affection they share. Storm never takes to anyone the way he has to Everly.

I lift her onto Storm's back and hop on behind her, grabbing hold of the reins. We begin our journey back to the castle at a steady pace. The time spent with Everly this afternoon has exceeded all of my expectations. Now, I am certain that she possesses magic. The question is, what magic?

Everly leans her back against my chest, and I soak in the feeling of her warmth. We've been riding peacefully for just over half an hour, but a slight disturbance in the air catches my attention.

The atmosphere crackles with magic, and Storm's hooves pound against the ground in agitation. I reach down and pat his side, letting him know I feel it, too.

My magic awakens, pulsating with a heightened sense of awareness. A delightful tingling sensation electrifies my skin, causing tiny prickles to dance across its surface. In an instant, I descend to the ground, my feet not making a sound as they land in the soft dirt. Effortlessly, I rise to my full height, my senses reaching out.

My eyes sweep across the area, taking in the sight of the forest before me. The trees begin to thin out as we approach the Fey Glade, but there is still plenty of cover for a lurker to be watching.

The forest stands still, holding its breath. Even the wind through the trees ceases to exist, leaving only an eerie silence.

"Maxon?" Everly's whisper reaches my ears, but before I can reply, a figure emerges from the midst of the trees. Familiarity washes over me, sending a jolt of recognition pulsing through my veins.

Without hesitation, I summon my sword. The obsidian blade materializes in my hand, the embodiment of my power. Its weight is familiar in my hand, a comforting extension of myself. When I channel my magic, it emanates an aura of darkness.

I cast a quick look up at Everly as she gasps, her hands instinctively flying to her mouth, her eyes wide. My heart swells with protectiveness, a fierce urge to shield her from any harm.

"Storm, take her to safety now," I command, my voice echoing with authority.

The urgency in my words is clear, mirroring the imminent danger that hangs over us. I don't watch her leave. I keep my gaze locked on the figure.

"Wait!" she cries, her voice filled with a mix of fear and frustration, but Storm doesn't hesitate, racing back toward the castle with lightning speed.

The glint of my sword catches the fading sunlight that filters through the trees. "What are you doing here, Alivar?"

"I've come for the human, of course."

"You can't have her."

Alivar's lips curl into a sinister smirk, a malevolent gleam dancing in his icy blue eyes. The air grows colder, as if shivering in response to the crown prince of seelie's aura of malice and cruelty.

"I hear she might be the Druid. You know, the one that was once promised to me."

Shock rolls through me at his casually spoken words, but my face remains stoic, not showing any outward reaction. I have suspected she might be, but I haven't been able to confirm my suspicions. Though that doesn't explain how he knows.

"Who told you that?"

"Tsk, tsk," he replies mockingly, running a hand through his white hair, the short strands standing up haphazardly. "One does not reveal his spies."

Red hot anger burns through me at the revelation. My magic lights up every nerve in my body. "Even if she were the princess, she was never promised to you, and you know it."

Alivar snorts, the air around him full of conceit. "We will see about that."

His hand sweeps outward in a swift motion, causing a chilling gust of wind to rush past me. The ground transforms into a glittering sheet of ice, rapidly advancing toward me. I swiftly dive to the side, feeling the cold air brushing against my skin, and easily roll to my feet, raising my obsidian sword, its weight reassuring, an extension of me.

As I explained to Everly, our powers are pulled from our magic, which is derived from the depths of our hearts. The blade I am able to summon from my magic is made of obsidian, a pitch-black volcanic glass that gleams with an otherworldly shine. Its edges are razor sharp, honed to perfection, and its surface is adorned with intricate carvings of ancient symbols. With each swing, it effortlessly cuts through the air, leaving behind a trail of shimmering black particles, like glittery shadows dancing in the moonlight. Its magical properties and mystical origins make it a formidable and deadly weapon, capable of piercing through even the strongest of defenses.

However, Alivar's heart is cold and devoid of mercy. The only magic that comes from him is cold and harsh, freezing the once flourishing meadow into a desolate tundra, turning vibrant flowers into delicate ice sculptures that shatter upon contact. His icy touch can drain the warmth from any living being.

"She isn't for you!" I snarl, feeling a surge of possessiveness and anger well up within me.

"What? Let me guess, she is yours?" His mocking tone has my jaw clenching. "If I kill you, then she will move on, eventually."

With a fierce snarl, I swiftly advance toward him, muscles tense and heart pounding. The sound of my boots hitting the ground reverberates through our surroundings as I close the distance. With lightning speed, I bring my sword down, but Alivar, just in time, produces one of his own.

The fury of the dragon fills my veins and I roar, lunging forward. Alivar side steps and spins. I watch as he summons his magic and sends a ball of ice hurling toward me. Raising my arms,

I slice at it with my sword, the obsidian blade cutting through any magic.

Undeterred, Alivar sends a surge of light shooting toward me, crackling and sizzling with malevolence, as it barrels in my direction. I raise an eyebrow at him, and I lift my sword in a wide arc, creating a shimmering shield that absorbs the deadly assault.

"Come, Alivar. It's been a while since we dueled, but I thought you might have upped your game."

With a flick of my wrist, a swirling vortex of wind and fire engulfs Alivar, the turbulent inferno devouring his roars of defiance. The scorching flames dance and lick at his skin, threatening to consume him, but his ice magic leaves him unmarred.

A gust of icy wind pushes away my flames, and Alivar glares at me as he strolls forward.

"Since when can you summon fire like that?" he growls.

I shrug, not sure if he's actually expecting an answer.

"What's the matter, princeling, can't handle the heat?" I taunt, sending him a wink.

Alivar's face contorts with offense, his jaw clenching and nostrils flaring. He throws spells at me, one after another, filling the air with crackling energy. With a swift motion, I raise my sword, slashing through each attack.

"Is this all you got, princeling?" I tease, knowing it will wind him up.

Alivar doesn't disappoint. He always has known how to hold his own. He stalks toward me, his own sword forming in his hand. Where mine is black obsidian, his is an icy white gem, like frozen water capturing the sunlight. I roll my shoulders and crack my neck before readying my sword. Our swords clash at the center, sending a cascade of sparks flying in every direction. Fire and ice collide with immense force, the impact rippling through our bodies. The sheer power fuels the adrenaline surging through my veins. I duck beneath his blade just in time, feeling the rush of air as it slices past. My feet barely touch the ground before I pivot smoothly around him.

Spinning my sword in one hand, I smirk at Alivar. "Very nice. So, you have been practicing."

He responds with a simultaneous strike and spell, icy tendrils lashing around my torso as I attempt to evade both. I struggle against the freezing restraints, my magic stirring beneath the surface. The earth trembles, splitting apart with a deafening crack, and the ice shatters, falling away in jagged shards. My sword is back in my grip in an instant, while my free arm ignites in a swirling inferno. Alivar lets out a furious cry, summoning a torrential downpour. The raindrops twist into razor-sharp ice, slicing through the air toward me. Each shard carries the weight of his resolve.

Releasing my sword, I sweep my arms outward, unleashing a blazing arc of fire. The flames expand into a searing shield, melting the ice before it can reach me. A sudden, sharp pain blossoms in my side. My breath catches as I glance down—Alivar has used a portal to close the distance, his dagger now buried deep in my flesh. A low growl escapes me as I rip the blade free. Fury fuels my every motion as I lunge. I slash through the air, aiming for his throat. His icy blue eyes widen as the blade skims his cheek, drawing a thin line of crimson.

Pain shoots through my body, but I refuse to yield. I push myself up, magic lashing out around me.

Dragon's fire.

A magic I've kept contained for a long time.

The wound on my side heals instantly as a layer of fire engulfs my body. I charge at him, dagger raised. Our blades clash, sparks igniting as we counter each strike. We dance back and forth, neither of us willing to back down.

The sound of thundering hooves breaks through our battle, taking advantage of Alivar's momentary distraction, I sweep his feet out from beneath him. Alivar curses as he hits the ground hard, but he's quick, rolling to his feet and creating a portal.

Sending a glare my way, Alivar growls. “Until next time, prince.”

Then, with a swift step, he vanishes into thin air.

Chapter Twenty-Six

Everly

Anxiously, I pace back and forth in front of the grand gates of the castle. Storm remained steadfast in his obedience, ignoring my every plea to turn back as we continued toward the castle at full speed. The moment the castle became visible, I began yelling and waving my arms, causing a chorus of shouts to erupt. The soldiers and guards, upon seeing Storm, quickly gathered to greet me.

Raiden flew to me, and his graceful descent was a spectacle I won't soon forget. Upon hearing what I had witnessed, he wasted no time hastily assembling a group of ten fae soldiers before departing swiftly. And now, they have been gone for what feels like an eternity, and my anxiety is growing with each passing moment. Like a finely-tuned machine ready for action, my senses have heightened as my body and mind have gone into overdrive.

"Stop pacing," Kian grumbles from where he stands leaning against the gate. "You're making everyone uneasy."

"Well, they should be here! Why aren't they back yet?"

Kian pushes his blonde hair from his face as he regards me. "You really are worried, aren't you?"

"Yes!" A tight knot coils in the depths of my stomach, a physical manifestation of the unease within me.

A chuckle escapes Kian's lips as he shakes his head. "The crown prince is more than capable of defending himself."

"But–"

I'm cut off by the thunderous sound of approaching hooves, and the trembling of the ground beneath our feet. Kian pushes himself away from the wall and joins me, his presence providing a sense of reassurance as the soldier's approach. My eyes catch Storm among the other horses, with Maxon on his back. A weight lifts from my chest, and I move without thinking.

"Everly!!" Kian shouts.

He's okay. I want to cry. I can feel the pressure building behind my eyes but refuse to let the tears fall.

The severity in Maxon's expression as I run toward them only adds to the fire coursing through my veins. The group gradually slows down and Maxon dismounts, his eyes never leaving mine. Ignoring the curious glances and hushed murmurs, I hurriedly make my way toward him and pull my arm back, delivering a firm punch to his arm. Shock registers on his face for a split second before he smirks, the silver ring in his eyes flaring to life.

"Stóirín?"

"How could you send me away like that?" I snap.

Maxon extends his hand toward me, but I forcefully push it away. I am not in the mood to be placated.

"I was worried!"

Maxon tilts his head, his violet eyes softening as his gaze bounces between my eyes. Slowly, he moves his hand to my face, his fingers sliding across my jaw, making my skin tingle. Refusing to succumb to his touch, I clench my jaw and pull my shoulders back. Maxon doesn't seem deterred. He cups my jaw, his touch sending a pulsating current of energy coursing through me.

"I refuse to let anything happen to you. I could not protect you and fight him at the same time. Alivar is dangerous, and he was there for you."

My head jerks back, making his hand fall. "Me?"

Raiden comes to Maxon's side, his face set in a stern frown. "The seelie crown prince has learned of your arrival. He thinks you are–"

"It's not important," Maxon growls, cutting Raiden off. "He can't have you."

My eyes narrow on Raiden. What was he going to say?

A throat clears, drawing our attention to Nolan. I haven't seen the queen's advisor in a few days, and he looks extremely irritated.

Maxon puts his hands on his hips, facing the fae. "Nolan, what can we do for you?"

"The queen wishes to meet with you about the seelie prince."

Maxon's jaw clenches, and the energy in the air instantly becomes charged. "I will be there shortly," he replies gruffly.

The weight of Nolan's stare hangs in the air, everyone remaining silent. Letting out a sigh, he bows his head in resignation. "Very well, your highness. I will inform the queen you are on your way."

Turning, he strolls away, back toward the castle. Kian moves swiftly and silently to my side. "I can take Everly back to the castle."

Maxon's hand gently grasps mine, pulling me closer to him. "No."

"But Maxon–" Raiden steps forward, ready to argue, but Maxon holds up his palm. "No. I will walk her. Go ahead . . . "

Kian and Raiden exchange looks, probably because I just gave us away with my outburst. But after a moment, they both turn and walk off toward the stables. Maxon doesn't budge until they are out of sight and the other soldiers have put a significant distance between themselves and us. Though some of them do cast curious looks at us as they go.

"I'm not sorry for sending you away from danger." Maxon's firm tone draws my attention.

"I could have helped."

"No, you couldn't have."

With a huff, I tug my hand free and start walking, Maxon easily falling into step beside me. I'm aware that my worry is manifesting as anger toward him, but my concern for his well-being outweighs everything else. My steps falter, the weight of my emotions overwhelming, as I come to the realization that I've fallen for him in such a short span of time.

"Stóirín, I can feel your conflicting emotions. Talk to me."

"It's absolutely frustrating how you can tell what I'm feeling so easily," I grumble.

Maxon's hand shoots out, wrapping around my upper arm as he pulls me to a stop. Refusing to look up at him, my eyes instead find a nice spot on the ground to stare at. Maxon inches closer, and I hold my breath.

"Your protection will always come first," he says softly.

My breath hisses out between my clenched teeth. "I don–"

The pounding of feet interrupts us as shouting breaks out. We turn as Rayna comes tearing around the corner of the garden.

"They've gone mad!" she shouts at us, her head whipping around behind her.

"What?" Maxon sounds every bit as confused as I am.

Hundreds of fluttering wings and squawks suddenly fill the air, making the hairs on my arms stand on end. I am terrified to find out what is responsible for that noise. Maxon extends his hand to me, pulling me back to stand behind him. My fingers grip the back of his tunic as a gray lizard-like bird whips past Rayna's head. She instinctively covers her head with both arms, shrieking as she ducks low. My eyes widen as the creature continues toward us, its beady eyes glinting in the light.

"Uhh, what is that?" I follow the creature with my eyes, watching it veer to the left, taking a wide circle around us.

Maxon draws his sword, his gaze locked on the creature. "That is a Vurien."

Before I can ask any more questions, my mouth drops open as a hundred of the tiny creatures fly around the corner from the garden, coming straight for us.

My heart thumps wildly in my chest as I watch the swarm of tiny creatures. Rayna reaches our side, panting. "They are usually harmless, but I don't know what's gotten into them. They don't venture from the caves."

"What do we do?" I ask, having to raise my voice to be heard over the shrieking.

"We need to get them rounded up and head them back toward the caves." Maxon ducks as one flies too close to his head.

"And how do we do that?" My tone is incredulous as I glance skyward to watch the small creatures. In the background, the castle seems gigantic with its stone walls reaching for the clouds.

Suddenly, a young woman with sparkling wings and vibrant blue hair appears out of thin air beside us. She looks at me inquisitively, her silver eyes twinkling mischievously, and I can't help but notice her sharp, pointed teeth. My eyes widen as I take her in, my breath catching and my skin tingling with nerves. She is a human-sized version of Nix.

Tucking some of her blue hair behind her pointed ear, her attention shifts to Maxon. "Need some assistance, Your Highness?"

Maxon chuckles and shakes his head at her. "Yes, that would be nice, Silver."

Rayna shrieks and steps back into me, bumping me out from behind Maxon. I regain my footing and gasp, ducking to avoid one of the scooping creatures. My heart goes out to the poor little creatures who have been disturbed and are now in an obvious state of panic.

Raiden and Zaria come bursting out the doors of the castle, their eyes widening on the mass of Vuriens flying around the courtyard. Zaria quickly turns, slamming the doors shut before any can make their way inside. The air fills with more shouts as the guards arrive, all of them coming to a grinding halt. Everyone seems to hesitate, uncertain of how to proceed.

I watch as Silver raises her hands, palms facing upward, and closes her eyes. If I look close enough, I can almost make out a slight aura surrounding her as I sense her magic fill the air.

Maxon catches my gaze. "She has the ability to put creatures asleep, though this many at one time could be a challenge."

Silver's responding snort makes me grin, and the tension loosens in my shoulders.

I watch as the Vuriens' frantic movements begin to slow, and they become sluggish. I take a step back to avoid one swooping down to land. My heart is in my throat as my foot slips on something wet and I fall backward, landing hard on the grass. A wave of embarrassment washes over me, and I hurriedly brush my hands off.

"Need a hand up?" Amusement coats Raiden's words as he tries to smother his smile. I glare up at him, but the only reaction I get is a loud, boisterous laugh. Maxon joins him and I growl at both of them before they each grab a hand and pull me to my feet.

"Go, head inside with Zaria. We will round them up." Maxon's words are gentle as he pushes me toward the castle.

Moving away from the group, I can't shake the feeling that the Vurien are deliberately tracking my every step.

A few of them swoop low enough to hook my hair with their tiny claws. Another flies at my face, veering to the side and nicking my ear with its teeth.

"Ouch!"

I bring my hand up and frown, feeling a stinging sensation. Pulling my fingers away, I see they are stained a deep red. It bit me!

"I thought you said they were harmless," I grumble as I raise my head.

Another creature breaks free of whatever magic Silver has been working, and flies at me. Quickly, I raise my hand, swatting the creature away, but its movements are fast and determined, immediately turning and coming right back. I feel a sharp flash of pain as its tiny teeth dig into my arm. I suck in a sharp breath, yanking it from my arm. Its small body thrashes as it screeches and twists like a demon in my grip. Clicking my tongue, I release my grasp on it as another comes flying right at me. All the oxygen abandons my lungs, and I swat it away frowning as more turn my way.

"What the–"

Suddenly, a large body connects with mine. I feel the wind rush past my face as I fly backward, strong arms instinctively wrapping around me as we twist mid-air before hitting the ground.

Before I can process what's happening, a large hand cups the back of my head, protecting me from the ground as his body rolls over mine, covering me completely. I know who it is from the scent that fills all my senses. I open my eyes to find Maxon's deep violet eyes looking down at me. He tucks his head, his breath hot against my cheek, and I feel the rumble of his anger in his chest. I nestle my head in the crook of his neck, inhaling his warm, comforting scent.

Someone squeals, and I hear the pounding of feet, but I can't make out anything past Maxon's massive form.

"Why are they trying to get to her?" Raiden yells.

Silver's response is lost in the cacophony of wings beating and screeching above us.

"What in the heavens is going on out here?!" someone bellows. "I want this taken care of now before they destroy something."

I'm not sure, but the voice sounds like Nolan.

"We need to draw them away!" Silver yells.

I feel my heart skip a beat when Maxon flinches. They are hurting him trying to get to me. A magical electric charge fills the air, making my skin tingle and my hairs stand up. Anxiety tightens around my chest at the thought of Maxon being hurt.

My vision wavers and my breathing becomes rapid, making Maxon pull back to look down at me.

In my mind's eye, I picture the vines on the castle walls growing and lengthening, weaving an intricate pattern around Maxon and I. Creating a barrier, a sanctuary.

Suddenly, it's as if the world has been silenced, and all that remains is a faint echo of sound.

Maxon slowly raises his head, his eyes scanning the area around us. "What in Aine?"

I blink, momentarily disoriented, as he lifts his weight off me, my jaw dropping in awe. Thick vines form a dome like barrier around us, just like I envisioned, shielding us from the outside world. As I sit up, one tendril snakes out and gently wraps around my wrist, caressing my palm as if checking to see if I'm okay.

Maxon kneels before me, and I can feel the weight of his gaze. I take my time to meet his eyes, not ready to answer the questions I know he must have. His expression is like a blank canvas, revealing nothing. His eyes dart around my face, lingering on the strands of hair that escaped my braid and are now tickling my cheeks. Slowly, his hand reaches up and touches my ear where the Vurien bit me. The warmth emanating from his touch banishes the slight throbbing I have been feeling. And when I reach up to touch my ear, it is completely healed, causing my eyes to just about pop out of my head.

"How?" I whisper in awe.

But Maxon's gaze is locked on my arm. He takes my wrist firmly in his grip, pulling my arm nearer to him. The warmth from his touch travels up my arm and settles in my chest. I take a peek at my arm to see what has caught his attention. My birthmark has darkened, the faint mark pulsing against my skin, almost like it's glowing. How? Why isn't the makeup working?

I'm ready to tear my arm away, but then his other hand appears and lightly traces the mark, causing my breathing to accelerate. My stomach flutters, and I'm completely captivated as his fingers move from my forearm to the inside of my elbow. They continue up, brushing my hair away from my shoulder and lingering on my neck. I peer up into his eyes, taken aback by how near we are.

His voice is deep and almost angry when he speaks. "You are her, aren't you?"

"I– I don't know who you're talking about."

Leaning forward, Maxon brings his face close to mine, our noses almost touching. My heart has been pounding from the moment he rolled on top of me, but now it feels as if it is going to explode out of my chest. Violet silver rimmed eyes fill my entire vision as we stare at each other.

I can't feel his emotions right now because my own are overriding everything. Maxon's chin dips as he leans in, making my breath catch as his nose runs along the column of my neck. Having his lips so close to my skin is making me dizzy.

"What– what are you doing?" I stutter nervously, clenching my hands in my lap to keep from grabbing him.

"Your scent is different. It's only a slight change, but I can smell it." He pulls back.

What? He knows my scent?

The revelation is so unexpected that my heart speeds up and all thoughts flee my mind. But was I not thinking the same of him moments ago? My lips part slightly, and his gaze falls to my mouth. The rapid thudding of my heart is making me feel lightheaded. I lean into his touch, my eyes falling closed when a loud thud makes me jerk back.

"Your Highness. Are you okay in there?" Raiden hollers, followed by two more hard thumps.

Maxon drops his hands, and I drag in a long-ragged breath, resisting the urge to fan my face.

"We're fine. What about the Vuriens?"

"Asleep. Some are already being rounded up and put in cages as we speak. Ready to be transported back to the caves."

Despite Raiden's voice being slightly muffled by the vines, we can still make out the distinct syllables of his words.

I shift my weight and move onto my knees. Normally, I would be filled with a sense of dread due to my claustrophobia, but it is surprisingly absent. I wonder if it's because Maxon is trapped here with me. We can't stand up, as the top of the dome is only a foot above my head. Running my hand over the vines, I feel a gentle tremor beneath my fingertips as they respond to my touch.

"Everly."

I swallow the lump in my throat, my cheeks flushing red, and give a low hum without looking at him.

"Stóirín, look at me."

I push down my nerves and lift my gaze at his command, immediately wishing I hadn't. My breath hitches, Maxon imposing figure seems even more so trapped in this dome. The air around him seems to crackle with tension. Something flickers in his eyes, and I swallow roughly. Whatever I think I saw in his eyes is gone too quickly for me to figure out. Gripping my chin with his fingers, he tips my head further back. A long, tense moment passes as his penetrating gaze roams over my face, as if searching for an answer to a question I don't know. Then his eyes ignite and my stomach hollows at the small rumbling growl that makes its way up his throat.

Maxon's fingers slide away from my chin to gently encircle my wrist, pulling me closer. His thumb moves in slow circles along the inside of my wrist, sending a tight, bewildering shiver through me. Simultaneously, his other hand reaches up and delicately cradles my face, filling the air with a subtle buzz of energy. The warmth emanating from his hand acts as a soothing balm, enveloping me in its comforting embrace. I let out a contented sigh and lean into his touch. Maxon's grin widens as a fiery intensity flickers behind his eyes. His hand then drops to my waist, and when I startle, Maxon only tightens his grip on my waist, as if restraining himself from pulling me onto his lap. I can feel his desire mirroring my own. If there weren't a group of people just beyond these vines, I have no doubt that he would have me undressed in an instant.

"You're so beautiful," his voice is a low hum in the silence.

I reach up to brush some hair off his forehead and delicately trace the intricate lines of the tattoo on his temple with my finger. Maxon's eyes fall shut at the touch and his jaw clenches. Worried I've done something wrong, I quickly drop my hand and mumble an apology.

Maxon's bright, jewel-like eyes shine as they look at me. "Don't say sorry for touching me. I want nothing more than for you to touch me."

A flurry of butterflies fills my stomach, and I move in closer. His hand reaches up and cradles my face as he leans in, and I can smell the comforting scent of his skin as my breath stalls in my lungs.

Before our lips can touch, a sharp pain pierces my chest, and I hear a loud thud from the dome as I break away from Maxon, gasping for air. Another thud hits the dome, and I scream out in pain, my hand gripping my chest.

Maxon frowns in confusion. “What’s wrong?” he demands, trying to grab hold of my shoulders.

A chill runs down my spine as my eyes widen with the understanding of what is occurring.

“Tell them to stop!” I plead.

“What?”

“The vines, they are chopping the vines, I can feel their pain. I’m still connected to them!” I gasp as another sharp pain steals my breath. I can feel tears rolling down my face and realization dawns in Maxon’s eyes.

“Raiden STOP!!” Maxon bellows.

A wave of relief sweeps over me as I sink down on the grass, lying down and welcoming the stillness that fills the air. I close my eyes and feel the tears still streaming down my cheeks. I picture the vine twisting and turning, scuttling back toward the castle wall. I feel a light caress on my cheek, and when I open my eyes, I am met with Maxon’s worried gaze and the azure of the sky.

Chaos erupts as the queen’s guards move in to surround us.

Chapter Twenty-Seven

Everly

Maxon's gaze hardens, and the muscles in his jaw tighten as his head snaps up. He scans the area, taking in the sight of the guards encircling us. The sound of their heavy boots echo, bleeding tension into the atmosphere, as they draw their swords. Raiden inches closer, his presence intensifying the situation. Maxon stands, his hand reaching out, intending to help me up. I swallow roughly and slip my hand in his, the touch of his warm palm providing a comforting reassurance amidst the chaos that now surrounds us.

What the hell is happening right now?

"I'm only going to say this once. Back down." Maxon's voice has taken on a menacingly calm tone, causing me to hold my breath. I scan the guards and catch a momentary flicker of hesitation in their eyes before it swiftly vanishes.

"We have our orders, Your Highness."

"Well, I'm giving you new ones," Maxon argues, taking a step forward, positioning himself slightly in front of me.

I sense Raiden shifting behind me, his intimidating presence unmistakable. They are putting themselves between me and the danger. The air is charged with tension as the guards remain still, their unmoving figures causing my heart to quicken.

Do they not follow Maxon?

I know the soldiers are loyal to Maxon, but are the guards loyal only to the queen?

Maxon's hand flexes and his obsidian sword swirls to life in his grasp.

Before anyone can make a move, a flash of white appears in my periphery. Maxon must spot it as well, because both of our heads turn, but whatever it is, it's gone.

My heart rate increases with another flash of white moving behind the guards.

What the–

A thunderous growl pierces the air. Heads turn in every direction, unable to pinpoint the source. Another growl follows shortly after.

"Maxon?" I breathe, my voice caught in my throat.

Out of nowhere, two white wolves soar over the guards and land with a thud in the empty space between us and the guards, their fur bristling. Maxon and Raiden move to intercept them, but I react faster, my fingers forcefully digging into their skin as I grab them.

"NO!" I shout in a panic.

Maxon falters, his intense gaze dropping to mine, and the two wolves turn, lowering their heads, emitting low menacing snarls at the guards.

"Don't hurt them," I implore urgently, moving toward the massive wolves.

"Everly, out of the way." Raiden's growl reverberates through the air as he tightens his grip on his sword.

"You can't hurt them!" I snap, blocking his way.

A low, menacing growl sounds from behind me, and I whip my head around to look over my shoulder. Maxon is edging closer to me, his footsteps cautious and deliberate. One of the wolves backs up to me, its head low and teeth bared, as it tries to protect me.

"He is safe," I whisper.

The wolf relaxes slightly as if understanding my words, moving its attention from Maxon and back to the guards who look as if they've seen a ghost.

Out of the corner of my eye, I see a guard readying his bow, and my panic manifests into anger in a split second.

I step forward and shoot him a warning glare. "Don't you dare!"

His eyes widen at my threat, and he slowly lowers the bow.

Raiden, still not convinced that they won't harm me, speaks low but clear. "Everly, step away. These are the white ghosts of the mountain. They are dangerous."

"They will not harm me."

"How could you possibly know that?" he scolds.

Disregarding the others, I shift my gaze to the wolves, taking in their sharp teeth and bristling fur as they prepare for combat.

I don't know how, but a sense of a familiar bond washes over me.

A tiny whimper catches my attention, and I halt my steps, straining my ears for the sound. I crouch down next to a bush and push the branches aside to reveal two quivering wolf pups, their snow-white fur muddled with brown dirt.

"Hey, it's okay. You're okay," I whisper gently, trying to reassure the pups I'm not there to hurt them. Brushing my wild, windblown hair from my face, I take a seat on the ground. I can feel the weight of their curious amber eyes as they watch my every move. The dirt beneath me is soft and pliant, almost like a cushion, as I cross my legs.

"I'm not going to hurt you. Where's your mother?" I whisper kindly.

The wolves' tails tuck between their legs as they look around nervously. After a moment of hesitation, one of them inches closer, its nose twitching as it sniffs the air. Holding my breath, I wait as they grow bolder and approach me. I tentatively extend my hand and run my fingers over its head, feeling the softness of its fur. Almost immediately, the pup dives into my lap, huddling against me. The other pup tilts its head at me and then stares at its sibling before slowly trotting over and seeking comfort as well.

Their wet noses and rough tongues tickle me, and I can't help but giggle. I know Mother and Father will be mad that I came out in the woods alone, but the trees were calling. Plus, if I didn't go beyond the boundaries, these poor pups would have been abandoned and helpless. I nibble on my lip, trying to figure out how I could stealthily bring the wolves into the castle and up to my room.

"You're mine now and I am yours. I will call you Nymeria and Anika."

I fall backward as they scramble up my body, their weight pressing down on me, but all I can feel is their relief.

Standing up, I begin walking toward home and usher the wolves to follow.

"Nymeria, Anika?" I whisper, tears stinging my eyes. Emotions I can't even begin to name surface, putting pressure on my chest, as both wolves snap their heads in my direction.

"Oh my gods, I remember you!" I rasp.

As one of the wolves steps forward, Maxon tenses, but I hold my arm out, signaling him to stay put. The wolf in front of me has a single green eye, which I know belongs to Anika. My lips curve into a tender smile as I open my arms, eager to embrace her. The wolf surges forward, and my arms instinctively wrap around her neck as I bury my face in her soft fur. I breathe her in, the comforting scent of familiarity wrapping around me. A soft warmth presses against my back and Nymeria's warm breath tickles my skin. My heart feels like it's about to burst with happiness.

I know these wolves.

They smell like home.

"What is happening right now?" Raiden's voice sounds extremely pissed off. I can feel the weight of everyone's eyes on me, their silent anticipation almost suffocating. Taking a deep breath, I stand and face the others, squaring my shoulders. Their faces show a range of emotions, from confusion to mistrust to fear. The queen's guards stand before me with faces twisted in fury as they raise their weapons again. Raiden and Maxon instinctively form a protective shield, blocking an easy path to me and the wolves. Raiden's wings span out, casting a shadow over us.

"Put your weapons down now!" Maxon barks.

He isn't facing me, but the threat in his stare is written across every face before us. His warning is emanating from his entire being.

Nolan moves to the front of the group, glaring at me. "She cannot be trusted, Your Highness."

"Bullshit. Put your weapons down. This is your final warning."

At Maxon's words, his own soldiers move in, surrounding the queen's guards. Their hands are poised on the hilts of their swords, ready to unsheathe them at a moment's notice, awaiting the orders of their commander and prince. Warmth fills me as Maxon's soldiers show how unwaveringly devoted they are to him, ready to confront the queen's guard at his command. Even so, if I can intervene—show them the wolves are no threat, that I am no threat—maybe they will back down.

"They won't hurt any of us!" I shout so everyone can hear.

"You don't know that," snaps Nolan. "And what of you? You've been lying to us the entire time."

"I honestly didn't know I could do that. I've never . . . " My voice trails off.

I don't know what to say.

What can I say?

Nolan steps forward, and Maxon's sword raises in his direction.

"The wolves are–"

I quickly step forward, laying a hand on Maxon's arm, and cut Nolan off. "As long as you are not a threat to me, they won't harm a soul. You have my word."

I will not let him harm them.

Nolan's face twists into a scowl. "Your words mean nothing, girl."

The air crackles and before I can take my next breath, Maxon blurs forward, and in a flash, Nolan is sent hurtling backward through the air before anyone can even react.

"Her words mean everything!" he roars.

Anger swirls like a savage storm around Maxon as he faces the guards. I step forward and gently place my hand on his back, feeling his instinctual need to shield and protect me.

I glance over my shoulder at Raiden, but he arches an eyebrow at the other guards. "Final warning. Back down, I can tell you now that the prince will not ask again."

In a synchronized motion, the queen's guards glance at one another. They all shift uneasily on their feet, like they know they are no match for Maxon's army. One by one, they sheath their swords.

Finally, Maxon turns to face me, his eyes locking with mine. Then they move over to Anika and Nymeria before finally settling on me again. Butterflies swarm through my stomach and chest, making my pulse flutter in anticipation.

"How do you know the white wolves?"

I give a small shrug, my shoulders barely lifting as I try to minimize the importance. "I know them because I am their guardian, and they are mine."

All eyes turn to me in astonishment, a heavy silence filling the air. The wolves sit on either side of me, my hands scratching between their ears. I feel the strength and power of their bodies next to me, and a deep sense of kinship.

Maxon studies me for several long moments before running a hand through his hair and letting out a deep sigh. "You are full of surprises."

The guards and soldiers shift nervously, their unease palpable. Without a word, Maxon raises his hands, commanding the attention of those gathered.

"Everly and the wolves are not a threat. Our primary concern is the Vurien. They need to be moved back to the caves." Then he looks to the guards, who are still surrounded by his men. "You will help. Everly and I will be going to see the queen."

Stepping closer, Maxon's hands find my neck, his touch both gentle and possessive as his thumbs stroke my jaw. Those violet eyes search my face. For what, I'm not sure. My breath catches when he tips my head back, those fingers sinking into my hair.

"Who exactly are you, Everly Baker?" he whispers, his mouth moving closer to mine.

"That's exactly what I want to know," snorts Raiden beside us.

Chapter Twenty-Eight

Maxon

My eyes lock with Raiden's, and the weight of the situation settles upon us. A wave of tension ripples through the air as everyone begins to gently pick up the Vuriens, placing them into cages. The scene is charged with confusion and distrust. It's evident in the furrowed brows and clenched jaws of those around us, all watchful of Everly. There is no doubt in my mind that she is the lost druid. I filled Raiden in on what Alivar had said and my thoughts about Everly being my mate before heading back to the castle. He seemed skeptical then, but now? I can practically hear the wheels turning in my best friend's head.

We both know that if Everly is my mate and the long-lost druid princess, it will undoubtedly trigger a cascade of questions and reactions. It won't be long before her family's loyal followers emerge from the shadows, seeking the truth and rallying behind their lost princess.

But we can't afford a massive rebellion, not in the fragile state our realm is already in. The consequences could be catastrophic, tearing apart the peace we have fought so hard to maintain over the years. We have to find a way to navigate this treacherous terrain, to spin the situation in a way that would quell the rising storm of uncertainty. The weight of the last rebellion, which claimed our parents' lives, has made me determined to prevent any further bloodshed.

But there is no turning back now. Everly's return is a reality, and we have to confront it head-on. The stakes are high, and failure is not an option.

Knowing I need to prepare myself for the challenges that lie ahead, I take a deep breath. Raiden gives me a subtle nod. He is with me. As for Everly, we will face the storm as a united front, relying on our trust and unwavering commitment to each other. The fate of our realm rests on our shoulders, and we will do everything in our power to ensure that the delicate balance remains intact.

I bite out a curse as Silver suddenly appears in front of us, Everly the focal point of her piercing silver gaze. Raiden's sister has always been an enigma of curiosity. The two white wolves draw nearer, and Silver's attention falls upon them, eliciting a wicked grin.

"I can't believe it, after all this time . . . " Silver trails off, shaking her head. "Leo owes me a bottle of ambrosia."

Raiden huffs out a laugh, crossing his arms.

"We haven't properly met." Everly steps closer, holding out her hand. "I'm Everly."

Silver looks down at Everly's hand in confusion, and then at me. I raise an eyebrow, waiting to see what she will do. Silver hates physical contact, or any show of affection, really. We never could figure out why. It's just who she is. The touch or being closer to someone always makes her skin crawl.

Slowly, Silver reaches out her hand and places it in Everly's. "I'm Silver. This one's little sister." Silver points her thumb over her shoulder at Raiden.

Everly's beautiful face lights up, and she looks absolutely giddy. "Really?"

"Yes. If you need any dirt on him, I have plenty."

Before any of us can reply to that, Nolan storms over, looking furious. I'm about to step in front of Everly when the two massive wolves leap forward, fangs bared. My arm instinctively wraps around Everly's waist, tugging her against me. Nolan draws to a stop, his gaze first on the wolves, then raising to meet mine.

"The queen. Now," he snarls, emphasizing each word.

"You do not give me orders, Nolan. Remember your place," I growl.

Everly gently runs her hand over the arm I have wrapped around her waist in a soothing motion. A refreshing sense of calm washes over me. Our connection is strengthening, weaving tighter like threads in a tapestry.

Nolan narrows his eyes on us before turning and storming away.

"You know he is going to snitch on you two," Raiden notes.

"I know," I grunt.

Everly turns to face me, her hands landing on my chest. "We should go before she gets impatient. I don't want her any madder at me."

After the day we've had, all I feel like doing is dragging her into bed.

"We will make sure everything goes smoothly out here." Raiden claps me on the shoulder, and I shoot him a grateful look.

Everly waves goodbye to Silver and Raiden. Then she looks about seeming to search for someone.

"What's wrong?"

"Oh, I was just wondering where Kian and Tristan are."

I sweep the area. "I'm not sure where they are."

Both went their separate ways when we left the gates. Surprisingly not drawn in by the commotion.

"Huh."

Everly casts worried glances behind us as the wolves trail us into the castle, their paws padding silently on the floor. "Are they okay to be in here?" she whispers.

"They are fine, though I wouldn't recommend bringing them into the war room."

"The war room!" she shouts, her voice echoing down the hall.

I laugh as her cheeks turn a rosy shade of red. "Relax, it's just where we meet to discuss important matters."

A few of the noble fae are milling about, whispering and casting distrusting looks at Everly as we make our way through the castle. One group in particular catch my eye. Madeline is talking with Lord Wallcliffe, their eyes narrowing on Everly as they whisper between themselves. Madeline's gaze moves to me, and her eyes widen.

"You're glaring," Everly murmurs under her breath.

With a grunt, I intertwine my fingers with hers, swiftly maneuvering through the crowded main halls. Stopping in front of the door of the war room, I turn Everly to face me, my hands cupping her shoulders. She's still in her black training clothes and her hair is a complete mess from the ordeal outside, but still she holds herself with poise.

"You ready for this?" I ask her.

"No. I'm never ready for a confrontation with this woman. She is scary."

"Scarier than me?" I inquire, a grin tugging the corner of my mouth.

"Definitely."

Leaning forward, I place a soft, lingering kiss on her forehead and step back. "You and me. We face everything together."

I hold my hand out for her and her brown eyes flicker with sparks of green. She takes my hand and then inhales deeply before looking over at the wolves.

"Nymeria and Anika, stay out here. I have Maxon. I will be fine."

Both wolves, their snow-white fur shining under the soft sunlight filtering through the tall windows, tilt their heads in unison, their piercing eyes fixed on Everly. The silence hangs in the air, broken only by the faint rustle of the sheer curtains swaying gently in the breeze. Finally, they sit down and stretch out on the floor, their heads resting on their paws. In that moment, I can feel the invisible threads of loyalty and love weaving between Everly and the wolves, binding them together in an unbreakable bond.

"We called these wolves the Ghosts of the Evergreen."

"Why?"

"They roam the area and the ruins of what I am assuming is your home. No one has ever been able to get a close enough look at them."

Everly's sadness flows down the bond, weighing heavily on my heart. "They've been alone for a long time," Everly whispers.

"We will figure out what happened. How you ended up in the mortal world." I lean over and gently kiss her on the temple. Everly nods, her eyebrows raised, and a hint of doubt in her eyes. I lift my hand, and the sound of my knuckles rapping against the surface of the door echoes around us.

"Enter."

I push open the door and see two of my aunt's personal guards and a very angry Nolan. Seems he's going to hold a grudge for getting thrown. I smirk at him, unable to help myself.

Nolan, his face contorted with anger, charges toward us, closing the distance in an instant. I position myself in front of Everly, feeling the rush of adrenaline coursing through my veins. My hand clasps firmly around the cold hilt of my sword as it materializes, its blade poised and ready to strike. Without hesitation, I direct it toward Nolan's neck, the tension in the air almost tangible.

"Not another step," I growl.

"Oh, boys. Calm down, would you. Nolan, we have much more pressing matters than your bruised ego."

Nolan grunts and turns away as I drop my arm, allowing my sword to disappear.

"How did you do that?" Everly's words are filled with awe.

"My sword?"

"Yes. It just appears. But it's different from the one you carry."

"I possess the ability to summon my sword, as it is an integral part of my magic. Additionally, I have a regular sword at my disposal."

"I thought your magic was fire."

"It is, but I was blessed with more than most when it comes to magic."

"Can we get on track?" my aunt's voice cuts in.

I shoot her a glare. "What's the rush?"

My aunt, with her eyes calculating and cold, completely disregards my presence and approaches Everly, whose body tenses up. In instinct, I reach out to get a feel of her emotions. As I connect with Everly's, I sense a mix of distrust, nervousness, and anger. The anger puzzles me. I understand the distrust and nervousness, but why the anger?

Lavina extends her hand to touch Everly's face, but Everly automatically retreats. I closely observe their interaction as they warily assess each other.

The air between them is thick with tension, as if a silent battle of wills is taking place. I can almost hear the unspoken questions passing between them—my aunt's curiosity about Everly's past, and Everly's doubts about Lavina's intentions.

"What have you been told?" I ask, breaking the silent standoff.

Lavina looks over at me, her gaze softening. I know she's harsh and cold, but I also know she cares.

"Only that Alivar ambushed you and Everly. That you two have been sleeping together, and Everly now has the Evergreen Ghosts in tow."

I purposely skip over the second part and go to the more pressing matter. "We can't let the seelie prince get a hold of Everly."

"How do you know it's me he wants?"

"Remember the story I told you about the deal the Seelie Court tried to make with the Druids regarding the princess? Alivar thinks if he can get his hands on you, he can force a marriage."

"He said that?" Everly gasps.

"Not in so many words, but Alivar thinks he can take what he wants."

"And right now, he wants you," Nolan adds, rubbing his temples.

"We need to confirm you *are* the princess," Lavina adds.

Everly extends her arm, the torn piece of her black shirt hanging open, revealing her rune. The rune imprinted onto her skin is a symbol of her pure druid bloodline, and seems to pulsate with power. My aunt swiftly seizes her arm, forcefully pulling it toward her. A frown forms on Everly's face while I struggle to contain my grin, relishing in the rare sight of my speechless aunt. With her deep violet eyes fixed on Everly, she then turns her gaze toward me.

"Tomorrow, I want you to accompany Everly to the ruins," she commands, her voice laced with urgency. "We must determine if it stirs any dormant memories. And remember, this must remain confidential." Her eyes briefly meet Nolan's, a silent understanding passing between them. "Understood?"

"Yes, your majesty." Nolan' his eyes remain fixed on Everly's mark. "But what of the coronation?"

Lavina curses and meets my gaze. "Can we push it back three days? That should give you enough time to return."

I bow my head. "Of course."

Chapter Twenty-Nine

Everly

With each step down the stairs, my palms grow clammy and my heart races faster. The weight of the unknown hangs heavily on my shoulders, and I can sense a similar tension in Kian's demeanor. His usually bright eyes are clouded with worry, mirroring my own internal struggle. Maxon and Tristan, always the practical ones, are busy securing the saddles and double-checking the supplies on the horses. Their efficiency only heightens my sense of unease.

I can't help but wonder what lies ahead for us. The journey we are about to embark upon is shrouded in mystery. Am I truly prepared for whatever awaits us in the Evergreens?

Doubts creep into my mind, fueling the nerves that are churning in my stomach. What if I'm not who they all think me to be?

I have no memory of my life before foster care, but the thought that I might be some kind of lost druid is absolutely insane. It seems completely impossible. I can't even start to comprehend the meaning, nor my feelings toward it. But had I not somehow connected with those vines . . . But amidst the uncertainty, there is also a glimmer of hope. I know deep down that this trip has the potential to change everything, to uncover truths I have never even considered. It's a chance to find myself, to prove my worth, and to discover the strength I never knew I possessed.

Dawn is breaking as I step out of the castle and make my way down to the garden. Lifting my face, I let the warm breeze caress my skin. Kian remains silent next to me, his unusually quiet demeanor making me nervous. I walk toward the elaborate garden, my fingers reaching for the flowers. Each one strains in my direction, as if begging to be touched. I smile and softly glide my hand over the rose bush, watching the flowers bloom. Color bursts forth, and I feel a jolt of energy as the red buds open.

"It's magic," a voice says behind me.

With a jolt, I turn to find Maxon a few feet away, his eyes locked on mine.

"That's what you are feeling," he explains.

I glance down at my hand, feeling the warmth of my magic tingling in my fingertips. I know it's true, and a slow smile spreads across my face as a wave of happiness washes over me.

Out of the corner of my eye, I catch a glimpse of Kian quietly slipping away.

I feel a tug in my chest pulling me toward Maxon. As I look up into his eyes, an overwhelming desire to be nearer to him consumes me. Instinctively, I move closer, coming to a stop directly in front of him. I raise my hand and gently trace the tattoo on his face, my other hand finding its place on his arm. Closing his eyes, he leans into my hand, and I can't help but smile. I let my hand lower to rest on his chest, my palm resting above his heart. His violet eyes slowly open, filled with an overwhelming heat and desire that takes my breath away.

"You are driving me absolutely crazy," he whispers.

I smile up at him, my cheeks warming under his intense gaze. His fingertips lightly graze my cheeks, sending a shiver down my spine.

"I love it when you blush," he breathes, bending his head, and drawing me closer as his lips press against mine in a warm, heated kiss.

Maxon's hands roam over my curves, pulling me closer and stoking the fire building in my veins. Suddenly, I'm swept off my feet and lifted into his arms. I let out an involuntary yelp, throwing my arms around his neck. One of his arms bands under my knees, the other behind my back. With a low chuckle, he makes my insides dance before leaning in to press a tender kiss on my forehead.

I feel the delicious warmth of his breath on my cheek as he grins down at me, running his nose along my temple. "I want to show you something."

"I can walk."

"I like holding you."

"I'm too heavy," I protest, feeling my cheeks burning again.

"No, you're not. You're perfect."

My mouth snaps shut at the sincerity in his voice.

I smile, kicking my feet a little as my long, simple blue dress gracefully cascades down his arm, and I tenderly run my fingers through his silky hair behind his neck.

"Where are you taking me?"

"You'll see." He takes off down the path, heading deeper into the garden where it grows a little wilder. I haven't been down this way yet. My mouth drops open and I gasp at the sight of the massive weeping willow trees surrounding a giant lake.

"Oh, my gosh."

Maxon gives me a gentle squeeze before placing me on my feet. Excitement bubbles inside me, and the wind seems to play around me in response. I laugh as the wind lifts my hair from around my shoulders, and I feel a gentle tug pulling me forward. I let out a gasp as my dress flutters around my legs. It's as if the wind is trying to speak to me.

Looking over my shoulder, I find Maxon standing with his arms crossed over his chest, watching me with a glimmer of amusement in his eyes.

I turn back toward the trees. They are absolutely breathtaking. What makes these weeping willows so beautiful is their unique coloring; some are a deep, majestic purple, while others are a pristine, snow white. The lake's surface glitters with the reflection of the branches and leaves skimming across its surface. I gaze out at the lake, captivated by its serene beauty. The sunlight glints off the ripples, creating a pattern of light and dark that resembles morse code, accompanied by the gentle sound of water lapping at the banks. I sense Maxon coming up behind me, his arms wrapping around my waist from behind, and sigh in contentment as I lean back against him.

"It's beautiful," I whisper.

Maxon spins me around and lifts me in his arms. I wrap my arms around his neck and he guides my legs around his waist, as he walks toward one of the weeping willow trees. My mind automatically goes to how secluded and hidden we'll be in there.

The branches part. Did I make that happen?. If so, I have no clue how I'm doing it. Maxon's eyes are alight with so many emotions as he stops and slowly sets me down on my feet, landing on the soft mossy earth beneath me. He removes his jacket and lays it on the ground. Then he pulls his white shirt off, exposing the powerful muscles beneath. I nervously gulp, trying to moisten my now dry mouth.

With a smirk, he carelessly tosses it aside and steps closer to me, his hands wrapping around my hips with a firm grip. His mouth descends on mine, his kiss like fire, consuming me and leaving me dizzy with desire. My body lights up instantly, craving skin to skin contact.

"Maxon," I pant, breaking the kiss.

I can feel the warmth of his breath on my skin as his lips trail down my neck and along my collarbone. His fingers slowly untie the ribbons of my dress. As soon as it is loosened enough, I step away and shimmy the dress down and over my hips, stepping out of it.

Maxon's eyes slowly travel down my body and back up, lingering on my mouth. Wearing nothing but panties, I feel the cool air caress my breasts, making my nipples perk. His gaze darkens as it drops to them, and he bites down on his lip with a groan. Before I can react, he is on me, pressing me down to the ground.

Although his movements are swift and unexpected, his touch is soft and gentle. His body covers mine and his lips close over my nipple as he cups my breast. I arch into his mouth, and his hair falls over my body, tickling my sides.

"Maxon . . . " I breathe, hooking my leg around his hip.

Maxon's hands are caressing every curve of my body, from the dip of my waist to the swell of my hips. I thought he'd hate my soft curves. Most of the fae have lithe bodies with long, slender limbs.

As if reading my thoughts, Maxon peers up at me. "Your curves are amazing, Stóirín," he assures me as he moves down my body. He nips at my waist, then my hip. "These curves drive me wild. All I want to do is touch you all the damn time."

Emotions flood me, and the way he is looking at me makes my heart soar. Maxon's teeth sink into my thigh, and I let out a gasp. Then, pulling my panties aside, his mouth covers me, his tongue swirling over my clit. I moan, my back arching as his tongue moves over me, devouring me. I feel a gentle pressure as his fingers move down to my entrance.

"Yes!" I moan arching my back in the soft mossy grass.

Maxon growls, gripping my panties in his teeth and tearing them a second before he thrusts two fingers inside me. I shiver, my muscles clamping down on his fingers as his mouth drops back down to my clit. My hands grip my hair as I ride all the feelings he's creating. Energy buzzes along my skin, sending me into a frenzy, my hips rocking into his mouth, as his fingers glide in and out.

Oh my god . . .

"Maxon!"

Molten hot lava flows through me, his name on repeat as bursts of light flare behind my eyes and I float on a wave of ecstasy.

I'm faintly aware of Maxon shifting and removing his pants. My heart is pounding wildly in my chest, and the sound of my heavy breathing fills the air around us in this haven we've created. His warm, naked body hovers over mine, and I reach for him, needing his skin to be pressed against mine. My hands cup his face, pulling his lips down to me. The moment our lips touch, Maxon's groan escapes into my mouth, his hips rocking into mine. A shiver runs through me as his cock slides hotly along my center.

I wrap my legs around his waist, rubbing my body against his. He doesn't wait another moment before pushing inside of me, and I gasp into his mouth as his thickness stretches me.

"Fuck, Everly," he growls, his eyes falling closed as he works his way in to the hilt.

My heart skips at the sound of my name being growled like that.

Once he is fully seated, he pauses, his muscles straining as he holds himself back. My body is trembling, and the stretch from his cock causes my inner walls to clench.

"Maxon," I breathe, making his eyes fly open. His gaze is like a physical force as our eyes connect. "Move."

Maxon withdraws and pushes back in, his body creating a gentle rhythm as he moves. He is driving me crazy, slowly building me up.

Our fingers intertwine, and Maxon pins them beside my head as we move together, feeling the warmth of each other's skin. Dropping his head, he sucks my nipple into his mouth, and I feel everything inside of me tighten.

Magic tingles across my skin, and that part deep inside of my very being reaches for him. It feels like my skin is electrified.

Maxon's eyes meet mine, the silver in them sparking and swirling against the deep violet. Magic hums in the air as we both tumble over that edge. His warmth fills me, and my muscles clench around him, taking everything he gives me. A million sparks of pleasure cascade through my body as I squeeze his hands, his gaze never leaving mine.

"Stóirín," he moans.

My heart races, pounding in my chest as I release my grip on his hands, and clasp his face. I kiss him desperately, pouring my heart and soul into the kiss, feeling something deep inside my chest click into place, and then there is a second heartbeat, right next to mine. Like an echo, and slowly they become synced.

Chapter Thirty

Everly

Maxon guides me toward the stables, the sound of hooves pounding the ground echoing in the distance. The scent of hay and damp earth fills the air, mingling with the sharper tang of sweat and leather. His sword is strapped to his back now, the hilt rising over his shoulder like a silent warning. There's a dangerous glint to his eye, something taut and restless beneath his usually controlled exterior, something that even sex couldn't dispel.

"Where are your wolves?" he asks, glancing down at me.

"I'm not actually sure. I figured they left to do their business this morning, but I'm sure they will show up again."

"Your Highness." A young fae boy runs toward us. "The others are waiting at the arch for you."

"Thank you, Gideon."

The young boy with curly red hair and bright blue eyes grins before bowing and quickly running back toward the stables.

"I have a surprise for you." Maxon turns his head, glancing down at me.

I can't help but bite my lip as a wave of butterflies fills my stomach. I don't know what this is between us, but I feel so damn lucky. I never had this sort of luck in my life. My earliest memories are not happy ones. I was the girl no one wanted around. I was always alone, overlooked, and unwanted. But then I walked through that damn faerie door, and everything changed. It's as if all the stars aligned and granted me this incredible stroke of luck. I have never experienced such joy, such happiness before. Maxon makes me feel seen, valued, and loved in a way I have never known. It's a beautiful mystery, this connection we share, and I will cherish every moment of it.

Maxon draws us to a stop and cups my face, his lips brushing across my forehead in a tender kiss that has my eyes closing, relishing the moment. "Stóirín, I can feel your emotions. What is going through your head?"

"Oh, I'm just thinking about how happy I've been since coming here." I try not to feel embarrassed admitting this.

Maxon makes a deep rumbling sound in his chest, and I pull back. There is something in his eyes I don't understand, but he doesn't give me time to ask. Seizing my hand once more, he tugs me in the direction of the stables. My feet struggle to keep up with his long strides. I try my best not to trip on the dress Zaria laid out for me today. The dress is a blend of white and dark green, with a bustier corset that enhances its beauty. It isn't as pretty as the other dresses, a more simplistic style, but still flows around my ankles. It reminds me of a dress from medieval times, and the longer sleeves provide coverage for my birthmark, now a deeper shade than before.

Reaching the other end of the stables, we step out into the sun again to see Tristan and Kian waiting for us, both on their horses already. The impatient look on Tristan's face immediately fills me with guilt for having made them wait so we could have sex.

My gaze shifts toward Storm, and an uncontrollable grin spreads across my face. He stands tall and majestic, his hooves gracefully tapping the ground in a rhythmic dance of excitement upon spotting us. As I observe his movements, a gasp escapes my lips as another horse emerges into my view. She is beautiful. Maxon guides me toward the group, his hand releasing mine as he confidently takes hold of the reins of the majestic, pure white horse.

"Everly, this is Nova." He strokes the horse's cheek. "She is yours."

"What?" I gasp, moving a step closer.

Tears well in my eyes, and my trembling hands lift to cover my mouth, my emotions getting the better of me. I'm hyper aware of the others watching and the sound of my own heartbeat. This is a moment like no other, as no one has ever given me something so extraordinary.

Maxon's eyes soften and he holds out a hand, beckoning me closer. "Come."

As soon as my fingers touch Nova, she pushes in closer, a spark of electricity moving between us. Without conscious thought, I run my hand down her neck. Her long, thick mane is gorgeous, so soft like silk, and it seems to shimmer in the sunlight.

Maxon stands close behind me. "Do you like her?"

"Like her? I love her," I admit, my throat clogged with emotion.

"But can you ride?" Kian teases.

I haven't thought about that. "Can't be too hard, right?"

Kian and Tristan laugh, and my gaze instantly whips to Tristan. "Oh my god, you laughed! You're smiling."

Tristan raises an eyebrow at me and shrugs. "I'm just looking forward to watching you try to ride on your own."

Kian's hand snaps out and smacks Tristan over the head. "Be nice, you frog."

I burst out laughing at the look of offense on Tristan's face.

"You are much more handsome when you smile," I tease, pressing my lips together when he scowls in my direction.

Maxon swiftly wraps an arm around my waist from behind, drawing me into his body, his lips dropping to my ear.

"I don't like that."

"What?" I question breathlessly.

"You thinking that other fae are handsome."

I startle, my eyes widening as I twist around to see his face. "Are you jealous?" I blurt.

Maxon doesn't answer, just stares back at me with an intensity that takes my breath away.

"Oh, you are jealous." A giddy feeling swamps my stomach. I don't know why that makes me so insanely happy, but it does.

The distinct sound of hooves fills the air, causing us to turn and see Raiden riding a massive gray horse as it comes around the side of the stables, followed closely by Anika and Nymeria.

"Want to tell me why I found these two tormenting the livestock?" Raiden grumbles.

I step from Maxon's arms and embrace each of my wolves. I can't help but nuzzle my face into their necks. I only have one memory of them, but I know deep in my heart they are family.

I look up at Raiden and shrug. "They were hungry."

"Right, well, maybe we need to find them something other than the livestock."

"Let's get you on Nova." Maxon says, interrupting.

Storm trots over and playfully nudges me with his snout. "Sorry, gorgeous boy, I haven't said hello yet, have I?" I get a soft nicker and another nudge, this time in the direction of Nova. "Oh, you want to go?" I laugh running a hand over his neck.

Maxon stands behind me and grips my waist, lifting me up onto Nova as Raiden grabs the reins. I swing my leg over and my heart slams into my chest when I almost go straight over the other side. Once seated, I look down to where Maxon's hand has a firm grip on my thigh.

"You good?"

Excitement fills me, making me slightly twitchy. I'm afraid that if I speak out loud, it will come out all squeaky, so I just nod.

"Wait!"

I snap my gaze up at Zaria as she comes running over, her curly brown hair flying in ribbons behind her.

"I want to come!" She pants.

The men trade looks, and Raiden shakes his head. "It's too dangerous."

Zaria snorts. "Everly is going."

"With three guards and the prince," Raiden argues. "And because she HAS to go."

Zaria stamps her foot, her hands landing on her hips. "Sounds like plenty of protection then."

I tap Maxon on the head, drawing his attention. "I want her to come."

He stares intently for a moment before giving a nod of understanding. "Raiden, she rides with you."

"What?" Zaria and Raiden yell in unison.

Maxon ignores them, swiftly mounting Storm, grabbing the reins and turning to face the group. He commands our attention, the aura surrounding him growing in magnitude, the silver in his eyes burning with a fierce determination. His every movement exudes a sense of power and authority, making a hushed silence fall over the group.

Maxon raises his voice, his words cutting through the air like a sharp blade. "You heard. We have a long trip ahead. It will take all day to get to the Evergreens, and we will be lucky to make it there before nightfall. We will need to spend the night."

The aura surrounding him seems to grow in magnitude, encompassing everyone. "The path to the Evergreen isn't an easy one, and there have been increased reports of deadlings and Bellowigs. I want you all to protect Everly with your life. In return, I will protect all of yours with mine." It's as if time itself stands still, the world bending to his will. In that moment, Maxon becomes a force to be reckoned with, a leader who will be neither ignored or underestimated.

I give Zaria a wink and she grins in return. Raiden huffs out in annoyance and holds an arm out for Zaria. She grabs hold of Raiden's hand and he pulls her up, and she settles in front of him. Raiden's arms encircle her and his wings flare before resting against his back again.

"Ready?" Maxon asks, coming up beside me.

"Yes." I take a deep breath of fresh air.

I'm ready for answers. At least, I think I am.

What if I'm simply an outsider, stumbling into a world where I don't truly belong?

The weight of uncertainty presses upon me, casting a shadow over my every step as I desperately seek answers to the question that haunts me: am I truly the long-lost Druid princess, or am I an imposter in this enigmatic realm? Is this all just wishful thinking?

Chapter Thirty-One

Everly

My eyes are instantly drawn upward as we enter the forest. The trees are covered with luminescent leaves that seem to shimmer with their own inner light as they stretch toward the sky in a harmonious ballet. Shafts of sunlight filter through the vibrant canopy, creating an enchanting play of shadows that move in time with the forest's mystical heartbeat. Flowers of every imaginable shape and color carpet the forest floor, their petals releasing fragrances that evoke the very essence of magic itself.

"I've never seen the forest quite so alive and colorful before," Zaria mutters.

"It's beautiful," I agree.

The further we travel the more the forest seems to breathe magic. Nymeria and Anika bound ahead silently, and within seconds they have completely disappeared. My pulse kicks up, and I tighten my grip on the reins as I search for them.

"Don't worry. They will stick close. They are the ghosts, remember," Maxon's voice reassures me.

I nod, relaxing my grip and trying to find calm in this beautiful scenery.

It amazes me how much the forest changes the longer we ride.

"The forest around the Evergreen is different from the others in Faerie. The druids' magic lives and breathes in this forest," Maxon explains, as if reading my thoughts. Dropping my gaze from the treetops, I peer over at him and smile. I try to reach out to see what he is feeling, but all I feel is contentment, and I'm not sure if it's mine or his.

Tristan and Kian are in the lead, followed by Maxon and me in the middle, with Raiden and Zaria trailing behind. Occasionally, I catch sight of Anika and Nymeria through the thick trees and foliage, fleeting glimpses of white. Nova and Storm stay close together while Maxon remains vigilant, scanning our surroundings with a watchful gaze. A sense of nervous energy permeates the air, making me feel unsettled. It's clear he is on high alert. They all are. But the silence that has encircled us weighs heavy, like a stone in my stomach, compelling me to break it and dispel the lingering tension.

Not sure how loud to speak, I reach out and poke Maxon's arm to draw his attention and whisper softly, "What are you looking for?"

"Nothing in particular."

Tristan twists around, catching my eye. "Well, I'm watching for bellowigs."

My eyes widen at his tone, and I'm almost too afraid to ask. "What's a bellowig?"

Maxon's violet eyes land on me, and he smirks before looking ahead. "They are rather large rodents. I think the best description that you would understand is flying squirrel."

The squirrels back home are cute creatures of grace and enchantment with large, expressive eyes, and velvety fur.

"Why would you be worried about running into them?"

Kian looks back at me and grins mischievously. "You're thinking of the cute human realm version, aren't you?"

"Well, yeah, what other version could there be?"

"The version that will claw you to pieces for a fresh meal," Zaria replies dryly.

I turn in my saddle and stare at her. "Say what now?"

"You heard her," Raiden grunts.

"What kind of squirrel is that?" I demand, looking back at Maxon, feeling slightly more panicked than before.

Maxon shrugs, as if not bothered. "The fae kind."

We all fall into silence again, and I do my best to push the images of the bellowig from my mind. Instead, I focus on my surroundings.

The air fills with the sweet symphony of unseen creatures. The delicate hum of fairy wings, the gentle rustle of leaves, the soft clopping of the horses, and the melodious songs of enchanted birds.

The forest grows denser the further in we go. The horses slow, Kian now taking the lead as we travel along the trail in a single line. My skin prickles with awareness when the temperature drops, and I look around in confusion. With every step we take, the forest grows quieter, as if holding its breath. Unease trickles down my spine, and I know the others can feel it, too.

Up ahead, Kian's horse rears, shaking its head and nearly throwing him off. He holds onto the reins, calming the horse with whispered words and rubbing its neck.

Storm snorts out loudly, startling me, and I feel Nova's muscles tense under me.

"Maxon," I whisper.

"I know," he answers, quickly dismounting from Storm.

A shiver runs down my spine, and I squeeze the reins tighter in my hands, doing my best to center myself.

Maxon turns in a slow circle, drawing his sword from his back. Raiden gets off his horse and blocks Zaria's path when she moves to follow. "Stay up there."

Zaria's eyes lock with mine, and she swallows audibly, her throat bobbing with a hint of anxiety. The fear in her eyes is unmistakable, and I wish I could reassure her everything is fine.

Nova nervously fidgets beneath me, and I gently stroke her neck, attempting to calm her. Storm must sense our unease, because he backs up, stopping at my side as Raiden and Maxon fan out, the ferns around us concealing most of their bodies. I glance over at Kian, who has drawn his bow and arrow.

Shit, what is happening right now?

Nova begins to prance nervously and backs up. My grip on her reins tighten, as Tristan approaches, silently maneuvering his horse to my side, coming to a halt beside Nova.

"If we–"

The sharp whistle of an arrow slicing through the air abruptly interrupts Tristan's words as it pierces his shoulder.

I gasp, lunging for him. "Shit."

I hold his shoulder as he reaches up and rips the arrow from his body, throwing it to the ground. Then the world around us erupts into chaos, the silence of the forest shattered as men came charging out from the trees. The scene before my eyes resembles something straight out of a movie.

So much is happening right now. I don't know what to do. We've found ourselves surrounded by a menacing group of at least twenty Outcasts, each holding a weapon.

A piercing howl tears through the air, and my eyes lock onto Anika and Nymeria, as they bound into the group, mercilessly bringing down the two nearest Outcasts. They land with such force that they appear to lose consciousness instantly.

Maxon swings his sword, slicing through each opponent that approaches him with the ease and grace of a dancer. Zaria's piercing shriek slices through the air, piercing the cacophony of clashing swords. My eyes snap to her, and I see a fae desperately attempting to pull her from the horse. In the blink of an eye, Kian's arrow swiftly finds its target, sinking deep into the fae's exposed neck. As the fae crumples to the ground in a lifeless heap, Zaria's wide, panicked eyes lock with mine.

Tristan manages to quickly and gracefully move from his horse to mine, his arms encircling me as he grabs the reins and kicks Nova in the side. As she rears up, Tristan instinctively presses against my back, ensuring we don't topple off. Then she shoots forward, and we are racing into the trees.

"Wait, where are we going?" I shout.

We can't leave the others. I can't leave them. Ice drenches my insides as we move further away from the group.

I hear Zaria scream again, and Kian curses, bellowing something to the others.

"We have to go back!" I plead.

"Maxon told me to get you out of there."

"When?" I yell.

I am getting super pissed now.

"Before we left!" Tristan growls.

The sound of the fighting fades and panic overrides everything else. Something dashes out in front of us, and I see a fae with his bow and arrow raised. Tristan ducks, pushing me down as an arrow wizzes past. I tilt my head up just as a ghastly, pasty gray figure lands on top of the fae, its teeth sinking into his neck. The deadling tears into skin and flesh, sending a spray of blood arcing through the air.

With a quick maneuver, Tristan steers Nova to the left, keeping a safe distance from the deadly creature.

"What the hell is a deadling doing topside?" he snaps.

"I never want to see one of those ever again." I shiver, my fingers sinking into Nova's mane. A spine-tingling guttural roar sounds behind us and Tristan curses.

I swallow roughly, choking on my words, a ball of fear clogging my throat. "Do I even want to know?"

"Probably not." Tristan urges Nova on faster.

"We need to go back to the others."

"Not an option right now, Everly."

"I can fight."

"Barely."

The sound of fast approaching footfalls has me glancing over my shoulder as the hideous milky eyes of the deadling meet mine. I swear my blood runs cold. "He's fast."

"They all are."

But how did I outrun one before? I look forward in time to duck under a low-hanging branch, its leaves slapping me in the face. A deep, bellowing noise fills the surroundings as Nova suddenly collides with something. My heart drops as she falls, sending Tristan and me sprawling on the ground, both of us rolling several times before coming to a stop. Tiny cuts litter my exposed skin, and my dress is coated in a thick layer of dirt as I hastily get up and rush to help Tristan stand.

With a swift motion, Tristan positions himself between me and the deadling, shielding me from any harm. Blood coats the creature's face, giving its grayish skin a gruesome appearance. It launches itself at us and Tristan moves fast, grabbing the creature around the neck and swinging onto its back. The deadling rears back, a high pitch screech emitting from its throat. I quickly release my dagger, which I have strapped to my waist, and run. Tristan's eyes meet mine, filling with panic when he realizes what I'm going to do.

With a quick duck, I evade the deadling's flailing arms and drive my weapon into its chest. The give of skin and bones makes bile rush up my throat. The deadling goes wild, and the unexpected backhand knocks me off balance, sending me sprawling across the ground. I groan disoriented by the bright lights flashing behind my eyes.

Digging my fingers into the soft dirt beneath me, I look up and see it sink its sharp nails into Tristan's side, flinging him off its back.

My breath catches in my throat as I struggle to my feet. I need to help him. My steps are off balance and I swear I hear Anika and Nymeria howling and barking in the distance.

The deadling abruptly turns toward me, and I instantly freeze in place. What should I do? I can't run.

Nova bursts through the trees, her white coat shimmering like diamonds despite the dirt coating her. Rearing up, she brings her hooves down on the deadling. My eyes widen in horror as it skilfully dodges the kick, swiftly climbing up her back and sinking its claws into her sides.

A scream rips from my throat and my heart beats wildly in my chest. “Nova!” Anger and devastation plummet me. I run forward, but Tristan is there, his arm wrapping around my waist and spinning me away.

“We need to run!” he shouts.

I desperately fought against his tight grasp. “Nova!”

In an instant, the deadling's focus snaps to me, and it relinquishes its grip on Nova. Launching from her back, it runs toward us with lightning speed. Tristan curses and snatches my dagger from my grasp. He meets the deadling head on, but my eyes won’t leave Nova. Without hesitation, I sprint toward her as she stumbles. She carefully eases herself down to the ground as I come to a stop beside her. My vision blurs and my nose stings as tears stream down my cheeks.

“Oh, Nova!” I cry, looking at her wounds.

I can’t tell how deep they are, but she’s bleeding so much. My hand instinctively moves to cover the puncture marks, and a sob escapes my lips, aware that there are additional wounds on her other side. Resting my head on her warm body, my tears dampening her soft coat, I feel the tell-tale tingle of magic moving through my body, and open my eyes to watch as, under my hands, appears a patch made of leaves and flower petals. Confusion floods my mind as I blink rapidly.

How did I patch up the wound? Can I do it on the other side? Jumping to my feet, I race around her. The sound of Tristan and the deadling fighting fills the air as I quickly lay my hands over the wound and close my eyes, trying to concentrate. My body warms again, and I sigh in relief, praying this will help her.

My eyes flutter open, and I find myself staring into the terrifying, milky white orbs of the deadling. A scream escapes my throat, echoing in the air as I frantically scramble away, my heart pounding in my chest.

Without warning, an obscured dark figure materializes before me, forcefully flinging the deadling through the air then igniting in a fiery blaze. It moves faster than I can track, colliding with the deadling. Its deafening screams reverberate through the air, assaulting my ears. I instinctively drop to a crouched position, covering my ears, seeking refuge from the piercing sound.

Suddenly, a profound silence descends upon us. My heart races, drowning out any other noise as it thumps relentlessly in my chest, accompanied by a rushing sensation in my ears. Slowly, I release my hands from my ears and rise to my feet. Standing just a few yards ahead of me is Maxon, his chest heaving. His eyes, like smoldering embers, cast a fiery glow that seems to set the air ablaze as ash dances around him, floating on the wind.

We both stand here panting. All we can do is stare at each other. Everything around us fades away as we close the distance between us. Maxon's hands cup my face as his mesmerizing eyes flicker over every inch of my face.

"I'm going to kill every single one of them again!" Maxon snarls, his whole body vibrating in anger.

Reaching up, I grip his wrists, the rapid flutter of his pulse beats under my fingertips.

"I'm okay."

His nostrils flare and his pupils dilate. "You're injured."

"I'm fine," I attempt to reassure him.

His head dips, and a rush of anticipation fills the air as our lips meet in a desperate kiss. The sound of my heart thumping echoes against my chest, and a wave of exhilaration washes over me, causing my stomach to swoop. Maxon lifts me up, my legs wrapping around his waist, providing a sense of security and connection. The kiss is consuming. It's as if I am his entire world.

Breaking the kiss, he traces a path with his lips along my jaw, sending shivers down my spine.

The gentle pressure of his fingers tangling in my hair at the back of my head has me releasing a deep breath. Bringing my face to his neck, he buries his face in mine, holding me securely against him. We stay like this for a long moment, arms wrapped firmly around each other. The taste of his kiss lingers on my lips as I breathe him in.

The sound of groaning reaches my ears, and I gasp. Drawing back, I push for Maxon to release me and drop my legs. Reluctantly, he lets go of me, and I spin around, searching for Tristan's familiar face. I spot him trying to prop himself up against a nearby tree. I make it all of two steps before my foot gets tangled in the fabric of my dress. With a frustrated growl, I grip my dress, feeling the fabric bunch in my fists as I sprint toward him.

Chapter Thirty-Two

Maxon

I am beyond pissed. I'm fucking livid.

With a group that big and armed, there is no way the Outcasts could have accidentally stumbled upon us. It's clear that someone informed them in advance of our journey. Only a select few knew our destination, but rumors may have spread through the grapevine to others they deemed trustworthy. A low menacing growl emanates from my throat, the sound reverberating through my chest, making the air ripple around me. Everly's wide brown eyes lock with mine over her shoulder as she tends to Tristan.

The insatiable need to shred something is so strong that I can feel it pulsating in my veins. My mate has been injured, bloodied, and nearly killed.

I was almost too late.

With my eyes squeezed shut, I clench my fists and inhale deeply, trying to find a sense of calm.

The sound of the others coming reaches my ears, their voices getting closer. Storm confidently leads the way, with Nymeria and Anika by his side. It is puzzling why the wolves made the choice to stay and lend us their assistance, rather than following Everly.

Both wolves trot over to her, their paws padding softly on the ground, and sandwich her between them. Their body language betrays their distress at seeing Everly in this state. Storm comes straight over to me, his head pushing into my shoulder as he snorts, obviously troubled.

"Shhh . . . I'm okay," I murmur, stroking down the bridge of his nose.

Raiden, Zaria, and Kian dismount from their horses, their boots hitting the ground with a thud. Everly manages to disengage herself from the wolves and hurries over to Zaria, meeting her halfway. Their embrace speaks volumes for their friendship, conveying an undeniable sense of relief that resonates through our bond.

"Is everyone okay?" I ask tersely.

There is a murmur of agreements from everyone, but Everly steps forward. Worry fills her eyes as she reaches for her wolves, sinking her hands into their fur. "No. Tristan has many wounds, and Nova was injured trying to protect me from a deadling."

With a grunt, Tristan pushes himself to his feet, leaning against the tree for balance. Everly spins, reaching out to assist him, and I can't control the burning jealousy that ignites in my stomach. I must make a noise, because Raiden steps into my path and places a firm hand on my shoulder.

"It's fine. Calm down."

My eyes narrow as I glare at him, my jaw locked and fists clenched.

"It's really fucking hard when she is covered in blood," I growl.

Understanding shines in Raiden's gaze and he squeezes my shoulder before stepping back. We face the group, with everyone's focus on me.

"This setback hasn't changed our orders. We are to get Everly to the Evergreen stronghold before nightfall."

"And we don't have a lot of time. We have already lost most of the daylight," Raiden adds.

I release a heavy sigh and direct my gaze toward the sky. He was right, the battle may have been short, but it still wasted precious time. We are now at least an hour or two behind schedule.

"What I want to know is why deadling's are topside. They disappeared indefinitely when the Shadoweaver was exiled." Tristan's voice sounds rough. His heavy gaze lands on Everly, and I bristle at the harshness of his expression. I can't help the surge of protectiveness that rises in my chest. I want to step forward and shield her from all those looks, but she needs to learn to hold her own. To navigate this world on her own, to stand tall amidst the scrutiny. Especially with my men. Yes, they have sworn to protect her for me, but I want them to swear it to her because they see her as worthy.

Kian clicks his tongue. "It is worrisome."

Everly frowns, her brows furrowing slightly, creating the most endearing expression of bewilderment. Her eyes widen in innocence, and her lips form a subtle pout that only adds to her charm. The way she tilts her head to the side, as if trying to make sense of the situation, is utterly adorable. It's in these moments of confusion that her true vulnerability shines through, making her irresistibly cute.

"Shadoweaver?" she asks.

"Yes," Tristan bites out. "Something has upset the balance. If the Shadoweaver has woken from his eternal slumber . . . "

"Who–"

"Do we have to talk about this here?" Zaria cuts Everly off, her eyes frantically scanning the area.

"Yes!" Tristan snaps.

Kian steps toward his friend. "Surely you heard the rumors, old man. Everly here is the long-lost princess. The last remaining full blood druid."

"We don't know that!" Raiden snaps, his wings spreading out behind him in agitation.

Zaria wraps her arms around her middle, shifting on her feet as Tristan looks around at us all.

"Are you fucking kidding me? That was her?" He points at Everly. "She made the vines move?"

"Well, dar . . . " Kian replies, rolling his eyes. "Why do you think the queen's guard surrounded them?"

Tristan's gaze focuses on me, but I set my jaw and return the stare. "Everyone was tight lipped about what happened," he grits out through clenched teeth.

I know they're all on edge, and with the attack just now, unsettled, but until I know for sure, I'm not going to say anything.

"We will continue this when we reach our destination," I reply instead.

I want out of this forest. Before we run into any more surprises. Yes, I probably should have confirmed these rumors before assigning Tristan and Kain to this mission, but I want to be sure.

I pivot and stride over to Nova, evaluating her injuries. Everly moves to my side, her hands clasped in front of her, fingers trembling slightly.

"Will she be okay?"

"Did you do this?" I gesture to the plant bandages covering the wounds.

"Oh. Umm, yes."

I crouch down and carefully peel back the layers, feeling a rush of surprise wash over me, before carefully placing it back over the now healed wound. From my position, I twist my body and gaze up at Everly, tilting my head in deep contemplation. I can't feel anything from her other than worry and confusion. With a sigh, I look back at Nova and feel the warmth of her snow-white coat against my hand as I stroke her before getting up.

"Will she be able to make the trip?" Everly asks, her voice cracking with emotions.

"Yes, she will make the trip just fine."

I run a hand over my face and walk to Nova's front. With a gentle tug on her reins, she responds by shifting her weight, testing the strength of her healed injuries, before standing.

Chapter Thirty-Three

Everly

My mouth drops open as I watch Nova stand. Crimson red blood mars the pristine beauty of her white coat on both sides. But she's standing, and my relief at that is instant.

"Oh my god, you're okay," I whisper, rushing forward. "She is okay, right?" I ask, looking at Maxon as I stroke her neck, feeling tears build in my eyes.

His face is like a mask, devoid of any discernible expression. Swallowing hard, I frown as a lump forms in my throat. "What's wrong?"

"Nothing. Here, let me help you up."

"I don't want to put any strain on her." I step back.

Maxon pauses, his eyes narrowing as he focuses his full attention on me. "Nova can handle it."

"No, I weigh too much. "

I frown as his jaw flexes, I'm not liking the way he is looking at me right now. "Why would you think that?" he questions.

"Ummm . . . " my fingers twist in my skirt and I drop my gaze.

"Well?"

"What do you mean?" I hiss, looking up at him. I can feel my anger rising, does he really not see? "I'm like three times the size of the other high fae women you're used to, that Nova is used to."

Maxon's eyes drop, taking in my body extremely slowly. Anger and desire swirl in my stomach. Argh, does he always have to make my emotions feel like a tangled web?

When his gaze lifts back to mine, his eyes are burning with longing, but the look on his face is less than impressed.

"Your body is shaped with elegant curves. You stand out among the rest. You're not heavy, not for me, and definitely not for the horse."

His words make my heart pound in my chest, causing a sickening feeling to wash over me. I feel like there are unsaid words, or it could just be my insecurities about my weight that have me feeling like this. Maxon has never once shown anything but an overwhelming attraction to the curves of my body. It's as if I have time-traveled back to high school, feeling just as low about myself as I did back then. I think my heightened emotions from our recent experience are clouding my judgment. With a slight tilt of his head, Maxon carefully observes every detail of my face.

"What's wrong? Why are you looking at me like that?" I snap.

I want to scream at him after everything we just went through. My emotions are already at an all-time high. Plus, I can't seem to get a read on his emotions, but I'm sure as hell he can sense mine just fine. Maxon tilts his head, his gaze never wavering. "Like what?"

I grit my teeth and push all my anger and frustration his way.

"Like you're pissed off at me. Tell me what I did? Because if it's leaving your side, Tristan told me that–"

Maxon tenderly grabs hold of my face, stalling my words as he drops his head, his lips softly brushing against mine, rendering me speechless.

"I'm not mad at you. I'm mad at the situation. And Everly, my Stóirín, you have to know how beautiful you are. Your curves set you apart from everyone else. I love the way you are." His hands drop from my face and skim down my neck, over my shoulders, and down my sides. Gripping my hips, he pulls me flush against him. "You have nothing to worry about. You are all I see. All I want. And I apologize if I gave off the impression that I was mad at you. I'm just trying to piece a few things together," he murmurs, reaching up and tucking some loose hair behind my ear.

"You were looking at me, weird," I sulk, needing him to know how he made me feel.

"I was trying to determine if you were aware of what you had done."

My eyes roam his face as I try to think of what he could possibly be talking about.

"But all I can feel is your confusion," he breathes with a heavy sigh.

Maxon takes a step back, extending his hand toward me, and I reach out to grasp it. Making our way to Nova's side, he tenderly removes the bandage I somehow managed to create. I draw in a sharp breath, feeling the rush of adrenaline as I push past him.

"Where is the wound?" I ask, running my fingers over her red-stained white coat. Nova's muscles twitch under my touch, eliciting a shiver down my spine, and when Maxon remains silent, I twist my body to catch a glimpse of his expression.

"You healed her."

"Me? What? No." My heart takes off, and a sick feeling settles in the pit of my stomach. There's no way.

The sound of the others talking over one another reaches my ears. Their voices grow louder as they debate on which way to go in the quickly fading daylight. Maxon rests his hand on my shoulder, squeezing gently.

"Don't worry, we will figure it out. For now, keep this between us." His voice holds an edge that makes my skin prickle.

Nodding, I swallow over the nerves building in my throat. What is happening to me?

I let him lead me over to the others. Zaria catches my eye, her furrowed brows reflecting her concerns. "Are you okay?" she asks gently.

"Yes," I reply hoarsely.

It seems like Tristan is healing just fine as he paces and runs a frustrated hand through his dark hair, leaving it tousled and unruly. Kian stands leaning against a tree, his ankles crossed and arms folded, observing Tristan's internal conflict.

"We need to head west." Maxon's voice is stern as he addresses everyone.

"But west will take us away from where we need to be," Raiden counters, looking confused.

"Yes, but it will take us around the bog."

Zaria moves toward Raiden's ash-colored horse and climbs on, her tail whipping back and forth. "Then let's go. I don't want to be in the forest when night falls."

I can't help but watch them as Raiden looks up at her, his expression melting into one of affection. "You'll be safe, Z."

Zaria lets out a snort, rolling her eyes.

Tristan shifts his attention toward me, his eyes narrowing with suspicion. "You coming here has set something in motion."

He doesn't sound mad, just distrusting, like I'm not who he thought I was. I open my mouth to reassure him but what could I say? A pang of sympathy moves through me at the worry etched on his face. I can sense that there is an underlying meaning to his reaction. Something I'm not privy to. Maxon steps in front of me, blocking my view with his broad back.

"She knows as much as we do at this point. The reason for going to the ruins is to see if it helps to bring up any memories."

"Memories of what?" Tristan counters.

Zaria pipes up, "Guys we need to get going."

I notice movement in the trees, and my eyes are drawn to a fleeting flicker of blue. Could it be?

The blue fox emerges from the trees, its vibrant fur contrasting against the green foliage. Faintly, I hear the voices of the others as they discuss the dilemma of navigating the bog or finding an alternative route. With a tilt of its head, the frostflare's unwavering gaze focuses on me. Its eyes begin to glow, casting an eerie light as it moves its head, as if inviting me to follow.

"Guys. I think it wants us to follow," I note, interrupting their bickering.

They all turn their gaze in the direction I'm pointing, and are struck silent.

"A frostflare hasn't been seen in centuries," whispers Zaria.

"Just like the damn deadlings," mutters Tristan.

I can't take my eyes off the stunning blue fox, mesmerized by the graceful swish of its tail. The strange white marking on its body emit a radiant glow, while its silver eyes shimmer with an otherworldly light.

'Follow.'

I startle at the whisper-like voice that softly echoes in my mind.

"I think it wants us to follow it," I stammer.

"How would you know?" Kian's tone is curious as he comes to stand next to me.

"It spoke to me," I whisper, as if in a trance.

The fox captures the attention of Nymeria and Anika, prompting them to pounce toward it, their barks echoing through the area as though they were inviting the fox to play. However, their enthusiasm quickly fades, and they turn their attention to us, waiting impatiently.

"Looks like we are following the mythical creature, then." With a warm chuckle, Kian squeezes my shoulder before gracefully mounting his horse.

Storm nudges my back, and I turn to see Maxon holding Nova's reins. A nervous flutter fills my stomach as we stare at each other.

"Everly, this is yours," Tristan startles me, holding out my dagger. With a weak smile, I reach for it, my hands slightly trembling.

"Thank you for keeping me safe, Tristan." My words are filled with genuine gratitude.

The weight of Tristan's stare hangs heavily in the air, creating an uncomfortable and suffocating silence. Without uttering a word, he nods and swiftly makes his way to his horse.

"He will be fine, don't worry," Maxon assures me. "Now let's get you on this horse."

"We're here," Maxon announces as the forest gives way to a set of open gates overgrown with roses and vines.

The horses' hooves echo around us as they step onto the stone road, entering a large courtyard teeming with greenery.

We draw to a stop at the base of the staircase leading up to the entrance. I swing my leg off Nova and land on the ground, but it's further away than I thought. I stumble backward, tensing as I prepare to land on my butt, but Maxon's there to stop my fall.

"Careful, Stóirín." Maxon's voice is deep and smooth like chocolate.

My heart warms at the name he has chosen to call me.

The others dismount and lead the horses over to the fountain for a drink. My gaze wanders over the area, taking it all in. The entire area is overgrown and falling apart, with the roses gradually engulfing most of the fountain. Amidst it all, one could barely make out the figure of a woman in the center, her hands lifted up, cradling a flower in offering to the gods.

Maxon moves around me, leading Storm and Nova toward the fountain. I turn my attention to the castle, my pulse kicking up. If the others are right, if I am who they think I am, then this is my home. The frostflare materializes again in front of the door to the castle, but only for a second before disappearing in a swirl of mist.

I'm so out of my element here. I still think it's completely plausible that I've hit my head and fallen into a dreamland. With cautious steps, I advance toward the damaged and forgotten castle, its ancient walls entangled in a lush tapestry of ferns and creeping vines. The towering trees loom above, casting dappled rays of sunlight on the grounds. A sense of anticipation hangs in the air, and I know the others are watching me, waiting for a flood of memories to consume my mind.

I don't want to disappoint anyone, and the pressure I feel makes my heart beat with trepidation. But as I focus on my surroundings, the ancient ruins and lush forests, I can't help but feel a deep connection to the land.

The whispering winds seem to carry echoes of long forgotten tales, and the mystical energy that permeates the air stirs something within me. Memories, fragmented and hazy, tease at the edge of my consciousness. Visions of ceremonies and rituals dance before my eyes, hinting at a past life intertwined with the druidic traditions of this realm. Yet, despite these signs, doubts begin to gnaw at my core. What if these feelings are mere illusions?

My pulse kicks up as I climb up the stairs, with the others trailing behind me. I place my hand on the door, and with a deep breath, I push it open. The door is heavy and solid, with a few large cracks running down the grains as if something forced its way inside. Ignoring that thought, I push myself to keep going, the sound of my heartbeat pounding in my ears. The foyer of the castle is breathtaking. The wall opposite us is made entirely of glass. Not just one sheet, but arches like you'd find in an old greenhouse. The forest has crept its way in, vines and wild flowers spreading across the marble floor. The castle is still and eerily silent, the kind of silence that leaves you uneasy. Where ghosts watch from the shadows and the dead whisper secrets of the past.

And I wonder just what secrets does this place hold?

Chapter Thirty-Four

Everly

I'm staring again.

But seriously, the man is a figment of my imagination; I'm sure of it. It honestly isn't my fault that my gaze keeps drifting to him every few seconds. Maxon's black breeches and tunic mold to his body perfectly. The air crackles with his energy, as if reaching for me. It's like we are two magnets constantly being pulled closer. As if sensing my stare, Maxon's piercing violet eyes lock onto mine, a mischievous smirk playing at the corners of his mouth, instantly transporting my mind back to our encounter beneath the weeping willow in the garden this morning. A surge of longing courses through me, causing my heart to somersault in my chest.

In that moment, Maxon's gaze takes on a devilish glint, like he can sense exactly where my thoughts have gone.

Blinking, my focus shifts to the mesmerizing sight of the crackling fire in front of me. After spending an hour walking around the main areas and the men clearing the rooms, we are confident it's a safe place to camp for the night.

However, I haven't recognized anything, and despite my denial, it bothers me quite a bit. I was really hoping this place would spark a memory, something that would give me some answers. I don't have a place where I truly belong. I was constantly being moved from one foster home to another until I reached the age of ten. After that, I endured seven years of pure hell with my permanent family. I sense Maxon's gaze on me, and it makes my skin tingle with awareness. I have a feeling he can detect my thoughts taking a dark turn. So, I take a deep breath and force myself to bury it all deep inside, at least until I'm alone. Then I'll unpack all these conflicting thoughts.

Once sure my emotions are locked down, I peer over at the men. My eyes immediately lock onto Maxon's, and a torrent of feelings pass between us until Raiden's throat-clearing breaks the spell. Embarrassment floods my cheeks, causing me to clench my thighs together and lower my gaze, hoping to conceal the intense flush of color I'm sure is covering my face right now.

"Hey, are you alright?" Zaria lays a hand on my arm.

I jump in surprise and glance at her. "I'm fine."

Standing, I wipe my hands on my skirt. "I'm going to look around some more. We haven't seen what's upstairs yet."

"Are you sure that's a good idea?" Her cat ears twitch, and my attention is drawn to Asrai, blinking those round dual colored eyes up at me.

"I'll be fine."

Suddenly, butterflies swarm my stomach, and I know Maxon is striding my way.

"I'll take you."

My heart leaps in my chest, and I curse my reaction to him, especially with so many eyes watching. "Thank you."

Giving Zaria a small wave, I consciously avoid looking at Kian, Tristan, or Raiden. I didn't need to see Kian's smirk, Tristan's scowl, or Raiden's all-knowing gaze. Silently, we move toward the stairs, with me taking the lead.

Even though I should be tired from the journey and the conflict, I can't shake this feeling of restlessness. "I'm anxious. I need to explore more of the castle. It still amazes me that it's the only building surrounded by the forest."

"You don't have to explain yourself to me. I completely understand, I'd be the same way. Does anything seem familiar to you?"

I pause briefly, attempting to decipher how I'm feeling. There's a lingering sensation, something weightless yet persistent, like the whisper of a name on the tip of my tongue. But I can't determine if it's recognition or just a figment of my imagination. Or hope.

Reaching the top of the stairs, my body moves on instinct—I automatically turn left and let out a sharp whistle. The sound slices through the silence, quick and precise.

Startled, I freeze. My breath catches in my throat as my mind scrambles to understand what just happened. Why did I do that? The act was so natural, so familiar, yet completely unintentional. Like muscle memory from a life I don't quite remember.

Nymeria and Anika bound up the stairs behind us, their paws utterly silent despite their size. Their presence is grounding, but it does little to settle the unease curling in my stomach. I lock eyes with Maxon, who had stopped mid-step to look at me with cautious curiosity. There's an unspoken question in his gaze, one I don't have an answer to. We continue down the hall, the sound of our footsteps echoing through the empty space, adding to the haunting aura. Walls once pristine are now adorned with intricate patterns of decay, with vines creeping up from the floor and intertwining with the cracks. The scent of dampness and age hangs in the air. And yet, despite the dilapidation, the beauty of the ceiling mural remains untouched. Delicate petals of vivid flowers bloom in a kaleidoscope of colors, their vibrant hues contrasting against the muted tones of the crumbling walls. The streams depicted flow gracefully, winding their way through the painted landscape and reflecting the ethereal moonlight that seeps in through the grand, arched windows. The combination of the subtle brushstrokes and the surreal illumination creates a mesmerizing scene, as if we have stepped into a dream world.

We walk for a few minutes, and I'm completely enthralled by the grandeur of the majestic halls. This castle is half the size of the one Maxon lives in, but it is no less spectacular. I take another left, and as a wave of familiarity washes over me, I pause, my gaze taking in the beautifully hand carved wooden doors in front of me. I rest my palm on the smooth surface and close my eyes.

Maxon's chest touches my back, and I feel him take a deep breath, his hands landing on my hips. "Are you okay, Stóirín?"

I open my mouth to speak, but his lips brush the curve of my cheek, stealing my words. Instead, I nod and push the doors open, feeling brave with Maxon at my back.

"Oh, wow . . . " I breathe.

Maxon's hands fall away as we step into the large bedroom. The room is a kaleidoscope of purples, blues, and greens. The window on the opposite side has wisteria and roses growing through it, the flowers a soft pink. A gentle breeze moves through the room from the broken window, making leaves scatter across the floor. To the left is a huge bed, leaves and flowers covering the surface from the towers of wisteria that have wrapped around the frame. Above the bed is a domed glass ceiling that showcases the stars and moon above, the forest seeming to leave that spot free. The room comes alive as Nymeria and Anika bound in, their paws skidding on the wooden floor, and they head straight for a luxurious daybed, where they settle down in a tight, cozy ball. Unable to resist, I grin at the two wolves.

How is it that I remember them?

I know who they are and what they are to me. But I can only recall that one memory of our lives together. It feels as if there is a barrier preventing me from accessing those memories.

I wander through the room, my fingers dancing over the furniture. Something tugs at my thoughts, and I desperately try to grasp at it.

Before I know it, my back is pressed against the dresser, Maxon's hands caging me in. His breathing is heavy as he looms over me. "Don't force it, Stóirín."

How could he possibly know I am hopelessly trying to grasp onto the fleeting feelings flashing through me? The memories that dance at the edge of my consciousness.

"Your desperation is filling the air." He leans closer, so close his nose is brushing against mine, those violet eyes holding me hostage.

"It will come to you. You just need to relax." His lips brush over mine, softly at first. "I know just how to make that happen."

I can't help but giggle, my hands sliding up his chest and looping around his neck. "I'm sure you do, *a chroí.*"

I freeze when the words leave my lips. Did I just speak–

My thoughts are cut short when Maxon's lips crash down on mine, devouring my mouth and clearing my head of all thoughts. Our clothes are discarded in seconds, abandoned in a messy heap on the floor.

Maxon's hands are everywhere, brushing against my skin. Each touch sends waves of pleasure rippling through me. Dropping to his knees, I feel the warmth of his breath as his mouth traces a path down my stomach, biting and nipping at my hip bone, then inner thighs, causing me to let out a surprised yelp. Peering up at me, his eyes glowing with lust, he smirks before covering my clit with his mouth.

A gasp escapes my mouth, and I can't help but bite down on my lower lip as my fingers find their way into his silky hair.

"Maxon," I breathe, tipping my head back. His hands spread my thighs more as he drives his tongue inside of me.

"Oh, my God." Fire whips through me, turning my blood to lava. How does he effortlessly stir such a whirlwind of emotions within me? I can't help but think of us being akin to the sun and the moon. The sun, with its radiant glow, caresses the earth, enveloping it in a comforting warmth. Meanwhile, the moon, in its gentle splendor, whispers tranquility to the world around.

Maxon slides his hand down my leg and hooks it over his shoulder and then does the same to the other leg. I let out a shriek mixed with a moan as he suddenly stands, effortlessly lifting me, with both hands gripping my ass and my legs over his shoulders. I grip his hair tighter in my fists as he turns, a growl rumbling from his chest as he continues to lick and suck as he walks toward the giant bed. Using his hands, he massages my ass cheek, rocking my hips against his mouth.

"Oh . . . " I moan, trembling.

I am so close, I'm delirious.

My hips are moving against his mouth, desperately seeking more.

I let out a scream as I find myself suddenly falling backward. The rush of air whips past me, making my heart race and my breath catch in my throat. With a resounding bounce, my body collides with the softness of the mattress beneath me. Leaves and flowers covering the bed sending an earthy aroma floating around us. In an instant, Maxon is upon me, his presence overwhelming, his tongue forcefully explores the depths of my mouth as he thrusts inside of me at the same moment. The intensity of his movements sends a jolt of both pleasure and pain coursing through my veins, like an explosive burst of sensations. I can't help but cry out, my voice muffled by his demanding kiss. My legs tighten around his hips as I eagerly match his thrusts, reaching a climax that consumes me entirely. Maxon breaks the kiss, his forehead dropping to mine as he lets out a savage growl, one that vibrates through both of us.

"Maxon!" I cry out, arching my chest against his, needing to be even closer.

"Fuck!" he groans, slamming into me. The force of his movements leaves me breathless as he relentlessly pounds into me, his groans echoing in my ears. I want to take control, to ride him, tease him. My eyes flash open, and I push against him. Understanding what I want, he rolls us so I'm on top.

The new angle causes him to sink even deeper into me, heightening the sensations coursing through my body.

"Oh my god!" I moan, tipping my head back as I rock my hips.

My nails dig into his chest, and his firm grip intensifies on my hips as he helps guide my movements. An overwhelmingly powerful mix of devotion and protectiveness leaves me breathless. It feels as if my heart is expanding in my chest, reaching for him. My skin tingles as warmth fills every part of me. I drop over his chest, my hair falling around us. Our eyes lock and a rush of butterflies flood my stomach.

"It was magic the way you came into my life. Each moment spent with you has a way of making the world seem a little more beautiful." Maxon holds either side of my neck as he lifts his hips to meet me.

My heart expands at his words, and I reach up, gripping his wrists. "From this moment until our last, I am yours, always," I vow.

As the words leave my lips, a radiant light explodes from within me, filling the air with a warm glow. Intense pleasure whips out so suddenly I have no time to prepare. With a growl that vibrates through the air, Maxon rolls us again, driving in harder, merging our bodies as one, as the glow wraps around us.

I experience every sensation that floods my body, reaching a point where it overflows like a brimming bucket of water, unable to contain it all. A cry escapes from my lips as Maxon's teeth sink into my neck, creating an intense connection between us, fueled by the pull of my blood. It's overwhelming, and yet somehow insufficient at the same time.

My vision turns white, and Maxon releases my neck, his mouth moving to mine, his hands sink into my hair, and he doesn't just kiss me, he devours me. The taste of my own blood lingers on his lips, sending a surge of wild exhilaration through me. I can feel the soft strands of his hair slipping between my fingers as I hold on. The push and pull of our bodies is completely harmonized. Maxon lifts from me, his forearms on the bed on either side of my head, those eyes more silver than violet.

"Everly, I am completely and unequivocally yours," he declares, his words carrying a sense of unwavering commitment.

“A chroí,” I breathe.

Magic swirls around us like a tornado, whipping and lashing throughout the room. I faintly hear glass breaking, my nail digging into Maxon’s back, arching my neck. Sharp teeth glide over my throat, sending a scattering of goosebumps across my skin.

Then everything goes black.

Chapter Thirty-Five

Everly

The air is suddenly filled with a deafening crack of thunder, so loud it shakes the ground. My bare feet slip in the mud underneath me, as my mother's tight grip on my hand pulls me along.

We run through the forest, lightning casting a stark, eerie light around us, and the sound of pounding hooves close behind. A chill spreads over me as I think about what would happen if they were to catch us.

I do my best to suppress my fear, but I feel like I am drowning in it. My mother veers to the left, pulling me with her. In one swift movement, she scoops me up and leaps over a fallen tree.

She spins, placing me on my feet, her face level with mine, "Listen to me, Everly. I want you to run. You run as fast as you can. Don't stop. Don't look back, just keep running."

"Mother, please!" I cry, clawing at her arms. "Don't leave me."

She shakes me firmly to get my attention. "Everly, listen. You have to go."

I stop crying and feel the warmth of my mother's gaze as I look into her moss green eyes. So many emotions flicker through them as she stares at me.

"I'm so sorry, Everly."

The sounds of howls filled the night air, and the horses drew nearer. Mother spins around, drawing her sword. She slowly looks around, her eyes carefully scanning the area. Spinning back to me swiftly, she places a tender kiss on my forehead before whispering words in an old, forgotten language. Pulling back, her eyes fill with tears, and I feel the pressure of her hands on my chest as she pushes me away. I stumble backward, my hand instinctively reaching for her as I fall. I watch in horror as an arrow pierces her chest and blood instantly spreads across the front of her dress.

Then I'm falling.

The world around me slips away, and I fall through the ground. I fall for only a few seconds before I am suddenly laying in a grassy meadow, the sun's heat warming my skin. I feel the warmth of the tears coursing down my cheeks. Sobs wracking my small body. My clothes are wet and muddy, and my mother's kiss still lingers on my skin. The longer I sit here, the more my memory begins to fade. Soon, I have no idea why I'm sitting in the middle of a grassy plain, or how I got here.

The world around me becomes engulfed in darkness. I sense my body being jostled around, and I'm lifted into the air for a moment before being cradled against a warm, solid chest.

"We can't stay here. It's not safe."

The haze around me makes the sound of murmured voices barely audible. I can feel the soothing warmth of the furs as they cocoon around me. The gentle, rhythmic sound of the horse's hooves beneath me lulls me into a peaceful state.

Chapter Thirty-Six

Everly

I startle awake when the door to my chambers smashes open, my guards racing in the room.

"Princess, you must come with us." Valric grabs my coat and ushers me from my bed. I look up into his worried purple orbs, my stomach twisting in fear.

"What's happening? Where's Mother and Father?" I ask.

Valric's face is a mask of indifference when he looks down at me. With a heavy sigh, he kneels in front of me, gripping my shoulders. "They are meeting us at the escape tunnel. You remember where that is?"

I nod, biting my lip, as tears well in my eyes.

"Good girl. Malarch will take you."

"I'm scared."

"I know, but you're a princess, and princesses are just as strong and brave as princes." With that, he stands and turns for the door, but I reach out, grabbing his hand.

"What about you?"

His long, silver locks brush against his face as he smiles down at me. "I'm going to lead them away from you."

"Who?"

"Just go, princess. Your parents are waiting."

Malarch draws his sword and moves swiftly to the secret escape tunnel hidden inside my wardrobe. He pushes the panel and ushers me inside. I cast a quick glance back at Valric, hoping I will see him again. He is my paladin, my friend, my family.

Malarch gently urges me forward. "Let's go, princess," he whispers.

I step into the dark tunnel, and Malarch shuts the panel behind us. Then he grabs my hand, and slowly, we make our way through the tunnel. I have so many questions on the tip of my five-year-old tongue, but I was taught that we weren't to make a sound in the tunnels.

We can barely see a few feet ahead of us. But soon enough, I can feel the breeze of fresh air caress my face. I breathe a sigh of relief and push down the urge to run ahead and see my parents.

Malarch pushes me behind him as the sound of shouted voices echoes through the air. He curses under his breath before turning and squatting in front of me. Malarch is a troll, the only one on the royal guard. His grayish skin and fathomless black eyes used to scare me, along with his sharp pointed teeth, but after a while, I grew to realize he is just a big teddy bear.

"Stay here. I'm going to see what's going on," he murmurs.

"Okay," I whisper back.

Malarch stares at me a beat longer, then slowly rises. He moves with purpose, his footsteps soundless against the earthen walls of the tunnel as he makes his way to where the tunnel ends in the forest. The tunnel fades to black, and I look around, not able to make anything out.

"Is she waking?"

I hear a faint voice, and feel a cool cloth being placed on my forehead.

"No. She is burning up though."

"What do we do?"

"There's nothing we can do. I think you two getting closer has triggered her Renascitur."

The voices fade, and I'm drifting again as pain overtakes my body once again.

Chapter Thirty-Seven

Everly

The sound of swords clashing and grunts reverberates through the air outside the tunnel. Slowly and quietly, I creep closer to the opening of the tunnel. How would anyone have known where the tunnel came out? Only the royal family and their personal guards had known of this tunnel. My hand landed on the wall of the tunnel and drew power and strength from the earth as I made my way toward the sounds.

Reaching the end of the tunnel, I spot my mother and Malarch standing back to back, fighting with three fae. They are all high fae, but I can't make out their clothes in the dark. I search the forest for my father, but I can't see him. One man makes it past my mother's defenses, his sword slicing her arm. A surge of anger and fear travels through me when she cries out. My body tenses, filling with primal energy. As I reach out my tiny hand, the vines obeyed my command, coiling around the fae's feet and dragging them away from my mother and Malarch. I watch as their swords try to hack away at the vines, but more just replace them. My mother's wild mossy eyes frantically scan the area, searching for me.

She runs over as soon as she spots me. "Everly, are you okay?" she asks hurriedly, checking me over.

"I'm okay, mother, but where is father?"

She meets my eyes and swallows roughly. "Honey . . . "

A rustling among the overgrown bushes makes me jump, though I can't discern the source.

"Incoming!" Malarch yells.

Dread and fear coil deep in my stomach as I tense for what's coming.

Bursting into the clearing is Valric. He has one arm around my father, helping him along. Blood covers the front of my father's white tunic, and his sword is hanging limply in his hand. Valric sees us and visibly relaxes.

The reprieve is short-lived as we all hear the whizzing sound of arrows being let loose. My mother covers me as a dozen arrows strike the surrounding ground. My mother's gasp echoes in my ear and I feel the warmth of her hands as she grabs mine and starts running, dragging me along behind her. I go to turn and look over my shoulder, but her sharp tug on my hand stops me.

"Don't look, Everly," she pleads.

Chapter Thirty-Eight

Everly

I'm struggling against the heaviness that is keeping me from moving. The frustration is building up within me, a fire fueled by the desire to break free from this weight. I command my fingers and toes to move, to twitch even slightly, but they seem trapped in this leaden state. The struggle against this unseen force is becoming not only physical but mental, as I battle the hopelessness that threatens to engulf me. The moment I feel my fingers twitching, a surge of relief flows through me, and once again when I realize my toes are responding to my commands. I part my mouth and take a shallow breath, slowly filling my lungs. I can just make out the faint sound of fabric shifting and a comforting touch of a hand lightly squeezing mine. The scent of lavender fills the air, mingling with the faint aroma of the garden back at the castle. Then there is the unmistakable scent of leather and cedarwood.

"Stóirín?" Maxon whispers, the velvety smooth timbre of his voice sending a shiver through me, making my stomach tumble.

My eyelids flutter allowing me to catch a glimpse of Maxon leaning over me. Slowly, I pry my eyes open, needing more than anything to see him. I blink against the dim light and whimper, fighting the urge to close my eyes again. A warm, gentle hand tenderly cups my face, and he leans in close to me, his face filling my vision. His tantalizing scent envelops me in its embrace. My heart thumps hard, and I feel as if I'm free falling as I stare into his deep violet eyes, the silver ring pulsing with magic.

From the depths of my being, a peculiar and indescribable emotion begins to rise, overwhelming my senses. I can feel him more distinctly now, as if his soul is intertwining with mine. His emotions, feelings, and heartbeat are nestled alongside mine. We are bonded, joined—as connected as two beings could be.

My palm moves up and covers his hand that is cupping my face as the word '*mine*' echoes through my head at the exact same time he whispers it.

Maxon drops his forehead, resting it on mine, his long dark hair falling around us, shielding us from the outside world.

"I'm so relieved you're awake," he murmurs, then gently brushes his lips against mine. Heat floods my body, and the all-consuming need to have him inside of me scorches my blood, tearing through my veins like molten lava.

Maxon groans, the sound filling the air as he swiftly stands and turns away from me.

"What's wrong?" I ask sitting up.

Maxon doesn't turn around, but I see the muscles under his tunic flex and bunch. "You're still recovering. I don't want to hurt you."

"You could never hurt me." I argue. "Wait . . . How long have I been asleep?"

I'm in my bed in my room at the castle, and the last thing I remember was being at the Evergreen's. How did we get back?

Maxon slowly turns and stares down at me. I can sense his worry, his concern, and his overwhelming relief, as if they were tangible emotions. His deep violet eyes look drained, the weight of exhaustion etched on his face.

"Four days."

It takes a moment for his words to fully sink in. "What?"

I push the sheets off my body and swing my legs off the bed, feeling the softness of the rug under my feet. Maxon steps forward to help me, but I hold up my hand to stop him. I don't know how I would react to him touching me right now. All I want to do is to press myself against him and feel his warmth surrounding me. Surrender to his body, get lost in his touches . . .

He clears his throat before asking, "What do you remember?"

I furrow my brow, trying to recall what happened right before I'd blacked out. Suddenly an onslaught of images flashes through my head, and desire has me clenching my thighs. Maxon rubs his hands over his face, cursing under his breath. My heart rate spikes as I remember our mind-blowing sex, the way he felt moving inside of me. My hand drifts up to my neck, my fingers tracing over the spot where he bit me, and another flood of warmth moves through me.

In an instant, I'm on my back in the bed, Maxon hovering over me, his eyes glowing more silver than violet as he stares down at me. Affection, lust, and need flash in his eyes as he grinds his hips against mine, making my eyes roll back. My hands instinctively reach for him. Maxon is quick, though. He grabs my wrists, pinning them above my head, leaning down to whisper in my ear.

"I'm holding back by a thread, Stóirín."

I turn my face toward his, my lips brushing his cheek. "But I want you."

Maxon groans, rocking his hips into mine again, making fireworks explode under my skin.

"A chroí," I moan, and we both freeze. "I said it again."

"You did. Do you know what it means?"

"My heart," I breathe, leaning up to place a kiss on his throat.

His hands spasm around my wrists before he releases them, placing a soft kiss on my neck before pushing off me. Immediately I miss his comforting weight and his scent and warmth. I could smell him all day, let my hands explore those defined planes with every curve and bulge of muscle.

Shit, I am so worked up with his arousal and mine combined, it's making it extremely hard to concentrate.

"The sex we had was amazing, but why was I asleep for four days?"

Maxon's restless pacing comes to a halt, strands of hair falling into his eyes, tempting me to reach out and brush them away.

"You went through Renascitur."

"Renascitur?"

"Yes, it's the fae version of puberty."

I laugh nervously, feeling my stomach twist in knots. "But I'm twenty-five years old."

"It doesn't matter. Your time spent in the human realm has had an impact on you. Being here and our mating has triggered the activation of your fae blood. We believe that when you were transported to the human realm, a potent spell was cast upon you, concealing your fae heritage and erasing certain memories. Our mating shattered the spell that was intertwined with your blood."

My mind whirls as I try to make sense of everything. I remember my dreams and the words my mother whispered before pushing me through the portal. Then another thought hits me, leaving me completely breathless. I had a mother and a father and they loved me; I wasn't abandoned.

Emotions clog my throat, and I stand abruptly. "I . . . need to use the bathroom."

Tears well in my eyes as I walk on shaky legs to the bathroom, needing to splash some cool water on my face. Almost as if in a trance, I lean over the sink, cupping the cool water in my hands, and splashing my face several times. Once the tap is turned off, I rest my palms on the smooth stone on either side of the sink, watching the water slowly drain away.

With a heavy sigh, I grab a towel, pressing it against my face to block out the world. A sharp pang of loss strikes with the realization that I lost my parents. I never knew for sure. I assumed they had died, but now . . . now I remember them clearly.

I glance up at my reflection in the mirror and my eyes go wide, my heart skipping a beat at the sudden shock. Stepping back, I lose my balance and accidentally knock several glass bottles off the nearby bench. The bottles collide with the ground, shattering into countless pieces, and sending shards of glass flying in every direction.

Maxon pushes through the door with such force it bangs against the wall, the sound reverberating around the room.

My wild gaze meets his. "What the hell happened to me?"

Maxon's features soften with understanding. "I'm sorry . . . I should have warned you, but it slipped my mind. I've seen you like this for three days." He walks over to me and cups the side of my neck, his thumb stroking my jaw in soothing motions.

"My eyes," I choke.

My mother's eyes . . .

"They are beautiful."

"They are the same as my mother's," I whisper.

Maxon's eyes search my face. "You remember?"

"Some . . . " I admit.

Moving closer, Maxon tips his face down to mine. I am not a small girl, but he always makes me feel safe and protected. That spark in my chest grows, slowly increasing in strength. I can feel its ghostly tendrils stretching toward him as if to embrace him. The tenderness of his touch sends a shiver down my spine. Then his lips crash down on mine, before I can even process the intent.

My heart races as I melt into his body, my hand sliding up his sides and around his broad back, pulling him tightly against me. The kiss is slow and gentle. The faint sound of our breathing is the only thing I can hear. We've had a lot of kisses, but this is beyond anything I've ever imagined. His other hand wraps around my waist, pulling me tighter against him. The thumb stroking my jaw stops and his fingers sink into my hair, tipping my head back further to deepen the kiss.

"You are mine, Stóirín," he breathes against my mouth.

My little treasure.

Resting my forehead against his chest, I can feel the steady beat of his heart. I let it calm me as I try to come to terms with my appearance. My eyes are now a vibrant mossy green with flecks of silver, just like my mother's. My hair seems longer, thicker and more radiant than before, while my ears have taken on a pointed shape. However, the most astonishing and surprising change is the tattoo on my right temple, an exact replica of Maxon's.

Chapter Thirty-Nine

Maxon

My heart thuds wildly in my chest as I take in her appearance, she looks like a fucking goddess fully awakened in her fae form. The sight alone drives me to the brink of madness. Everly was stunning before, but now there is just something magical surrounding her. Of course, it could just be that we are now mated, and the sensation of seeing my mark on her face has intensified my desire beyond measure. So, I excuse myself, allowing Everly to step into the shower in fear that I might lose control.

Watching her transform over the past few days has been truly astounding. It's as if a light has been ignited within her, illuminating her true self. Did I panic when she lost consciousness after our bonding? Fuck, yes . . .

Actually, I became a bit unhinged until Zaria explained the situation to me.

Her body had gone through a lot. The spell that was keeping her identity hidden was also preventing her Renascitur, which usually happens slowly over time, but it hit her all at once, putting her body into shock. Had we not bonded, I would hate to think of the pain she would have felt. But because we had, I was able to do my best to temper the pain and soothe her while she slept.

When I hear the shower turn on, I start pacing the room. I should feel relieved she's awake, but all I can sense is a cloud of confusion. Everly's confusion. She is bound to have questions. And they're questions I cannot answer.

Fuck, *I* have questions.

Like how the fuck did the druid fucking princess end up hidden in the human realm for twenty fucking years?

A knock at the door has me calling on my sword, my protective instincts flaring to the surface. The door opens, and Zaria's wide eyes meet mine, her gaze flickering to the sword in my hand. Sensing her discomfort, I release a heavy sigh, realizing that my reaction may have been too extreme. I drop my arm, and the weight of the sword dissipates as it vanishes into thin air. Zaria's expression softens slightly as she watches me.

"I didn't mean to startle you, Zaria. Please, come in."

Zaria clears her throat and slips inside, shutting the door behind her. Then her eyes travel to the empty bed.

"She's awake?"

"Yes."

Zaria's shoulders drop, her voice barely audible. "Thank the goddess, Aine. I was getting worried. Does she remember anything?"

I run a hand through my hair and slump down in the chair. "Some, I think. She was shocked by her appearance. I don't even know how to explain what it means to be fully mated or fae."

"You'll figure it out."

I huff a laugh. "Glad you think so."

"Just be honest with her. A lot has changed. Her whole life was taken from her. She would have felt the effect of being stuck in the human realm. Though she might not have understood it."

I nod, leaning forward and resting my elbows on my knees. "At least we know how she was able to transport herself through the portal. She has so much untrained power."

Zaria looks worried as she makes quick work of stripping the sheets from the bed and rolling them up.

"What's bothering you, Z?"

Her head snaps up, and her face lights up with a wide grin. "You haven't called me that since we were kids."

I rest my chin in my hand and smile. "I remember you spying on Raiden and me, before you joined our friend circle. You were quite good at it, which is probably why Raiden chose you as his in-house spy."

Zaria's face flushes, and she clears her throat. "I did not spy on you two."

I tip my head back and let out a laugh. "You were not fooling anyone, Z. Your crush on Raiden was so obvious."

A pillow flies at my face, and I swiftly catch it before it can hit. With a mischievous grin, Zaria sticks her tongue out at me and proceeds to fluff up another pillow.

"It's okay, Z. You two suit each other."

Her ears twitch and she stops making the bed to stare at me. "You really think so?"

"Of course."

Zaria bites her lip, a brief moment of hesitation passing through her, before she nods and continues her task. I furrow my brow and rise to my feet, striding over to lend her a hand.

"Tell me, have you or Nix come any closer to who the mole is?"

"No. It's blooming hard because everyone is damn suspicious!"

I grunt, reminded of the constant deception that defines life in the high fae court.

"I was sure Nix would have weeded them out by now. Speaking of Nix, where is she?"

"She went off with Nero. I think Silver went with them."

"Nero?" I question straightening up.

"Oh yes, the shapeshifter now has a name. He would like to be called Nero, not the Puca or trickster."

"Well, that's new. I thought he liked his names."

"Right!"

"Wonder what brought on that change," I muse, placing the pillows neatly on the bed.

Zaria shrugs, then places her hands on her hips. "You really didn't have to help."

"It was no problem," I offer.

We hear the shower turn off, and Zaria collects the dirty sheets from the floor.

"I will leave you to it and bring food. I'm sure she is starving."

"Thanks, Z."

The door clicks shut behind her as the bathroom door opens and Everly walks out in a pink silk robe, her hair in a towel on top of her head.

"Feel better?" I ask.

Everly walks toward me with a dreamy expression, her steps unsteady and gaze unfocused. I move toward her and scoop her into my arms, carrying her over to the sofa. I can feel the mix of confusion and awe emanating from her.

"What's wrong?"

"I have your mark," she murmurs.

A grin spreads across my face as a sense of pride and contentment swells within me. "You do."

A joyful spark lights up her now mossy green eyes. "That means I'm your true mate?"

A gentle tenderness envelops my heart, and I sense her delicate heartbeat echoing in harmony with mine. The air fills with a soft hum, as if the universe itself is whispering its approval. The sight of her radiant smile coupled with the warmth in her eyes, assures me that we were destined to be together. From the very moment our paths crossed, my soul recognized hers, entwining us in an unbreakable bond. Though initially bewildered by our differences—her humanity, my royalty—I knew deep down that I was willing to embrace any path that led me to her.

"It does. We were always meant to be. I knew my soul recognized yours the moment we meet. I was just confused because you were human, but I was willing to take you anyway. I was determined to convince you to remain here, by my side. The longer you were here, the more sure I became that I loved you. That I have been falling in love with you since the moment I scooped you up in the Fey Glades."

The fragrance of blooming flowers heightens the atmosphere, adding a touch of ethereal magic to our conversation, and I realize that the sweet scent is drifting from her. Her smile is soft as she runs her fingers over her birthmark.

“It's funny, back at the Evergreen Castle, I thought that we were reminiscent of the sun and the moon, and this mark always looked like a unique combination of a sun and moon to me, together in a winding pattern of vines. It was us all along. Marking me as a druid and you as my mate.”

My hand reaches out, gripping her wrist, I bring it to my mouth and kiss it softly.

“Entwined together by fate,” I whisper against her soft skin.

A loud knock at the door has me sliding her from my lap and standing. “Enter.”

Zaria enters with a food cart, her smile wide as she beams at Everly.

Everly stands up immediately, and I can feel her excitement as she rushes over to Zaria. Their bodies collide in a tight embrace. Zaria pulls away, her hands gently cupping Everly’s face.

“You look beautiful!” she laughs, blinking away tears.

“Thanks,” Everly replies quietly.

I see Raiden slip in followed by Nymeria and Anika before shutting the door. By the look on his face, we aren’t going to like what he had to say.

“I hate to interrupt, but the queen wishes to see you both.”

Chapter Forty

Everly

From the wardrobe, Zaria pulls out a beautiful pink dress that catches the light. My breath catches, and my heart races as I take in the stunning elegance of the dress she holds up. The top of the dress sparkles with silver glitter, with a sweetheart neckline and delicate, thin straps. The silver flows down, turning light pink at the smallest part of my waist and gradually getting darker. It flares out like a ballgown at my waist, layers upon layers of tulle with glittering rhinestones scattered throughout. It is gorgeous.

Nymeria and Anika trot over, their ears perked up as they curiously tilt their heads, studying the dress. I grin and reach out, stroking their heads. "It's beautiful, right?"

Both wolves bow their heads in agreement, sandwiching me between them. I can't believe they are alive, that they have survived alone for this long. They were still only pups when my parents were killed.

"Let's put it on, then." Zaria grins.

"This is too pretty to wear now. This is a special occasion dress." I laugh.

"This is a special occasion. You need to go out there and show everyone who you are."

I swallow over the emotions rising in my throat and run my fingers over the dress again.

"Okay," I whisper.

The twinkling rhinestones scattered amidst the fabric send a rainbow of colors reflecting off the walls as the soft rays of sunlight streaming through the curtains reach it. As Zaria takes it from the hanger, the whole feel of the dress adds a touch of enchantment to the room. It is a sight to behold.

Zaria places it on the ground, opening the top wide for me to step into it. Slowly she pulls it up my body, and I slip my arms in the straps, staring at my reflection in awe.

I find myself lost in my reflection, my fingers idly toying with the soft tulle of my skirt. My eyes tracing a path over my face, taking in my now pointed ears and green eyes. The mating mark that makes my stomach fill with butterflies. It's impossible not to think back to how mindblowing the sex had been before I passed out. I want to get him back in bed. A blush covers my cheeks and Zaria clears her throat. Blinking, I meet her gaze in the mirror.

"Do you like it?" she asks nervously.

"I love it."

I spin around, admiring how the skirt fans out around me, catching the sunlight on the sparkling gems.

Zaria claps her hands together, her eyes brimming with tears.

Startled, I pause and grab her hands.

"What's wrong?"

"It's just . . . I knew you were her. I was hoping . . . " she trails off and our attention drops to my arm where my birthmark is now fully displayed in dark raised lines.

There's movement in Zaria's hair before Asrai peeps out, offering me a shy wave.

"Come. We must not keep her majesty waiting too long." Zaria reaches out and runs her fingers through my hair. "I think we can leave your hair down. It looks magical."

I peek in the mirror one more time, marveling at the beauty of the dress.

This dress makes me feel like a princess.

I turn to follow Zaria and see Asrai signing. *'You are a princess.'*

My step falters mid-step. How did she know what I was thinking?

"Wait, one more thing." I rush over to the bed and reach under the mattress, pulling out my dagger—the one that Raiden gave me. My eyes shift downward to my dress, and a frown immediately forms on my face. Where on earth am I going to put it?

"Here." Zaria steps forward, holding out her hand.

I give her the dagger, and as she takes it, she reveals a hidden flap in my bodice. The perfect size for a dagger.

I beam at her. "Perfect." Turning to face Nymeria and Anika, who are following close behind, I add, "You two stay here."

Both wolves let out exasperated sighs and sit, their unwavering gazes focused on me.

"Don't look at me like that," I whine. "Just stay out of trouble."

Stepping out into the hall, I see Tristan first, then warm solid arms spin me, and I'm wrapped in Kian's embrace.

"You scared the shit out of us, princess."

With my arms pinned to my side, there isn't much to do but hang here.

"I'd apologize, but . . . not my fault."

"Let her go, you brute," Tristan's gruff voice pipes up from behind.

I grin as Kian puts me back on my feet, his hands landing on my shoulders, as he takes in my appearance. "He said you'd changed, but I wasn't expecting this."

I flush, feeling my cheeks heat, and shrug my shoulders.

"The crown prince wouldn't let anyone but Nix and Zaria in the room," Kian continues with a frown.

Tristan grabs my hand, breaking Kian's hold, and pulls me into a hug. I'm so surprised and shocked by the gesture I don't immediately move. Then hesitantly, I lift my arms, giving him a gentle squeeze. My eyes dart to Kian and Zaria, both of whom are smothering their amusement behind their hands.

"Don't scare us like that again," Tristan says gruffly before letting me go.

"Yes, the prince almost went into a rage when you blacked out," Kian grouses.

Surprised, I step back and look at each of them. "He did?"

"Yep, would have destroyed what was left of the Evergreens palace if Zaria hadn't reassured him you were okay."

"We weren't allowed anywhere near you. Tristan tried once and almost lost his head." Kian laughs.

My eyes widen and dart to Tristan.

"What?" I croak.

Tristan grabs his neck, looking slightly uncomfortable. "It was my mistake."

Zaria snorts. "If Raiden hadn't intervened, you'd be headless."

"How are you joking about this?" I shriek, completely horrified.

'Stóirín, what's wrong?'

Maxon's voice in my head startles me, and I snap my mouth shut.

'How are you in my head?'

'The bond lets us speak to each other. I can feel your distress. What's happening?'

'You almost killed your friend because he got too close to me?'

I feel his exasperation through our shared link. *'He did not heed my warning.'*

'That doesn't mean you behead him!' I berate.

Maxon hums down the link, and I roll my eyes.

"Are you even listening to me?" Kian's voice breaks me from the spell.

"Of course she is. She just rolled her eyes at you." Tristan's tone conveys how bored he is with the conversation.

"We really should be going," Zaria points out.

Kian holds out his arm to me and I beam, looping my arm in his.

"Be careful. You are literally playing with fire," Trisan mumbles and begins leading the way.

Zaria falls into step next to me as we head toward Queen Lavina's part of the castle.

"How are you feeling?" Kian asks, drawing my attention.

"I feel great, actually. I'm not as shocked about the changes as one would be because I remember my time from before."

"You do?" Zaria asks.

Tristan casts me a questioning look over his shoulder.

"My eyes are just like my mothers." I grin softly.

Making our way around the corner, we come to the open doors to the main sitting area. Just inside, Madeline and Maxon stand close together, their voices hushed as they engage in conversation. My grip involuntarily tightens on Kian's arm, and I do my best to keep my face neutral as a surge of jealousy burns in the pit of my stomach. Connecting with the bond, I immediately sense Maxon's heightened alertness as well as his overall state of calm.

Somehow, knowing he's calm helps me relax, but it doesn't stop the sharp words building on my tongue. My fingers twitch with anticipation as I reach for the dagger hidden within my bodice. Kian pats my hand, snapping me out of my haze.

"You have nothing to worry about," he reassures me with a smile. "She is a snake, and he knows it, plus you are his true mate."

I look up into his lavender eyes and feel a sense of kinship. "Thank you."

"Anytime, princess." He grins, giving me a wink.

As soon as we enter the room, a distinct tension fills the air, causing my skin to prickle. In an instant, Kian is forcefully torn away from my side and sent crashing into the closest wall. The room echoes with the sound of the impact, and several gasps. Maxon's movements are a blur of agility, his hand gripping Kian's shirt tightly, their bodies pressed together before Maxon forcefully slams him against the wall and holds him there.

In a moment of panic, I let out a yelp and rush forward. I bump into Madeline in my haste, causing her to stumble off balance.

"Maxon! Stop this. What are you doing?" I snap angrily, grabbing his arm.

"He should know better than to flirt with you," Maxon growls.

"Maxon, he is my friend, and someone you trust to protect me."

Maxon's eyes flare brightly. "Maybe that's something I need to reconsider."

"No, it's not!"

"Told him he was playing with fire," Tristan mumbles under his breath, but I hear it clear as day.

I glare over my shoulder at him, and using strength I didn't realize I possessed, I pry Maxon away from Kian. The moment our eyes connect, a bolt of lightning shoots through my veins, and he is on me in a second, his mouth fusing with mine. The touch of his lips makes everything else fade into oblivion.

I barely hear the door click shut as Maxon swiftly lifts me, slamming my back against the wall. My legs instinctively wrap around his waist, drawing us closer. His lips, heated and passionate, trace a trail down my neck. Without hesitation, he pulls down the top of my dress, snapping the delicate straps, revealing my breasts. Reaching up, his warm hands cup my breasts, his hips pin me in place before he takes my nipple into his mouth and sucks hard, pleasure pulling at my core like a string. Then, switching to the other, he does it again. I move my hips against his, craving that intense and pleasurable friction, but this damn dress is hindering my movements.

"I knew I couldn't wait to have you," Maxon growls, his eyes blazing in desire. "Should have fucked you in the shower."

My heart squeezes in my chest as he drops me to my feet and spins me, my palms landing on the wall as he gathers up my dress. His fingers find me soaking wet, and he lets out a low rumbling sound, biting down on my shoulder.

A moan slips from my lips as I shudder, pushing against his hand. Maxon doesn't waste a second, and pushes two fingers inside me, his warm breath skating over my neck as he bites down.

"You look so fucking sexy."

I moan, pressing backward into his hand as waves of pleasure wash over me. Every nerve ending in my body is sparking. Maxon builds me up, his lips kissing down my spine, and up my neck as his fingers move in and out.

"Maxon . . . " I breathe, my stomach tightens as warmth floods me.

"I got you."

Maxon removes his fingers, positioning himself at my entrance. Gripping my hips, he pulls me into him, and with a forceful thrust, he enters me. The intensity leaves no room for tenderness or sweetness. It's a raw declaration of possession.

I arch my back as he buries himself deep within me. He withdraws and slams into me again, over and over. His grunts and groans, making me lightheaded. With each forceful thrust, my fingers press hard into the wall, my toes curling in my flats, and the coil in my stomach growing even tighter. The sensations are driving me closer to the brink.

Maxon leans in close, his breath brushing over the sensitive skin of my neck. "Don't you fucking come yet. We are coming together, Stóirín."

"Oh, God . . . " I moan.

Maxon's hand wraps around my throat, and he pulls me flush against him, my back plastered to his front as he pounds into me at a dizzying pace, the tulle from my skirt bunching around us.

"I am no god." His voice is gravely and harsh.

My head turns to his, my hands gripping the arm holding my throat. His other hand holds my hip in a deathly grip. My mouth hovers next to his, our eyes hooded.

"A Chroí . . . " *My heart.*

Maxon's mouth slams down over mine. Our tongues dance together, our breaths growing heavy and rapid. The air around us crackles with electric energy, charged with the heat of desire. His hand moves from my hip and presses into my lower belly. A warmth floods my core, and I whimper into his mouth.

"That's it . . . " Maxson whispers harshly against my mouth. "Good girl."

Thank god Maxon is holding me up, because my legs start to shake and his grip around my throat tightens just slightly, sending a rush of endorphins through me, making me dizzy.

"Fuck!" Maxon roars, feeling me squeeze around his cock.

Thrusting even harder, his hand slips lower, rubbing over my clit. I cry out, my head slamming into his shoulder as waves of ecstasy wash over me.

"Maxon. I'm . . . I'm . . . "

"I know. I'm right here with you."

Even though this dress is hindering our movement, it isn't stopping us.

Not one bit.

Maxon's teeth bite down on my ear. "Come," he commands.

I would have laughed if my body didn't respond instantly. That coil snaps and light whips from our bodies, dancing and entwining around us. Fire erupts along Maxon's skin, and I jolt, but it doesn't burn me. We ride out the waves, and I can feel Maxon slowing his movements, prolonging the pleasure and relishing the sensation of my walls gripping him.

Breathing heavily, Maxon falls forward and pins me against the wall once more. My chest and face are tightly pressed against the cool surface, my heart racing. The fire dissipates, and I sigh, but am not able to draw in a breath.

'You're squishing me.'

Maxon chuckles, his dark hair falling over my shoulders as he kisses my shoulder gently before stepping away. He fastens his pants up before turning me and cupping my face, his eyes searching mine.

"That's never happened before."

"What? Jumping me in front of a room of people? Cause we have to face them now when they know exactly what just happened. Oh no . . . " I groan, covering my face with my hands. "We were not quiet."

"Shh . . . " Maxon tugs my hands away and leans forward, feathering light kisses all over my face. "I mean the fire."

"Oh . . . " I breathe as his lips trail over my collarbone.

"Fuck, you smell amazing," he growls against my skin, sending goosebumps scattering.

"Maxon."

"Right. Sorry." Maxon takes a step back, a smirk on his devilishly handsome face.

I try to hide my grin as I pull my dress back up, adjusting my boobs. The tulle fabric is crinkled, but with a little effort, I manage to smooth it out. Not much I can do for the broken straps though.

"Our bond is still new."

I raise an eyebrow, hoping he'll explain.

"It's why I acted as I did," he continues.

"Well, you can't just go cave man on everyone who comes near me, Maxon. I still need friends."

Maxon nods and steps up to me, his hands running through my hair, smoothing it out before letting his hand trail over our mate mark.

"You're so beautiful, even more so with my mark on you."

Just as I'm about to reply, the heavy doors to the sitting room burst open with a resounding bang. Queen Lavina enters, her presence immediately commanding attention. Her piercing eyes scan the room, locking onto the two of us, and with a flicker of annoyance. She clicks her tongue.

"You two done?"

Mortification sweeps over me swiftly, and I duck my head. Maxon quickly places a kiss on my forehead before turning and addressing his aunt.

"Yes. Thank you for asking."

Queen Lavina snorts with amusement, the sound echoing through the room as she pours herself a drink and takes a long sip.

"It's your coronation tomorrow. Are you ready?"

I startle. "Wait . . . you were supposed to be crowned king two days ago."

'I moved it back.'

"Yes, I'm ready."

Queen Lavina's eyes swing to me, pinning me to the spot. "Are you ready for what it means to be queen?"

Huh . . . Queen? I just found out I'm a lost druid princess.

Maxon's hand grips mine, our fingers entwining. "She will be fine. There is no rush."

Queen Lavina raises a perfect eyebrow at us and flickers her wrist.

"A druid princess, born under a crescent moon's gentle glow, shall wield power unmeasured in realms both high and low.
With magic deep within, she'll rise, her destiny unknown,
To shake the faerie realm, where mystic secrets are sown.
Her heart a beacon of the woods, her spirit strong and free,
She'll dance with stars and call the winds.
Beneath the moon's enchanting light, she'll rise to claim her throne,
Uniting realms of faerie, her power fully grown.
With wisdom, love, and courage, she'll mend what once was torn,
For in her hands, the faerie world shall be reborn."

I blink as if in a trance as she recites the prophecy Kian had told me about.

"What has the prophecy got to do with any of this? We don't know that it's talking about Everly." Maxon crosses his arms.

"Don't we?" Queen Lavina volleys back, throwing back the rest of her drink and placing the glass down.

"Is there any way to determine if I'm the one in the prophecy?"

Both turn their piercing stares on me, their eyes filled with anticipation and concern. The queen's attention lingers on my arm, where my birthmark stands out vividly, commanding attention. A heavy sigh escapes her lips, echoing through the room as she paces back and forth. The sound of her footsteps reverberates, creating an air of unease. Tension hangs around her. Her agitated movements, so unlike her usual composed demeanor, speak volumes about her inner turmoil.

"The night before your castle was raided, there was an incident. Do you remember?"

I furrow my brow and tilt my head in confusion as I look at her. "An incident?"

"Yes, in the village closest to the Evergreen's."

I blink. "What was the name of this village?"

Queen Lavina stops pacing and stares at me, the violet in her eyes glowing otherworldly. "Pinehelm."

Images flash in my mind's eye. A younger version of me running happily through the streets, my mother following behind me. Then the sudden sound of shouting, as a group of men surrounded us. They were trying to grab me, I remember being terrified. As the chaos ensued, my younger self found solace in the embrace of nature. I called for it in desperation with tears in my eyes as my mother fought the men. Sensing my distress, the forest burst forth with life, as if responding to my silent plea for help. Trees stretched their branches protectively, forming a shield around me. Plants and vines snaked their way through the village, entangling the hands of the men who sought to harm me. Animals, sensing danger, unleashed their primal instincts, defending me with their teeth and claws, as if I were their own flesh and blood. Water rushed through the streets, cleansing away the darkness and carrying away the fear that had gripped me. The once tranquil village became a battleground between nature and those who intended to cause me harm, as the elements unleashed their fury upon them. The sound of shouting and the sight of people fleeing in terror filled the air, a stark contrast to the joyful laughter that graced the streets moments ago.

"No." I shake my head, backing up. "I couldn't have."

Queen Lavina's expression becomes tender, her whole demeanor changing before my eyes. "It wasn't your fault. You were only a child. But the other high fae were scared of what you would become. If you weren't to be married off to the courts to control, then you were to be put to death."

I gasp, my hands covering my mouth as tears burn my eyes. "My parents are dead because of me," I whisper.

Maxon's arms wrap protectively around me from behind. "You are not to blame here," he murmurs.

"Kinda feels like I am," I choke out over the lump in my throat.

All of a sudden, the door bangs open, causing us all to jump. Nolan burst into the room, his face flushed and his gaze urgent as he quickly makes his way over to us.

"Nolan, what is the meaning of this?" Queen Lavina demands, her expression pinched.

"Your Majesty, Your Highness, there has been a breach."

"A breach?" I echo, as Maxon steps forward.

"Where?" he demands.

"The north village of Escalle is seeing an influx of deadlings. Someone said they were being commanded by a dark army."

Queen Lavina takes hurried steps toward Nolan, the skirts of her long purple gown swishing around her ankles, drawing my attention. The fabric looks so soft, so pretty. Wait, why am I thinking about her skirt? Nolan has said something about deadlings in the village.

I look up and blink. Something isn't right. Everything around me dissolves into darkness, swirling and engulfing my senses.

I battle through the dense, thick mist, the darkness permeating my mind as much as the battlefield. Shadows dance, mocking my every move. Sweat drips down my brow, as I grip the sword in my hand. My heart pounds in a rhythmic drumbeat of fear and determination.

A surge of power courses through my veins, ignited in my chest, and fire lights up my sword. My eyes glow in its reflection, and as I look around, the mist lifts. I take a step forward, pausing as two shapes come barreling toward me. I brace myself, but relief has me sagging where I stand as Nymeria and Anika wrap around me, their beautiful snow white fur covered in blood, both black and red.

Firm hands are on my shoulders, shaking me, and I blink. The room around me comes into focus, but it's Maxon's furious expression that has my full attention.

"What was that?" I ask.

"You tell us, dear," Queen Lavina answers.

Maxon's thumb grazes my cheek, drawing my attention. "What did you see?"

"The room faded, and I was somewhere else. The air was thick with an unsettling black mist that obscured my vision. I was dirty and bloody, as if I had been in battle," I explain.

Maxon places a tender kiss on my head before turning to Nolan and his aunt. "Black mist, black army . . . Does that mean he's awake?"

Nolan curses, running a hand over his short blonde hair, making it stand up in a disheveled mess.

"Wait, who's awake?" I ask, dread curling in my stomach.

"Do you think he sensed her awakening?" Queen Lavina demands.

"Possibly. If she is the one the prophecy spoke of, then it could mean he'd sense her power and wants her for himself."

What the hell? What were they talking about?

"We can't let him have her. If he does, it will spell catastrophe. The realm will fall," Nolan states.

My insides burn with anger, a fiery and weighty sensation, causing me to tightly clench my fists. Maxon turns his body toward me, his eyes full of curiosity, obviously sensing my emotions.

'WHO?' I demand down the bond.

"Sorry, Stóirín. We think that your arrival may have been felt by the Shadoweaver."

"Well, shit, that sounds ominous." I twist the tulle of my skirt in my fingers. Isn't that what Tristan said when he saw the dealings?

"If she is the one in the prophecy and this is a sign the Shadoweaver has awoken, then we need to move quickly," Nolan urges.

"First things first. Raiden and I, along with some of my men, are going to go to the north village of Escalle to see what damage has been done, to see if we can find any clues of what we're dealing with. We need to be sure, and I won't believe anything unless I see it for myself."

Alarm shoots through me, and I step forward at the same time as Nolan questions, "Are you sure that's wise?"

"What about your coronation?!" Queen Lavina shrieks.

"I'm going with you," I add.

Maxon shakes his head. "This is important. Coronation can wait until I return." Then, turning to me, he sighs heavily, and I know what's coming. "You need to stay here where it's safe."

"Maxon, you cannot keep putting this off. The people are waiting," the queen scolds.

Maxon raises his hands in a placating manner. "I know they are waiting, but this is more important."

Queen Lavina narrows her eyes and the two seem to have a silent conversation. Finally, Queen Lavina relents and shakes her head.

"Fine." She sighs, exasperated. "Go do what you must, but the moment you return, we need to give the people what they want, Maxon."

Maxon bows deeply, a twinkle in his eye as he straightens up. "Didn't think you'd be so eager to be rid of the crown, Aunt Livy."

Queen Lavina's smile lights up the room, a rare sight that leaves me in awe. I think this is the first time I've seen her smile, and it brightens up her entire face. The corners of her lips curl upward, revealing a warmth I didn't expect. As I observe her, a sense of reassurance washes over me, as if I've misjudged her all along. It's clear now that she genuinely cares for her people and has a deep affection for Maxon.

"It was never my crown," she answers softly.

Smiling, I look around the room. Nolan is gone.

Chapter Forty-One

Everly

Kian and Tristan have been ordered to stay behind and guard me. I'm pissed to have been left behind, but dress in the battle gear Zaria had made for me. I am so glad to no longer be in men's clothes. These pants are molded to my legs and have special clips for my knives. The black long-sleeved shirt is loose, but the black corset that laces over the top of it is fitted. I turn to the mirror and smile as I make quick work of braiding my hair. By the time I'm finished, my arms are aching. My hair has grown at least a few inches since being here, and it's so much thicker.

I run my hands down my body and twist left and right, taking in my reflection. I look badass.

At the sound of my whistle, Nymeria and Anika abandon their spots on the daybed out on the balcony and eagerly trot over to me. The wolves are incredibly tall, their heads easily reaching my chest, making it effortless for me to nuzzle their necks.

"Ready?" I ask them.

Silently, they head toward the door, and I shadow their movements, stepping out into the hall. Tristan and Kian take me in, their eyes widening in surprise.

"Well shit, princess. You look like a warrior," Kian remarks.

I swallow roughly and pull my shoulders back. "It's time to train."

"Are you sure?" Tristan eyes me incredulously.

"Of course."

The two share a knowing look before giving me a nod. Feeling more confident than I probably should, I lead the way outside toward the training arena. It's mostly empty, with only a handful of soldiers sparring. A few cast cautionary looks my way, their eyes probing and assessing. The mate mark on the side of my face burns with their attention, and I release a sigh.

Nix comes flying over, a trail of glitter following in her wake. "I heard you were awake!"

"Nix!" I grin.

"Wow, look at you," she says, letting out a low whistle. "Sorry I've been MIA. Nero had me working on something with Silver."

"Where is Nero now?" Tristan inquires.

"Human realm. Silly Puca went and swore to protect the Daughter of Light. He was only supposed to check on her for a close friend, apparently, but then he got attached."

My mouth falls open in disbelief. "Wait, Nero can go to the human realm? I thought the gate was closed?"

Nix smiles, and the corners of her mouth curl up in an unsettling way. "Nero doesn't need a gate. Neither does Silver."

Umm, okay. I wish I knew that information earlier. "Who is the Daughter of Light?"

Nix shrugs. "Some goddess who is about to end some long-winded feud of bad blood between her family and another god."

I blink several times at her cavalier tone. "How can you talk about something like that so calmly?"

"No skin off my nose." Nix grins at me, putting those sharp teeth on full display.

"Right . . . " I give her a long look.

How can the fae be so . . . unaffected?

Then I remember Nix's words from when we first met: *Us fae are selfish, spiteful, manipulative, and easily offended creatures.*

Tristan starts walking off, calling over his shoulder. "Come on. You wanted to train. Let's train."

"Okay." I nod.

Kian bumps my shoulder with his and grins. "I'll keep your mind so busy you won't even think of the prince once, and you'll be too exhausted afterward."

I roll my eyes at him and take off to do my laps, leaving him to catch up.

We drill hand to hand combat techniques for what feels like hours, sweat pouring off us as we move across the mat. Kian's voice is a constant stream of guidance, pushing me to refine my skills.

Finally, he signals a break, and I collapse onto a nearby bench, gasping for air. Tristan's grizzly face breaks into a rare smile. "You're getting there, princess. Remember, it's not about how hard you hit; it's about how well you can control the fight."

"Do you have to call me that?" I pant.

I don't need *both* of them calling me princess.

"Of course not. I could call you consort."

Kian shoves a bottle of water in my face, and I gratefully take it, glaring at Tristan. "Do not call me that."

"Princess it is."

Does he always have to be such a pain in the ass?

Tristan's violet eyes sparkle, reflecting the light as he gently brushes a few strands of his dark hair away from his face. His beard is neatly trimmed, and it is evident that he had a restful night's sleep, as the once-present dark circles under his eyes have completely vanished.

"Ready for actual swords today?" Kian asks.

I jolt, sitting up straight. "Really?"

"I need to see if you can handle the weight and keep your balance."

Tristan snickers, the sound infectious, light-hearted. I turned to give him the stink eye, but am unable to stop my smile. It's good to see him relaxed for a change.

"What's so funny?" I question.

"Nothing," he replies, leaning back against the stand and crossing his arms. "This is just going to be fun to watch. And we won't have to worry about you going anywhere for the next couple of days, because I doubt you'll be able to move."

I huff in annoyance, and Nix chuckles. "You'll be fine. Zaria has a special tonic for your bath."

"Don't ruin my fun, fairy," Tristan adds.

Nix pokes her tongue out at him, and I shake my head, standing on weak legs.

Kian grins as he looks down at my legs. "You good?"

"Totally."

Kian looks like he doesn't believe me, but I just need to get moving again. Passing me a sword, he moves away and waits for me to follow. My hands instinctively adjust their grip, adapting to the weight they now bear. It was much different from the wooden swords we had been using.

"Ready?" he asks.

I give a nod, expecting him to ease me in, but he doesn't. Kian rushes me immediately. Alarmed, I instinctively recoil as his sword swings toward me, the sharp sound of metal cutting through the air. I barely manage to evade the first attack when he swings again, and I react just in time to block his attack.

Kian shakes his head, a soft sigh escaping his lips. "Faster."

Determination fills my veins, and I narrow my eyes, taking a deep breath. We both step forward simultaneously, swords clashing. The force of the impact jars my arms, and I try not to wince. We both pivot away and immediately lunge at the same time coming face to face, this time our swords lock together.

"Good. Again." Kian steps away.

The sun bears down on us, casting long shadows that dance with every movement. Beads of sweat trickle down my forehead, stinging my eyes, but I can't afford to blink. Kian isn't letting me catch my breath.

With a swift parry, I deflect his strike; the vibrations coursing through my arms. My muscles scream in protest as we circle each other.

I am hell-bent on getting stronger; I know I need to. It seems no matter how hard I try, I can't shake the image from yesterday's vision from my mind, and it's making me feel sick to my stomach. I know, deep down, a darkness lies on the horizon, and it's coming for me. For all of us.

"Concentrate!" Tristan barks.

"Shut up!" I snap.

I focus on Kian, watching for the slightest opening. Kian steps forward, and I counter with a quick sidestep, narrowly avoiding the deadly edge of his blade. The world seems to slow as I step forward, my sword slicing through the air with perfect precision, but he blocks with lightning reflexes.

"Impressive." He gives me a wink.

We clash again and again, each strike fueled by adrenaline. My breath comes in ragged gasps, and my arms tremble from the relentless exertion. But I can't back down. Not now.

I take deliberate steps sideways, my sword held in front as we circle each other. Kian winks at me again, his calm demeanor still there, though I can make out the sheen of sweat on his forehead, which fills me with a small sense of satisfaction.

Kian deftly feints to the left, tricking me as he swiftly moves from the right, expertly sweeping my feet from under me. The impact of hitting the dirt sends a rush of air escaping my lungs, leaving me momentarily breathless. With a determined glare, I stare at Kian, his sword poised at my throat. The scent of the earth lingers in the air, mixing with the faint smell of sweat.

With a confident smile, Kian sheaths his sword, his dimples adding charm to his expression. "That was amazing. I didn't know you had it in you."

I grunt, letting go of my sword and closing my eyes. My chest heaves with exhaustion, and my body throbs with pain as I blink up at the sky.

Kian looks down at me, his body casting a shadow over me. "You okay down there?"

"Peachy."

Nix flies over, landing on his shoulder. "I don't think a tonic bath is going to cut it."

Kian chuckles playfully and holds a handout for me.

I push it away. "Can't. Not yet."

Tristan walks over and slaps Kian on the back. "You're an excellent teacher."

"Not just a pretty face, eh?"

Tristan shakes his head and stares down at me, curiosity shining in his periwinkle eyes. "You did well. I'm surprised. Are you sure this is your first time with a sword?"

I draw in a deep breath and slowly let it out, my hands resting at my sides. I'm about to say, *of course*, when a memory pops into my mind. It was Valric going through defense maneuvers with me; I was only four or five. My father had gifted me a sword for my birthday, and I wanted to learn.

The sudden clicking sound startles me, and I instinctively blink. Kian is squatting down, snapping his fingers in front of my face.

"There you are," he sighs.

"Back it up." With a forceful shove, I push him away and fight against the weight that keeps me down as I struggle to sit up. "I'm good. Something from my past just came back to me."

"What was it?" Nix floats down to land on my knee as I cross my legs.

"My paladin. Valric. He was teaching me how to use defense moves with a sword. So, answering your question, no, this wasn't my first time with a sword."

Tristan blinks, his expression frozen somewhere between disbelief and awe. "Your paladin was Valric?"

"Umm . . . maybe?"

Nymeria and Anika make their way over, nudging me back and forth. I groan, too drained to protest, my limbs heavy and unresponsive. The idea of moving even a fraction more is unbearable. I'm too scared to even try to lift my arms. "I think I'll just sleep out here tonight."

"Oh, no you don't," Tristan grumbles, rolling his eyes before crouching down. Before I can protest, he loops his arms around me and hauls me up, setting me unceremoniously on my feet. The world tilts, my legs threatening to give out.

"You need to walk it off," he insists, keeping a firm grip around my waist to steady me.

"Easy for you to say," I grumble, barely able to keep my head from lolling to the side.

Nix suddenly appears in front of me, her face so close I nearly flinch. She studies me for a moment, then nods as if making a mental note.

"I'll let Zaria know to prepare the bath."

Before I can thank her, she's gone. Tristan's arm is still around my waist, keeping me steady on my feet, my arm around his shoulders.

Chapter Forty-Two

Everly

Zaria's brown eyes take me in, and she bursts out laughing before covering her mouth, her eyes widening in shock. "I apologize. I didn't mean to laugh, but . . . " she trails off.

I attempt to wave her off, but my arms are like limp noodles. "It's fine. I know exactly how I'm feeling, so I'm sure I look much worse."

"Nix told me to get a bath ready for you, and I've added the tonics to help with restoring energy and muscle recovery."

Kian's attention bounces around the group. "I think you're in excellent hands. I'm going to clean up myself."

"She will manage without you for a while," Tristan retorts sarcastically.

Ignoring them, I shuffle toward the bathroom.

"Do you need help?" Zaria calls out, but I wave her off.

"I'll be outside," I hear Tristan say.

"I'm going to shower," Kian adds.

"Well, I'm going to be eating." Nix flies for the cart of food. "I love Rayna's baking."

"It's not for you. It's Everly's!" Zaria snaps.

I reach the bathroom and gently close the door, shutting out the noise of the outside world. A heavy sigh escapes my lips, my body feels drained and weary. Not to mention, the constant presence of the others has left me utterly exhausted. My social battery is running on empty, desperately in need of recharging. The only company I crave is Maxon's. He has only been gone a day, but I already ache for the way his eyes sparkle with mischief, and his smirk lights up my insides.

With a sigh, I push away from the door, stepping over to the bath. The delicate aroma of lavender and oranges permeates the bathroom, soothing my senses. Slowly, I peel off my clothes, my trembling muscles protesting with each movement.

I sink into the inviting warmth of the water, feeling its comforting embrace seep into my weary muscles. The sweet smells rising from the water combine in a fragrant symphony that dances around me. With a gentle sigh, I surrender to the tranquility, closing my eyes and reclining, allowing my head to find solace and respite. As I lay there, I run my hands over my arms, washing away any dust and dirt that clings to me. Sinking a little deeper into the water, I feel a sense of weightlessness as I let out a soft moan. If only Maxon were here to enjoy this moment with me.

I desperately want to know what's happening. It's why I kept myself busy training all day. I'd do my head in worrying otherwise.

Who is this elusive Shadoweaver that whispers fear into the hearts of all who hear his name?

As I lie here longer, my eyes drift shut, a wave of sleepiness making my limbs feel heavy. A cool breeze washes over me, and I notice a change in the air temperature. I furrow my brows and sink deeper into the water. Oddly, there is no window in the bathroom, ruling out the possibility of a breeze. Abruptly, my eyes flicker open, and my heart pounds fiercely in my chest. A strange awareness prickles at the edge of my senses, and before I can fully process it, I find myself locking eyes with a pair of piercing violet-blue orbs.

A stranger. Inside my bathroom.

A scream rips from my throat before I can stop it, pure instinct taking over as panic surges through my veins. I fling my hands up, scrambling backward in the tub, but my body acts on something far more primal—something unfamiliar yet terrifyingly natural. The water moves. It rises in an instant, a shimmering barrier forming between us as if answering some silent command I never issued. The intruder takes a sharp step back, clearly startled, but I barely register it over the sheer force of adrenaline flooding my system. The bathroom door bangs open, and Zaria bursts in, her face going slack in shock. Her lips move, shouting something, but I can't hear her over the furious pounding in my ears. Anger quickly overtakes the initial terror, a fire igniting inside me. I snatch a towel from the side, wrapping it hastily around myself as Tristan and Nix shove their way in behind Zaria. Their gazes immediately lock onto the shimmering wall of water still hanging in the air, separating me from the intruder. I tighten my grip on the towel, my breathing ragged. My entire body is trembling—not just from fear but from the power still humming in the air around me. I don't know how, but I can feel it. Feel the magic woven through the liquid barrier, the way it bends and shifts, waiting.

My gaze snaps to the figure on the other side.

"Who the hell are you?" I snap, my voice sharp, unyielding.

The stranger tilts their head slightly, their face partially obscured by the rippling distortion of the water. There's something unnerving about the way their gaze latches onto me—not just watching, but studying. Calculating.

A sudden tension coils in my muscles. I take a menacing step forward, my fingers curling into fists at my sides. Was it him who moved the water? Or was it me?

I don't know. And that terrifies me.

Tristan moves beside me, close but not touching, his presence solid and grounding. His voice is low, steady, but edged with something sharp.

"That, princess, is an intruder. The Seelie Prince, to be precise."

His words land like a punch to the gut.

The Seelie Prince.

A shiver runs down my spine as I inhale sharply, my pulse thundering. How the hell was he able to get in here?

"Prince Maxon will have your head for being in here with his mate!" Tristan yells over the noise of the water.

Reaching out with my mind, I am able to trace the intricate threads of magic, revealing that it's my power that controls the water. Carefully, I reclaim the magic, observing how the water level steadily decreases before my eyes.

"The prince isn't here, and I was hoping to be gone with the druid before he found out, but it seems I was ill-informed of her current state of progression and mating status."

As the water disperses, the seelie prince comes into view, his appearance becoming clear. His long, silvery hair was intricately braided away from his face, and he wears a cold, calculated expression. Surprisingly, his presence exudes a more sinister aura than the Outcasts I encountered upon my arrival.

"How did you know Maxon wasn't here?" I command, crossing my arms over my chest.

"Same way I knew what room you were in," he smirks.

Irritation bubbles up inside of me, causing my face to grow flushed with anger, and a strong desire wells up within me to wipe that arrogant smirk from his face. Nix lands on my shoulder, and I can feel the weight of her hand gripping my wet hair.

"You should leave while you can," she warns calmly.

Leave?

"Like hell!" I hiss.

No, we need to find out who is feeding him information. Maxon will want to know.

"Everly," Nix whispers.

"No. You should stay and wait for Maxon to return." I am fuming. "Better yet, let me make you comfortable."

The storm inside me rages, each thunderous heartbeat echoing the intensity of my emotions. Zaria and Tristan are caught off guard as vines suddenly erupt from the open door behind us, knocking them off balance in their pursuit of the seelie prince. With an eye roll, he produces a sword, slicing at the vines, but the tingle of magic in my blood grows stronger and the vines grow again. His eyes dart to mine in shock, and I can see the disbelief reflected in his expression, if only for a second. Then he waves a hand in the air, and a shimmering ripple distorts the atmosphere. Tristan lets out a loud curse and races toward him, just as the prince steps through and disappears.

"Fuck!" Tristan bellows, running a frustrated hand through his hair.

Zaria stands off to the side, her usually radiant brown skin now appearing pale and her face filled with concern.

I storm into the bedroom, my frustration crackling around me like an oncoming storm. My hands move on their own, yanking open the wardrobe with a sharp tug. I don't bother to sift through the options—just rip a handful of clothes free and toss them onto the bed.

Without a second thought, I drop the towel, caring little for modesty. My skin is still damp from the bath, droplets trailing down my back as I step into a pair of tight, black breeches, the fabric hugging my legs like a second skin. Practical. Unyielding. Exactly what I need right now.

Next, I reach for the gorgeous blue long-sleeved dress I had Zaria make for me. The deep sapphire fabric gleams under the candlelight, deceptively delicate in appearance but designed for more than just beauty. Secret slits run up both sides, hidden so well they'd never be noticed—until I needed them. I pull it over my head, the soft material sliding over my body like liquid silk. Before I can struggle with the laces at the back, Zaria is there, moving quickly. Her fingers work with practiced ease, tightening the fabric until it hugs my curves, securing everything firmly in place.

I let out a sharp exhale, rolling my shoulders as irritation and annoyance **swirl** around me, thick and oppressive. My jaw clenches, my eyes burning with barely restrained fury as I turn to face them.

"How did he get into the castle?"

The words lash out like a whip, cutting through the silence. Because someone let him in. And I was going to find out who.

"Someone would have had to let him in, but it could only be someone of high stature," Tristan replies stiffly.

I storm over to where I keep the dagger Raiden gifted me and a few knives and quickly strap them on; the dagger at my back and two knives at my thigh.

"I want the traitor found," I snarl, not recognizing my own voice.

I slip on my boots, the familiar weight grounding me as I stand tall. Zaria and Tristan both stare at me oddly.

"What?" I question.

Zaria is the first to respond, shaking her head. "Nothing."

"Just what are you going to do? You look like you're dressing for a fight."

"We have a traitor in the castle, one who let in the enemy. They need to be found."

"Maxon has it under control. Nix has been spying on the nobles and Zaria has–"

I blink, scanning the area. "Where is Nix?" I interrupt.

Glancing around, Zaria and Tristan frown.

Zaria's face pales. "I don't know," she replies uneasily.

"Why would she tell the seelie prince to leave before it was too late?"

Zaria looks off to the side. "If he was caught here in the castle. It would be a declaration of war."

Understanding dawns, no one wants that war is the last thing anyone wants.

"I'm going looking for the traitor. Kian should be back by now . . ."

"Yes, he should." Tristan sighs. "I need to inform the queen immediately of what just happened."

My fists clench tightly, the knuckles turning white as anger courses through my veins. The exhaustion that weighed me down earlier evaporates, replaced by a renewed energy that propels me forward. I want to take action. My muscles tense, coiling like a predator ready to strike, as steely determination settles deep within my bones. I will find this traitor and deliver them to Maxon. Opening the door to the hall, I feel Tristan's palm forcefully land on it, closing it with a heavy thud before I can step foot outside.

"What are you doing?"

"Stopping you."

"No shit. Why?"

Tristan steps back and raises his palms when Nymeria and Anika approach, their heads lowered and fangs bared.

"Just let me inform the queen first, and when Kian gets here–"

"Argh!" I yell in annoyance, cutting him off.

"I understand your frustration."

I let out a harsh laugh. "Oh, did you open your eyes during a relaxing bath to find a stranger hovering over you?"

Tristan rubs the back of his neck. "No, but–"

"But nothing! I'm going to find the answers we need, and I won't be discrete."

The way I'm acting should startle me. I don't know where this person has come from. This is very unlike me. I typically shy away from conflict, but my personal space was invaded while I was in a vulnerable state, and a surge of instincts has overwhelmed me.

"Look, we need to be slow and strategic, like a mushroom."

His words are enough to give me pause, and I glare at him in confusion. "What?"

'Stóirín?'

'Maxon?'

'What's wrong? I can feel your emotions from miles away.'

I give Tristan a hard stare and walk off toward the balcony. *'We had an intruder in the castle.'*

Maxon's fury ignites my own, but I can also sense a tinge of alarm race through him.

'Who? Are you okay?'

'I'm fine. I promise.' I hesitate, not wanting to cause him any further distress.

I literally feel Maxon's growl in my chest.

'Tell me, Stóirín.'

'The seelie prince found his way into my chambers.'

'What?' Maxon's voice in my head is calm, but the emotions hammering my senses are anything but.

'Everything is fine.'

'Everything is not fine. I won't be back until tomorrow.'

Nymeria and Anika come to sit next to me as I peer out over the gardens below.

'I miss you,' I whisper.

'I miss you too, Storin.'

A flicker of movement catches my attention in the garden below. "What is that?"

Tristan and Zaria approach the balcony.

"Where?" Tristan asks.

I point to where I thought I saw the flash of movement, but nothing is there. With a sigh I push off the stone ledge and make my way back inside just as the doors to my chamber open and Kian appears.

He looks at each of us in turn, running a hand over his still-wet hair, looking almost sheepish.

"What's with the expressions? And why are you dressed in that?" he asks, concern in his voice.

"There is a traitor in the castle," Tristan answers for me.

Kian frowns. "We know that. Maxon has had Nix and Zaria spying since we returned from the Evergreens."

"Well, spying isn't working!" I snap, magic whipping from my body creating a wave of tension in the air.

"Prince Alivar was here," Tristan explains.

"Here? As in, this room?"

I grunt, plonking myself down on the sofa. "Fucker saw me naked."

Kian's eyes widen and he snaps his head to Tristan. "What the fuck, man?"

"I didn't know he could portal into the bathroom. Did you?"

"The bathroom!? Maxon is going to kill us." Kian groans, tipping his head back.

I scowl at Kian. "Where were you?"

Kian stops in his tracks. "Me?"

"Yes. Your room is down the hall, and that was an awfully long shower. Not saying you can't take your time, but you seemed nervous when you walked in," I state.

"I uhh . . . was occupied."

"Doing what?"

Kian looks to Tristan pleadingly, and I glance between the two of them. Tristan lets out an exasperated sigh. "He was relieving some tension with a lady."

"Oh." My eyebrows raise, then it really clicks. "Oh . . . "

Well, now, I feel stupid.

"Madeline cornered me, and–"

My eyes snap up, anger burning in the pit of my stomach and something like betrayal stings my insides. "Madeline?"

"Yes." Kian looks at Tristan and Zaria, puzzled.

I don't know why, but a feeling of dread or worry gnaws at my insides. Actually, I know why. Madeline is a power hungry, manipulative bitch. I know it. They know it. She locked me up and tried to hurt me when I had done nothing to her. Though, even she couldn't have known what locking me in a cupboard would do. She is cruel and cold. How could he want to sleep with her? Didn't he himself say she is a snake?

"I see your face. It wasn't like that. It was purely transactional."

"Do you think she was keeping you distracted?" Zaria pipes up.

Is Madeline the traitor?

Kian opens his mouth and closes it, but Tristan gestures for him to continue.

"I don't know. She has never shown an interest in me before, and she did seem pushy."

My pulse quickens, and I leap to my feet. "She could be the traitor. We need to find her."

Tristan appears in front of me. "Hold your horses. Let's think about this. I need to speak with Nolan and the queen first before we approach Madeline."

"Why?"

"Because if it is her, then we will need to go about this in the right way."

Frustration wells up, and I can feel tears building in my eyes, making my nose burn. Nymeria and Anika circle around me and gently nudge me back toward the sofa. I drop down and rest my head in my hands.

"This sucks."

"Here, this will help you relax," Zaria offers, handing me a cup of herbal tea.

I bring it to my nose and sniff it.

"One of us will stay in here with you. Alivar has already portalled in once, nothing is stopping him from trying again."

"Well, he saw I was mated, and he can't claim me, so he should leave me alone, right?" I reply, taking a sip.

"Not necessarily. The mating bond can be broken, or there are ways around it. He could kill Maxon, though that would prove extremely difficult."

"He wouldn't though, right?" By the time the words are out, my heart is thundering in my chest.

"No, he wouldn't do that," Kian rushes to reassure me.

Tristan folds his arms. "The fact you are mated is only a hurdle, not a roadblock."

"Well, that's just great, isn't it?" I reply, throwing my hands in the air.

"No, I don't know if you were listening, but it is terrible." Tristan eyes me as if I were a little crazy.

"I was being sarcastic, you douche."

"Okay, I think Everly needs rest. Why don't you two head out?" Zaria steps between us.

"That's fine. I'm going to find Nolan and see if I can get in to see the queen." Tristan squeezes my shoulder as he passes.

"Fine, but I'm sleeping in these clothes," I reply.

“I will stay right here.” Kian plonks down on the sofa.

“Whatever,” I grumble.

Chapter Forty-Three

Maxon

I slam my fist into the closest tree, feeling the flames dance along my skin as my fury overpowers my emotions.

"That fucker!" I bellow, my voice echoing around the clearing.

I need to get back to the castle. I should never have left Everly behind. The weight of my decision presses on me like a stone in my chest. I was aware that Alivar had a spy within the castle's walls, but the betrayal stings more sharply than I could have anticipated. How could they allow him access, jeopardizing the safety of everyone within?

Fury surges through me, a seething anger that threatens to consume my soul. The mere thought of someone in the castle aiding Alivar in his nefarious plans fuels my desire for vengeance. Whoever betrayed me will pay a heavy price, and the castle's halls will echo with their cries for mercy.

The thought of Alivar's failed attempt to take Everly flashes in my mind, mingling with the emotions I felt from her. Relief blends with the rage, a strange concoction of emotions.

I can't comprehend why he failed in his attempts to take her, but the respite from imminent danger to Everly brings at least a momentary calm.

The bond with Everly is already growing stronger, connecting us on a profound level, and the mere thought of her in danger has sent me spiraling into a maelstrom of fear and protectiveness.

I lean against the tree, my chest heaving, and close my eyes, taking several deep breaths in an attempt to quell the storm within. The scent of damp earth and distant rain calms my senses as I focus on the rhythm of my breathing.

With each inhale and exhale, I gather the fragments of my composure. With my determination solidified, a steely resolve settles over me. The traitor in our midst will face justice, and Everly will be protected at all costs.

I push off the tree, my steps purposeful, ready to confront all that threatens to engulf us. I can sense the intensity of my men's stares as I walk back and forth in the small clearing.

We are camped just outside of Escalle. The town lies in ruins as survivors recount the terrifying events. According to their descriptions, a horde of deadlings descended upon them, while an army of dark figures ominously stood on the distant horizon, observing the chaos. All witnesses recount seeing shadows swirling and weaving around the revenants as they stood guard, a silent presence.

The most disturbing part is the dark beast they've described, with glowing ruby red eyes, pacing among the army. Without a doubt, the Shadoweaver has awakened, and its pet is lurking in our realm, searching for something. But just because the Shadoweaver is awake, doesn't mean he has been freed from his prison.

"What is it?" Raiden's voice is urgent as he makes his way over.

"Fucking Alivar tried to take Everly tonight."

Raiden's brows slam down, his wings flaring outward. "How do you know that? I didn't see a messenger."

"Everly told me."

"You can mind speak over this distance?" His voice is incredulous.

"Looks like it. I could sense her heightened emotions and was able to hold the connection for a brief time."

"Well, shit. That will come in handy."

"Someone allowed him access to the fucking castle, Raiden!"

Raiden's eyes harden. "And we will find them."

"I'm heading back." I stalk over Storm.

"We only arrived a few hours ago!" Raiden snaps, following me.

"I don't care. I never should have left her behind."

"Don't be a fool."

I spin my face inches from Raiden. "She is my mate."

"We need to get to the bottom of what happened here."

"We know what happened here," I growl.

Raiden lets out a deep sigh and runs his hand through his hair, right between his horns.

"I will gather the men and explain what has happened."

"Thanks. I will go and talk to the villagers. We will leave half the soldiers here to help the survivors in any way they can. These men will provide necessary aid such as medical assistance, distributing food and water, and assisting with search and rescue efforts. They will also help in setting up temporary shelters and providing emotional support to those affected by the disaster. They are to ensure the safety and well-being of the survivors until we can send more help. I want to ride full speed all night, so only those who can keep up are to come."

Raiden nods in agreement and turns, his footsteps crunching on the forest floor as he makes his way over to the campsite to gather the soldiers.

Chapter Forty-Four

Everly

Restless, I shift in bed. Kian's currently sprawled lazily on the sofa, the gentle sound of his snores filling the room. I punch my pillow a few times and flop back down. Nymeria and Anika are curled up at the end of the bed, fast asleep. Seeing everyone else sleeping so peacefully only intensifies my frustration.

Rolling over, I wince as the two knives on my thigh dig awkwardly into my leg. This isn't working. The tea may have relaxed me, but I can't get comfortable. Maxon's absence had left a void, a longing for his strong arms to envelop me in their embrace.

Climbing from the bed as quietly as I can, I tiptoe toward the secret passage, doing my best not to disturb either the wolves or Kian. Without looking back, I hold my breath as I press the small stone button on the wall. The door slides open and I make my way toward Maxon's room in the dark. The only sound to be heard is my breathing and the soft click of my boot on the stone floor. My fingers trace the wall as I walk, the stone smooth and cool beneath my hand. I find the lever in the dark and pull. The moment the door slides open, I'm greeted by Maxon's unmistakable scent.

For the first time since he left yesterday, I feel at peace. Without bothering to remove my boots, I crawl onto the bed and collapse. The softness of the bed cushions me, providing a comfort I've been seeking. Within seconds, my eyelids grow heavy, weighed down by the fatigue that has accumulated throughout the previous day. The gentle rhythm of my breath matches the peaceful silence in the room. I feel the outside world slowly fading away as my body sinks deeper into relaxation. Thoughts and worries dissolve into the abyss of my subconscious, replaced by a blissful stillness. I pull the blanket up to my chin, the warmth of it adding to the sense of comfort, lulling me further into a state of blissful surrender. Tendrils of sleep wrap around my mind, gently pulling me toward its realm. The world around me becomes distant and blurry as my consciousness drifts away, succumbing to the irresistible pull of slumber.

'Come to me . . . '

With a jolt, I wake to find myself standing amidst the dense, eerie darkness of the forest, where shadows dance and whisper. Slowly, I pivot. The unsettling silence is broken only by the rustling of leaves and the distant hoot of an owl. An icy shiver runs down my spine, my heart pounding in my chest, as I realize I am still clad in the same clothes I fell asleep in—a chilling confirmation that I am trapped in a nightmarish realm.

'Come to me, Everly . . . '

The piercing glow of those red eyes, haunting me since my first night in these woods, flicker and shift around me.

"Everly!" a familiar voice yells from somewhere far away.

The voice sounds so real.

I watch the horrible black beast approach, its ruby red eyes glowing in the darkness, its hot breath misting in front of it. I tremble in fear, the blood freezing in my veins.

'Everly . . . ' the voice sings followed by a chuckle.

"Everly, wake up!"

I shoot up in bed, my eyes scanning the room frantically. Maxon's room. Tristan and Kian are standing over me, concern lining their faces. The room is darker than normal, vines covering the windows and doors to the balcony. One vine trembles as it snakes over the sheets toward me, wrapping around my wrist as if to soothe me.

"I'm okay," I mumble, trying to adjust to being woken so suddenly. Though I'm glad I'm not facing that hellish beast again. "It was just a nightmare."

My voice wavers slightly, and I repeat it again, not sure if I'm trying to convince them or me. Kian and Tristan exchange worried glances.

I scrub my hands over my face, causing the vines that have wrapped around my wrist to loosen their grip. As the tingling sensation of magic slowly fades away, a sense of relief washes over me. The emerald green leaves that have entangled the balcony within their thorny embrace now begin to recede. Reflecting on the experience, I realize how terrifying that dream was. My heart is pounding so hard in my chest, it seems like it's about to burst free. The lingering fear has engraved itself into my mind, sending shivers down my spine. It feels as though the nightmare has seeped into reality, leaving me feeling utterly vulnerable and on edge.

"I spoke to the queen last night, and she is currently questioning Madeline. We will know soon enough if she is the traitor," Tristan's voice breaks through my inner thoughts.

I swing my legs from the bed and stand. I have an overwhelming desire to be there, to lock eyes with her and see it for myself. The countless years of being mistreated and bullied in foster care left a lasting impact. I have finally reached a point where I refuse to let anyone think they can treat others badly without facing the repercussions.

"Then let's go."

With each step I take toward the door, my footsteps resonate with a resounding echo, a declaration of my unwavering commitment to dealing with the traitor. The world around me fades into insignificance as my focus sharpens, honing in on the task at hand. Nothing else matters now except finding the one responsible for Maxon's betrayal.

Before I can reach the door, sounds erupt in the halls, and some screams. I halt and suddenly Kian and Tristan grab me, dragging me to the door, both drawing their swords.

The piercing screams resonate through the hall, causing a surge of adrenaline as I try to free myself.

"We have to help!" I yell.

Kian's eyes dart between me and Tristan, and a silent understanding passes between them. A sense of unease hangs in the air, making it hard to breathe.

"Your safety comes first," Tristan argues.

Shock has my mouth dropping open in protest. "No. We need to see what's happening."

"We will go. You stay here."

"What? No. I can help."

"We are wasting time!" Kian snaps his eyes darting toward the door.

"You will wait here." Tristan growls a second before Kian lifts me.

"Let me go, Kian!"

"This is for your own safety."

Before I can comprehend what he is planning, Kian swiftly places me in the wardrobe. My mind slows down, and it takes me a moment to gather my wits. Before I can even utter a word of protest, they swiftly close the door, trapping me inside and filling me with sheer terror. I manage to push myself onto my knees, desperately pounding on the door. Through the narrow crack, I catch a glimpse of Kian securing something around the handles, and then both he and Tristan exit the room, leaving me behind in a state of confusion and fear.

A surge of adrenaline courses through me, causing my heart to race uncontrollably. Betrayal slices through my chest at how easily they left me in here. My stomach churns, and spots begin to dance before my eyes. Digging my nails into the door, I drop my head, resting it on the wooden surface.

Why? Why would they do this?

I needed to get out.

"Please . . . " I whisper into the dark.

I can feel tears begin to roll down my face, and I know I need to be stronger than this. They will come back. They weren't like my foster brother. But still I desperately try to push on the doors, but they only budge a tiny bit, held closed by whatever they have tied them shut with. I try calling out, but my voice emerges as a raspy wheeze, fear clogging my throat. I bang my fists on the doors, resting my head on the cool, smooth surface.

Shouts can still be heard from outside, and I know something is wrong. A knot tightens in my stomach, a primal instinct warning me that danger lurks just beyond.

Is this Madeline's doing? Alivar?

My chest squeezes painfully as I only manage to draw in the smallest amount of air. I lean all my weight against the doors and begin whispering the lullaby my mother sang to me as a child, my eyes falling closed.

I don't know how much time has passed before the doors are suddenly ripped open, and I fall forward. My heart stalls as I brace for the impact, but strong, secure arms wrap around me, catching me as I fall. The relief that consumes me is instantaneous, and I find myself unable to suppress the sobs that emerge from deep within my chest. Maxon's arms spasm around me, and his resounding growl moves over my skin.

"Shit!" Raiden curses, his voice sounding furious. "Who the fuck put her in there?!" he bellows.

I don't lift my head from where I've buried it in Maxon's neck as he rocks me. I can sense his confusion at my reaction, but only Raiden knows of my fear.

Maxon's large palm smooths over the back of my head as he carries me over to the sofa and takes a seat with me in his lap.

"Stóirín?" he whispers, his deep, rough voice full of emotion.

I can't sense his emotions right now. My own are front and center, overriding everything else, embarrassment now replacing the fear I was trying to overcome moments ago.

The sound of Kian's voice reaches my ears. "I just needed her to stay put and not leave the room while we checked out what was happening. I didn't think she'd react like that."

"You should never lock someone up unless it's in the dungeons for a fucking crime. That's where I should send you two for the shit you just pulled. Everly cannot be locked up!" Raiden yells, the walls seeming to tremble with his anger.

"Stóirín, talk to me."

I know I need to explain myself, but now it feels incredibly foolish.

"You are not foolish," Maxon growls.

My heart skips a beat, and I pull back enough to meet his gaze. I can feel my eyes are puffy from crying, and wish like anything that I could be rid of this damn fear.

"Seeing you like this breaks me." Maxon leans down, rubbing his nose along mine.

I wrap my arms around him, holding him as tight as I can for several moments before taking a deep breath and turning to face the room. Slowly, I raise my eyes to look over at Raiden. The fury burning in his eyes steals my breath. I push from Maxon's lap and make my way over to him, wrapping my arms around his massive form.

"It's okay," I whisper into his chest.

"It's not," he replies, his voice harsh and gruff. "I should throw them in the dungeons."

"They didn't know."

"I still don't even know," Maxon snarls as he stands.

He's still in his fighting gear, his armor still hugging his frame. He looks stunning, a vision of striking handsomeness that makes me feel like the luckiest woman alive. His features stand out even more thanks to the way his long, dark hair is pulled back in a half-up, half-down style.

Dragging my eyes from him, I face everyone. My hands rub down my pants nervously. "It's silly, really."

"Don't do that," Raiden snaps. "Your fear should not be diminished or trivialized."

"Right." My eyes drop to the floor. "Look, I'm scared of being trapped in small spaces, especially in the dark."

"You have claustrophobia?" Maxon asks gently.

"Yes, it stems from my childhood. My foster brother frequently locked me away, sometimes for long periods of time. He enjoyed–" I pause, feeling the tension in the room grow. Maxon's eyes are glowing, and not just the violet and silver combination I'm used to. Flames swirl and twirl in their depths, creating a mesmerizing spectacle.

His attention snaps to Raiden. "You knew about this?"

"Don't blame him. I asked him not to tell anyone. He was being a good friend," I answer before Raiden can.

Maxon storms over to me, taking my hand in his. "Where does he live?"

"What?"

"This foster brother."

"What? No."

"Tell me."

Instead, I push up on my toes, my lips meeting his in a soft embrace. "It's very sexy of you, wanting to avenge me, but please just forget it. He isn't worth it."

"But you are," Maxon states firmly, his expression softening as he stares down at me. His fingers thread through my hair as he pulls me closer. Butterflies swarm my stomach and I rest my cheek on his chest, listening to his heartbeat as it beats in sync with mine.

"Everly." Kian's tone is low, pleading.

Reluctantly, I shift my body in Maxon's arms, unsure of what to expect.

Kian's eyes hold a deep remorse, a silent admission of regret. "I'm so sorry I put you in there. Had I known, we never would have done that."

"I know," I whisper.

"We are truly remorseful, and are ashamed of our actions," Tristan adds softly.

'Want me to put them in the dungeons for the night?' Maxon offers, his deep voice caressing my mind.

'No, we have more important things to do.'

'You sure? Because I really want to see them in there for upsetting you.'

I squeeze his arm, which is still wrapped around my waist. *'I'm sure.'*

The door to Maxon's chambers bangs open, making all of us jump. Within a second, I am swiftly maneuvered behind Maxon, and his sword is drawn.

"Thank the goddess Aine, you're all here!" Zaria says.

"We've been looking everywhere!" Nix agrees.

As I step out from behind Maxon, my eyes land on a disheveled-looking Zaria, flanked by Nix and Rayna.

"What are you guys doing back already?" Nix asks, glancing from Maxon to Raiden.

"We heard about Alivar," Maxon growls.

"How?" Zaria asks.

"Everly."

"You can mindspeak over that great of a distance?" Tristan breathes, his wide purple eyes bouncing between us.

"Seems like it," Maxon responds.

"That's amazing!" Rayna gushes. "But why haven't you confirmed your mating status? It is obvious from Everly's markings, but I thought this would be something you'd be shouting from the rooftops."

"There has been a lot going on, and I didn't want to overwhelm Everly."

"Right. Your memories returning and the prophecy." Her casually spoken statement catches me off guard, and I blink in surprise.

"Sorry, I told her." Zaria looks contrite.

That's when I notice Zaria is bleeding from a cut on her arm. The vivid crimson of her blood catches my attention, standing out against her sage dress. My eyes zero in on the gash, the sight of it sending a surge of concern through me. It seems I'm not the only one to notice. Raiden, with a determined stride, storms over to her. Zaria's brown eyes widen in surprise as Raiden gently lifts her arm. I can't see his face; all I can see is the tension radiating from his shoulders.

"What happened?" His snarl echoes through the room, startling Rayna and causing her to retreat a step.

"An arrow nicked me. It will heal soon enough."

"It would heal quicker if you could shift," Raiden snaps.

Hurt lines Zaria's eyes, and I can see tears building. A sharp pain pierces my chest at her obvious distress. Maxon's attention shifts to me, as if he can feel the weight of my pain.

Zaria's tail pokes Raiden in the chest twice. "You don't think I know that?"

"I didn't mean–"

"Yes, you did."

Raiden reaches up, cupping her neck, his thumbs grazing her jaw. “I didn’t.”

Then, surprising us all, Raiden leans down, dropping a gentle kiss on her forehead. My heart swoons, and my gaze catches Maxon’s, his lips tipping up in a knowing smirk.

Zaria and Raiden take a step back, creating a space between them. I watch as Zaria makes her way toward me, her hands sending a chill through my skin as she clutches mine. Zaria is never cold. As a shifter, her body heat keeps her warm, even in the coldest of temperatures.

"Are you okay?" Her concern is evident in her voice. “I tried searching for you when you weren’t in your room, but then with the Outcasts and everything, I needed to get to Rayna.”

“There is no need to explain. I was fine. I came through the tunnels to Maxon’s chambers when I couldn’t sleep.”

Raiden snorts. “She was not fine. These fools locked her in a wardrobe to stop her from leaving the room when the commotion started.”

Zaria’s ears twitch, understanding lighting her feline eyes.

“Raiden told you?” I whispered.

“Yes. But I swear I have told no one.”

“It’s fine.”

Tristan steps forward. “Would you stop saying everything is fine? It’s not fine.”

“He is right,” Maxon agrees, his eyes narrowing on him.

Ignoring them, I pull Zaria down next to me on the sofa and tilt her arm so I can see the gash better.

“It’s still weeping blood,” I murmur. “And you’re cold to the touch.”

“I know . . . ” Zaria sighs. “I suspect the arrow was poisoned.”

I reach up, covering the cut with my palm, and close my eyes. The tell-tale tingle sensation of magic moves through me, and I feel my body warm. The room goes completely silent, and I open my eyes to see a green leafy bandage forming around her arm. The glow of the green magic is visible as it swirls around her arm. Moving my hand, I sigh and look up into Zaria's shocked face.

In the reflection of her eyes, I see mine are glowing a vibrant green. The unexpectedness of it takes me by surprise, leaving me momentarily breathless.

"You can heal now?" Kian asks as he comes around the sofa and leans down to inspect Zaria's arm.

"Yes." I shrug.

"Holy shit," Rayna breathes.

Feeling embarrassed and hating being the center of attention, I stand and clear my throat. "What happened out there?"

"Outcasts stormed the castle," Raiden surmises.

"They were looking for something." Rayna takes a seat next to her sister. "Moving from room to room."

"Do we know what?" Kian inquires.

"Nope, but Madeline is dead, and so are a few other nobles." Zaria's words make me jolt.

I'm overwhelmed by a sinking feeling, as if a heavy weight has settled in my chest. Surprisingly, her death fails to bring me any sense of relief. "What?"

"Was she the target?" Tristan asks. "We suspected her of being Alivar's spy."

"Alivar wouldn't kill his spy. They'd be no use to him dead, and I can't see him working with the Outcasts either."

"True, but if the spy was about to be discovered . . . " Kian considers.

Maxon paces. "It just doesn't seem like something he'd do."

I frown, sensing Maxon's inner turmoil. "You seem to act like you know him well."

"We were close as children."

My eyes bulge. "Really?"

"Yes, before the uprising. After your parents were killed, everyone settled on sides. The realm was divided. Seelie, unseelie, Outcasts . . . There was a line drawn, and we weren't to cross it. Like I'd mentioned before, the Druids kept the peace."

"But because of their fear of me and what I could do, they waged war?"

"Exactly."

I see Asrai float up and land on Raiden's head, holding onto one of his horns. Her orbed eyes take in the room before landing on me.

'Madeline wasn't the traitor,' she signs.

My pulse kicks up a notch. *'Do you know who it is?'*

Asrai shakes her head and hides behind Raiden's horn just as the doors to Maxon's chamber bang open for a second time. Nolan strolls in, an air of urgency surrounding him. He draws up short, his eyes widening in surprise, as he catches sight of all of us, his face paling when he spots Maxon.

"Maxon, y- you're back?" he stammers.

We all frown at Nolan as he stands there. "Yes, I only just arrived as the Outcasts were fleeing."

"The queen will want to debrief you about Escalle," he replies, composing himself.

"I will get to her soon enough."

My curiosity gets the better of me. "Why are you here?"

"To summon His Highness."

"But you weren't aware he was back," I note, feeling my heart trip up.

The blood drains from Nolan's face, and he backs up as if realizing his mistake. "Right."

My awareness shifts to Asrai, and I quickly realize that she is visibly shaking.

"It's you," I murmur, my eyes drifting back to Nolan. "You're the traitor."

Unease slithers down my spine, and everyone in the room freezes as they all turn their attention to Nolan. Understanding ripples through the room, followed by disbelief.

One second Maxon is beside me, next he's across the room, his hand around Nolan's throat. "How long?" he demands.

Nolan doesn't answer.

"I'm giving you five seconds to answer me, Nolan."

Chapter Forty-Five

Maxon

My grip tightens around Nolan's neck. He couldn't be the spy. He was my father's best friend and closest confidant. Acting as a father figure, he has mentored me since my parents' passing.

"Nolan?" I growl in warning.

"Maxon, he was there when we made plans to go to the Evergreens. He had ample amount of time to let the Outcasts know what was happening. And with your departure to Escalle . . .'

I shake my head, not wanting to believe her. A tight knot forms in my stomach. The thought of Nolan being the spy sends a rush of betrayal through my veins.

"Tell me it's not you giving information to the Outcasts."

I see Raiden move swiftly, positioning himself to block the exit. There is no response from Nolan as he stares at me. It's true. A surge of rage courses through me, and with a thunderous bellow, I launch Nolan into the air, his body crashing against the wall above the fireplace. Slumped over, Nolan lands on the floor before attempting to push himself back up. My obsidian sword materializes in my hand, and I stalk toward him.

"Answer me, Nolan."

Before Nolan even has a chance to answer, the secret passage opens, and three fae come strolling into the room, drawing up short when they see everyone gathered here. Kian, Tristan, and Raiden all draw their weapons. I let go of Nolan and face the new threat.

"Who are you?" I growl, striding toward them. "And how did you know the passages?"

I place myself between them and the rest of the room. The man in front is frozen, his gaze locked on someone behind me. The two other fae are younger, and shift nervously on their feet. One sees Nolan and pales. A cold sensation washes over me when I realize the leader's stare is fixated on Everly.

"Don't look at her. Look at me!"

The man's violet eyes snap to mine. His long silver hair is messily pulled back, and a scar runs down his cheek, the skin red and puckered. Meaning he was cut using a spelled blade. He wouldn't have been able to heal as he normally would, and judging by the shade of his eyes, he is strong.

"Apologies, Your Highness." The man bows his head. "Seems Nolan misinformed us of your absence."

I lock eyes with Nolan, and he winces under the intensity of my gaze.

"Val, I don't know where she could be–" A woman enters the room behind the three fae, a look of panic on her face as she comes to a stop. It's one of my aunt's lady's maids.

I inhale sharply, my fist tightening around the handle of my obsidian sword. "Someone better tell me what the fuck is going on!" I bellow.

Everly's touch on my back jolts me out of my anger-induced haze, making me aware of her own emotions. I glance over my shoulder at her, and notice the glistening tears in her eyes.

"I know you," she whispers.

"How could you know these fae? They are Outcasts and traitors!" Tristan spits.

Everly moves to my side, her eyes remaining fixed on the man with the striking silver hair. Looking into his eyes, I am immediately struck by the depth of emotion they convey.

Who was he to her?

"Princess Vera." His voice is tender as he inclines his head.

Everly gasps, her hands covering her mouth. "Valric!"

The fae smiles warmly at her and sheaths his sword. "At your service."

"What? No fucking way!" Tristan growls.

"How are you here?" Everly asks him, and I can see she is holding herself back from going to him.

"I've been waiting a long time for your return."

"You're her paladin?" Kian sounds stunned.

Her paladin?

I shake my head. It seems in my absence I've missed out on a few things. "You storm my castle and kill my people, all to get to Everly?" I snarl.

The lady's maid shifts on her feet, and I see Nolan discreetly shake his head at her. Without hesitation, I point my sword in her direction. "Don't even think about running or I'll cut you from navel to neck."

Her throat bobs and she drops her eyes, exposing her neck. Everly's anger builds again, I can sense the shift in her energy.

"Eve, right?" she asks the woman.

The woman's head tilts upward, and she responds with a nod.

"So, it was you and Nolan, then? You allowed the seelie prince access to my rooms. Informed the Outcasts of our movements."

Her eyes widen. "The seelie prince was here?"

With a subtle nod from me, Raiden has Eve by the throat, his dagger positioned over her heart.

Valric and Nolan advance, the gleaming tip of my sword aimed directly at Valric's throat. Valric hesitantly raises his hands, while Nolan stands frozen in place, the weight of tension palpable in the atmosphere.

"We have a lot to discuss. Answer my questions and she will live," I growl.

Valric looks pissed but join the fucking club. The flames of my fire are flickering dangerously under my skin, and I am barely keeping it at bay. The amount of anger and betrayal surging through me is inconceivable.

Tristan and Kian come to stand at my back, Everly between the two of them. I glare at the two fae behind Valric.

"All of you, sit," I order, nodding to the daybed.

All three men walk over and reluctantly take a seat. Before anyone can utter another word, Nymeria and Anika smash through my chamber doors, the magic wards visibly wavering. The wards don't let anyone in my chambers who wishes me harm. But just because they don't mean me harm at that moment doesn't guarantee their intentions won't turn malicious.

In a moment of panic, everyone freezes, and Rayna lets out a frightened yelp, instinctively seeking protection behind Zaria, who stands from the sofa to face the wolves.

"Perfect timing, you two," I greet the wolves. "Mind making sure no one moves?"

The wolves snarl in the direction of the three Outcasts, and trot forward, coming to sit at either side of Everly and myself.

Glancing at the person I've relied on for years, I lock eyes with Nolan, the light from the swaying curtains casting shadows on his face.

"Nolan," I demand, the sound of my voice echoing through the quiet room, "I want to know every detail of your recent activities."

"Maxon, I did this for you. Can't you see she was bewitching you? She doesn't belong here. She is one of them."

I reach out through the bond, and I'm overwhelmed by Everly's hurt and rejection. It only fuels the fiery rage that simmers in the pit of my stomach.

"Nolan. Everly is part of me, part of my soul. To plot to have her taken from me is treason," I seethe.

The shock of the situation causes Nolan's face to go ashen, resembling the paleness of a ghost.

"Tristan, Kian, take him to the dungeons before I do something I may or may not regret." My voice is barely more than a feral growl.

"Wait!" Everly links her fingers with mine. "Did you conspire with the seelie prince?"

Nolan jerks his head back, his brows lowering in confusion. "What?"

Everly sighs. *'He isn't Alivar's spy.'*

'We can't be sure yet. He will need to be questioned.'

Looking down at Everly, I find myself leaning in and lightly kissing her forehead, savoring the smoothness of her skin against my lips and the scent of her hair. I breathe in the tranquility she brings, allowing it to soothe me. Gazing at us, Nolan stands tall, exuding an air of confidence. Confidence he has no right in feeling, even if it is an act. Even after all this time knowing Nolan, I never once thought he was capable of this, and yet here we are.

"Go!" I snap, fire burning in my eyes.

Nolan is escorted out of my chambers without argument. I grind my teeth together and watch the door close behind them. Giving Everly's hand a gentle squeeze, we both turn to face Valric.

"Why are you here?" I try my best to sound calm, and not at all like I want to rip his head off his shoulders. Which is still a possibility.

Valric's gaze lingers on Everly's hand still firmly clasped in mine, as if trying to make sense of something before he finally looks up. He immediately looks at Everly, and I despise how he watches her. I hate that it even bothers me.

"We are here to take you to our encampment."

"Like fuck," I growl, magic infusing my words.

"I'm not going with you." Everly is remarkably calm as she responds. "My home is here."

Everly's words, though a soothing balm to the raging fire inside of me, have the opposite effect on Valric, who jerks to his feet.

"He is the enemy. You cannot stay here!" Valric yells, slashing his hand toward me.

Nymeria and Anika bare their fangs, growls rumbling from their bodies. Before I have a chance to lash out at Valric, Everly drops my hand and marches toward him, her finger poking him in the chest several times.

"Enemy? He is my mate, and I will not leave. Peace once existed in this realm. Division was never meant to happen."

"It's the court's fault there is division. They attacked us. They killed your parents. Don't you remember!"

Everly flinches, and instinctively I extend my arm, encircling her chest, bringing her close to me. A wave of pain and sadness overwhelms our bond, and I send Valric a sharp look as I channel my love and comfort to Everly

Her hands reach up, gripping my arm tightly. "I am perfectly safe here. It's your attempts to reach me that have put me in danger. That was you in the forest, wasn't it? Would you have killed my friends to take me?"

Eve gasps, the lines on her face etched with weariness. "You ambushed them?"

"She belongs with us," Valric snaps.

Everly shakes her head. "You've changed."

"I lost everything the day your parents died. The day you disappeared."

"You say it like it's my fault," Everly whispers.

And I know she is thinking of what my aunt told her.

'What happened in Pinehelm wasn't your fault. They attacked first.'

'But it was my magic that sent everyone into a fear-induced frenzy. What if it happens again?'

'I won't let anything happen to you, Stóirín. I swear.'

Chapter Forty-Six

Everly

Maxon's words do little to soothe the fear gripping my chest. I still don't understand my magic and what I am capable of. Raiden releases his grip on Eve and gestures for her to take a seat. Maxon's arm is still tightly wrapped around my waist, as if he's afraid I'll run away with the Outcasts.

"It wasn't your fault," Valric replies, his tone softening.

I stare at him, trying to figure out if he's being sincere. When no one breaks the tense silence that has fallen over the room, Valric continues.

"You look so much like your mother."

Anger fills my chest, and I give him a pointed look. I am done. I don't want to talk to him anymore. The thought of continuing the conversation with him makes me feel nauseous. When I first recognized him, my heart leaped with overwhelming happiness. But to learn what he's done, what he is willing to do to get to me is heartbreaking.

"You need to leave," I state matter of factly.

Maxon's arm falls from where it was banned around my chest, and his fingers link with mine.

'Speak your truth, Stóirín. I will back you.'

As my eyes shift back to Valric, a surge of confidence and determination courses through me, making me stand taller. I can sense Maxon's unwavering support, assuring me that he will back me up every step of the way. It ignites a fire within me, pushing me to rise above any doubts or fears.

Valric stands there, blinking at me in confusion as if I were speaking another language. Maybe that would work better anyway.

"Please, just leave," I say again, this time in my native tongue.

Valric's eyes widen in astonishment, causing the other Outcasts to gape in disbelief.

"But you are our queen," one of them argues, rising to his feet.

With a menacing growl, Nymeria lunges at him, causing him to instinctively raise his hands.

"I may be your queen one day, but for now, we have bigger things to deal with. I will bring peace again, but it won't be by force. I will not leave my home again, and my home is here."

Valric's eyes harden as he looks over my head at Maxon. "Will you let us leave?" he snaps.

"If she wishes it, then yes."

Valric's jaw tenses up, and then he looks over at Eve. "What of Eve?"

"She can stay if that's what she wants," I reply.

Maxon tenses behind me, and Valric's eyes widen with uncertainty as he stares at us for a long beat.

'You sure?' Maxon asks.

'I don't think she is here to harm me or force me to leave. I know her. I just can't remember yet.'

'Okay.'

"Raiden, see our guests out. Nymeria and Anika, make sure they leave the castle grounds," Maxon commands.

Once they have left, Maxon turns to Zaria and Rayna. "Can you please escort Eve back to her room, the castle is on lockdown until I say."

Both nod and quickly usher Eve out the door. The soft click of the door shutting has my shoulders sagging. As if trying to ward off a headache, Maxon rubs his temples with a furrowed brow. My heart aches for him, and instinctively I reach out and grasp his hand, gently guiding him to the sofa and sit him down. Straddling his lap, I sink my fingers into his hair and gently run my finger through the dark, silky strands.

"I'm sorry," I whisper, dropping my forehead to his.

'What for?'

'For everything. All that's happened is because I arrived here.'

'Don't ever apologize for coming into my life, Stóirín. There is no life without you.'

Maxon's arms wrap around my back, and he draws me into his chest, my arms going around his neck. I press my cheek to his as we nuzzle each other. This is where I belong.

This is home.

In Maxon's arms.

It doesn't matter where I am as long as he is beside me.

"What stopped Alivar from taking you?" Maxon's voice is gruff as he speaks.

"I did."

I feel his shock down the bond, and he pulls back, cupping my face, his eyes searching my face. "How? Alivar is strong, and he could have easily portalled you away before anyone knew you were gone."

I shrug. "I think we were both shocked. I somehow managed to create a wall of water between us."

"Water?"

Oh shit.

"Hmmmhmmm . . . "

"Everly, where exactly were you? You said your chambers."

"It doesn't matter," I reply, dropping a kiss to his lips.

His hands drop to my thighs, the move distracting me.

"It does to me," his voice rumbles in his chest.

I gently place my fingers on his chest, absentmindedly running them over the texture of the leather. I bite my lip, knowing he is going to lose it. "I was in the bathroom."

"And why would he be shocked?"

I tip my head back and groan, feeling my cheeks heat. "I was in the bath."

Instantly, I can feel his anger and possessiveness flood our bond.

"He also saw my mark. He knows I'm yours," I rush to reassure him.

Maxon's grip on my thighs is firm and the low growl that comes from his chest sends a pulse of awareness through me. Desire surges through my veins, electrifying every inch of my body. The silver ring flares in his iris, his magic rising to the surface. Hot, dark and beautifully sexy. It skates over my skin, leaving goosebumps in its wake. With a tight grip on my wrists, he brings my hands to his mouth and tenderly kisses each of my fingertips. The sensations send my heart into a frenzy, beating wildly in my chest.

In an instant, his hands drop mine and move up my body, cupping my breasts. His touch is like adding gasoline to an already burning fire. A barely audible groan escapes my mouth and I rock against his hard cock.

This is definitely not the time for this, but I can't stop.

The friction of the fabric as I rock against him sends a swell of heat through my core. One of Maxon's hands moves to my hip, his grip almost painful as he pulls me into him. The other hand sinks into my hair and cups the back of my head. I open my eyes, meeting with his intense and unwavering gaze. His lips hover just an inch away from mine, and I can feel the warmth of his breath. My tongue instinctively darts out, moistening my lips, wanting nothing more than to close the breath of space between us.

"You belong with me," he growls, then his lips crash down on mine.

I moan into the kiss, our movements becoming frantic as I grind on his lap. I am so close; I am dizzy with need.

Love and possession wrap around my heart as Maxon deepens the kiss, his tongue driving into my mouth. My stomach dips violently at the feel of his tongue sliding against mine, setting me off.

Maxon's kiss muffles my cries as I come apart, trembling on his lap. I'm panting and shaky, collapsing my forehead on his shoulder.

'That was . . . wow. You didn't even take my clothes off.'

Maxon chuckles, the sound bringing a warmth to my chest and a smile to my lips.

Chapter Forty-Seven

Everly

A knock at the door has us breaking apart. Maxon slides me from his lap onto the sofa, giving me a quick kiss as he stands.

"Wait here."

He strides over to the door and opens it. Nymeria follows closely behind, her paws softly padding on the ground. My face lights up with a smile. The wolves have developed a love and protectiveness toward Maxon, similar to how they feel toward me.

Maxon steps aside and lets Raiden in, followed by Tristan, Kian, and Nix.

"They want to know about Escalle," Raiden explains, crossing his arms and flaring his wings slightly. Something I've noticed he does when he is irritated.

Maxon's eyes flash, and I can sense his reluctance as he and Raiden share a look.

"What did you discover in Escalle?" Tristan questions.

"Is it bad?" I ask.

Maxon rubs his fingers over his forehead as if trying to rid himself of the impending headache. "The town was indeed taken out by a horde of deadlings, leaving behind a trail of destruction and the stench of decay. It was worse than I thought it would be."

"They are trying to get our attention. They want something," Raiden adds.

All eyes turn to me. None hold any accusations, but I feel it all the same. Guilt has a way of slithering inside of you, taking up space and snuffing out your light.

Nix flutters down and lands on my knee. "This isn't your fault. The Shadoweaver would have sensed your arrival, and he would have sent a scout out looking for you. He has been locked away for centuries, dormant. Only waking when someone with enough power came along to break him free from his prison."

"Are you sure it's this Shadoweaver?' I ask.

"The Shadoweaver's pet was among the army, so it's safe to say this is his doing."

"He might be trying to draw Everly out. Or doing this to make us give her up," Tristan muses.

Maxon's eyes narrow as he shoots a sharp glare in his direction.

"The Shadoweaver has a pet?" I ask, incredulous.

Maxon nods, crossing his arms over his broad chest. "A black creature that is half demon, half beast. Crimson eyes and shrouded in darkness. It is said to be able to shift between demon and beast form, though no one has lived to tell what the demon form is."

With a sudden jolt, I sprang to my feet, overwhelmed by a wave of panic coursing through my veins. "The first night I was here, I saw that beast with the red eyes!" I exclaim, my hands trembling. "I dreamed of it last night. If it is the servant of the Shadoweaver, then it would have told him of my arrival here in Faerie."

Nix looks completely horrified. "It saw you?"

I nod, unable to speak. It's like my throat is closing up. Within a second, Maxon is in front of me. His hands firmly planted on my shoulders, he bends down to peer directly into my eyes.

"Hey. It's okay. You're safe. Calm down," he whispers gently.

As I struggle to catch my breath, I tightly grasp his wrist, locking eyes with him as I mirror his deep, deliberate breaths.

"That's it," he coos. "Deep breaths."

With a soft, sweeping motion, his thumbs graze my cheeks, prompting me to close my eyes and savor the sensation. Maxon straightens and pulls me into his chest. Once I'm composed and have my emotions under control, I turn around and face the room. Nymeria and Anika each nudge my hands, and I swipe my hands over their heads, wanting nothing more than to bury my face in their fur and hide.

"So, the Shadoweaver needs me in order to break free from his prison?" I look around the room.

Kian rubs the back of his neck, avoiding me. With a fierce expression, Raiden confidently takes a step forward. "He will not get to you." He raises a fist to his heart and bows. "I swear on my life to protect you until my dying breath."

My heart slams hard against my chest, and the air seems to be sucked from the room. I sense Maxon's gratitude and affection through the bond at his friend's spoken words.

With a courageous stride, Tristan steps forward, his fist held high against his chest. "I, too, will give my life freely to protect you, Everly Baker, from all threats."

The words of the fae are binding, and I feel its weight settle on my shoulders. There is no way out of the oath except through death. My eyes fill with tears, so many emotions overwhelming me. The last twenty-four hours has been a rollercoaster at best, and a shit show at worst.

"Well, you know how much I hate being left out." Kian winks and steps next to Tristan, raising his fist to cover his heart. "Princess, I give my word you'll be safe with me."

With a smile playing on my lips, I nod my head in acknowledgement.

Maxon walks purposefully past me, heading toward the three fae soldiers he trusted with my life. He clasps each of them on the shoulder, leaning in to whisper words that elude my ears.

Several loud bangs reverberate against the door, and Raiden walks over, swinging the door open. I feel a gentle flutter as Nix lands on my shoulder.

"I'm jealous of all these hot fae men swearing to protect you with their life."

I chuckle, the sound escaping my lips in a soft huff. I watch as a tall man with dark skin walks in. He is covered in brands, and his long black hair flows around his shoulders.

"The Puca insisted." Raiden's eyes roll.

"Nero," the man corrects.

Raiden frowns. "Right, Nero."

"Thank you," Nero replies with a wink, making him blink.

"Nero. What are you doing here?" I ask, giving him a warm smile.

Nero bows and straightens up with a grin. "I heard you had fully awoken. I wanted to come and see for myself. And I was in the area for the coronation of our king."

"You two know each other?" Maxon asks.

"Nero saved me from a horrible dance with Lord Wallcliffe."

The sensation of Maxon's irritation slowly spreads through our bond, like a subtle current. Not at Nero, but at Lord Wallcliffe. It appears that the man is not well-liked by anyone. I remember something the others mentioned about Nero before and step forward eagerly.

"Nero, can you get a message to my friends back in the human realm?"

"Of course."

"Mia and Scarlett shouldn't be hard to find. Knowing my friends, they would undoubtedly be searching for me. Do you want the address?"

Nero shakes his head. "I already know where they are."

"How?"

Nero winks. "When I heard the lost druid princess had returned through the gate from the human realm, I wanted to know how she had been living all these years. Your friends, as you say, were very easy to find. They have not given up hope in finding you. Stirring up quite a ruckus."

My eyes sting with tears, and my heart feels heavy with the pain I've caused them, but also grateful they haven't given up on me. Taking a deep breath, I quickly wipe away my tears.

"Could you let them know I'm safe and I'm happy?"

"They won't believe me for a second." Nero raises an eyebrow.

That's true they would probably kidnap him to get answers. I chew my lip and look out the window. "Tell them . . . Tell them, the weather is beautiful here. There is no need for the blue umbrella."

Everyone in the room trades confused looks, but Nero grins, the brands on his body swirling. "Done."

"Thank you," I whisper, doing my best to hold back tears. When I initially began going on my hikes, the girls would consistently urge me to bring along additional supplies. Back when I used to live with them, Scarlett would often attempt to secretly slip a blue umbrella into my backpack, along with a bag of skittles, and a rape whistle.

Nero tilts his head, studying me. "How do you feel? I see you and the crown prince wasted no time in joining."

A red blush heats my face, and I lift my fingers to my own markings on my face. "Well, when you know, you know," I murmur.

"Touché."

"How did you know who I was?" I ask.

"Makeup can't hide the birthmark of druid royalty from everyone, princess."

"Oh."

Maxon leans over, his warm breath tickling my skin, and gently presses his lips against my temple. "I'm going to go and fill my aunt in about Nolan. Tristan and Kian will stay with you."

"Okay," I breathe.

I watch him and Raiden exit and Nero bows. "I will leave you to it, princess, and we will see each other again."

Chapter Forty-Eight

Everly

My heart races as fear grips me tightly with its boney fingers, making it difficult to breathe. The black mist seems to suffocate the air around me, its dense presence enveloping everything in its path. I strain my eyes, desperately trying to pierce through the darkness, but it's futile. The world has been swallowed whole by this ethereal abyss.

A chill runs down my spine as a tingling sensation crawls across my skin. The tiny hairs on my arms stand up. What is happening? The air feels heavy, as if every molecule were infused with a sense of impending doom.

I reach up to touch my face, only to find it smeared with dirt and streaks of dried blood. It's as though I have emerged from a fierce battle, a battle I can't recall.

My body aches with the weariness of a warrior who has fought tirelessly. My muscles throb, evidence of the physical exertion I have endured. I can taste the metallic tang of blood in my mouth, a bitter reminder of the violence that surrounded me. The adrenaline is still coursing through my veins, heightening my senses and amplifying every sound, every heartbeat.

Yet, amidst the chaos and confusion, a glimmer of resilience flickers to life within me. Despite the crushing darkness, I find the strength to push forward, to navigate through the unknown. I know that I have to find a way to dispel the black mist, to reclaim my clarity and regain control over my surroundings.

With determined resolve, I take a step forward, my body trembling but my spirit unyielding. I refuse to let the darkness consume me completely.

Chapter Forty-Nine

Everly

Gazing out at the stars, I stand with my hands resting on the stone balcony, and soak in the fresh air. Looking down, I catch glimpses of white as Nymeria and Anika gracefully bound through the gardens. I am pleasantly surprised by the significant improvement in my eyesight since the spell that was affecting my druid magic was removed.

Abruptly, my stomach fills with butterflies, a sure sign that Maxon is close. I hear the chamber doors open and the air suddenly becomes charged with Maxon's energy as he enters, and without hesitation, he dismisses Kian and Tristan. I smile into the night, happy he has returned. It's been a long day. I was told five fae were killed in the raid yesterday, and one was indeed Madeline, who had only left the queen's chambers moments before.

Maxon's hand touches mine as he comes to stand next to me, our pinkies linking.

"I have something for you," he whispers.

Before I can respond, he slides something in front of me. I glance down, and see a small box glistening in the moonlight. My eyes quickly meet his with a look of surprise.

"It took me longer than I thought it would to pick. That's why I missed dinner." He smirks.

Looking down, I slowly lift the lid of the box, feeling a mix of curiosity and excitement bubbling up inside me. Inside sits a ring, its diamond sparkling under the moonlight. A web of thin golden vines forms the circle of the ring, crawling up and intertwining with each other. My heart swells and thumps hard in my chest, making me feel lightheaded.

It's beautiful.

I try to speak, but I can't form words. My eyes are glued to the ring.

Maxon takes the ring from the box and drops to his knee. "I want to do this right. You are my mate and the other half of my soul. I want to make you my wife and queen."

My eyes fill with tears as he takes hold of my hand, placing the ring on my finger, and I fight to hold back the sob that threatens to escape my throat.

"I want us to grow together, uniting the fractured pieces of this realm, and filling our home with the laughter and footsteps of our children. Everly, will you do me the honor of becoming my wife?"

I nod my head over and over, a sob breaking free as I dive into his arms.

"Yes," I whisper into his neck. "Yes."

I didn't expect to feel such overwhelming emotions by this question, we are already mates. However, it was like the cherry on top, bringing undeniable happiness to my soul. Maxon's arms enveloped me tightly, burying his head in my neck. My heart, a wild drumbeat, thunders in my chest, threatening to break free from its confines. It echoes in my ears, drowning out the rest of the world. I feel a rush of adrenaline, a surge of energy coursing through my veins, as if the universe itself is pulsating in time with our connection.

"I love you, Stóirín."

"I love you too, a chroí."

Pulling away, I pepper his face with kisses, my hands firmly grasping his cheeks.

Maxon's growl reverberates through me as his lips press against mine, the kiss filled with desire and hunger. His hands go under my ass, and he stands, lifting me into the air. My dress is a simple silk gown, but it has slits all the way up so I can easily wrap my legs around his waist as he carries me inside.

The sensation of Maxon's tongue against mine sends a flurry of tingles throughout my body, and I can't help but grind against him in response. He gently places me on the bed before swiftly unfastening his swords and daggers. The moment he finishes, I lunge at him, my fingers seizing his shirt and tearing it apart. My hands immediately drop to his belt, but Maxon clasps my wrists in one hand and lifts them above my head as he walks me backward. The back of my knees hit the bed, and I fall, Maxon's body following mine. The weight of his body feels like pure bliss, and all I crave is the sensation of his skin pressed against mine.

Leaning up, I gently graze my lips against his, teasingly nipping at his bottom lip. There is a flickering fire burning deep in my chest, warming my entire being. Maxon's hand presses my wrists into the mattress, his other hands ripping down the top of my dress, letting my breasts spill out. I squirm as he drops his head, sucking one nipple into his mouth while grinding his hips into mine.

"Maxon," I moan.

"Yes, Stóirín?"

"I need your skin against mine now," I whine.

Maxon lifts his head, eyes more silver than violet as he smirks, sending a riot of butterflies through my stomach. Rising to his feet in one swift move, he kicks off his boots and rips his pants off. My god, he is absolute perfection. And he is mine.

I slowly stand, my hands landing on his abdomen, my finger tracing the dips and swell of his muscles. Maxon shivers under my touch, and I smile playfully before repeating the motion. I squeal when he growls, spinning me around and tearing my dress from the neck down. Shocked, I drop my eyes to the tattered remains of my new dress piled at my feet. His arms come around me and firm hands cup my breasts, pulling me back into his chest. His lips tease along my neck as he pinches my nipples, and I press myself into him, rubbing my ass against his cock. Maxon's hands slowly release my breasts, and drop to my pants to skillfully guide me as I step out of them. He then stands, turning me to face him once more.

"You are so incredibly beautiful," he whispers, gripping my throat and tilting my head back.

Then his mouth is on mine, owning this kiss, owning me.

I whimper into his mouth, the need and desire more than I can handle. I've never felt like this before, like if he didn't touch me, I'd burn up.

Our hands glide over each other in a sensual dance, wanting to explore every inch of bare skin.

Breaking the kiss, Maxon carefully guides me down onto the bed. His lips start to explore my stomach before he firmly holds onto my thighs, gently spreading my legs apart. Slowly, his mouth moves along my inner thighs, occasionally nipping at my skin, eliciting a surprised yelp from me. I look down into his eyes, a wicked glimmer holding me captive as his mouth covers my clit. Waves of pleasure cascade over me, causing my mouth to drop open in sheer ecstasy. My head falls back onto the bed, and my hands instinctively find purchase in Maxon's hair as he devours me with an insatiable hunger. My legs tremble as warmth spreads to every part of my body, a bright light filling the room as I come apart.

Maxon growls, driving his tongue deeper into me, feeling my walls clench around him. The noise he makes is inhuman, and only makes another orgasm crash over me. I cry out into the room, barely aware of the words coming from my mouth.

Maxon withdraws and grabs my ankles, flipping me onto my stomach and covers my body with his. I moan, pushing my ass into him as he slides his cock against my wet pussy.

"I could die happy hearing you come apart like that," he admits, his voice rough and sexy, his arms caging me in.

"Please don't."

A dark chuckle escapes him as he mischievously nips at my ear, causing an instant shiver and a new wave of tremors that sweep over my body.

"I could do that every day. You taste fucking divine, my queen." He grabs my chin, bending my head back, his tongue driving into my mouth.

The taste of myself lingers on his lips as we kiss, and I let out a whimper of anticipation as his tip teases my entrance. Maxon releases my chin, his hands now gripping my waist as he pushes into me, his movements deliberate and gradual. My head drops between my shoulders, and I grip the sheets tightly in my fists as he slowly stretches me. Maxon pushes in as far as he can go, and a low rumble comes from deep in his throat, his hips rotating and grinding into me. A rush of heat floods my core, and I can't help but start panting in response.

"Maxon, faster," I moan.

I'd do it, but his grip on my waist doesn't allow me to move. He is in complete control. Maxon's hands squeeze my waist as he leans over me, drawing out and sliding back in. All his movements are leisurely and controlled, making me delirious. The words coming from me are incoherent as Maxon works my body. Somehow, without his cock leaving me, he maneuvers my legs, so I am now on my back, his cock still buried deep in me. Fire burns in his eyes as he stares down at me, the flames dancing in the depths. I've never seen anything so magnificent.

My hands reach up and cup his face, and he drops to his elbows as he cages me in, his eyes never leaving mine. I lift my hips up, to meet his, my legs wrapping around his waist, grinding against him with each thrust of his cock. The overwhelming sensations make my eyes involuntarily flutter shut as he moves.

"Open your eyes," Maxon growls, nipping my bottom lip.

My heart skips a beat and my eyes open, dazed.

"I want you to see what you do to me."

I nod, my fingers tracing the contours of his sides. Our movements quicken and grow increasingly desperate.

"Maxon," I pant, my heart thumping hard as my body becomes a live wire.

Maxon's jaw clenches, his movements becoming more aggressive, and he starts slamming into me with even greater intensity. Flames burst along his body as white light erupts from my chest. My fingers dig into his biceps as his head tips back, a roar filling the air. Every muscle in his body is taut. The sensation of his cum filling me sends me hurling over the edge, both of us shuddering with the intensity of our orgasm. Maxon continues to move, though much slower, drawing out every tremor and spasm, before collapsing on me.

His head falls to my shoulder, soft kisses brushing over my skin. "That was . . . "

"Amazing," I finish for him, tilting my head to give him more room.

Softly, I trail my fingers up and down his back in leisurely strokes. My heart is filled with an overwhelming surge of love and affection. I lift my left hand up and stare at the ring, unable to stop the smile that spreads across my face.

CHAPTER FIFTY

Everly

Standing beside Raiden, I feel the warmth of the sun on my skin as Kian and Tristan stand confidently behind me. From our vantage point on the side stage, we absorb the vibrant atmosphere that surrounds us. The air is filled with anticipation and excitement as thousands of eager onlookers gather to witness Maxon ascend the throne. The sound of cheers and applause fills the air, mingling with the soft melodies of the musicians playing nearby. Amidst the crowd, the scent of fresh flowers wafts, infusing a tinge of sweetness into the already electric atmosphere. I am so proud of him, and even though she is well versed in hiding her feelings, I can see the tears in Lavina's eyes as she watches on like a proud mother. With every step Maxon takes toward the throne, the crowd's adoration for him swells, creating an undeniable energy that passes through the air.

Raiden leans over to whisper in my ear. "The crown is a bit much, don't you think?"

I cover my mouth and chuckle. "It is a bit flashy. I don't think it's Maxon's style."

Raiden grins. "He will get matching crowns made more to his liking for the two of you."

His words slam into me, reminding me of the implications of being with Maxon. Even though, according to Valric, I am queen to my own people. I look out over the crowd gathered and feel nerves replacing my excitement from moments ago. So much has changed in such a short amount of time.

As the crowd grows quiet, I shift my attention back to the raised dais. Maxon stands tall, his formal attire accentuating his commanding presence, his long black cloak flowing as he moves, the dragon emblem proudly displayed over his heart.

"My people, as your new king, I pledge my unwavering devotion to the prosperity of our realm. I stand before you not as an individual, but as a protector of the great magic that courses through the veins of our kingdom. With immense gratitude and humility, I accept the mantle of kingship bestowed upon me by the sacred will of our people. I hope to be everything you wish for in a good ruler, but today, we are not only here to celebrate my ascension as king but also welcome the radiant heartbeat of our beloved kingdom—the enchanting soul who has chosen to stand by my side, your future queen and my beloved fiancée."

My heart skips a beat, and I find myself frozen as Maxon's eyes meet mine. A smile graces his face as he reaches out his hand toward me.

"That's your cue, princess," Kian mutters from behind me.

'This wasn't part of the plan,' I hiss down the bond.

With a small shrug, Maxon's eyes spark with amusement. *'I'm improvising, plus you're too beautiful not to show off.'*

Face burning, I step forward with a low grumble, and Raiden comes to my side, offering his hand to assist me up the three steps onto the dais. I shoot him a grateful smile, then proceed to walk over to Maxon. Reaching for his hand, a gentle warmth spreads through my fingers. With a burst of excitement, Nymeria and Anika come bounding up behind me, their tongues lolling out of their mouths. Some of the fae closest to the dais gasp in shock at the two wolves circling Maxon and me before laying at our feet.

Feeling the weight of all these eyes on me, my fight or flight instincts are kicking into high gear. Among the crowd, I notice a few fae, and my gaze meets that of a small family of gray-skinned creatures in the front row. Their frowns are evident, but the youngest, a little girl, has the biggest smile on her face, which brings me some much-needed relief from my anxiety.

'Don't be scared. I got you.'

I release a soft, content sigh, my lips curling into a smile. *'Because it's just so easy to do.'*

'Trust me, Stóirín.'

The crowd has been silent the entire time since Maxon called me to his side, only faint murmurs among a few. As Maxon addresses the crowd once more, I intertwine my arm with his, drawing on his warmth and strength.

"It is with immense pleasure that I introduce to you my heart and soul, Everly Baker. The last druid princess, daughter of King Oleander."

Cheers erupt from the crowd, along with murmurs of excitement and shock.

Lavina steps forward, and the crowd takes a moment to calm down. When they do, she faces us, and I am really confused by the look she is giving us. I really thought she hated me.

'She did in the beginning when she thought you were a human spy, here to lure me down the wrong path.'

I jolt inwardly. *'Well, now I'm a druid she is approving then?'*

'Yes.'

I can't stop my eyes from rolling.

"Your presence here today marks not only a union of hearts but a fusion of destinies, intertwining the fate of two souls who have found solace and strength in each other's embrace.

"Together, Maxon and Everly, you stand as a testament to the enduring magic of love in our fae realm. Your union heralds a new chapter in our history—one that promises prosperity, unity, and an abundance of joy for generations to come."

I look out over all those gathered, my eyes drawn to the back of the crowd, where a hooded figure stands motionless, their face obscured by the shadows. I can feel the unwavering focus as if they can see right into the depths of my soul, and I know it's Valric.

Thoughts race through my mind, each one like a jagged puzzle piece, trying to fit together the fragments of Valric's motives. Does he believe I have abandoned him? Is he hurt by my choice to stay with Maxon? The uncertainty gnaws at me, fueling my inner turmoil. The weight of guilt presses down on my shoulders, making it difficult to draw a steady breath. Deep down, I still care for Valric. The bond we once shared cannot be easily severed. He still is my true paladin, bound by oath to keep me safe.

In the midst of the crowd, Zaria and Rayna spot me and make their way over. It is impossible to miss their huge, bright smiles, which brings a sense of joy to me. The festivities are in full swing, with music and dancing, while I am completely exhausted and barely able to stand. I notice I don't possess the same level of energy as these fae creatures. I also haven't spent a lot of time outside as of late, and I really need to recharge in the garden. As a druid, my magic flows from the very essence of the natural world, and being surrounded by its beauty is essential for me to recharge and restore my abilities. No wonder I was so drawn to the gardens when I first arrived, and hiked in the human world every weekend. The vibrant colors, soothing scents, and the gentle rustling of leaves have always captivated me. Little did I know that it was more than just a personal preference; it was an instinctual need to connect with nature and replenish my druidic powers.

"Everly!" Rayna laughs, wrapping her arms around me. "You look absolutely amazing in this dress."

The bubbly shifter playfully spins me around, and I feel a rush of dizziness as my surroundings become a blur. I lose my balance and stumble to the side, but Zaria is there in an instant, grabbing hold of my arm to steady me.

"You okay?"

"I wasn't expecting that." I laugh.

Zaria's eyes linger on my dress, and a warm smile spreads across her face. "The shimmering gold and vibrant green colors truly work wonders on you. It really makes your skin glow and captivates the hue of your green eyes."

I lower my gaze toward the exquisite ball dress, expertly chosen by Zaria, and glide my fingers delicately across the velvety smoothness of the satin fabric, relishing its gentle caress against my skin. The off-the-shoulder ballgown accentuates my curves beautifully, hugging my upper body, while gracefully flaring at the waist like a classic gown.

"I can't believe the king put you on the spot like that." Rayna's brown eyes are sparkling. "Everyone was wondering who the gorgeous fae was with the king's personal guards. The whole of Skora is so excited to have the lost princess here and marrying our king."

My fingers instinctively graze my pointed ear, a tangible reminder that I am still adjusting to these unfamiliar traits.

"Not everyone," I murmur, having caught the cautious stares of some.

Zaria waves her hand. "There are always some who will oppose. We all know the prophecy. Just like we all know your magic will not destroy the realm. The past occurrences are not going to be repeated. I don't know who brainwashed the others into their plans to kill your family, but the king would not let that happen again. He would slaughter any who try, and I'd be right there with him."

Rayna and I stare at Zaria for a moment. Even Asrai seems shocked by her outburst. Her dual-colored eyes are wide in disbelief.

"Wow, Z. Really going for it there." Rayna nervously glances around.

"Well, it's true. Everly has us at her back, and anyone who tries to harm her under false accusations will meet their end swiftly."

I reach for Zaria's hand, my chest swelling with a mix of emotions that I am suddenly finding it hard to contain.

"I'm so lucky to have you as a friend." Sniffing, I can't help but feel a burning sensation in my eyes. "Great, now I'm going to cry." I laugh.

Rayna grins. "You two are cute. But seriously, Z, easy on the talk, you need to be cautious. There are people who don't want the courts to reconcile. They prefer this division, and we still haven't identified the spy."

Somehow, with everything that has been going on, I forgot about the spy. As of now, Nolan is locked away in the dungeons, eagerly anticipating Maxon's decision regarding his punishment. Nonetheless, we are still unable to make any progress in uncovering the identity of the individual providing information to the unseelie prince.

"I won't apologize!" Zaria snaps, her ears twitching in annoyance.

"I'm not asking you to. Just be cautious," Rayna begs.

Zaria sighs heavily and nods. "Fine. I'll keep quiet."

"Thank you." Rayna looks around and spots some of her friends and waves. "Do you mind if I go see my friends?"

"Of course not," Zaria and I answer together.

Smiling, I look at her. "Jinx."

"Huh?"

"Never mind." I wave her off.

Rayna embraces Zaria, giving her a brief hug before waving goodbye. The moment Rayna waves goodbye and excitedly heads toward her friends, Zaria swiftly turns and looks directly at me.

"What's wrong?" Zaria asks, pulling me aside.

"Huh?"

She gives me a knowing look. “Look, we have only known each other for, like, a few weeks, but I can tell something is wrong. Plus, you look a little pale. Are you sick?”

My cheeks flush with warmth as I inch closer to her. “Is there somewhere we can talk? In private.”

Concern shines in Zaria’s big brown eyes, her tail swishing back and forth. “Sure, come with me.”

She grabs my hand in hers and leads me through the crowd of people, toward a side door. Pushing it open, we slip outside onto a small balcony, which seems to be empty.

“Right, what’s wrong?” She turns to me.

"I'm– It's–" I stammer, my eyes shifting to Zaria, trying to determine if this is a common occurrence among shifters or fae. I've gone through my Renascitur, and now I'm uncertain about what lies ahead.

Zaria patiently waits for me to collect my thoughts. I adore her for being so understanding.

“I have my period!” I blurt.

Zaria’s eyes narrow and she tilts her head to the side, as if what I’m saying makes no sense to her.

I know I’m bright red right now, but I’m going to have to be blunt.

“I’m bleeding . . . down there,” I whisper, pointing.

Zaria’s eyes widen, her mouth forming an O shape. “Oh, right. We call it the Cycle of Brigid.”

I wrinkle my nose in response. “Isn’t she a goddess?”

Zaria's laughter fills the air, and I notice Asrai trying to stifle her own amusement, her hand pressed against her lips.

“Yes. She was the goddess of spring, the dawn, and fertility.”

‘Each marking a new beginning,’ Asrai signs.

"Well, thank the goddess. You know what I'm talking about." My shoulders slump with relief. "I need painkillers and to get out of this dress. My cramps are killing me," I groan.

"Do I need to send for a healer?"

"No. I just need some rest. Can we sneak away? You can rejoin the party. I just need help out of this dress."

"Of course. Let's get you comfortable." Zaria links her arm in mine.

We step back inside, where Kian and Tristan are waiting by the doors.

"You ladies, okay?" Kian asks, eyeing us suspiciously.

"I'm heading back to my room."

"Already?" Tristan frowns.

"Yes, is that okay with you?" I snap, whipping my head in his direction.

Tristan raises an eyebrow at me in question, and I close my eyes, breathing through a cramp. This tight dress really wasn't helping. I cling onto Zaria's arm and once the cramp has passed, I open my eyes and look at Tristan.

"Sorry, but I'm done for the night. Once you escort me back, you can come back to the festivities if you wish."

Kian and Tristan share a look. But Zaria and I don't wait for them before making our way toward Maxon's chambers.

"Can we come in?" Kian asks, as Zaria is about to close the door.

"No." Zaria and I speak at the same time.

Closing the door, Zaria turns to me and smiles softly. "Let's get you out of that dress."

"Please!" I groan.

A sheen of sweat forms on my skin as the cramps ramp up their intensity.

The pain is so intense that I double over, clutching my stomach. "Motherfucker," I grit, my breathing turning heavy.

Zaria places a comforting hand on my back. "Has it always been this bad?"

"Yes, always."

"Let's get this dress off, and I'll get you some herbal tea."

I nod and stand straight so she can unlace the dress.

'Stóirín is everything okay? Tristan just informed me you are turning in for the night?'

'A chroí, I'm fine. I am in our room. Please enjoy your night.'

'I will be there soon.'

'No. You have just been crowned king. Stay. Your people need to see you.'

I can feel his hesitation, his need to see I'm okay.

So I close my eyes and send my love and affection through the bond. *'I'll be here when you return. I promise.'*

'Okay, my love.'

A wave of adoration washes over me, momentarily easing the pain.

"There." Zaria tugs the dress down, and I step out of it and settle myself on the comfortable bed.

Zaria disappears and returns with a stack of clothes and lady items. Thank the goddess. I head to the bathroom and shower, pulling on the clothes Zaria gave me. They must be Maxon's, as huge as they are on me, but as I lift them to my nose and smell, a wave of peace moves through me, relaxing my tense muscles.

"The smell of your mate will ease the pain," Zaria explains, when she sees me sniffing Maxon's clothes.

"Oh, well that's handy." I smile.

I lie down in Maxon's bed after Zaria has given me an herbal tea to help with the cramping. Hugging his pillow to my chest, I curl into a ball. My cramps may have dulled, but they're still bothering me.

Just as I'm drifting off to sleep, I hear the chamber doors creaking open and instantly sense Maxon entering the room. That swarm of butterflies that usually appear when he is near grows.

The bed dips behind me, and his fingers stroke my hair. "Stóirín, are you okay? Zaria tells me you are unwell?"

I roll my head so I can see him when I talk. "I'm okay, just female issues," I whisper.

Maxon's brows furrow and his jaw clenches. "What do you mean? Did someone hurt you?"

I grin and reach up, sliding my hand over his jaw. "No. It's . . . " What did Zaria call it? "You fae call it the cycle of Brigid."

Maxon's eyes blaze in the dark, and I feel his confusion for a moment before his features smooth out and understanding softens his features. Standing from the bed, I watch him disappear into the bathroom and then return several minutes later. He's carrying what looks to be a small pillow. He quickly strips off his clothes, leaving on his briefs, and climbs into bed behind me. Placing the heated pillow on my lower stomach, he presses against my back, his body molding perfectly around mine. I let out a deep sigh of contentment, instantly feeling the tension melt away from my body.

Chapter Fifty-One

Everly

Maxon left early this morning to meet with the lords of the Winter and Autumn Courts, accompanied by Raiden. I'm unsure what is being discussed today, but I can sense Maxon's reluctance to leave. Today is his first day as king, and I couldn't be happier for him. I know he's worried, he couldn't hide that from me even if he wanted to. I can feel his doubts and the pressure to be perfect, but everyone loves him. He is already an exceptional leader and a formidable warrior.

With Nix sitting silently on my shoulder, I stroll through the gardens, my bare feet sinking into the soft green grass. Inhaling deeply, I savor the scent of flowers and the soft, velvety touch of petals brushing against my fingertips. Now that I understand my magic a little better, I take my time watching as the flowers respond to my touch, unfurling their petals and releasing a sweet fragrance into the air. Nearby, a few curious birds flutter closer to investigate. I already feel a hundred times better than yesterday; the tea Zaria gave me, combined with Maxon's comforting embrace throughout the night, feels like the perfect remedy for PMS.

Tristan and Kian wait at the edge of the gardens, their disapproving frowns unmistakable when I asked them not to follow.

Nix playfully kicks her legs as the soft branches and leaves of the weeping willow sway around us, as if they're attempting to tickle us. A sense of familiarity comes over me, a rush of memories flooding my mind, taking me back in time to my childhood.

"Everly?" Nix's soft voice whispers.

"Yes?"

With a gentle push from my shoulder, she effortlessly flies in front of me, twisting her long, brown hair in her hands. "Are you happy you found your way back here?"

"Yes. Of course."

"Do you miss your old life?"

Her question stirs up a whirlwind of emotions inside me. Do I miss my old life? Not at all. Throughout my childhood, I lacked the presence of someone who genuinely cared for me. I felt small and insignificant growing up in the human world, but ever since arriving here, I've had countless people who embraced me with genuine concern for my well being. That was before they discovered my true identity.

"No. Do I miss Scarlett and Mia? Absolutely."

"Will you leave us?"

I stare at Nix, a frown slowly creeping onto my face. This isn't like her at all. "No. I don't plan on leaving. Why?"

Nix shrugs, looking uncomfortable. I start walking again, and she follows with a trail of fairy dust falling behind her.

"I hear you can make gems with your fairy dust."

"Sometimes. Depends on what I'm trying to do."

"Can you make one for me?" A butterfly floats closer, and I lift my hand.

Nix stops. "You want me to make you a gem?"

With a twist of my body, I face her, the butterfly resting gracefully on my finger. The sunlight catches its wings, revealing a mesmerizing shimmer of white and blue.

"Only if you want to," I answer, not wanting to pressure her.

"I can do that." She beams.

Her attention is drawn to something behind me, her big blue eyes widening in surprise. A mischievous grin spreads across her face, exposing all those sharp teeth. "See ya. Wouldn't wanna be ya!"

Then she is gone.

Shaking my head, I twist back around, and I'm surprised to see the queen, or rather, Lavina, staring back at me. Bloody Nix, she calls that a warning.

Drawing in a breath, I smile, though I'm nervous. "Lavina, so lovely to see you."

"No, it's not. You are a terrible liar." Her violet eyes, usually filled with a sternness, are surprisingly clear and calm today. Reaching upward, she glides her hand over her already impeccable bun. I can't help but feel like she is checking to make sure the crown is gone.

"Oh." That's the only response I can muster.

"I wanted to see if we could get to know one another. There is this restaurant in Skora that I love, would you join me for lunch?"

Chapter Fifty-Two

Everly

Kian and Tristan follow on horseback as Lavina and I ride in a carriage on the short trip through the castle gates and across the meadow that separates the castle from the city. Skora is so beautiful. Vibrant wildflowers paint the landscape, while the gentle breeze causes the long reeds of grass to sway and whisper.

"You know, it's never looked this magnificent before," Lavina remarks, surprising me.

We haven't spoken a word to each other since she asked me for lunch. I don't think I even answered that question verbally; I just nodded like a weirdo.

"It's truly beautiful," I breathe.

"It's all you, you know."

"I'm not sure how."

"Your presence here. The plants and wildlife can feel you; they are drawn to you. They feed you magic, and in return, you allow them to thrive. With time, you'll be able to communicate with them."

My mouth drops open. "How . . . How could you possibly know that?"

Lavina's eyes flicker with sadness, which baffles me completely. Turning around, she gazes out over the meadow, completely disregarding my question. Our conversation over, it seems.

Before long, I'm seated at a quaint and cozy restaurant. To my surprise, the place exudes a warm and inviting ambiance that is completely unexpected. Soft music fills the air, gently blending with the murmur of conversations. The walls are white stone with tall wood arched ceilings, and various climbers winding around the beams.

"Not what you were expecting?" Lavina's voice draws my attention from across the small table.

Twisting my ring on my finger I give a half smile. "I expected some high-class, fancy restaurant that would have made me uncomfortable."

The former queen's face beams in delight. "I'm glad I could surprise you. So, Maxon tells me you have no family in the human realm?"

My eyebrows raise at the unexpected question. "Uhh . . . no. But Mia and Scarlett are like sisters to me. We would do anything for each other."

"I'm sorry you had to spend so long in that world. I wish things had been different."

Once again, I find myself at a loss for words, completely taken aback.

Tucking my hair behind my ear, my fingers stalling on the points. "So do I," I agree.

The ground rumbles beneath me, and my eyes are drawn to the glasses on the table as they vibrate with the tremors. With a frown, I raise my eyes to see a dark silhouette blotting out the gentle rays of light that were pouring into the room through the front window. Suddenly, a blinding flash and a deafening explosion shatter the tranquility, plunging the restaurant into pitch-blackness.

Black smoke billows in my face, the explosion ringing through my ears as I try to draw in a breath, only to cough as inky tendrils of black mist weave their way through my nostrils and down my throat.

I fan the air in front of my face, gasping, as I grasp the edge of the table, trying to see what is happening. My name echoes through the air, urging me to summon the strength to rise. The ringing in my ears is subsiding, but that explosion took out the front of the restaurant. Lavina gets to her feet, looking around in confusion, and I spot Kian and Tristan with their swords drawn, standing where the front doors used to be.

'Stóirín, where are you?'

I rub my head, trying to recall the name of the restaurant, my fingers tracing the cut on my forehead. '*Your aunt's favorite restaurant.'*

'Stay where you are. I'm on my way.'

'Where are you?'

Before he can answer, the walls tremble as an earth-shattering roar reverberates from outside, causing fragments of debris to rain down upon us. I crouch, covering my head as bits of debris fall around me. When everything stills, I slowly stand and shift my attention to the shattered windows. A gasp escapes my lips, leaving my mouth agape in utter disbelief.

At the far end of the street looms a massive giant in tattered clothes. I can sense his menacing presence from here, and it sends shivers down my spine. Suddenly, with thunderous footsteps, the colossal figure lunges forward, his massive arms flailing through the air, brushing against terrified bystanders desperately fleeing the street for safety.

Lavina stumbles toward me and grabs my arm, tugging me through the destroyed restaurant. "We need to get out of here!"

Reaching the back door, we both push, but something is blocking it. Probably rubble from the crumbling building. Together, we push relentlessly, exerting all our strength, until it finally yields, and we burst out onto the sidewalk. The warmth of the sunlight instantly embraces us, and I shield my eyes from the blinding light. The piercing screams and frantic yelling reverberate through the cobblestone streets.

"What is happening?" I breathe.

"Look." Lavina draws my attention to where she is pointing, and I see something that takes my breath away.

Maxon and Raiden are in the street, their swords gleaming, readying themselves for battle. The obsidian sword forms in Maxon's spare hand, his face set in a murderous glare. My heart races as at least a dozen deadlings slam into them.

Maxon's movements are a sight to behold as he flawlessly wields both swords. The two of them are moving so fast, I can't keep track. The sound of steel slicing through the air creates a symphony of danger and skill, an impressive show that I would admire if his life weren't hanging in the balance.

My breath catches in my throat as a flood of people rush into the streets, heading straight toward the approaching deadlings. Above the chaos, I hear Maxon's furious roar, resonating with an overwhelming power. Raiden swiftly soars into the sky as flames engulf Maxon's body. He unleashes a scorching wave, engulfing the deadlings in a fiery inferno. The air fills with their agonizing shrieks, echoing as their bodies convulse in a futile attempt to escape the searing flames.

"We need to leave!" Lavina grabs my hand again.

"What about Kian and Tristan?!"

"They will catch up."

Together, we sprint toward the castle. My hair flows behind me like ribbons, and I'm grateful for the fighting attire I'm wearing; it allows for effortless movement and speed. We reach a corner and come to a sudden halt. A shiver runs down my spine and my blood freezes at the sight before us.

Deadlings. Their elongated limbs and sharp claws lunge at groups of soldiers and civilians. The air is filled with their menacing howls. I spot Tristan and Kian, both their swords glinting in the sunlight as they slice cleanly through the deadlings' bodies, severing limbs, and silencing their eerie screeches.

How did they get in front of us?

However, their efforts are in vain. The defeated deadlings seem to be replaced almost immediately by new ones emerging from the shadows and surrounding them with an unrelenting force. The group of soldiers is outnumbered.

"We need to do something!" I implore over the noise to Lavina.

Before I have time to move or even draw in my next breath, Lavina suddenly shifts, placing herself in front of me, blood dribbling down her chin. The long sharp claws of a deadling are buried in her neck, the other in her chest. Shock washes over me, leaving me rooted to the spot in complete stillness. Lavina's purple eyes flare, and she spins, reaching for the creature. As she does, its claws tear from her chest, and slice open her neck. Her fingers wrap around its unnatural head, and with a quick twist, she snaps its neck. The crack seems to echo around us, and the deadling falls to the ground with a muted thud.

Lavina turns to face me, her face ashen as blood bubbles in her mouth, spilling down her chin. Blood spreads rapidly over her dress as we stand here, staring at each other. My brain finally catches up to the events that have just unfolded, and I let out a piercing cry. Terror seizes my heart in a fierce grip, and I stretch my arms out to catch her before she hits the ground, slowly lowering her.

"Why?" I beg her, desperately trying to cover her wound and stop the bleeding.

"Shhh . . . It's okay, Vera."

I jump in surprise at her words, mentioning the nickname reserved for those who were closest to me in my childhood.

"What did you call me?"

Her voice is strained as she speaks. "Your mother and I . . . grew up together. We were"—she swallows—"best friends for a long time. I wanted to tell you." Her expression is filled with regret. "I was going to tell you."

It becomes hard to breathe as a feeling of sorrow overwhelms my heart. She knew my mother?

A sob breaks free, and I gently stroke her hair, trying to offer her comfort.

"I used to visit her a lot when you were very young." The barest hint of a smile tugs at the corners of her lips. "I loved your mother dearly . . . I could never let harm come to her child."

"I'm so sorry," I weep, lifting her to my chest.

"Take care of him." A soft wheeze escapes her throat a moment before her eyes turn glassy.

No.

No. No. No. How could this happen?

'Everly? What's wrong?' Maxon's desperate voice fills my head.

'Oh my god, Maxon, I'm so sorry. I'm so sorry. I didn't see it coming and she, she . . . '

I hear shouts from the soldiers, and look up, seeing two deadlings closing in on me. My connection with Maxon is lost, and I gently rest Lavina's head on the ground before standing. My heart pounds in my chest, threatening to burst through my ribcage as a surge of emotions courses through me. Screams and shouts echo through the streets as smoke rises in the air.

The air crackles with magic as the fae use their abilities to push back the hordes of deadlings. Shifters lunge at them, their sharp claws aiming to bring them down swiftly.

My gaze drops to my blood-soaked hands, the chaos around me becoming muted. This feels unreal. Wrong. Turning my hands over, my eyes travel up my arms that are streaked with Lavina's blood. My fingers tremble. Anger surges through me, a searing rage that burns like wildfire in my veins. My vision sharpens, and magic floods every inch of my body. More shouts. I snap my head up, locking eyes with a deadling as it lunges through the air at me, claws reaching out. Time seems to slow, and in a fluid motion, I pull my dagger from its sheath at my waist. Stepping into the attack, I grab the deadling by the throat. Its icy skin beneath my grip, I drive the blade into its temple, a scream ripping from my throat.

Without missing a beat, I yank the dagger free and sprint forward, my attention locked on another deadling, my feet pounding against the ground. I duck beneath its outstretched claw and come up behind it, both hands around the hilt as I plunge my dagger into the base of its neck. The impact sends a shock through my arms, but there's no time to think. The fight isn't over yet.

A hand lands on my shoulder and I spin, ready to attack, but Kian blocks my arm. "Hey, it's me."

Ignoring him completely, I drop my arm and press forward, making my way to the soldiers. I extend my hand to the fountain in the middle of the square, and a powerful column of water emerges, shooting sky high. With intense focus, I tilt my head and silently convey a message into the earth. Within seconds, vines erupt along the ground, ripping the deadlings away from the soldiers. Their claws scrape along the ground as the vines drag them toward the water.

The noise of their howls and screeches fade into the background as the column of water engulfs them, drowning out their cries. The vines slowly retreat back into the ground. I watch as a face appears in the water, mirroring the one I witnessed that day by the stream when I first encountered the frostflare. Its ethereal smile graces my vision, before the water cascades down, mercilessly falling through the air. The deafening sound of the crashing water mingles with the sickening thud of lifeless bodies sprawling upon the unforgiving stone.

"That's one way of doing it . . . " Kian mutters, coming to stand next to me.

"She is dead." My voice cracks on the admission.

"I know, princess."

I look up into his lavender eyes. I want to burst into tears, but at this moment, there is no room for an emotional breakdown. Not as the sounds of terror still rage through Skora.

'Maxon?'

'I'm here. Are you safe?'

'Yes.'

'Good. Get back to the castle.'

With a frown, I scan the wounded. *'No.'*

'Everly.' My name comes out like a curse.

'I'm helping. I can help.'

'No, I need you safe.'

'I know.'

I know Maxon can sense my decision through our bond, just like I can feel his alarm. With determination, I start running toward the piercing screams that are echoing in the distance. Adrenaline fuels my every step.

"Everly, where are you going?!" Tristan bellows. "The castle is the other way!"

"To help!"

The sound of Kian's curse reaches my ears, and in a matter of seconds, he is right beside me. "Are you sure?"

I glare at him in response, and he nods, pride filling his gaze.

I am no longer a helpless human.

I never was.

I am a powerful druid princess.

I won't hide behind walls.

I won't use others as a shield.

I embrace my true identity.

The air crackles with magic, the energy pulsing through my veins, ready to be unleashed.

The scent of earth and magic fill my nostrils, and I brace myself.

In an instant, Tristan materializes on my other side, giving me a resolute nod. "Let's do this, princess."

Chapter Fifty-Three

Everly

We round the next street corner—into hell.

A wall of soldiers stands ahead, their weapons drawn, forming a rigid line of defense. Beyond them, the **deadlings** emerge from the forest, creeping out like shadows brought to life. Their hollow eyes gleam with hunger, their twisted limbs jerking unnaturally as they advance.

A low growl rumbles from Tristan's chest. Without hesitation, he hurls his sword toward me.

I snatch it from the air with ease, my fingers closing around the hilt as if the weapon has always belonged there. Since my change, everything feels sharper—faster. I give the blade a practiced spin, testing its weight, the cool steel an extension of my own body.

I glance at Tristan. A single nod passes between us. No words. No hesitation.

I step forward.

The soldiers stiffen as I move among them, shifting in uneasy surprise. A ripple of murmurs rises—doubt, confusion. What is she doing? Why is she here? Their uncertainty buzzes in the air like a swarm of wasps. Stretching my free arm out, I extend my palm toward the ground, the cool breeze brushing against my skin. With unwavering concentration, I summon my magic, feeling a sudden surge of power flow through me, causing the earth to tremble beneath my feet. My breaths are sawing in and out as I try to concentrate. There's a deafening roar as a shockwave echoes through the air, rattling my eardrums. I watch as the earth rolls and buckles, a wave of energy radiating outward toward the approaching deadlings. The ground rises and falls under them forcefully, propelling them backward, their bodies soaring through the sky.

It only provides a brief respite, but I'm hopeful that it will allow more women and children to make it to the protection of the castle walls.

I can almost taste the tension in the air as the soldiers brace themselves for the impending onslaught. The deadlings, with their sullen flesh and milky white eyes, advance relentlessly, driven by their need to kill. In the dimness of the tree's shadows, I swear I catch a glimpse of the black beast's piercing crimson eyes.

With Tristan's sword in hand, I take a deep breath, steeling myself for what lies ahead. The first wave of deadlings lunge toward us, and I swing the sword with all my might, the blade slicing through the air, cleaving through their grotesque bodies. A mixture of fear, adrenaline, and an unwavering desire to survive fuels each and every strike.

Grinding my teeth together, I deftly sidestep, kick, and dodge the relentless creatures that are intent on ripping me to shreds. With each step, the metallic scent of blood fills the air, staining my face and clothes. It fills me with a sense of desperation, urging me to keep going despite the overwhelming odds stacked against me.

I catch glimpses of Kian and Tristan, their faces lined with determination as they fight alongside me, their own weapons carving a path through the encroaching hordes. We move in sync, relying on our training and instinct, as we desperately try to push back the onslaught.

Sweat trickles down my forehead, mingling with the dirt and grime already covering my face. The cut on my head has sealed, leaving behind a crusted layer of blood.

"Everly!" Raiden's voice climbs above the chaos.

Spinning on my heel, I see him running toward me. Hope rises in my chest. If Raiden is here, Maxon must be close. I can barely feel him through the bond with all the adrenaline pumping through my veins.

My heart jumps to my throat, and I try to scream out as a deadling comes out of nowhere, jumping on his back. The creature grips his wings and tries tearing them from his back, but Raiden is quick, dislodging it in one swift movement, sending it hurling into the wall of a nearby building. Raiden looks furious, his whole being vibrating in anger, black blood smearing his face and chest.

Another approaches him, and I watch with wide eyes as he swiftly grabs it by the throat, crushing its windpipe and tossing it aside like a rag doll. Our eyes meet from a distance, and I immediately start making my way over to him, desperately needing to find Maxon. But a sinking feeling washes over me when Raiden's face turns pale, and he shouts something at me. I spin around and come face to face with . . .

What the hell am I looking at right now?

I tilt my head back in confusion. Standing before me is an enormous creature with bluish skin, imposing horns, and charred clothing. Its looming hand hangs in the air, casting a shadow over me. Before I have a chance to react, it comes crashing down, sending me hurtling across the uneven cobblestone road. My sword falls from my grasp, the breath knocked out of me. The impact sends a searing pain through my head, like a hot knife slicing through my skull. With a groan escaping my lips, I gently extend my hand to feel the warm, sticky blood trickling from the new gash on my forehead. Just great.

Despite the shock, I gather my strength and slowly stand, my legs wobbling as I cling to a planter box for support. A hiss emanates from my left, and I catch sight of a sinister black smoke weaving its way through the street, heading directly for me. I glance back at the beast that knocked me into next week only to see Raiden engaged in a fierce battle with it.

With a flick of my wrist, vines burst from the ground, snaking their way around the monstrous creature's wrists and ankles, immobilizing it.

I know I only need conscious thought to get them to act, but I squeeze my fists anyway, making the vines tighten their grip, trying to hold it down. With a thunderous roar, it forcefully tears through the vines, breaking them into pieces. Damn it!

"Everly! Maxon is near the south gates, at the wharf. GO!" Raiden's voice booms over the chaos.

I nod sharply, knowing he'll fight better if I'm out of the way. With a deep inhale, I push off, sprinting toward the south gate, my pulse hammering so hard I can feel it throbbing in my fingertips.

A piercing howl erupts to my left. Before I can react, Nymeria and Anika burst from a narrow alley, their powerful forms falling into step beside me. Their once-pristine white coats are now streaked with blackish-red, soaked in blood—but not theirs.

Relief flutters in my chest, even as my lungs burn. "It's good to see you two," I whisper between ragged breaths.

We skid to a stop at the south gate. My hands brace against my hips as I gulp down air, my chest heaving. With Nymeria and Anika at my side, a strange energy courses through me—a raw, undeniable sense of purpose. I feel alive.

And then I sense him. Maxon.

The bond hums with his presence—strong, unbroken. He's close, unharmed, moving fast.

All around us, the streets are a war zone. Fae battle fiercely, their magic crackling through the air, the scent of blood thickening with every passing second. My gaze sweeps the battlefield—and then I see him. At the end of the street, near the wharf gates, Maxon is fighting.

Deadlings close in, lunging, snarling—but he moves like a storm, his blade flashing, his power radiating with every strike. He's holding his ground.

For the first time since this nightmare began, something inside me loosens. A weight I didn't even realize I was carrying **lifts.**

He's okay.

As I look around, my eyes land on a cluster of children gathered beneath a cart. I sprint over, with Nymeria and Anika close behind, their paws pounding against the ground. My heart races as I kneel down and come face-to-face with multiple pairs of glowing yellow eyes, their tiny frames shaking with fear. Shifters.

"I know you're all scared, but you need to get to the safety of the castle. The way should be clear."

It looks like we're driving the deadlings back.

The children huddle closer together beneath the cart, shaking their heads in fear. My heart races. I know they are scared, but it's crucial for them to reach the castle. Nymeria exhales impatiently, her paw scraping the ground.

I lock eyes with her. "Can you carry these kids to safety on your backs?"

Both wolves nod simultaneously, their eyes glinting with understanding.

My fingers grip the wood, and I lean back down. "Let's go. My wolves will take you to the castle, where you can find your parents. If you stay here, you'll be in danger."

The four little shifters exchange glances, then cautiously emerge from beneath the cart. I release a deep breath, a wave of relief washing over me, as I extend my hand to help them up. Their small hands slip into mine, and I can't help but feel a surge of protectiveness. Carefully, I lift each one of them up onto Nymeria and Anika's backs.

"Keep them safe."

Nymeria and Anika both bow their heads in understanding, and I watch them leave.

I hear a roar that sounds like my name. My stomach twists like someone wringing out a wet towel. Amidst the chaotic scene at the gates, my eyes lock onto Maxon's. His burning like embers, piercing and deadly. As he strides toward me, a nearby building erupts in a violent explosion. I instinctively duck, shielding my head from the onslaught of flying debris. The air is filled with the acrid scent of smoke, mingling with the metallic taste of fear in my mouth. As I rise to my feet, panting heavily, my ears still ringing, a dense cloud of smoke and rubble obscures my vision. Suddenly, a dark mass crashes into me, engulfing me in complete darkness.

Chapter Fifty-Four

Everly

I hit the stone ground hard, the impact rattling my bones and making my teeth slam together. Shit. That hurt.

Pain explodes through me, radiating from every limb as I lie there, stunned, blinking up at the sky. The world feels distant, disjointed, as if my body hasn't quite caught up with reality yet. A sharp hiss escapes through my clenched teeth as I force myself upright, every movement sending a fresh wave of agony through me. My breaths come in ragged gasps, shallow and uneven. Something's wrong. My ribs—fractured, maybe even broken.

I clutch my arm beneath my chest, trying to steady the wild pounding of my heart as my gaze sweeps my surroundings. Where am I?

How far have I been carried?

Pacing directly ahead of me is the gigantic black wolf with crimson eyes that gleam in the black depths. I grip my dagger tighter in my hand, holding it in front of me. If I die, I die fighting. Even though the Shadoweaver wants me, no one specified if that was dead or alive. Either way, I am not about to make it easy.

An eerie chuckle rings through the empty street, but my attention remains fixed on the red eyes before me. The beast disperses, smoke twists and twirls, transforming into a solid form, leaving my mouth agape. With her pale white skin contrasting with the thick black bands wrapped around her throat, the wolf had shifted into a woman. The wind tousles her long black hair, creating a mesmerizing, billowing effect. Clad in a white silk kimono adorned with red flowers, her arms and chest smeared in blood, she grips tightly in her left hand a katana. My throat tightens as our eyes lock once more, and I swallow awkwardly. The intensity of her glowing red eyes captivates me, while her malicious smirk sends a chilling shiver down my spine.

"I can see you shaking like a leaf from here, princess," the woman taunts, tilting her head in a predatory way.

"What are you doing here?" I'm proud that my voice doesn't tremble.

The woman brings her arm to her mouth, a sly grin forming as she licks the blood from her arm and tastes it.

I scowl, narrowing my eyes on her. She's taunting me.

"I'm here for you, of course." Blood coats her teeth.

My scalp prickles, and tightens, as a sense of foreboding hits me. "I won't go with you."

With a wicked grin, she tips her head back and lets out a chillingly sinister laugh that has the hair rising on my arms.

"That's so cute. You think you have a choice."

"There is always a choice," I snap. "If you are his soldiers, then why are you trying to kill me?"

The woman bites her lip to stop her smile from spreading. "We aren't trying to kill you, silly. We just need to bring you back alive, though he never said how alive you needed to be."

I reach out with my mind, drawing upon the ancient strength of the trees and the twisting vines that coil deep beneath the earth. The air is suddenly alive with movement—branches snap, twigs crack, and roots groan as they shift at my command. In my mind's eye, I see them before they even take shape—four figures rising from the chaos, their bodies sculpted from woven vines and splintered wood, their limbs twisting into humanoid forms. Maidens. Warriors.

As the last strand of ivy entwines into place, they stand beside me, each gripping a bow, their arrows already nocked and aimed at the demon before me. She watches with amusement, her eyes flashing with something that makes my stomach turn—delight.

"Oh, this will be interesting," she purrs, rolling her shoulders as if warming up. "I always did like a challenge."

Her katana gleams in the dim light as she lifts it, tilting her head with an easy smirk. Then, with a sharp crack, she rolls her neck from side to side, the sound making my skin crawl. There's something sickeningly casual about the way she moves, her confidence oozing from every step, every shift of her weight. Arrogance. A trait that suits a monster like her.

Then, she moves.

With a single, forceful push against the ground, she propels herself into the air, closing the distance between us at blinding speed.

The thwack of bowstrings snapping fills the air as my maidens unleash their arrows, a relentless storm of sharpened wood aimed straight at her heart.

But she is faster.

Her katana becomes a silver blur as she spins mid-air, deflecting each arrow with effortless precision. Not one touches her. Every motion is smooth, calculated—a dance of death, each step choreographed with a grace that shouldn't belong to something so monstrous.

Then, like a blade through paper, she cuts through the first maiden.

The woven figure crumbles instantly, vines snapping and falling lifelessly to the earth.

One by one, she carves through them, her katana slicing with unrelenting ease. The last warrior barely has time to draw her bow before the demon's blade cleaves her in two.

My breath catches as the final remnants of my creations wither into nothing. My fingers flex and curl into fists, and I feel the weight of realization sinking in. I am not going to be able to fight her and win.

Her long black hair whips around her face when she faces me. "Impressive. But you'll need to do better than that. Or you could just give up and come with me now, save all this drama."

"I'm not going anywhere."

The woman bursts into black smoke and slithers around me, before reforming closer than before.

"What are you?" I whisper harshly.

"A demon." She shrugs casually. "You can call me, Yumekui."

'Everly, where are you?' Maxon's voice reaches through the bond.

'I think I'm near the eastern border.'

'Raiden and I are on our way.'

'I'm not alone. His pet is here.'

The bond between us trembles with Maxon's panic, sending a rush of anxiety surging through me.

'I'm almost there.'

The demon spins, coming at me faster than I can track. Her katana slices through the air, and searing hot pain spreads across my chest, leaving me gasping for breath. The ground buckles under me, sending me flying backward. My arms shoot out to my sides for balance as I skid backward along the ground. I can't help but glare at the long, crimson line that extends from my left shoulder to the top of my right breast.

The demon smirks, a wicked glimmer entering her eyes as she lifts her blade to her mouth, licking off my blood.

Her crimson eyes glaze over, turning completely black. "Hmm, very nice. Maybe once *he* is done with you, there will be enough left for me. Though, probably not. He doesn't share. What a shame."

Overwhelmed by anger and disgust, instinct takes over and my arm raises, the air propelling her forcefully into a nearby building. The wall gives way upon impact, collapsing around her with a deafening crash. Completely exhausted, I stumble forward, my legs feeling like jelly. The ability to call upon my magic is slipping away, growing more elusive by the second. I'm not sure I have another attack left in me.

Emerging from the debris, the demon gracefully brushes off the dirt from her kimono. "You are stronger than they were."

When I don't answer her, she grins. It only makes me want to send her flying into another wall. "It was so easy getting into the heads of the unseelie king and the seelie queen."

I jerk forward a step, my pulse spiking. "What?"

"The original plan was to have everyone kill each other after they kill your entire family. Then I'd swoop in and rescue you and bring you to *him*. But that mother of yours.," she spits, anger flashing in her eyes. "She went and ruined everything."

"You were the reason my family was killed? That Maxon's parents died?"

"Of course. Even though my original plan failed, all is well. I felt you the moment you stepped through the gate. I've been hunting you ever since. You see, we need your blood to unlock the chains holding *him* prisoner. Then he will tear this world apart, molding it into his. Mold you into his."

I freeze in horror, unable to move or even think. The sound of her laughter pulses around me, turning my blood to ice. I blink at her and watch as she bursts into a dark mass of shadows and comes barreling my way. There is no way to avoid it.

My vision is momentarily filled with a burst of vibrant color as a ball of fire crashes into the demon, sending them both hurtling into the side of a building.

The sound of fighting reverberates, making the very air tremble with violence. I catch a glimpse of Maxon amidst the scattered rubble. My heart lurches in my chest as he fights with the demon.

With lightning speed, his obsidian sword slashes through the air, almost too quick for my eyes to follow. Flames flicker in his eyes, igniting a fury in his movements. He is channeling his dragon fire, and he's not holding back.

A noise draws my attention away from them, and I turn to see an army of dark figures approaching. The sound of their footfalls echoes all around, the sound bouncing off the empty streets.

I hear my name, and I spin around in terror as Rayna comes sprinting toward me from between two buildings.

"Everly!" she screams, her big brown eyes locked on mine.

Dread. That is all I can feel as I put my hands up to block her path to me. But my magic is depleted. I hear a shrill whistle and feel the hair around my face move as the arrow narrowly misses my face, hitting Rayna in the chest. Her body jolts and her steps falter, the light fading from her eyes before she even hits the ground. A scream erupts from my throat, and I feel like my heart is being torn from my chest. I take a step toward her, but my movement halts abruptly as Yumekui's sinister laugh rings through the air. I whip my attention toward the building where Maxon is fighting her. The moment I lay eyes on him, my stomach drops, and cold dread slips through my veins.

Maxon's knees buckle beneath him as he struggles to stay upright. Dirt and blood coat every inch of his clothes and skin. But it's the dense tendrils of swirling shadows enveloping him that cause my heart to freeze in fear. They are suffocating the flames that danced over him, smothering his fire. Maxon strains against the restraints, attempting to break free, his attention shifting from the oncoming army to meet my gaze.

"Everly, run!" he bellows, the command clear.

Tears stream down my face, as panic overtakes all thought. "MAXON!!"

Shadows snake around his throat and pour into his mouth, stalling anymore words. My heart stalls in my chest, squeezing painfully as I watch his eyes grow wide in alarm.

"Maxon!" I scream.

The moment I start running for him, an icy cold hand grabs hold of my arm, making my heart race even faster. I spin on my attacker, and I fight. I fight hard, because Maxon needs me.

"Everly, stop." Alivar's furious gaze meets mine.

"Let me go!" I snarl, trying to pry my arm free from his grip.

"There is nothing we can do. We need to regroup!"

"Fuck you!" I yell, swing my fist at his face.

Alivar dodges all my attempts, and I growl in frustration. This is a waste of time. With a burst of energy, I spin, slipping from his grasp. I run toward Maxon, my heart pounding in desperation.

The demon emerges, obstructing my way and preventing me from reaching Maxon. Alivar grabs my arm again, but I'm to focused on the demon in front of me to care this time.

'We only need you,' she whispers in my head. *'You can save him.'*

"Alivar. Take her!!!" Maxon roars, the sound shaking the buildings, as he struggles against the blinds.

Nooooooo . . .

My elbow connects with his chin, and I push his arm away, lunging forward. But somehow, he manages to snag the back of my dress, pulling me back. I stumble backward into Alivar as Nymeria and Anika bolt past me toward Maxon.

'We will go with him, mother.'

'We will protect him for you.'

Twin voices echo in my mind. Nymeria and Anika.

Their voices give me enough pause that Alivar gains the upper hand, swinging me over his shoulder and creating a portal. As he steps through, I hear Raiden bellow, the sound slicing through my chest, and piercing my heart.

I can hear the sound of thundering footsteps in the distance, but they are too late. The last thing I hear before the portal closes is the familiar pounding of hooves. Storm.

Alivar continues forward, and I stop struggling, all my fight leaving me. A blistering cold wind cuts through us, and I am met with an unsettling silence and a blinding white that overwhelms my senses. Alivar places me on my feet in the snow, an icy wind whipping my hair across my face. Anger, guilt, and anguish tear at me, making it hard to breathe. I double over, a scream ripping from my throat.

Oh my god. The pain is unbearable. It's searing through my veins like lighting.

What's going to happen to him? To everyone? What about Rayna? Lavina?

This is all my fault!

Hands land on my shoulders, and I abruptly stand and start shoving Alivar in the chest.

"Don't touch me! Don't fucking touch me!" I scream over and over, my voice cracking as emotions rip apart my chest.

Alivar doesn't react, he just takes it. Takes every push, every hit as I wear myself out. Falling to the ground on my knees in the snow, I sob. I hear Alivar sigh, and I turn my eyes up to him as he squats in front of me, his hands clasped between his knees. He studies me for a moment before speaking.

"Not all is lost. We will get him back."

The feeling of shock courses through my body, and I find myself unable to look away from Alivar's icy stare.

"What?" My voice is hoarse and scratchy.

"A woman can be broken down, piece by piece. But will you remain broken, or fight?" His head cocks to the side. "A real woman will pick up the pieces, rebuild herself, and come back stronger than ever. The same can be said for a kingdom."

I blink at him, trying to decipher what he is saying.

"Are you a real woman, Everly? Are you going to pick up the pieces? Fight for Maxon? Fight for your people? Fight for this realm?"

His words worm their way into my heart. I will fight until my last breath for every one of my friends. Maxon? He needs me to be strong, so I will be strong. Wiping the tears from my cheeks, I slowly stand up, and stare at Alivar as he stands with me, my resolve growing like a seed inside of me.

"I'm going to fight." I clench my fists at my sides.

Alivar crosses his arms, a smirk appearing on his face. "Good."

"And you're going to help me? Or kidnap me?" Caution bleeds into my tone.

Alivar shrugs, his blonde hair whipping across his face. "You're his. I won't take you from him. I won't lie and say I wasn't disappointed, though. Once Skora is secure, I will take you back to your friends, and together we will work this out."

A frigid breeze wraps around me, causing me to cross my arms over my chest, seeking warmth.

"How will you know when it is secure?"

"Once my inside man tells me." He smirks.

My eyes widen, and I abruptly take a step forward. "Who is your spy?"

My anger simmers within me, radiating heat throughout my body, and warming me up.

"You will find out soon enough. Now, come." Alivar turns and walks toward a small cabin I only just noticed.

Pivoting, I look out over the white, snow-covered hills, wondering where exactly that demon has taken Maxon.

"I'm coming for you, Maxon. I will find you. I will not stop until we are together again."

The cold stings my cheeks, and my breath forms clouds in front of my face. I hope my words will carry on the wind and reach Maxon.

To be continued…..

www.ingramcontent.com/pod-product-compliance
Lightning Source LLC
Chambersburg PA
CBHW070540310726
48982CB00010B/1421/J

* 9 7 8 0 6 4 5 5 8 2 9 8 7 *